Praise for Di

"Book after book, Duvall brings her readers complex, juvenile... romance, danger and loyalty."
—RT Book Reviews

"Duvall's storytelling is simply spellbinding."
—Tome Tender

"Dianne Duvall does an amazing job of blending paranormal with humor, romance, action, and violence to give you a story you won't want to put down."
—The SubClub Books

Praise for Dianne's
Immortal Guardians Books

"Crackles with energy, originality, and a memorable take-no-prisoners heroine."
—Publishers Weekly

"Fans of terrific paranormal romance have hit the jackpot with Duvall and her electrifying series."
—RT Book Reviews

"This series is earth-shattering awesome and Dianne has quickly become one of my favorite authors. Each of these stories… has been heart-stopping, intense, humorous and powerfully romantic."
—Reading Between the Wines Book Club

"Full of fascinating characters, a unique and wonderfully imaginative premise, and scorching hot relationships."
—The Romance Reviews

"Fans of paranormal romance who haven't discovered this series yet are really missing out on something extraordinary."
—Long and Short Reviews

"This series boasts numerous characters, a deep back story, and extensive worldbuilding… [Ethan] boasts the glowing charms of Twilight's Edward Cullen and the vicious durability of the X-Men's Wolverine."
—Kirkus Reviews

"Paranormal romance fans who enjoy series like J.R. Ward's Black Dagger Brotherhood will definitely want to invest time in the Immortal Guardians series."
—All Things Urban Fantasy

"Ms. Duvall brings together a rich world and a wonderful group of characters… This is a great series."
—Night Owl Reviews

"It was non-stop get-up-and-go from the very first page, and instantly you just adore these characters… This was paranormal at its finest."
—Book Reader Chronicles

Praise for Dianne's
The Gifted Ones Books

Titles by Dianne Duvall

The Gifted Ones

A SORCERESS OF HIS OWN

RENDEZVOUS WITH YESTERDAY

Immortal Guardians

DARKNESS DAWNS

NIGHT REIGNS

PHANTOM SHADOWS

IN STILL DARKNESS

DARKNESS RISES

NIGHT UNBOUND

PHANTOM EMBRACE

SHADOWS STRIKE

BLADE OF DARKNESS

AWAKEN THE DARKNESS

Anthologies

PREDATORY

(includes *In Still Darkness*)

ON THE HUNT

(includes *Phantom Embrace*)

DEATH OF DARKNESS

NEW YORK TIMES BESTSELLING AUTHOR

DIANNE DUVALL

Immortal
Guardians

DEATH OF DARKNESS
Copyright © 2019 by Dianne Duvall

Published by Dianne Duvall, 2019
www.DianneDuvall.com
Editor: Anne Victory
Cover Art by: Damonza

E-book ISBN: 978–0986417184
Print ISBN: 978–0986417191

For my family

Author's Note

Dear Reader,

Seth's character has been with me for a very long time. He first appeared in *A Sorceress of His Own*, which—despite its later release—actually predated my Immortal Guardians series. My curiosity about who he was and why he was different played a large role in driving me to create the Immortal Guardians series. I have wanted to tell his story ever since that first appearance and have received more requests for his book than for any other character's. That he resonates with so many of you means more to me than you know.

Many Immortal Guardians fans have expressed their concern that Seth's book might end the series. Rest assured, it will not. As some of you have no doubt seen me say online, I'm having way too much fun with these characters to give them up. And there are quite a few immortals who are still fervently hoping I will tell their tale.

Thank you so much for your interest. I hope you will enjoy Seth's story.

—Dianne Duvall

Acknowledgements

First, I would like to thank everyone who requested this book. I absolutely loved writing it. I would also like to once more thank Crystal and my fabulous Street Team for your continued support and for holding down the fort when I'm working hard to meet a deadline. I've said it before and I'll say it again: you all rock!

Many thanks also go to the members of my Dianne Duvall Books Group on Facebook. I've been having so much fun with you. You've made it my favorite place to visit on the internet. Any readers who enjoy my Immortal Guardians and/or The Gifted Ones series are welcome to join. We'd love to see you there.

Special thanks go to Anne Victory, who is always a joy to work with. I'd also like to thank the proofreader, formatter, and other behind-the-scenes individuals who helped me bring you *Death of Darkness*.

I also thank all of the bloggers and reviewers who help spread the word about my books, introducing them to new readers. I thank the readers who recommend them to friends, family, and even virtual strangers. I appreciate you all so much. And, of course, I'd like to thank my Facebook and Twitter friends and blog followers who share in my excitement with every release and make me laugh and smile even when I'm stressing over deadlines. You're the best!

Chapter One

SETH SENSED A PRESENCE BEHIND *him and turned.*

A woman stared up at him. Her light brown hair fell several inches past slender shoulders in a thick mass bereft of curls. Her pretty face — free of makeup — boasted a short, pert nose and full pink lips that drew and held his gaze. Clear lip balm coated them, keeping them temptingly soft and carrying the scent of coconuts to him. Though her lips turned up in a smile, her hazel eyes remained somber, conveying an emotion Seth couldn't identify.

She reached her arms out to someone he didn't see, then drew Adira to her chest.

The beautiful toddler went trustingly, bouncing in the woman's arms and giving her a big grin. But the toddler's joy soon faded as she met the woman's gaze. Her bright green eyes solemn, Adira rested a hand on the woman's cheek and acquired a look of concentration that Seth had come to associate with her reading someone. The tiny child bore many gifts. He still wasn't sure whether she examined the other person's thoughts during these moments or read their emotions like Stanislav and Bastien. Perhaps she perused their past the way Bastien's sister Catherine could by touching objects. Or did she try to glimpse their future like Dana?

Whatever Adira saw in the woman kept the grin from returning to her plump face.

Seth shifted his gaze back to the woman, who no longer smiled. Who was she?

She turned her gaze up to meet his... and Seth found he couldn't look away. There was something about her, something —

Skillet's "Monster" abruptly blared. Adira and the woman both looked around as though seeking the source of the music.

Seth jerked awake and stared up at the ceiling.

But the image of the woman in his dream was slow to fade. She seemed… familiar in some way, as if he had met her before. But he could find no memory of her.

Who was she? And why had she been holding Adira?

When the music continued, he slid the cell phone on the bedside table an irritated look. Resignation slithered through him as he grabbed it. "Yes?"

"Seth!" a relieved American male voice blurted with relief. "I, uh… Shit!" Metal clanged in the background. A clatter followed, most likely from the phone on the other end falling to the ground.

Seth glanced at the clock as he rose fully clothed from the bed. Twenty minutes of sleep. He supposed it was better than nothing. But damn, he was tired.

"I might have bitten off more than I can chew," Sean admitted, his voice distanced, confirming Seth's guess that he had dropped the phone. More clanging ensued. Someone howled in pain. "I could really use your—"

Grabbing his katanas, Seth teleported to NCCU's campus where Sean, one of the youngest Immortal Guardians currently stationed in North Carolina, was fighting five vampires.

"—help," Sean finished. A beep sounded. Relief filled his blood-streaked face as he swung at two vampires in front of him, then spun to block the attack of three more behind him. "Watch the phone, asshole! Watch the phone!" he shouted.

The vampire in front of him looked down at the cell phone that lay in the grass at his feet. Sneering, he raised his foot to stomp on it.

The move cost him his head.

Amusement sifting through him, Seth swiftly dispatched three of the remaining vampires while Sean took out the last.

As soon as his opponent fell, Sean bent and retrieved his phone, then grinned in triumph. "Ha! Not a scratch on it."

Seth shook his head. "Why are you hunting alone?"

Sean's look turned sheepish as he wiped blood off the device and tucked it into an inner pocket of his long coat. "Do you want *my* answer or the one my Second would give you?"

"Your Second. Nicole is an excellent judge of character." Seth walked around the corpses at their feet, studying each slack face intently before the peculiar symbiotic virus that inhabited the vampires could distort their features by devouring their hosts from the inside out in a desperate bid to continue living.

Sean's shoulders slumped. "Because I'm hardheaded."

Seth would've laughed if he weren't so concerned. These were dangerous times. He had already lost two Immortal Guardians in recent years. He didn't want to lose another. "Was I unclear in my instructions?"

Sean shifted his feet. "No." Bending, he began to retrieve his swords and daggers.

Seth had heard more than one Immortal Guardian grumble that he sometimes made them feel like children being upbraided by a parent. That was how Sean appeared now. Seth was the self-proclaimed leader of the Immortal Guardians, the oldest and most powerful amongst them. And David, Seth's second-in-command, had reminded him not long ago that they all viewed him as a father figure. So he couldn't help the authoritative tone he sometimes took.

"Until we locate and defeat Gershom," he said, "none of you should hunt alone."

Sean wiped the blood from each blade before he returned them to sheaths inside his coat. "I know."

"And yet here you are, hunting alone." Seth cleaned his own weapons before sheathing them. "Why?"

The younger man shook his head. "It's going to sound lame."

"I'm sure it will."

Sean laughed, his countenance lightening as some of the tension in his posture eased. "Krysta hunted and killed psychotic vampires for seven years before she met Étienne."

"Not without your help," Seth reminded him.

"Some help I was," he muttered, his amusement dying. He and his sister Krysta, like all Immortal Guardians, had been born *gifted ones*. The advanced DNA they hadn't known they possessed had lent them both special abilities. Sean could heal with his hands. Krysta could see auras. And while Krysta had always believed her gift useless when compared to her brother's, it had ultimately enabled her to become the only mortal in history to successfully hunt and slay vampires without immortal aid *and* live to tell the tale. Vampires' auras shifted before they did, enabling her to anticipate their movements and giving her a way to battle the vampires—who moved so swiftly they appeared but a blur to mortals—on a more equal footing.

Sean had lacked that edge and had not fared well in battle the few times he and Krysta had hunted together before their transformations. So his role in eradicating the vampire menace had been reduced to letting Krysta do the fighting while he waited to heal whatever wounds she incurred.

Seth shook his head. "She couldn't have slain as many vampires as she did had you not enabled her to live to fight another day. I know your past." He had thoroughly examined the man's thoughts and memories before allowing Étienne to transform him. "You saved her life countless times."

"So she could go out the next night and risk it again while I sat on my ass in the car and studied instead of fighting by her side." He had been a med student at Duke University when the Immortal Guardians disrupted their lives.

"I know how much it ate you up inside," Seth told the younger man softly, "having to sit on the sidelines."

"And now you're telling me I can't hunt without a babysitter."

The vampires' bodies shriveled up like mummies as the virus infecting them—the same that infected immortals—continued to do its work. Their bloody clothing began to flatten out as their bodies sank in on themselves.

"You don't need a babysitter," Seth countered. "*Bastien* needed a babysitter."

Seemingly against his will, Sean smiled. "Don't let *him* hear you say that. He thinks Richart was there to guard him because the other immortals all wanted him dead."

"There was that, too," Seth admitted. "But my primary purpose in assigning Richart to hunt with him was to keep him in check." The immortal black sheep was forever getting into trouble. "The only reason I wish you to hunt in pairs now is to ensure your safety as well as that of your hunting partner. You know the dangers we currently face."

"Yes, but—"

"Gershom has the sedative." The only one that could knock an immortal out instantly and leave him or her completely vulnerable.

"I know."

"And we believe he is raising his own army of immortals."

"I know."

"And yet you hunt alone with not even your Second as backup to call me if you're tranqed. Why?"

He sighed. "The married couples are already paired up. Krysta hunts with Étienne. Aidan hunts with Dana, Zach with Lisette, Roland with Sarah, and Ethan with Heather. Bastien has been guarding network headquarters and hanging out with Melanie and the vampires." The network currently housed seven vampires who had surrendered to the immortals, hoping doctors like Melanie could prevent them from losing their sanity. "Marcus is afraid to leave Ami's side and only hunts in brief spurts now."

"That's understandable, considering she nearly died right in front of him."

"Absolutely. And he's there to keep Adira and Michael safe."

Seth saw where this was going. "You could hunt with Jared." Almost as old as Seth, Jared had only recently joined their ranks.

Sean grimaced. "I did. For a while. But…"

Seth arched a brow in question.

Sean threw up his hands. "The man won't stop talking!"

Seth fought a laugh.

"I mean, he is *obsessed* with movies."

"Because he spent thousands of years refraining from interacting with humans. Movies and books were the only glimpse he had into their lives and world." Except when he had been monitoring Seth and his Immortal Guardians.

"And he asks *so* many questions."

Seth shrugged. "He's curious about this life he was not allowed to explore before."

"But some of those questions are way too personal for my liking."

"Well… wouldn't *you* be interested in learning more if you were his age and had refrained from sexual activity all your life?"

"Yes. But why doesn't he just put himself out there and start dating?"

Sobering, Seth pointed an imperious finger at him. "Don't you dare put that idea in his head. I have enough chaos in my life. I don't need Jared's dating to muck it up any more."

Sean winced. "I… might have already mentioned it to him. More than once."

Seth loosed a beleaguered sigh. "Of course you did."

"Sorry."

"You'll just have to hunt with Chaak or Imhotep then. Both are elders and so powerful I've been allowing them to hunt alone. I'm sure neither would mind partnering with you."

He grimaced. "Those guys are the antithesis of Jared. They're *too* quiet. Sometimes eerily so."

Seth regarded him with exasperation. "Then hunt with your sister and Étienne."

Sean sighed in defeat. "Do I have to?"

"It's not a punishment, Sean. It's for your safety."

"Fine. But only if you tell Étienne to stop talking dirty to her telepathically when I'm around."

Seth shook his head, feeling like the father figure they all considered him. *Étienne,* he called telepathically.

Yes? the French immortal responded.

Stop talking dirty to Krysta telepathically when her brother is around.

A laugh filtered through his head. *Seriously?*

Yes. I've told Sean I want him to hunt with you two, and he's chafing over needing what he considers a babysitter. Don't exacerbate things by making him feel uncomfortable.

It makes him uncomfortable? he asked with surprise.

Are you saying it doesn't make you uncomfortable when Zach gets handsy with Lisette in your presence?

Ugh. You're right. I'll stop.

Seth turned to Sean. "It's done."

Sean's eyebrows shot up. "Really?"

"Yes."

"Thanks." He motioned to what was left of the vampires at their feet. "I take it none of these were immortals? I thought the guy in the green shirt kinda looked like one of the missing *gifted ones.* And he had brown eyes that glowed amber." Almost all immortals did.

"No. But thank you for calling me. I would still like to capture rather than kill the immortals under Gershom's control." The bastard had kidnapped and transformed a dozen *gifted ones*. Seth could only assume the worst — that he intended to pit them against Seth's Immortal Guardians and inflict as much damage as possible before he used them to kick-start Armageddon. Gershom wanted to watch the world burn and was doing everything he could think of to make that happen. But he harbored a baffling hatred toward Seth at the same time and had struck some heavy blows since embarking upon his quest.

Sean began to collect the vampires' fallen weapons. "I don't have Ethan's picture-perfect recall. So if I see even the slightest resemblance, I figure I should call you."

"I appreciate that." Seth motioned to the empty clothing at their feet. "Can you take care of this on your own?"

Sean shook his head. "I need to call Reordon and have him send over a cleanup crew. I want to make sure none of the security cameras caught anything."

Chris Reordon was the head of the East Coast division of the human network that aided Immortal Guardians.

Seth nodded. He didn't know how Chris and the network did it, but they could work miracles when it came to keeping anything related to Immortal Guardians, vampires, or *gifted ones* from reaching humans. Chris had once even managed to completely quash an incident that took place in Times Square.

There seemed to be little he and his techno wizards couldn't do. *Hmm.*

The woman from Seth's dream strolled to the forefront of his mind.

Tilting his head, Seth studied Sean thoughtfully. If anyone could tell him who the woman was, it would be Chris.

"What?" Sean asked.

"Nothing. You just gave me an idea. Go ahead and call Reordon. Do you want me to wait until the crew arrives?"

"No, I've got this."

Nodding, Seth teleported to the study in David's home.

David's Second, Darnell, sat at his desk, typing on a laptop. A beep sounded in his pocket. "Hi, Seth," he said without looking up.

Seth's mood darkened. Chris's techno wizards had come up

with a device all immortals and their Seconds could carry in their pockets that would beep once whenever Seth was near them. Chris had said the alarms were linked in some way to a coin-sized object Chris asked Seth to always keep with him. No other copies of the coin existed. And the developer who had created the coin had allowed Seth to erase knowledge of it from his memory so Gershom couldn't duplicate it.

Since Gershom could shape-shift and had impersonated Seth in the past, it was the only way most of them could tell Seth was himself when he appeared and not Gershom.

It infuriated him that such was necessary.

Darnell glanced at him over the laptop. "It's only until we defeat Gershom. Don't let it upset you."

He shook his head. "I think Chris is right."

"About what?"

"You've been spending too much time with David and me. Our *paranormal whozeewhatzit*, as he calls it, is beginning to wear off on you."

Darnell laughed and leaned back in his chair. "Anything I can help you with?"

"I need paper and a pencil."

Rising, Darnell strolled past Seth to Ami's desk. "Sounds like *Chris's* whozeewhatzit is starting to wear off on *you*."

Seth smiled. Though Chris was a technological genius, the man carried a stubby number two pencil and a small notebook around with him everywhere he went and preferred to jot things down the old-fashioned way when ideas came to him. "Maybe so."

The overhead light glinted on Darnell's shaved brown head as he bent and opened a drawer. Stacks of paper resided therein. "How much do you need?"

"Just a sheet."

After retrieving the paper, Darnell closed the drawer and drew a regular pencil out of a can full of multicolored ones on top of the desk.

Footsteps approached in the hallway.

Sheldon, Richart's young Second, poked his head in. "Hey, Darnell? Where did Roland end up coming down on letting Michael play with weapons? Was he for it or against it?"

Darnell handed the paper and pencil to Seth, then headed for the doorway. "Are they sharp or dull?"

"Dull," Sheldon answered, stepping back to let Darnell pass. "Or dull-*ish*." Both men left Seth's sight. "I mean, it'll still hurt if he pokes himself in the eye, but the blade won't cut him."

Seth shook his head and let their voices fall away as he set the piece of paper on the desk. Leaning down, he sketched the woman from his dream at preternatural speeds. It was a good likeness, resembling her almost as well as a black-and-white photograph would.

He studied her. She was pretty. Not in a glamorous, perfectly coiffed, expertly made-up, Hollywood kind of way, but in a fresh-faced, girl-next-door kind of way. Again he felt that odd sense of familiarity, as if he had seen her before, *outside* of the dream. But he couldn't recall when or where.

Nor could he erase her from his thoughts.

Setting the pencil down, he drew out his cell phone and dialed Chris Reordon's number.

"Reordon," Chris answered absently.

"It's Seth. I need a moment of your time."

"Sure. I'm in my office. Let me turn off the alarm." A slight pause ensued. "Okay. You're good."

Seth pocketed his phone and teleported to Chris's office.

A beep sounded. Seated behind his massive desk, Chris nodded a greeting, then tapped a key on his computer.

After network headquarters had been breached by a certain Immortal Guardian bent on mischief two or three years earlier, Chris had installed a security feature that would sound an alarm anytime someone teleported into the building.

Rising, the blond strolled around his desk and approached Seth. "What can I do for you?"

"Do any of your contacts have access to facial recognition databases?"

"Yes." Chris had fostered relationships with individuals in just about every law enforcement and government agency there was (including those swathed in secrecy) in his quest to provide Immortal Guardians with all they needed.

"If you give them a picture, can they use it to identify a person?"

"Many times, yes."

"Can they do it with a drawing?"

"Depends on how good the drawing is."

"It's good." He said it factually, not boastfully. Seth had been sketching people for thousands of years. He had long since perfected the craft.

He handed Chris the drawing.

Chris turned away. His chin lowered as he examined the picture on his way back to his desk. "I'll get this to them immediately and..." Halting, he swung around and held up the paper. "Actually, I don't have to. I know who this woman is."

Surprise coursed through Seth. "You do?"

"Yeah. Leah Somerson. She owns Little Gifts, Ami's favorite shop. She sells children's clothing and toys. Baby stuff, too. Ami takes Adira there fairly often because Leah has storytime twice a week to entertain the kids while their parents shop." His lips turned up in a half smile. "And to advertise the books she sells, no doubt."

Leah Somerson. He now had a name to place with the face, but it didn't sound familiar. "What do you know of her?"

Shrugging, Chris leaned back against his desk. "She's originally from Colorado. A widow. No kids. Lives alone above her shop. Total workaholic. And she's never had any affiliations with mercenaries or anyone else who would raise a red flag."

"So you've looked into her background?"

"As soon as Ami started taking Adira to Little Gifts." It proved yet again that Chris thought of everything when it came to ensuring the safety of the Immortal Guardians and those who worked with them. "I found nothing suspicious. Why? Did something happen?"

Seth shook his head. "I had a dream in which she was holding Adira."

"And you want to ensure it wasn't a warning?"

"Something like that." He *did* have prophetic dreams on occasion. "But I was sleeping at David's place, so it was probably just Adira's dream infiltrating mine since she knows her."

"Probably," Chris agreed, then nodded toward a nearby doorway.

Seth followed him into a large conference room dominated by a very long, sleek table with dozens of chairs pulled up to it.

"But," Chris said as soon as he closed the door. Though sound from the rest of the building was escorted in via hidden speakers, nothing inside this room could be heard outside it.

"But?" Seth queried.

"Gershom has proven to be a wily bastard. And he has used people as his puppets in the past."

"You're thinking of Dr. Whetsman." Gershom was nearly as powerful as Seth, his gifts as numerous and varied. One of those gifts, unfortunately, was telepathy that was so strong he could compel others to do his bidding… as he had with Dr. Whetsman, a researcher here at the network, with grim results.

"Yes. Not that he has to do that anymore," Chris added. "We know now that Gershom has become incredibly adept at shape-shifting. If he can fool an immortal who has known you for three thousand years into believing he's you, I doubt he would have any difficulty posing as the proprietress of Little Gifts. Who would know it wasn't her?"

"Ami would," Seth murmured. Ami could detect and identify the unique energy signature every individual possessed, something even Seth couldn't do. "She would know in a heartbeat if Gershom impersonated the woman."

"True."

Seth sighed. This was what it had come to. This was what Gershom had wrought with his perfidy. Ami couldn't even take Adira shopping without Seth worrying that the woman who owned the shop wasn't who she appeared to be.

"Is there any action you'd like me to take?" Chris asked.

"No. It's probably nothing. Just a dream."

"A dream that could possibly foreshadow the future?"

"Or a dream manifested by Adira's subconscious after a recent visit to the store."

Chris shook his head. "Fucking Gershom. We have to get that bastard, Seth. I'm tired of suspecting every*one* of every*thing*."

Guilt once more assailed Seth over not having accomplished that feat yet. "As am I." Skillet's "Monster" rang out from his pocket. Sighing, he answered his phone. "Yes?"

"Seth!" a male cried. "It's Caleb. I could use your help."

Seth looked at Chris. "I'm needed in Canada."

Chris nodded.

Seth teleported to Toronto. A beep sounded.

Caleb, a relatively young immortal at three hundred years old, was fighting seven vampires.

Drawing his katanas, Seth effortlessly ended the life of a vampire intent on hamstringing Caleb, then remained at his back while the two of them worked together to dispatch the rest.

When the last vampire fell, Caleb turned to him with a smile. "Thank you."

Seth nodded. "Why are you hunting alone?"

Caleb held up both hands, which were bloody fists still curled around the hilts of his sais. "I'm not."

The sound of someone approaching at preternatural speeds reached Seth's ears.

Multiple someones.

His frown deepening, he whirled in that direction and raised his katanas. A blurred form raced toward him and skidded to a stop beyond his reach.

"He wasn't hunting alone," Gerard declared breathlessly with a faint French accent. "I was hunting with him. I took off chasing three vampires who tried to flee, but they led me into an ambush and—"

"Duck," Seth ordered.

Gerard ducked.

Seth leapt past him and swung his weapons at the half dozen vampires lunging toward Gerard's back. Far swifter and stronger, Seth struck every target without receiving so much as a scratch in return, opening arteries and severing limbs. Blood slapped him in the face and splattered his clothing. Sputtering in disgust, he stopped.

Six bodies dropped to the ground around him.

Seth looked down at the blood that painted him. "Well, shit."

Gerard and Caleb laughed, then grinned unrepentantly when he tossed them a disgruntled scowl.

Grumbling under his breath, Seth retrieved a clean handkerchief from his back pocket and wiped his blades clean before sheathing them. He would've swabbed some of the blood from his face but couldn't find a clean spot on the cloth.

Caleb stepped forward and offered him a handkerchief. "Here."

"Thank you." Seth diligently applied it to his face and neck. "Next time stay together. The vampires fleeing the scene could've led you into something worse than an ambush."

Gerard nodded. "We will."

Skillet's "Monster" blared from Seth's pocket. Handing Caleb the handkerchief, Seth answered his phone.

"Seth! *Necesito ayuda!*"

Seth glanced at the Canadian immortals. "Leo needs me in Mexico." He teleported away before they could respond. Leo's Second had suffered serious wounds while coming to his aid and was bleeding out. Seth healed him with a touch and teleported both to the network headquarters in Mexico City.

An immortal in Seattle required Seth's aid next. Then more calls came in, summoning him to New Zealand, Venezuela, Colombia, French Polynesia, Brazil, Hawaii, Argentina. He slew more vampires. He healed Immortal Guardians who had been gravely wounded. And through it all, his mind kept returning to the drawing in his pocket and the woman it portrayed.

Leah Somerson. Why did her pretty yet somber face inspire this dueling sense of familiarity and unfamiliarity? *Had* he seen her before? Perhaps long enough ago that he'd forgotten?

Waving Javier over, Seth gently clasped the arm that hung limply at the immortal's side and raised it enough to give him a better grasp on the shoulder wound.

Javier grunted in pain, his jaw clenching.

Seth's hand heated as he healed the wound, stopping the outpouring of blood and sealing the deep gash.

Javier's muscles relaxed. "Gracias."

Smiling, Seth patted his back. "De nada." He looked over at Javier's hunting companion. "Oliver."

Oliver crossed to him and stood still while Seth healed the head wound he'd suffered. "Gracias."

Seth waved his thanks away and stepped back. Glancing down, he grimaced at the wealth of blood that saturated his clothing and painted his skin. He should take a moment to change. Bidding the others good hunting, he teleported to his bedroom in David's home and headed into the bathroom where the clothing he doffed would be less likely to stain the floor.

He kicked off his boots first and wiggled his toes. Thousands of years and he still hated wearing shoes. Shucking his pants, he tossed them in the laundry hamper Darnell kept in there for him. His coat, shirt, and boxers followed. The coat might need to be replaced. It had taken a beating in recent months. It was probably time he sent it to the network, where employees would clean it, mend the tears, and donate it to a homeless shelter along with the other clothing discarded by Immortal Guardians.

He started for the shower, then swore. Facing the sink, he quickly washed his hands, dried them, and returned to the hamper. A moment later, he dug the drawing of Leah out of his coat pocket and unfolded it.

Not a speck of blood marred it.

He stared at her image for a full minute, then folded the paper once more and set it aside. Reaching into the large shower, he turned the faucet. Water pounded tile. Steam began to rise as he stepped in and closed the glass door. A long sigh escaped him as he stepped beneath the hard spray. The ceilings and shower fixtures in all of David's and Seth's homes were higher than normal, so he didn't have to duck to fit his six-foot-eight-inch form beneath the showerhead.

Fatigue pummeled him, a constant annoyance. As always, Seth pushed it aside.

He didn't know what Gershom's game plan was this time, but it seemed to have begun with simply wreaking fucking havoc by dramatically increasing the vampire population worldwide. There were only so many Immortal Guardians sprinkled around the globe who could fight to keep vampires from preying upon humans. When the vampires' numbers overwhelmed those immortals, they called Seth in to take up the slack.

And he had been taking up a *lot* of slack lately.

Though he would've liked to linger beneath the hot water, Seth lathered up and rinsed at preternatural speeds. Stepping out, he dried off just as quickly.

It only took a few seconds to don his usual black cargo pants, black shirt, and his spare black coat. Grumbling a bit, he slid his big feet back into his worn boots and pocketed his cell phone. Miraculously, it hadn't rung the whole time he was showering, so maybe he'd have time to look in on Ami and Adira before he was called away again.

After giving the drawing of Leah another long look, he tucked it in his back pocket, opened his bedroom door, and stepped out into the hallway.

Thumps and thuds carried up the staircase from the basement. Darnell must be sparring with the other Seconds, keeping their skills sharp for whatever battle they would face next.

Seth strode along the hallway, heading for the living room.

"Hi, Seth," a female voice called as he passed David's study.

He stopped. A smile dawned as he backtracked and peered through the doorway.

His adopted daughter Ami sat on the floor, playing with her daughter Adira. Her husband Marcus, a British immortal who was over eight hundred years old, sat cross-legged beside her. An impressive structure comprised of stacked wooden blocks of various shapes and sizes rose between the three of them.

Adira turned toward the doorway, a block clutched in one plump hand. Her adorable little face lit up. "Baba!" Jumping up, the toddler raced forward.

His heart lightening, Seth bent and scooped her into his arms. "Hello, sweetheart. How's my girl tonight?"

Instead of responding verbally, she sent him a slew of mental images of the things she'd done that day.

"Been having fun, have you?"

She nodded with a big grin, setting her bright orange curls to bouncing.

The front door opened.

Seth glanced over as David entered and closed the door behind him.

David nodded to him. "Ami said she wants to see me. Did she summon you as well?" His deep voice carried a hint of an Egyptian accent.

"No. I just stopped in for a shower."

Adira bounced in his arms and held her free hand out to David.

"Abaye! Abaye!"

David smiled. "Hello, poppet. Did you miss me?"

"Yes," she declared as if months, not hours, had passed since she'd last seen him.

Stopping beside Seth, David clasped her hand and brought it to his lips for a kiss. "You've had a busy day, I see."

She nodded.

Seth gave David a quick once-over. His clothing—nearly identical to Seth's—bore no rips or wet splotches. His dark-as-midnight skin appeared unscathed. And his pencil-thin dreadlocks were still neatly tied back at the base of his neck, falling in a thick mass to his hips.

Good. Whatever had called him away must have left him unharmed.

"Hi, David," Ami called. "Would you two join us for a minute?"

"Of course," David agreed.

Seth followed him into the study, only then noticing Zach sprawled on one of the sofas. "What are you doing here?"

As ancient as Seth, Zach jerked a thumb over one shoulder. "I go where she goes."

Lisette's head suddenly popped up from behind the sofa. "Found it," she called with a smile as she held up a cylindrical block. "Hi, Seth."

He nodded. "Lisette."

The pretty French immortal rounded the sofa and dropped the block on the floor beside the others. When Ami rose and approached Seth, Lisette moved to stand behind her. Both appeared to have something on their minds.

Seth arched a brow. "What's up?"

Ami caught and held his gaze. "You need a break."

Lisette nodded. "And we're here to ensure you take one."

Seth frowned. "No, I don't. I'm fine."

"Bullshit," Zach commented. "You're exhausted."

Marcus scowled at the elder. "Damn it, Zach, watch your language."

Ami sighed. "Marcus, honey…"

"What?" He winced. "Oh. Right. Sorry, sweetling. Don't say *damn it*, Adira."

"Okay, Daddy," Adira promised with a sweet smile as she reached over and toyed with one of David's dreadlocks.

David's lips twitched.

Ami returned her attention to Seth. "You need rest."

"I don't have time," he told her honestly.

"Well, if you won't rest, you'll at least take a break from the constant problem solving and life saving," Ami declared, her chin thrusting forward. "Zach has agreed to field your calls for a couple of hours."

Seth looked at Zach.

Zach shrugged. "Lisette can talk me into doing just about anything."

Lisette winked. "You bet I can."

Seth returned his focus to Ami. "And what will I be doing while Zach is alternately annoying and terrorizing any Immortal Guardian who calls me for help?"

"Adira needs some new clothes. Most of hers are stained from playing in Sarah's garden."

He stared at her. "So... you want me to relax by going shopping?"

Zach tried and failed to stifle a laugh.

Seth cut him a glare.

"Yes," Ami responded.

"Why don't you and Marcus take her?" As much as he'd love to spend some downtime with Adira, he needed to keep looking for Gershom and the *gifted ones* he'd transformed.

Ami's gaze slid away as she looked to one side, then the other. Up at the ceiling. Down at the floor. "Because I need to... stay here and... train the Seconds while Darnell redirects your calls. And Marcus wants to... hunt tonight."

Amusement rose. Ami was a terrible liar.

Lisette leaned to one side behind her and caught Seth's eye. *Don't*, she ordered telepathically as she narrowed her eyes.

Don't what?

Don't ask Ami why she and Marcus aren't taking her themselves. They need some alone time, and she's too embarrassed to tell you.

Seth glanced over the women's heads at Marcus, whose gaze was firmly fixed on Ami's ass. His face reflected blatant longing.

Do you know how long it's been since the two of them have made love? Lisette asked, drawing his gaze once more.

No. And didn't care to. Ami really *was* like a daughter to him, so he was content to remain oblivious to certain aspects of her marriage.

You know Adira hasn't wanted to let her mommy out of her sight since Gershom hurt her.

Seth ground his teeth. The bastard had slit Ami's throat while Ami held Adira in her arms.

Most days she still sleeps between them in their bed when they retire, Lisette continued. *So take Adira shopping and let them have a couple of hours together. Spend some time with your granddaughter and do something frivolous. You really* could *use a break from your duties. I know you better than you think.*

Thanks to Zach.

Seth eyed the women thoughtfully. They might have actually given him an opportunity to personally appease his curiosity regarding the mysterious Leah Somerson. He glanced at David. *Did you catch all that?*

Yes.

Do you want to come?

His eyebrows rose. *Really? Don't you want me to help Zach field your calls?*

No. I've something else in mind.

All right.

Seth smiled at Ami. "Okay. We'll take her shopping."

Her face lit with a grin. "Thank you." Ami was only five feet tall, so when she rose onto her toes, Seth still had to lean down so she could kiss his cheek. "You're the best." She handed him a slip of paper. "Here's the address of Little Gifts, our favorite store. You three have fun."

Seth nodded. He would inform David of their other agenda on the way there and finally determine why he couldn't stop thinking about Leah.

Chapter Two

L EAH LIFTED ONE OF THE large boxes that had been delivered earlier onto the table in the back room and grabbed her box cutter.

A bell sounded out front.

"Holy hell," Brittney murmured behind her. "I think I'm in love."

Leah smiled. "You know that's like the third or fourth time you've said that today, right?"

"I know," the twenty-five-year-old said, "but this time I may actually mean it."

Leah shook her head as she applied the utility knife to the box before her.

"Wow. You gotta come look at this guy. Seriously. He is freaking *hot*."

The bell above the door at the front of the shop dinged again.

"Okay, now I'm a two-timing bitch," Brittney declared, "because another guy just walked in and I'm totally in love with him, too."

Leah laughed. "You need to get laid."

"I do. I really do. It's been forever."

She shook her head. "I'm almost afraid to ask. How long is forever to you?"

Brittney cast her a sheepish smile. "Three months."

Leah sighed. "Damn, you make me feel old."

The younger woman grinned and returned her attention to the monitor. "Seriously, you've got to come over here and take a look at these guys. They are unbelievably hot."

Sighing, Leah crossed to stand beside Brittney. "Wow," she parroted as she stared at the screen. "They really *are* gorgeous."

One of the men bore beautiful skin as dark as night and had to be at least six and a half feet tall. Long, thin dreadlocks were drawn back at the nape of his neck and fell to his hips. His features were as flawless as his skin, his build that of a professional athlete. Broad shoulders. Slender hips. A thickly muscled chest. She'd guess his arms and legs were equally muscled, but they were mostly concealed by a long black coat.

His companion stepped up beside him... and Leah's breath caught.

He was an inch or so taller than the first man with skin that held a nice tan. He, too, boasted broad shoulders and a muscular build. His black hair was tied back much like the other man's and fell past his waist. And his features were striking, particularly when he smiled down at the toddler he held in his arms.

Damn it. Why are the good guys always taken?

She blinked, surprised when the thought flitted through her mind. She wasn't looking for a man. Why should it matter if he was taken?

"Look at that beautiful bone structure," Brittney murmured. "I bet he's from Africa. The other guy kinda reminds me of the Italian exchange student I dated last year, but older. That's it. I'm going out there."

Leah reached out and caught her arm when Brittney started forward. "No, you're not."

"Oh, come on. Both those guys look totally doable, and I haven't had sex in ages. I call dibs on the African guy."

"Would you keep your damn voice down?" Leah hissed. "Sheesh."

"Okay, okay. If you want the African guy, I'll take the other one."

"He's holding a baby!"

"I don't care. I need sex, and I'm guessing those guys can *really* deliver."

"Well, too bad. I'm finally operating in the black. And the last thing I need is for you to go out there and spark a sexual harassment lawsuit. Stay here and finish unpacking the merchandise."

"Spoilsport," Brittney grumbled.

Ignoring her, Leah handed her the utility knife and strolled out into the store.

Both men looked up as she entered.

"Hi," she greeted them brightly. "How are you tonight?"

Both returned her smile.

"We're well, thank you," the taller one replied in what she thought might be a British accent. "And you?"

She shrugged. "Can't complain. Is it still raining?"

"Just a drizzle," his dark companion offered.

"I'm Leah." She held her hand out to the black man, whose features and accent made her wonder if Brittney might be right and he was indeed from Africa. "Welcome to my establishment."

"Thank you. It's a pleasure to meet you. I'm David." Instead of shaking her hand, he bowed over it and brought it to his lips for a kiss.

"Oh." Leah suddenly felt as flustered as a teenaged wallflower who had just been approached by the coolest boy in school.

The other man shifted the slumbering baby in his arms and did the same, clasping her hand in his much larger one and bringing it to his lips for a kiss. "I'm Seth. It's nice to meet you, Leah."

Her heartbeat picked up. "It's nice to meet you, too," she managed to squeeze out. Why was she so flustered? As soon as he released her hand, she pressed it to one of her hot cheeks. "I'm blushing, aren't I?"

His smile broadened. "Yes."

"Charmingly," David added.

The heat in her face intensified. "Don't say that! You'll only make it worse."

They laughed.

"That's the first time a man has ever kissed my hand," she confided.

"Shameful," David declared.

"A travesty," Seth agreed with a grin.

Leah laughed, really liking these guys. "Why don't I take your coats and hang them up for you? I keep it pretty warm in here for the little ones who run around in diapers and bare feet."

They exchanged a glance, then shrugged.

Leah moved to stand behind David, admiring his dreadlocks as he shrugged out of his coat. "I know you probably hear this a lot," she murmured, reaching up to grip his collar and tug the coat down his thickly muscled arms, "but you have beautiful hair." And how cool was it to have to reach *up* to help him? Leah was five foot ten, so there weren't many men she had to look up to like this.

"Thank you."

She stepped away long enough to hang his coat on the coatrack near the register. "Do women drive you crazy, asking if they can touch it all the time?"

As she returned, David reached out and took the toddler from his friend. His brown eyes twinkled with amusement. "No. Most women find me a bit... intimidating."

She winked. "Shameful. But it's their loss."

Both men chuckled.

The toddler stirred and buried her face in David's neck.

Leah turned to Seth and motioned for him to give her his back.

Again he exchanged a glance with David.

What was he thinking?

<hr />

Seth started to peel off his coat.

Just as she had with David, Leah reached up and helped him remove it. Her fingers brushed the back of his neck as she reached for the collar to give it a tug, leaving a slight tingling in their wake.

When he turned around to face her, Seth found her staring at his ponytail. "Wow. Your hair is beautiful, too."

Surprised, he smiled. "Thank you." When was the last time a woman had paid him a compliment? Not the blatantly sexual I-want-to-do-you kind, but a simple, genuine one?

He couldn't remember.

Leah sent them both a wry smile. "I suddenly feel the need to run out and buy better shampoo and conditioner... along with a slew of curling irons."

"I assure you there's no need," he told her. "You have lovely hair." She really did. Thick and straight, it shone beneath the overhead lights as it fell down her back almost to her waist.

"You're just trying to get me to blush again," she quipped, turning away.

Seth chuckled again and met David's gaze as she left them to hang up his coat. *She's not at all intimidated by us, is she?* he commented telepathically.

Not a bit, David agreed. *It's a refreshing change.*

It really was. Even people who didn't know they were immortal seemed to sense their power and more often than not gave them a wide berth.

Are you reading her thoughts? Seth asked him. He had described his dream to David on the way over, mentioning his and Chris's concerns.

Yes. I haven't found anything suspicious. No signs of mind control by Gershom or such.

That was a relief. The dream must have been what he had hoped—just Adira's infiltrating his own.

"So what can I help you with tonight?" Leah asked as she returned. "Or would you prefer that I leave you alone to browse? I won't be offended if you don't want company."

Seth retrieved the list Ami had pressed into his hand before they'd left. It was a pretty lengthy one. "I think we'll just browse if you'll point us in the direction of toddler clothing."

"Sure. It's right over there by the dressing rooms. Girls on the right. Boys on the left. Gender neutral in the middle."

"Thank you."

"Let me know if you need anything." She crossed to a clothing rack on wheels located near the back of the shop. Drawing it forward, she stopped, removed some pants from it, and inserted them into one of the floor racks, then moved on to do the same at the next one.

Seth's gaze lingered on her for a moment. She was tall—a little less than a foot shorter than his six-foot-eight-inch frame—and slender, with full breasts and hips that formed an appealing hourglass shape. She had a natural beauty that was unclouded by makeup. And he again felt that odd sense of familiarity, as if he'd seen her before. Not in his dream. Somewhere else. But he still could unearth no memory of her.

Tearing his eyes away so she wouldn't catch him staring, he meandered through the clothing racks with David until they reached the designated area. A sea of pink, purple, and white fabric decorated one side. Blue, gray, and black dominated the other. Green and yellow grew in the middle.

So many racks surrounded them. And he knew *nothing* about buying clothing for toddlers.

"What are we looking for?" David asked.

Seth consulted the list in his hand. "The first item is…" He frowned. "Does this say skirts or shorts?" He held out the paper.

David frowned down at it. "It looks like it says skorts."

"What the hell is a skort?"

Feminine laughter sounded behind them. Low and warm, it made him smile before he even looked over and found Leah regarding them with good-natured amusement. "A skort is a skirt with shorts attached." Setting the pants she held aside, she joined them and motioned to a rack a few yards away. "See?" Choosing a purple skirt with pink and white polka dots, she held it up, then lifted the hem to show them the shorts sewn beneath. "This way the girls can wear skirts to the playground without flashing their panties or diapers when they're on the slide. That sort of thing."

Seth took the proffered garment. "That's actually quite clever."

David agreed, and Leah returned to her sorting.

Seth and David picked out several skorts in the size Ami had designated and moved on to the pants. Then the dresses. Seth retrieved a basket from the front of the store and deposited his load in it.

Leah continued to distribute articles of clothing to this rack or that. Though she said nothing more, leaving them to their murmuring and perusing, he was very aware of her movements. Every glance she sent their way. Every twitch of her lips when they said something that amused her.

"What's next?" David asked.

"Sleepwear."

"I heard Sarah tell Roland to make sure he bought organic sleepwear. Something about flame retardants."

Flame retardants?

Seth looked at Leah.

Smiling, she pointed to a rack beside her. "The organic sleepwear is over here. I also have some sleepwear there" — she pointed to a rack beyond it — "that isn't made from organic fabrics but doesn't contain the flame retardants. Just look for the yellow tag that says it isn't flame resistant and should be close fitting."

"Thank you."

They crossed to the racks she recommended.

Seth had to admit Ami was right. Though he didn't feel right shopping while so much danger lurked in the Immortal Guardians' world, it did succeed in taking his mind off things and provided him with a bit of a mental break. He couldn't fume over Gershom's determination to launch Armageddon when he was concentrating on what Adira would be comfortable in, what would look cute on her, and what wouldn't make Marcus declare all children's clothing designers pedophiles because he thought the shorts and skirts inappropriately short.

While he considered a pair of pajamas with a giraffe printed on them, he became aware of Leah moving closer. Plastic and metal clicked and clacked as she placed more hangers on the rack behind him.

The clacking stopped. The store quieted.

He paused. Leah stood behind him and to one side. He heard her heartbeat close by. Smelled her strawberry-scented shampoo and her lip balm, which carried the same aroma of coconuts as it had in his dream.

From the corner of his eye, he saw her take a large but deliberately casual step forward to stand between him and David.

Looking at neither of them, she clasped her hands behind her back and just stood there. A faint smile lit her pretty face as she rocked forward and backward the slightest bit on her toes, turning her head one way and the other as though she were merely passing time while waiting for the bus to arrive. She even nodded as though she'd been carrying on an internal conversation and drawn a conclusion that pleased her.

Seth looked over her head at David. *What's she doing?*

David shook his head, appearing equally puzzled. *I have no idea.*

Are you still reading her thoughts?

No. Are you?

No. It was something else from which he'd dearly needed to take a break. His search for Gershom and the newly transformed immortals the bastard held had required him to perform a great deal of mind reading in recent months. He had wanted to enjoy a little peace and quiet for a change and had opted to leave the mind reading to David tonight.

Leah chose that moment to look up at him.

Seth arched a brow. "Afraid we intend to pocket some of the merchandise?"

Laughing, she offered him another smile. "No. I'm sorry. I couldn't resist. I just wanted to see what it was like."

He shared another quizzical glance with David. "What *what* is like?"

She shrugged. "Being short. When I was in high school, I always envied the petite girls. You know, the ones who were only an inch or so above five feet and never had to worry about being rebuffed by guys who were shorter than they were."

Seth stared at her, perplexed. "Guys rebuffed you for being taller than they were?" She really was quite lovely. He would've thought the boys would've been vigorously competing for her attention.

"Oh yeah. Quite a few times," she told him.

"Why?" David asked. "You'd think they'd *like* being shorter than you."

Seth nodded. "It would put their faces right at breast level."

"Exactly!" she said with a grin. "That's what I thought, too. But that ended up not being the case. At all. So I've always wondered what it would be like to be one of those tiny women who always has to look *up* at the men around them."

Seth raised his eyebrows. "And?"

She grinned. "I like it. I haven't felt this small since I was thirteen."

Both men chuckled.

"You would love the rest of our family then," David told her as he held up a pajama set to examine. "Every male is over six feet tall."

She nudged him with her elbow. "You shouldn't have told me that. Now I'm going to crash your family reunions."

Seth smiled as she retrieved her rolling garment rack and moved on.

I like her, David said.

I do, too, he admitted. He'd smiled more in the past fifteen minutes than he had in...

Well, it had been a while. Adira could always make him smile. Ami could, too. But Leah seemed to have a unique talent for eliciting full-blown grins.

Probably because she really *didn't* seem intimidated by him. That was rare. *Very* rare. Hell, immortal men and women he had known for hundreds—if not thousands—of years still maintained a certain reserved distance when dealing with him. And that included Lisette, upon whose sofa he had sprawled while trying to catch a few minutes of downtime. Her husband Zach was as old as Seth and nearly as powerful, but Lisette had never completely shed that hint of distance, that deference or respect, that had always been present when she interacted with him. There were very clear lines she wouldn't cross.

"I see now why Marcus is convinced all children's clothing designers are pedophiles," David grumbled.

Seth looked over and found David holding up a small nightgown that was cut more like a woman's.

Again Leah laughed, drawing his gaze. "I've heard many a daddy say the same." Then her brow furrowed. "Wait. Did you say Marcus?"

David glanced at her. "Yes."

Leaning to one side, she studied Adira's hair as though hoping she could glimpse the toddler's features. Her gaze then settled upon Seth. "You said your name is Seth?"

"Yes."

Her eyebrows rose. "You're *the* Seth?"

Seth cast David an uncertain glance as suspicion rose. "I'm not sure what you mean by that. Did Ami mention me?"

"No." The surprise in her eyes gave way to amusement as her lips twitched. "Sheldon did. Usually in sentences that begin with *Seth would kick my butt if...*"

He laughed.

Leah strolled over to join them once more. "I didn't realize that was Adira."

Seth nodded. "She's our granddaughter. Ami is our adopted daughter."

"Oh," she responded. And the single syllable conveyed something that sounded almost like disappointment.

Had he said something wrong?

David caught his eye. "She thinks we're gay." *And she's attracted to you, hence the disappointment.*

Seth's eyebrows flew up again as he regarded Leah with surprise. "We're not gay."

She wagged an index finger back and forth between them. "You two aren't a couple?"

"No. David and I are as close as brothers. When we found Ami and discovered she had lost her own family, we welcomed her into ours."

Adira stirred.

Seth reached out and took Adira from David, settling her against his chest. "Though I didn't officially adopt her, Ami is like a daughter to me. To us both really."

"And Adira is like your granddaughter," she said, smiling when Adira sleepily opened her eyes and gave Leah a glance. "Okay. That makes more sense, because you do *not* look old enough to be a grandfather. Neither one of you. You don't even look old enough to be Ami's father."

"I'm older than I look," he admitted.

Leaning toward him, she said in a conspiratorial whisper, "I wish I could say the same, but I'm pretty sure I look my age."

Adira straightened in Seth's arms and stared at Leah.

"Hi there, cutie," Leah said and waggled her fingers.

Her cheeks plumping with a big grin, Adira thrust her arms out and lunged toward Leah.

Eyes widening, Leah hurried to catch Adira, inadvertently trapping Seth's arm between the toddler and her breasts. "Oh! You gotta give me a little warning before you do that, sweetie," she said on a laugh.

"I'm sorry." Seth wasn't sure if he should retrieve Adira or relinquish her and extricate his arm. "Shall I take her back?"

"No, it's okay," Leah responded with a good-natured smile.

"She likes to sit in my lap when Ami brings her to storytime. So she knows me. Let me just... Here... How's that?" She held Adira slightly away from her body so Seth could slide his arm out.

Behind her, David's face creased with a grin while Seth tried to minimize contact with her as he withdrew his arm. But she had lovely full breasts and hadn't left him much space.

Really? David asked telepathically, his dark eyes twinkling with amusement. *Trying to cop a feel at your age?*

Seth shook his head. *You've been spending too much time with Sheldon.*

David's laughter filled his head.

She really did have beautiful breasts though. Seth was surprised to feel another tingle of awareness slither through him.

Adira giggled and bounced in Leah's arms.

"I'm excited to see you, too," Leah said.

Suddenly, male voices began to sing rhythmic *dos* to the accompaniment of piano and drums in the sprightly tune "I've Got My Love to Keep Me Warm."

Brow furrowing, David reached into his back pocket and withdrew his cell phone. He shared a concerned look with Seth.

Zach was supposed to be fielding their calls, so this wouldn't be good.

"Yes?" David answered.

"Sorry to interrupt up your downtime," Darnell said without preamble, "but Edward has been wounded pretty badly in Norfolk."

Seth's preternaturally sharp hearing allowed him to hear both sides of the conversation.

"How badly?" David asked.

"He nearly lost an arm. It's still attached, but even with blood infusions it'll probably take at least a day for the virus to mend vessels, ligaments, muscle, and bone enough to take the edge off his pain. Zach had to teleport to Chile. Vampires were overwhelming two immortals there. And I've sent three more calls his way since. Aidan had to teleport to Ontario for the same reason." Both immortals were powerful healers as well as teleporters.

David frowned. "I assume Aidan took Dana with him."

"Yes. And Roland and Sarah were both injured earlier, so I'm thinking Roland shouldn't do any more healing tonight."

If he did, Seth knew Edward's wound would open on Roland's body. Such always happened when younger immortals pushed their healing gift too far. And Roland was only nine and a half centuries old, give or take a decade.

"All right," David said. "I'm on my way."

Seth sighed mentally. So much for getting some downtime. *I'll do it,* he told David telepathically.

David shook his head as he pocketed the phone. *No, you won't. You really* do *need a break.*

Leah smiled. "I love the Mills Brothers. It's so cool that you listen to them. I think it's a shame that so many kids today refuse to listen to music produced before they were born. They're really missing out on some great stuff."

"I agree," David said with a smile, then caught Seth's eye. *She thinks we're a mere twenty-eight or thirty years old to her forty-six.* Another twinkle of amusement entered his dark brown gaze. *And that you're very handsome.* "I'm afraid I have to leave. Something has arisen that requires my immediate attention. But it has been a pleasure meeting you, Leah."

"A pleasure meeting you, too."

Seth caught David's eye. "Call me if you need me."

Nodding, David crossed the store, grabbed his coat off the coatrack, then slipped outside.

Adira squirmed in Leah's arms, wanting down.

Leah lowered her until her little sneaker-clad feet touched the floor.

Adira toddled away, patting the garments that brushed her head and shoulders.

Straightening, Leah watched her for a moment, then turned back to Seth. "I guess I'll get back to work."

Was that disappointment he felt upon hearing her words? He really was enjoying her company.

Adira turned around and toddled back. Grasping Leah's fingers, she reached out, took Seth's hand, and placed Leah's in it.

Seth instinctively curled his fingers around Leah's.

Satisfied, Adira turned and toddled off once more.

"Oh," Leah said with a surprised chuckle. "Well. Maybe not."

Seth was surprised, too. What was Adira thinking?

He glanced at Leah. Should he apologize? "Sorry about that."

"No worries," she said with another charming smile. Raising their clasped hands, she turned them so his was on top and slid her free hand over it. "Oooh. Look how big your hand is."

How many times had he heard Tracy or one of the other mortal women he frequently encountered think *Oooh. Look how big his hands are. You know what they say: big hands, big feet, big package* in much the same tone as Leah's.

Seth couldn't help it. He barked out a laugh.

Leah's eyes widened. "Wait. I didn't mean that the way it sounded."

"It sounded as if you like that my hands are so big."

She flushed. "I do, but I didn't mean it like you think."

"How do I think you meant it?" he asked with exaggerated innocence.

Face red, she laughed. "Stop making me blush. I just meant I like that you're so big. Not just your hands. But all over." Again her eyes widened. "I mean, not *all* over, but—"

Laughing, he took pity on her. "It's all right. I understood what you meant the first time."

Smiling, she squinted up at him. "You like to tease, don't you?"

"Guilty as charged." Many immortals did. It helped lighten what could otherwise be a dark existence.

She caressed his hand again, sending little tingles through it. "My hand actually looks small in yours. That's so cool."

It did. And the sensations her soft touch inspired unnerved him a bit. His pulse even picked up.

Seth eyed her curiously. "You really dislike your size so much?" He thought it a shame. She was a beautiful woman.

Shrugging, she released his hand and let hers fall to her sides. "When someone gives you a complex in high school, it tends to stick with you."

Adira reappeared as if by magic. Taking Leah's hand, she again placed it in Seth's, then moved away.

The two looked at each other and smiled.

Leah nodded after Adira. "Maybe she's hoping I'll distract you so she can take her time looking over the toys she plans to coax you into buying before you leave."

Seth winked. "Or maybe she just heard you say you like my big hands."

She laughed.

———◦◦◦———

Damn, he was handsome, Leah thought. *Funny, too.* And his long fingers twining through hers felt really good. Maybe *too* good. She hadn't held a man's hand in almost a decade. She'd forgotten how nice it could be. How such a simple touch could speed her pulse… as it did now. That surprised the hell out of her.

Seth released her hand. And she thought he seemed almost as reluctant as she to sever the contact. But surely she was mistaken. A man with his astonishing good looks would not suffer a dearth of female attention. Women probably touched him all the time.

How weird was it that she envied them?

Adira returned. Taking Leah's hand, she again placed it in Seth's and held them together for a moment as if to say *I want you to hold hands. Seriously. Is it really that difficult for you to understand?*

As the adorable little redhead left them once more, Leah met Seth's gaze. He had nice eyes. So dark a brown they were almost black.

"I'm sorry," he said with a baffled shake of his head. "She's never done this before."

"That's okay. No need to apologize. I think it's cute." She watched Adira meander through the racks until she stood before the wall of toys behind Leah's storytime bench. "Looks like I was right," she told Seth with a grin.

"Apparently so."

"Well…" She shrugged. "I'm up for taking a break from work and don't mind holding a handsome man's hand while doing so. Why don't I help you knock out that list of yours?"

He smiled. "Sounds good. Particularly since I haven't held a beautiful woman's hand in a long time."

"I find that *very* hard to believe, and I know I'm not beautiful. But I'll let you get away with saying it because it's good for my ego."

He laughed.

She even liked his laugh, so deep and rumbly she could almost feel it.

As they worked their way through the racks, comparing nightgowns and dresses for Adira, he slid his thumb back and forth across the back of her hand in an absent caress. When she made him laugh, he squeezed her hand. His brown eyes twinkled. And his lips stretched in an appealing grin, flashing straight white teeth.

He made *her* laugh, too, with his penchant for teasing.

Leah didn't think she had ever had so much fun helping a customer find what he wanted. She didn't even realize until they had found everything on his list that he and Adira had stayed twenty minutes past closing time.

Leah couldn't have cared less. Smiling up at him, she nodded toward Adira. "Shall we see what toys she's picked out?"

He nodded.

Still holding hands, they weaved their way through the racks to stand beside the toddler.

"See anything you want, poppet?" Seth asked, his deep voice full of affection.

Leah waited for Adira to start pointing to a multitude of toys. She had seen a *lot* of battles erupt between parent and child when the child wanted more toys than the parent wished to purchase.

Adira crossed to the substantial section of stuffed animals and chose a buffalo. A large smile wreathing her face, she returned and stared up at Seth.

Still holding Leah's hand, he knelt in front of his granddaughter. "That's a handsome fellow." He drew his free hand down over its back. "So soft. Did you know that some bison are taller than I am?"

Adira's eyes widened as she shook her head.

Smiling, Seth rose. "I'll have to take you to Yellowstone to see them. Any other toys you'd like?"

Hugging the buffalo to her chest, Adira smiled. "No."

He nodded and turned to Leah. "It's cute. I don't believe I've ever seen a stuffed bison before."

She agreed. "I like that company. They make a lot of stuffed animals that you don't normally see in the big stores and donate part of the proceeds to preserving those species."

"Excellent. Perhaps I can coax her into buying more the next time we're here."

Leah shouldn't be so happy to hear he intended to return but couldn't help it. He was fun to be around. Fun to talk to. And a tease, as she'd accused him earlier. She also shouldn't be disappointed about having to release his hand when she rang up their purchases, but silently admitted she was.

"It was a pleasure to meet you, Leah," Seth said as he tugged on his coat.

"A pleasure to meet you, too."

Adira held her arms up for a hug. Once Leah complied and stepped back, the two headed out into the night.

Watching them walk away—Seth carrying a multitude of bags with one hand and holding Adira's little hand in the other—Leah sighed. What an adorable sight. Seth smiled down at Adira while she hopped along beside him, still clutching her beloved buffalo.

When Leah could no longer see them, she turned back to face the interior of the store and found Brittney standing in the doorway to the back room.

Brittney's eyes were wide. "That was freaking *awesome!*" Her pink lips stretched in a huge grin. "I mean that was so cute! The way she made you guys hold hands the whole time he was here."

Leah smiled.

"And he is so freaking gorgeous! Seriously, this has to be a sign. You totally have to hook up with him."

Shaking her head, Leah returned to the rack of clothing she had abandoned when Adira insisted she hold Seth's hand. "Yes, he is gorgeous… and at least sixteen years younger than I am."

"So get your cougar on, girl, and go jump that!" Brittney challenged. "You look a lot younger than you are."

"Statements like that only make me feel older. Get back to work."

Brittney's shoulders slumped. "Fine."

Leah smiled and, despite her assistant's grumbling, continued to do so the rest of the night.

Chapter Three

S ETH BRACED HIS HANDS AGAINST the tile and sighed as hot water pounded his tight shoulders. Steam rose around him as crimson liquid sluiced down his form and slithered into the drain. None of the blood was his. All of it was vampire. After twelve hours of teleporting all over the globe to aid his Immortal Guardians, he had once more stopped in at David's for a shower.

Never in his thousands of years of living had he seen vampires amass such numbers. Gershom had done a hell of a job mind-controlling every vamp he could find so the vampire would transform rather than kill its victims. And Immortal Guardians were paying the price.

Fatigue pulled at him as he reached for the shampoo. He hadn't managed to snag much sleep in the week since he had visited Little Gifts. Just a half hour here or an hour there. And he did so at David's home, wanting to be close to Ami and Adira even if he wasn't able to spend time with them.

Until Zach had joined their ranks, David had been the second oldest and most powerful Immortal Guardian on the planet. Possessed of a warm and generous nature, David opened his homes throughout the world to all immortals and their Seconds or mortal guards, wanting them to have a place in which they could gather together and stave off the loneliness that often accompanied this existence. David was, in fact, largely responsible for the fact that Immortal Guardians considered each other family.

Seth did the same, but was often kept so busy that he rarely visited his homes. And now that Ami and her family lived with

David in North Carolina, Seth spent every moment he could there instead. He really did love Ami as deeply as he would a daughter, perhaps because she reminded him a great deal of his own... of the daughter he'd lost along with his wife and son so long ago.

Though he would love to linger in the shower, Seth finished lathering up, rinsed off, then stepped out and grabbed a towel. A minute later, he ran a comb through his long, thick hair and tied it back with a strip of leather. Gershom had been spawning such chaos that even when he slept, Seth wore standard Immortal Guardian hunting garb: black cargo pants, a black T-shirt, and black boots. When he reached for his coat, he paused. Digging in one pocket, he pulled out the drawing he'd made of Leah and unfolded it.

Her pretty face was somber in the drawing, as it had been in the dream. He had not seen that expression once while he had spoken with her. Instead, she had laughed and teased and winked at him while her hazel eyes sparkled.

He liked her... and hoped like hell Gershom had no plans to use her in whatever new scheme his madness birthed.

Giving in to impulse, Seth strode into the bedroom and grabbed the paper and pencil Darnell had left on the bedside table. It only took him a moment to sketch Leah again. This time she tilted her head back as if she were looking up at him. Her lips formed an enchanting smile. Her pretty eyes danced with amusement.

Once he finished, Seth smiled, too. Much better. Folding both drawings, he donned his coat and slipped them into the pocket, refusing to explore why he wanted to keep the sketches with him.

The sun had risen. The other immortals staying at David's home would have retired for the day and succumbed to slumber. Unfortunately for Seth, it was always night somewhere. Even now, Immortal Guardians on the other side of the globe embarked upon their nightly hunts and engaged in fierce battles. And some of them would inevitably call, requiring his assistance.

Perhaps he could sneak in a nap before his phone rang again. Maybe snag something to eat first. Leaving the soundproof bedroom David reserved for him, Seth strode down the hallway toward the front of the large one-story home. The living room it opened onto was huge, boasting numerous sofas, love seats, wingback chairs, and coffee tables to accommodate the powerful warriors who gathered together each night as their hunts wound down and dawn approached. Most of those stationed in the area had been spending their days here at David's. All were very protective of Ami, the first mortal woman to conceive and give birth to an Immortal Guardian's baby. All adored Adira. And all obsessed over their safety nearly as much as Seth and David did.

Marcus exited the kitchen as Seth approached it. "Hi, Seth." He tucked a colorful stainless steel water bottle into a Doc McStuffins backpack. A pink stuffed unicorn dangled on a clip from one of the straps.

Seth nodded. "Marcus." He'd known the British immortal for 850 years, give or take, ever since a vampire had transformed Marcus against his will. When Seth had assigned Ami to serve as Marcus's Second, he hadn't expected the two to fall in love. "What are you up to?"

"Ami wants to take Adira to storytime at Little Gifts."

Seth perked up a bit at the mention of the store, his mind going straight to Leah. "Oh?"

Nodding, Marcus adjusted the strap of the backpack on his shoulder. "I just tanked up on blood to ensure the sun won't harm me. Wouldn't want to walk in looking like a lobster." He smiled. And damned if he didn't appear more relaxed than Seth had seen him in weeks. "Hey, thank you, by the way, for the other night."

"Don't mention it," Seth responded and held up a hand when Marcus started to speak again. "I mean it. Don't mention it. Ami really is like a daughter to me."

Marcus laughed. "I know."

Seth couldn't help but frown though. "I didn't realize Adira was still insisting on sleeping with the two of you."

A shadow passed over Marcus's features as he sobered. "She's reluctant to let Ami stray too far. I was actually surprised she left her mother long enough to go shopping with you. I think that's the first time she's let Ami out of her sight since it happened. Did she really do as well as you said?"

"Yes." Seth had mentioned nothing about Adira wanting him to hold hands with Leah after David had left. He hadn't told David either and wondered absently if David had read it in Adira's thoughts. "She seemed to have a nice time." *He* sure as hell had. "What did you mean by mostly? Is she still dreaming of her mother being harmed?"

"No. Those nightmares finally faded away. But the others — the ones about the mystery man being tortured — still return every once in a while."

Seth's frown deepened. Adira had been having those nightmares ever since she was in the womb. They still had no idea who they were about because the dreams were always from the man's point of view, so none of them ever saw his face.

"Do you think it's one of Gershom's immortals?" Marcus asked hesitantly. "She's displayed some precognitive abilities. That would explain her having dreamed about him before Gershom kidnapped him."

"I don't know," Seth replied honestly. "Where is Ami now?"

"Getting Adira ready to go."

"Will Michael be going, too?"

"No. Not today. He didn't sleep well last night."

The toddler Roland and Sarah had adopted after Gershom killed his mother was settling in well but still had rough days now and then.

"Why don't I take Adira to storytime for you?" Seth asked, then wondered what the hell he was doing.

Wouldn't hurt to check the place out one more time, would it? a voice in his head argued. *Just because Gershom didn't interfere with Leah's life before you met her doesn't mean he won't in the future. What if the dream* wasn't *simply Adira's infiltrating your own? Wouldn't it be wise to keep an eye on Leah? Check in? Ascertain how she's doing? Ensure nothing has changed?*

It seemed a weak premise, but damn it, he wanted to see her again.

Marcus stared at him. "Really? You would do that? You don't mind?"

The blatant hope that lit the younger man's face filled him with guilt. Seth had been so furious at himself for not protecting Ami better and so concerned about Adira that he hadn't devoted much thought to how Marcus was coping. Adira wasn't the only one who had almost lost Ami. Marcus had nearly lost her, too. And he had been subverting his own need to touch her and hold her close all this time in order to ensure his daughter's needs were fulfilled.

"Of course I don't mind," Seth said, glad now that he'd offered. "What do you say?"

His lips stretching in a wide grin, Marcus leaned forward, hugged Seth tight, and exclaimed in a boyish voice, "I say you're the best dad ever!"

Smiling, Seth shook his head and gave him a shove. "Oh, fuck off."

Marcus laughed.

"I'm not even going to ask," a deep voice said dryly behind them.

Seth turned as Zach strolled out of the hallway. "Perfect timing. I need you to field my calls for a couple of hours."

"Okay." Zach stopped beside them. "What's up?" As usual, he wore black leather pants and boots but no shirt that would constrict his large dark wings.

"Nothing," Seth said, taking the bag from Marcus and looping it over his shoulder. "I'm just going to take Adira on an outing." *Marcus and Ami need time alone,* he told Zach telepathically.

Zach arched a brow. *Again?*

Yes. And don't make any smart-ass remarks. Do you remember how you felt when you nearly lost Lisette? The way you refused to let go of her and — once you did — needed to touch her as often as you could to convince yourself she was okay?

He tilted his head to one side. *Yes. I wouldn't even let go of her long enough to let her brothers hug her at first.*

Well, Marcus hasn't been able to do that since nearly losing Ami, because he's been putting Adira's need to be close to her mother first.

Oh. Zach looked at Marcus. *Poor bastard. Yes. Let's give them some time alone together then.*

The quick capitulation surprised Seth. Zach had changed a *lot* since he'd fallen in love with Lisette.

Ami entered the hallway from the basement stairwell, Adira perched on her hip. "Okay," she told them as she approached. "We're ready to go."

Marcus smiled and rested a hand on her back when she stopped beside him. "Change of plans. Seth is going to take her."

Ami's eyebrows rose as she looked up at Seth. "Really?"

Seth smiled. "As you said last week, I could use some downtime." He held his arms out to Adira. "What do you think, poppet? Would you like me to take you to storytime today?"

Adira hugged Ami tightly, then nodded and leaned toward him.

"That's my girl," he said, feeling lighter already. "Zach, tell Darnell to redirect my calls, will you?"

"All right."

Marcus leaned forward and pressed a kiss to Adira's cheek. "Have fun."

Grinning, she bounced on Seth's hip. "Okay, Daddy."

And Seth thought there might have been a little *bounce* to his step as he strode through the front door, as happy as Adira.

He was really looking forward to seeing Leah.

———◦◦◦———

Upon hearing the bell on the front door ding again, Leah glanced over the many bodies milling around her shop and felt her heart do a funny little skip. Seth entered, Adira in his arms, a Doc McStuffins backpack looped over one shoulder.

Every female in the store glanced over, went still, and stared.

He made quite an impression. While the other adults present wore clothing in a variety of colors and the children raced about in pretty pastels, Seth wore a black T-shirt and black cargo pants that did little to hide his muscular physique. His long obsidian hair was drawn back from his face and tied at the nape of his neck. Though it was only eleven in the morning, his strong jaw bore a five-o'clock shadow that, coupled with the dark shades that hid his eyes, only enhanced his rugged beauty.

Hell, even a couple of the dads present stopped and stared.

Reaching up, he removed the sunglasses and glanced around the store.

Adira spotted Leah first and waved with a big grin.

When Seth followed the toddler's gaze and found Leah, his friendly smile filled her stomach with butterflies.

She waved back.

"Holy crap," someone whispered in her ear.

Leah glanced over her shoulder at Mandy, another of her

employees.

"Is that the guy Brittney told me about? The one whose little girl made you hold hands for like an hour?"

"Yes."

"I am so freaking jealous."

Leah rolled her eyes. "You're married, Mandy."

"Yes, I am… and dearly wish Paul was built like that. If he was, I would never let the man out of bed and would weigh twenty pounds less from all the extra calories I'd burn ravaging his hot body every chance I could get."

Laughing, Leah wound her way through the crowd. Some of those present were regular customers. Some were new. She stopped short when two preschoolers darted in front of her, then continued on to greet Seth. "Hi." She waggled her fingers at Adira. "Hi, cutie."

Adira lunged toward her again with a giggle.

Leah hastily grabbed her and held her close. "Whoa!" she said on a laugh. "I thought you were going to give me a little warning next time."

"I'm so sorry," Seth said as he gently extricated his arm. "She usually only does that with family."

Leah caught her breath when the back of his hand brushed against her breast. She could tell he hadn't done it on purpose, but that didn't stop her body from tingling in the wake of his touch. "That's okay. It just caught me off guard." She smiled. "Again."

Adira bounced in her arms.

Leah grinned. "She *really* likes storytime."

Seth smiled. "So I see."

"Ami isn't coming today?"

He shook his head. "I volunteered to bring Adira."

He did? To see *her* again maybe? Leah wondered, then mentally shook her head. Of course not. "We're about to begin. Do you want her to stay with me while I read? I don't mind if she does."

Seth looked at Adira. "What do you say, poppet? Do you want to stay with Miss Leah, or do you want to sit with Baba?"

Adira rested her head on Leah's chest.

His smile widened. "Looks like she's made her choice."

Leah chuckled. "Are you sure you don't mind?"

"Not at all. I'll just find a quiet corner to lean in and stay out of everyone's way."

Everyone being the women who surreptitiously edged closer, hoping to sit beside him. Leah shook her head. "There are chairs over there for parents who don't want to sit on the floor with the kids."

"Thank you." Offering her a brief bow, he started to walk away.

Adira reached out and grabbed his arm. "No, Baba."

He turned back. "Did you change your mind?" Unperturbed, he reached for the toddler with a smile full of affection.

Even *that* made butterflies flutter in Leah's belly. The man was just too damned handsome. And she loved that he was good with children.

Adira shook her head. "Come read, Baba."

His eyebrows flew up. "Oh. No, sweetheart. This is Miss Leah's storytime. Remember? We're here to listen to *her* read today."

"Both," Adira responded and looked at Leah with a hopeful smile. "Both?"

Leah glanced at Seth.

He cast her an apologetic look. "I'm sorry. I haven't been spending as much time with her as I usually do and she probably just—"

Leah waved a hand. "Don't worry about it. If you'd like to give it a try and don't mind an audience, we can both read the story. You can be the raccoon and I'll be the rabbit."

He looked uncertain. "I don't want to interfere with your routine."

"You wouldn't be. Mandy reads with me sometimes. The kids get a kick out of hearing us do different voices." Although Leah suspected the *moms* would be the ones who got a kick out of today's reading if Seth joined her. "And every once in a while I ask the parents if any of them would like to read with me."

Still he hesitated. "You really don't mind?"

"Not at all."

Smiling, he shrugged his broad shoulders. "All right then."

Adira giggled with glee and bounced on Leah's hip.

Laughing, Leah led Seth to the area she'd cleared for storytime. Seth waited for Leah to sit on the bench, then seated himself beside her, his muscled arm brushing her shoulder.

It did not surprise Leah at all when the mothers all opted to sit in a close circle with the children today instead of milling about the store or chatting softly by the coffee machine. What *did* surprise her was Seth himself. He was a fantastic storyteller! In the past, the parents who had gamely read stories with her had been pretty stilted readers. Seth, on the other hand, read Raccoon's dialogue with such character and humor, his facial expressions as entertaining as his voice, that the two of them soon had even the parents laughing, enthralled by the story.

He must read to Adira a lot at home.

The thought made Leah smile. What a great guy.

And that great guy seemed oblivious to the way the other women in the store devoured him with their eyes. When storytime ended, Seth quietly guided Adira over to the stuffed animals.

Leah headed for the cash register.

But Mandy was already ringing people up and refused to step back. Widening her eyes, she jerked her head in Seth's direction. "Are you crazy?" she whispered. "Get over there."

Clearly she was of the same mind as Brittney and thought that Leah should pounce on him. Leah would've disabused her of that notion if she hadn't noticed Mandy's customer watching them both with interest.

Shaking her head, she made her way over to Seth and Adira. "Anyone catch her eye today?" she asked cheerfully.

Seth smiled. "I suspect a black-footed ferret will be going home with us this time."

Adira turned away from the stuffed animals. Grabbing Leah's hand, she placed it in Seth's, then returned her attention to the stuffies.

When Seth opened his mouth to apologize, Leah held up her free hand. "It's fine. I don't mind. I still think it's cute." She narrowed her eyes playfully. "Or is this how you pick up women — by having Adira woo them for you?"

He laughed. "I'm afraid I'm not that clever."

She suspected he was very clever indeed but knew he was innocent of the laughable charge.

Adira picked up the black-footed ferret and hugged it to her chest.

Seth smiled down at her and ran his free hand over her bright curls. "Anything else?"

Grinning, the toddler shook her head.

A tinny version of Skillet's "Monster" suddenly competed with the murmurings of customers.

Frowning, Seth reached into a back pocket and drew out his cell phone. "I'm sorry. It's work. I have to take this."

"Okay."

"Yes?" he answered.

Leah wondered if she should slip away or—

Seth stiffened. "How many?" His brows drew down. "Where's Zach?"

Adira's little face sobered as though she too sensed something was wrong.

"All right," Seth said brusquely. "We'll leave now. It'll take me a few minutes, so tell him to just sit on them until I get there." He pocketed his phone. "I'm sorry. An emergency has arisen at work. We have to go."

"No problem. Do you still want the ferret? I can either hold it for you for later or open the second register and check you out faster."

"We'll take it now," he said. But his mind clearly lay on whatever work crisis had arisen.

Sorry to see him leave so soon, Leah hurried to the unoccupied register and rang up his purchase.

<hr />

As soon as Seth deposited Adira in Marcus's arms, he called Felix and teleported to his location in Perth.

A beep sounded.

Seth turned in a half circle. His eyebrows rose when he located the Aussie immortal.

Felix sat cross-legged atop three vampires he had stacked on top of each other. The bottom two were unconscious, most likely tranqed. The top one spewed out a steady stream of curses.

Unaffected, Felix continued to stare at his cell phone.

What was he doing—reading an e-book?

Seth shook his head, amusement rising. "When I told Darnell I wanted you to sit on them until I got here, I didn't mean literally."

Felix looked up with a grin and tucked his phone away. "Sorry about that. I wanted to finish the chapter." Rising, he stood atop the vamps and stretched.

The vampire under his feet expelled several more epithets.

Chuckling, Seth strolled forward. "Which one did you think you recognized from the missing immortals' pictures?"

Felix nudged the complainer with a boot. "This drongo here. He's American and has our hair and eye color. I thought he might be the bloke from California."

Seth studied the furious man. "No. He's a vampire."

Felix grunted. "I can kill him then?"

The vampire's eyes widened.

Seth gave the vamp's mind a quick scan, then nodded. "Yes. He was an asshole *before* he was infected with the virus and isn't fighting the madness at all. He's embracing it."

Felix snorted in contempt. "I was *hoping* he wasn't an immortal. Two minutes in his company and I already wanted to kick his ass."

"Where is Aari?"

"Off taking a piss."

A twig snapped in the distance, far enough away that even Felix couldn't hear it.

But Seth could and arched a brow. "Are you sure?"

"Deadset. Why?"

"You'll know in a moment." Drawing his katanas, he turned to the trees that lay to the east.

Seconds later, Felix swore, stepped off the vampires, and drew his own weapons.

Judging by the oncoming clamor, Aari was racing back toward them with several vampires in hot pursuit.

Aari burst from the surrounding foliage. "Incoming!" he shouted.

Over a dozen vampires followed, eyes glowing, teeth bared, weapons raised.

Seth leapt forward to meet them and swung both swords.

Only a couple of these were newly turned. The rest were off their fucking nut, reeking of sweat and the blood of their victims. *Many* victims.

Seth read each mind before he ended each life. None were worth saving. None had fought the insanity the virus spawned as it damaged their brains. All had embraced it willingly, eager to use their new strength and speed to terrorize and torture any unfortunate human they captured.

Aari and Felix fought by Seth's side, slaying as many as Seth did.

When the last vampire fell, so did silence.

Even the insects remained quiet for a time.

"Crikey," Felix breathed.

Aari nodded. "I don't know where the hell they came from."

Seth pointed his sword at the so-called drongo, who had gained his feet during the melee only to be run through by one of his cronies. "That one texted them."

Aari grimaced. "Fucking cell phones. Hunting vampires was a hell of a lot less complicated before they came along."

Seth shrugged. "But they've made it easier for you to contact me when you need help."

"True." Aari studied the disintegrating vampire. "I'm guessing he wasn't a missing immortal?"

"No." Seth wiped his blades clean and sheathed them.

"Anyone else have any luck finding one?" Felix asked.

"Not yet."

A heavy pall blanketed them.

"Monster" broke it. Seth glanced at the screen. "Duty calls, gentlemen."

Both nodded.

As soon as the immortal on the other end of the call requested his aid, Seth teleported away. The next ten hours or so proceeded the way most did now. Seth teleported from place to place, aiding Immortal Guardians who—thanks to Gershom's sorry ass—found themselves fighting an unusually high number of vampires. He healed immortals, healed Seconds, and aided a network division head in cleaning up a mess when police arrived on the scene of a battle before the network's cleanup crew could get there. That had taken some time. Neither of the two immortals on the scene had been telepaths, and the police officers hadn't believed the cover story they concocted. One officer called for backup seconds before

Seth arrived. Seth had to alter the policemen's memories, clean up the scene, and help with purging any reference to the incident from all reports, recordings, and files.

Modern technology could really put a crimp in things.

He stopped in at David's shortly after nine p.m. North Carolina time for another shower. Hunger gnawed at him. He hadn't eaten anything since breakfast and had expended a lot of energy teleporting all over the world and leaping into one battle after another. As soon as he was dressed, he headed for the kitchen and grabbed a sandwich from the fridge. He didn't even take time to sit at the table, he just stood over the sink and wolfed it down while he waited for his phone to ring again.

Marcus poked his head in the kitchen. "Hey, Seth?"

Mouth full, Seth raised his eyebrows.

"You haven't by any chance seen Adira's favorite unicorn toy, have you?"

He swallowed. "The little pink one?"

"Yeah."

"No."

Marcus swore.

"Where was the last place you saw it?" Maybe he would have enough time to help look for it before the next call came in.

"I clipped it to her Doc McStuffins backpack right before you took Adira to storytime."

"It wasn't there when I brought her back?"

"I don't know. I didn't notice. But I've looked all over the house and can't find it."

Zach strolled into the kitchen, his stride loose and languid. A smile toyed with the edges of his lips.

Seth arched a brow. "You look very pleased with yourself."

He smiled. "I am." Opening the refrigerator, he took two foot-long sandwiches off the pile Sheldon had prepared and left for anyone who wanted one. "I got bloody on my last foray to aid your Immortal Guardians and Lisette just kindly helped me wash it off."

Seth grunted as he took another bite. Clearly the two had done more than soap each other up. "Can you take my calls for a couple of minutes?"

"Sure. What's up?"

"I think Adira's unicorn toy might have fallen off her backpack during our outing earlier. I want to retrace our steps and see if I can find it."

"No problem. Want me to tell Darnell?"

Seth shook his head as he swallowed the last of his sandwich. "It shouldn't take me long. Let's just exchange phones."

"Thanks, Seth," Marcus said.

Nodding, Seth teleported to an alley near Little Gifts, then walked the rest of the way in case anyone was still out and about. All was quiet, however, the street deserted. Apparently the businesses in the area shut down early on weeknights.

Had Little Gifts already done so, too?

Seth hesitated when he reached the front of the store. It did indeed appear closed.

Stepping back into the shadows, he stared through the front window.

Leah was working diligently as usual, her back to him as music played over the speakers inside. Seth didn't recognize the tune. Something with a snappy beat that fell under the category of pop music, he supposed. Not really to his liking... until Leah began to move to it. Singing under her breath, she hung several dresses up on one of the racks adorning the wall between the dressing rooms. Her head started to nod, her hips to move.

Then the volume abruptly increased, all but drowning out her voice.

Seconds later, her assistant danced out of the back room, mouthing the words, bouncing on her toes, first one leg then the other while she flipped her hair from side to side in a way he remembered teenaged girls doing in the eighties. Or was it the sixties?

Hell, he couldn't remember. When you were thousands of years old, the decades tended to blend together.

Leah laughed as Brittney danced over to her. Then Leah set the dresses down and started mimicking her.

Seth's lips stretched in a wide smile as he watched the women dance and laugh and twirl and goof around, each trying to outdo the other. How carefree they seemed. He envied them that.

The song ended and another began.

"Why are you so chipper tonight?" Leah asked, nearly yelling to be heard over the music.

"I have a hot date!" Brittney called back. "And I mean *hoooooot!*" She sang out the last word like an opera singer.

Laughing, Leah shook her head and shooed her away. "Go have fun. I'll see you tomorrow."

Brittney blew her a kiss and waved as she dug some keys out of the purse he hadn't noticed hanging from one shoulder. Unlocking the door, she stepped outside, locked it with her keys, and turned.

Glancing up, she gasped and stopped short. Her eyes flew wide. "Shit! You scared the crap out of me!"

Seth tucked his hands in his pockets, something he often did to try to put mortals at ease, and offered her a slight bow. "My apologies. I didn't mean to startle you."

Frowning, she adjusted the purse strap on her shoulder. "What are you doing out here, lurking in the shadows? You aren't a creepy stalker, are you?"

He smiled. "No. Adira's favorite unicorn toy has gone missing. The last time I saw it, it was attached to the backpack we brought to storytime earlier, so I've been retracing my steps in hopes of finding it."

Her expression cleared. "Oh. Well, why didn't you knock? The music was loud, but we would've still heard you."

He shrugged and offered her a sheepish smile. "The two of you were dancing and having such a nice time. I hated to intrude."

She glanced back at the store.

Seth followed her gaze. Leah danced slightly in place to the next tune, her hips swaying as she hung up some dresses. Though the movements were more subdued, she was no less appealing.

Brittney returned her attention to Seth and gave him a sly smile. "She's hot, isn't she?"

"Yes, she is." He saw no reason to deny it.

"She's single, too. You should totally hit that."

His smile vanished. He frowned. "I don't hit women." And was insulted that she would believe he did.

Her mouth fell open. "Oh my gosh," she said in hushed tones of amazement as a huge smile dawned. "You don't know what that means. That's so cute! You guys are *perfect* for each other."

His scowl deepened.

She laughed. "By *hit that,* I meant sleep with her. Or seduce her. But in a good way, not an asshole kind of way."

I wish, he thought, then went still inside. He hadn't so much as wanted to hold hands with a woman since he'd lost his wife, and he'd been celibate for thousands of years.

He looked at Leah. He had definitely enjoyed holding Leah's hand the other night though. And earlier today, too. But... "I don't think that's in the cards."

Her smile dimmed. "If it's because she's older than you —"

"It isn't," he assured her. Like Leah, Brittney believed he was as young as he looked, which was around thirty years old.

"Then what's stopping you?" She wasn't one to let a subject drop, was she?

"I'm not currently looking to enter into a relationship," Seth recited automatically, surprised by how much the words felt like a lie. What was wrong with him tonight?

Brittney tilted her head to one side. "Yeah. Neither is Leah. But I've seen you two together. There's something there that's worth exploring... even if you just end up being friends with benefits."

That term he knew.

Her expression darkening, the younger woman closed the distance between them and craned her neck to look up at him. "*But,*" she warned ominously, "if you hurt her, I will fucking kill you. Leah is good people." Tough words belied by the anxious racing of her pulse as she awaited his response.

Seth admired both her devotion to Leah and her courage. Most people were nervous around him. Some outright feared him at a glance. Even the women who had boldly offered themselves to him over the many long years had often done so because fear excited them. It was one of the reasons he had empathized with Lord Dillon so many centuries ago.

And it was one of the reasons Seth liked Leah. She seemed completely unfazed by the leashed power everyone else sensed and steered clear of. "I know she is," he told Brittney. "I have no desire to hurt her." And hoped Leah's association with Ami and Adira would not inspire Gershom to attempt to do so.

Brittney stared at him long and hard, then smiled and stepped back. "Okay then." Her keys jingled as she leaned over and unlocked the door for him. "Have a nice night."

Again he bowed. "Thank you. You, too."

Her heels clacked as she strolled up the sidewalk, turned a corner, and left his sight.

Seth stood a moment longer, watching Leah through one of the large front windows of her shop. His preternaturally sharp senses allowed him to hear her humming along with the tune she danced to, singing softly when she remembered the lyrics. This one he recognized as a Stevie Wonder song: "Faith."

She had a lovely voice, staying on pitch as she sang along with the female singer, though Leah sang an octave lower than the other woman. And she moved like she was born to dance. Seth couldn't keep his gaze from traveling down her back to her narrow waist and the hips that rocked and swayed to the music as her feet moved.

Almost of their own volition, *his* feet carried him to the door.

Chapter Four

S ETH ENTERED LITTLE GIFTS, USING telekinesis to silence the bell overhead so it wouldn't *ding* and alert Leah to his presence.

Her back still to him, she stretched up to hang some little blouses on another rack. As she lowered her hands, she drew them down her sides in a sensual stroke and began to move more to the music, believing herself alone.

Seth crossed his arms over his chest, leaned against the wall, and just enjoyed watching her. She wore a pink T-shirt that hugged her hourglass figure. Every time she raised her hands to hang more garments, his gaze went to the breasts he could glimpse the sides of as she twisted and rocked to the beat. Full breasts he'd brushed his arm against. Twice. Full breasts that would fit perfectly in his hands.

Her jeans clung to a shapely ass and legs that seemed to go on forever, ending in feet tucked into sneakers instead of high heels. She was so self-conscious about her height that Seth doubted she ever wore the latter.

Personally, he thought her height perfect.

Leah grabbed some blue T-shirts. Hips still swaying enticingly, she spun around, then jerked to a halt and let out a squeak of surprise. A wide range of emotions swept across her expressive features as she stared at him. Fear at discovering she wasn't alone. Recognition and relief. Pleasure at seeing him again. Then a great deal of embarrassment.

Smiling, he mouthed, "Caught you."

Cheeks flushing, she laughed and raised the T-shirts to hide her face.

The music faded as the song drew to an end.

"Brittney let me in," he said. "I hope you don't mind."

She lowered the shirts. "Not at all. But I really wish you hadn't seen that."

"Why? You're a wonderful dancer."

Acoustic guitar music began to play.

"You're just trying to make me blush again," she called over the music.

He grinned. What was it about her that seemed to instantly lighten his spirits?

Drums joined the guitar, providing a Latin beat.

Setting the shirts aside, she started to move toward the back room, no doubt intending to lower the volume. After just a couple of steps, however, she stopped and looked back at him. She eyed him speculatively, then extended a hand to him.

Seth tilted his head, unsure of her meaning. Did she want him to accompany her to the back room?

Turning her lithe body to face him, one hand still extended, she began to move her feet in a salsa step that was damned alluring as her hips joined in.

Surprise flashed through him. She was asking him to dance?

Smiling, he shook his head.

Narrowing her eyes playfully, she held out her other hand as well, waggling her fingers in a *come on, you know you want to* gesture.

His heart gave an odd little leap. He *did,* he realized with a great deal of surprise. He *did* want to.

Seth straightened away from the wall and would later wonder what imp had seized control of his mind and body. Because all it took was one more waggle of her fingers to compel him to doff his coat.

The simple truth, however, was that he liked her. Whatever light burned inside her called to him and alleviated—at least for a time—the darkness that seemed to constantly dog his footsteps.

What the hell are you doing? the voice of reason inquired.

Ignoring it, he hung up his coat.

Leah's pretty face brightened with a delighted smile.

Abandoning his cares, his concerns, and his many obligations, Seth strode toward her.

Her eyes widened when he shoved weighted racks of clothing to either side as he did, clearing a dance floor for them.

A man began to sing in Spanish. Seth recognized this tune, too. "Bamboleo."

As soon as he was within touching distance, he took Leah's hands and drew her close. Their feet began to move in tandem, their hips to sway. Seth knew many of the steps she chose and followed them easily. Salsa. Merengue. Bachata. And the two of them danced as though they'd been doing so together for years. Always touching.

Leah laughed as he twirled her around and around and back again. Seth grinned, his heart light. Tugging her closer, he slid an arm around her waist and settled his hand above those sexy as hell, swaying hips. She grinned back and smoothed a hand up his chest, curling it around the back of his neck. His skin began to tingle, his heart to race. He spun her again, then again and again before he drew her against him — this time with her back to his front. As they moved, he rested a hand on her flat stomach, slipping it up and splaying his fingers until his thumb rested just beneath her tempting breasts.

His pulse leapt. Her hair brushed his chin as he drew in a deep breath. Her scent hit him like an aphrodisiac as she inched closer, her ass brushing against him as their hips touched, rocking from side to side.

Fire flashed through him, heating his blood as long-dormant lust struck hard.

Seth spun her away to put a little distance between them, clasping both her hands as they returned to the salsa. She seemed completely unaware of the effect she had on him, caught up in the moment, the music, and the dance.

He twirled her again, grinning when she laughed.

She moved around behind him and stepped up close. Her pelvis brushed his ass as she slid an arm around him, splaying her fingers on his chest.

Holy hell, it felt good. He had missed a woman's touch. And Leah's affected him so strongly that it was all he could do not to moan. Slipping his hand back between their bodies, he clasped her free hand, ducked, and twirled under their arms to face her, then spun her around and around. When he stopped, she danced away a bit, raising her arms high as she sent him a flirtatious smile.

It's not personal, that annoyingly reasonable voice tried to warn him. *She isn't flirting with you. It's just the dance.*

Seth ignored it and moved forward. Resting his hands on her hips, he drew her close, too tempted to resist.

She stared up at him, her face flushed, her heart pounding as loudly as his beneath the music.

So beautiful.

He slipped a thigh between hers, hips still moving to the beat.

Her other thigh slipped between his as her breasts brushed against him. Wrapping her arms around his neck, she closed her eyes and nuzzled his chest.

Seth wrapped his other arm around her and settled his hand on the small of her back, as close as he dared to her lovely ass. He wanted so badly to slide his hand down, palm the firm flesh there, and urge her even closer against his hard body. But she had asked him to dance, not to grind on her and simulate sex.

He spun her away from him, afraid he might be making her uneasy.

But she smiled, unoffended, when she looked up at him. "Tease," she called good-naturedly.

Laughing, he relaxed back into the dance and sent her into a flurry of spins that ended with him bending her back over his arm in a deep dip as the music ended.

Both were breathless.

Seth straightened, keeping his arms around her until she was steady, then stepped back.

Neither spoke.

Loud trumpets and drums introduced the next song.

Turning, Leah hurried into the back room. The volume lowered.

Seth... didn't know what to think as he struggled to bring his body back under control. What had just happened?

Leah returned. "That was awesome!" she exclaimed with an infectious grin. "I mean, that was so much fun!"

He laughed. "Yes, it was."

"You really know how to dance," she said, admiration sparkling in her pretty hazel eyes.

"As do you," he replied. "Thank you for coaxing me into joining you."

"Thank you for the dance. Whew!" Fanning her face, she reached back to lift her hair off her neck. Perspiration added a slight sheen to her lovely skin. "I needed that. I'm a total workaholic and have been so stressed lately."

"Me, too," he admitted. "I can't remember the last time I enjoyed myself so much."

"Well, anytime you want to do it again, feel free to drop by."

He stared at her, his heart jackhammering in his chest. "Really?"

"Sure."

That was damned tempting.

A trebly version of R.E.M.'s "It's the End of the World as We Know It" suddenly sounded. Seth frowned as he dug Zach's phone out of his pocket. "I'm sorry. I have to take this."

"Okay."

He answered the call. "Yes?"

"Seth?" Bastien asked.

"Yes?"

"Is Zach fielding your calls?" the British immortal asked.

"Yes. Why? Is there a problem?"

Zach spoke in the background. "He thought I was Gershom."

Frowning, Seth turned and paced away a couple of steps. "You what?"

"I thought he was Gershom," Bastien confirmed. "When I called you, Zach appeared instead. The gadget didn't beep and confirm he was him the way it tells me you're you. And Darnell didn't warn me he was redirecting my call, so... yeah. I thought he was Gershom. So did Cliff."

Seth did swear then and reached up to rub his forehead. He hadn't thought about the device he now had to carry all the time or the reassurance it offered those he helped. "Is Cliff okay?" The young vampire was fiercely protective of those he loved. If he thought there was even a chance Zach was Gershom and intended Bastien harm, Cliff would've probably succumbed to the madness he battled and attacked.

~ 56 ~

"Yeah," Bastien said, his voice telling Seth otherwise.

Even though he was the most powerful healer on the planet, Seth had been unable to prevent the progressive brain damage the virus caused in humans from slowly robbing Cliff of his sanity. The young vampire had been valiantly fighting tooth and nail to keep it at bay so Melanie and the other researchers at the network could continue their search for a cure. But he was losing the battle. Something like this could affect Cliff for days.

He's all right, Zach spoke in Seth's head. *I didn't hurt him, and I am infusing him with calm even as we speak.*

Thank you. "Do you need me?" he asked Bastien.

"No. I just thought I should check before I attacked Zach and fucked him up."

Zach laughed in the background. "As if you could."

"Sorry to bother you," Bastien said and ended the call.

Leah watched Seth pocket the phone and did her best to keep her smile friendly and carefree. But her body still burned from his touch.

Holy crap, he set her on fire. She didn't know why so many people believed really tall men—at least those who didn't play professional sports—were clumsy or awkward. Seth moved more smoothly than her dance instructor had, his glorious muscles flexing and rippling beneath his tight T-shirt. Those big hands of his had made her breath catch and sent desire coursing through her. The way his thumb had brushed the underside of her breast, the touch as light as a feather. His long fingers gliding down her back and coming damned close to cupping her ass. And when he had slipped his thigh between hers...

Sensation had shot through her as he'd brushed against her. Her nipples were still tight from it, her body throbbing with need. But it had just been a dance. And she didn't want him to see how strongly it had affected her.

"Everything okay?" she asked when he turned to face her.

He nodded. "Just work. As usual."

As she watched him approach, she couldn't help but notice he looked as if whatever information the call had conveyed had sucked some of the fun out of the night for him.

She could relate. She didn't want to see the fun end either. Speaking of which… "I wasn't trying to *get my cougar on* as Brittney would say, by the way, when I invited you to drop by anytime you want to dance."

He stared at her. "I'm sorry. I don't know what that means."

She really did love that she had to look up at him. He was so tall that she'd actually felt his chin brush the top of her head when she had nuzzled his chest.

Oh shit. Mortification struck. She was forty-six and had just nuzzled the chest of what appeared to be a twenty-eight or thirty-year-old man! "I don't want you to think I'm a cougar." Most men his age would be appalled if a woman almost as old as their mother hit on them.

Uncertainty crossed his handsome features. "I still don't know what that means."

She smiled. He said it as though he feared not knowing would offend her. "Cougars are what some people call older women who pursue younger men."

His eyebrows shot up. "Oh." A smile dawned on his handsome face. "Well, you've no worries there. You aren't older than me."

She laughed. "Yes, I am."

He slid his hands into his pockets. "I'm older than I look, remember?"

What was he — thirty-one? Thirty-two? That was still younger than her kid brother.

Leah shook her head, amused. "How old do you think I am?" she asked curiously. "And don't round down or lie because you're afraid you'll insult me or hurt my feelings."

He flashed her a grin. "You're saying you want me to be blunt?"

"Absolutely."

"All right." He assumed an exaggeratedly somber expression. Raising a hand, he stroked his chin as he narrowed his eyes and studied her like a scientist might a whiteboard sporting a particularly difficult equation.

She fought a smile.

"Let's see." That dark gaze of his followed a slow path down her body to her feet, then back up again.

Sheesh. How could he amuse her one second, then turn her on the next with just a look?

"You have a lovely, tight, fit body," he said, admiration glinting in his eyes, "and the same energy level as your assistant, who I'm guessing is… twenty-five or thereabouts?"

"Twenty-five is right," she said, surprised he'd guessed Brittney's age correctly and trying not to feel so pleased that he liked her body.

Closing the distance between them, he touched a fingertip to her chin and nudged it up.

She drew in a breath. He smelled good. No cologne. Just him. Just Seth.

He pursed his lips thoughtfully. "Pale, perfect skin. No signs of crow's-feet or laugh lines."

"Because my pale skin sunburns if I spend more than five minutes in the sun," she said dryly. "So I always covered up instead of laying out and tanning like my friends did when I was younger." Such tended to age the skin faster, she knew.

"No gray hairs."

"You can thank a certain hair dye for that."

His lips twitched as he released her and stepped back. "If I had to guess, based solely on your appearance, I would say you're thirty years old. The fact that you own a successful and thriving business, however, leads me to believe you're a decade or more older."

"You think I look thirty years old?"

He nodded.

"Wow, Seth. You're my new best friend."

He laughed.

R.E.M.'s "It's the End of the World as We Know It" arose once more.

Irritation darkened his features as he shook his head. "I'm sorry. It's work again. I have to take this."

She nodded.

"Yes?" he answered. "Yes." A moment passed as he listened. "I know. I'm sorry. I neglected to take that into consideration." He shook his head but didn't speak as his gaze lowered to his big boots. She could actually see the muscles in his shoulders begin to tighten as tension returned. "Aside from that, all is well?" He nodded. "All right." Sighing he pocketed the phone.

"Bad news?" she asked tentatively.

For the first time since he'd entered, the smile he sent her looked tired. And his eyes carried so much weariness that it almost convinced her he really *was* older than he looked. "No. I shouldn't have taken time off, I guess."

"Well, personally, I'm glad you did. Because it made *me* take a little time off, too."

His spirits seemed to lighten. "Then I'm happy I did."

"What line of business are you in?"

"Private security. And like you, I run my own business, so…"

"You're a total workaholic, too?"

He nodded.

"It's the End of the World as We Know It" again began to play.

"Damn it!" he ground out.

She bit her lip.

Offering her a little grimace of remorse, he touched her arm in a light caress. "Forgive me. I'm enjoying myself and hate for work to intrude."

She smiled. "Don't worry about it. I understand. I really do."

He drew the phone from his pocket and answered it. "Yes, Zach is fielding my calls." Turning, he strolled away, head down. His hair was so long and shiny and silky, drawn back in a thick ponytail and falling past his waist. She could almost imagine gripping it in a fist while he took her in his arms and—

"Yes," he murmured.

Her heart sank a little when he reached out with his free hand, grabbed one of the racks of clothing he'd moved earlier, and effortlessly pulled it back into position. Damn, he was strong. Those things were weighted and heavy enough for kids to hang on without tipping them over. Yet he moved them as easily as she did the little plastic chairs she sometimes used for storytime.

"No. The fault is mine," he said.

She had a feeling he was once more thinking *It's my fault for taking time off.* Poor guy.

He moved another rack. "Everything is fine otherwise?" And moved another rack. "All right. Zach, I know you're listening. Meet me at David's. This isn't going to work. I shall be there shortly."

She even liked the way he talked. Not just the accent, but the words and phrases he chose.

Pocketing his phone, he turned to face her. "I'm afraid I must leave."

"That's too bad." *Crap.* She hadn't meant to say that out loud.

He smiled. "My sentiments exactly."

Leah strolled past him as he finished moving the last few racks back into place. Lifting his coat from the hook by the door, she held it up for him.

"Thank you." Giving her his back, he slid his arms into the sleeves and shrugged it on.

Leah couldn't resist touching him one last time and did so in the guise of brushing lint off a broad shoulder. "I didn't ask what brought you here tonight."

"Adira's favorite unicorn toy is missing. I thought perhaps we had left it behind earlier."

"Is it pink with a key chain clip and a flower on its butt?"

Grinning, he faced her. "Yes."

"I found it earlier." She headed around the counter to fetch it from the lost-and-found box she kept there. "Here it is." She held it out to him.

Seth took it with another thank-you. Before she could withdraw her hand, he caught it and pressed a kiss to the back of it. "Thank you again for the dance."

Her pulse raced at the touch of his lips and the feel of his large fingers giving hers an affectionate squeeze. Heat rose in her cheeks. "You love to make me blush, don't you?"

He winked. "Guilty as charged." Stepping back, he bowed. "Have a lovely night, Leah."

"You, too."

Opening the door, he stepped out into the night.

Leah retrieved her keys from the cash register and moved to lock the door. As she did so, she glanced through the window to get a last look at Seth... and saw only empty street. Frowning, she moved closer until her nose nearly touched the glass, then looked in both directions.

He was gone. No sign of him walking away. No car pulling

away from the curb. Nothing.

She locked both locks on the door. "That's weird," she mumbled.

Reaching over, she grabbed the rod and turned it to close the blinds, then did the same on the larger windows.

A sigh escaped her. Oh well. It had been a fun interlude.

Seth teleported to David's home as soon as he left Leah's store.

Zach was already there, smiling down at Lisette, who played with Adira on the living room floor. When he caught sight of Seth, he frowned. "You look pissed."

Seth shook his head. He was, but he didn't want to talk about it. "Here." He tossed Zach his phone and caught the one Zach slung toward him. He wasn't even sure if it was anger he felt or exhaustion. Or maybe disappointment, which didn't make any sense at all.

Zach shared a glance with his wife. "It wasn't a big thing, Seth. Next time we'll do what we did this morning and have Darnell and Chris take your calls before diverting them to me so the immortals will know whom to expect. We just skipped that step this time."

And Seth had needlessly alarmed his Immortal Guardians because he'd volunteered to look for a stuffed unicorn so he could see Leah again. "I wasn't thinking," he muttered, furious at himself. Cliff's mental state was fragile. What if Zach and Bastien hadn't been able to walk him back from the edge this time?

Zach frowned. "Seth—"

Skillet's "Monster" interrupted him as Seth's cell phone rang. "Yes," he answered.

Harsh breathing and the clang of weapons carried over the line. "Seth! I could use your help," an immortal stationed in Scotland called.

Reaching into his pocket, Seth drew out the little unicorn and tossed it to Lisette. Then he raced to his bedroom, retrieved his katanas, and teleported to Glasgow.

"I'm worried about Seth," Lisette said a couple of weeks later.

"I am, too," Zach admitted.

The two of them lay in bed, their skin still damp from the vigorous lovemaking they'd enjoyed. Zach was stretched out on his back with Lisette curled up against his side, her head resting on his shoulder. He didn't think he would ever grow tired of her touch. He loved the feel of her fingers stroking his chest in languid movements and the way her toes tickled his shins.

He combed his fingers through her long, silky hair.

"Has he said anything to you?" she asked softly.

"No." Seth wasn't saying much to *anyone*. He had been quieter of late. Withdrawn. Zach had thought perhaps fatigue weighed him down on top of everything else, but Seth had refused to let Zach field his calls so he could get some rest. It was almost as if he feared something dire would happen if he relaxed his vigilance even for a moment.

"I wish we could find the missing *gifted ones* for him," she murmured.

"Immortals," he corrected. "The missing immortals."

She sighed. "I still can't believe Gershom transformed them. How could he even do that when he isn't infected with the virus himself?" That was something the other immortals didn't know. Seth, Zach, and Gershom—and the rest of the ancients deemed Others—were not infected with the virus. Their immortality had instead been granted them at birth.

It still bothered Zach that he couldn't share the source of it with Lisette. But if he did, anyone with telepathic abilities would be able to pluck the information from her thoughts. And as Seth often said, violence always followed when humans learned the truth of who and what the Others were.

David knew the source of their immortality. But everyone else believed the virus had transformed them as it had the rest of Seth's Immortal Guardians.

"Gershom must have extracted the virus from the vampire army he raised in Russia," Zach surmised.

She nodded. "Not being able to find the immortals and rescue them is killing Seth."

Again Zach nodded. But something else niggled at him. The last time Zach had fielded Seth's calls—the night Seth had taken a few minutes off to fetch Adira's favorite toy—Seth had returned to

David's home carrying the scent of a woman. Zach had assumed at the time that it had been some human he'd plucked from a vampire's grasp or perhaps a female immortal he'd aided earlier in the night, but… what if it hadn't been? That *did* seem to be the night that had initiated the disturbing silence that now cloaked him.

"It's the End of the World as We Know It" broke the silence.

Zach retrieved his cell phone from the bedside table and answered it. "Yes?"

"It's Reordon. I need a few minutes of your time."

"When?"

"Now, if possible."

"All right."

"Can you bring David with you?"

"I don't want to leave the house unguarded."

"It won't be. That house is chock-full of immortals sleeping for the day. Ami will alert them if Gershom makes an appearance."

"Nevertheless, we should wait until Seth returns."

"Actually, I don't want Seth to know about this."

Suspicion rose. Gently extricating himself from Lisette's warm body, Zach stood. *I'll be back in a moment,* he told her telepathically.

Her eyebrows shot up as he grabbed a katana and teleported to the origin of the call.

A second later, he found himself standing in a large, unfamiliar, circular room that bore no windows.

Chris Reordon leaned against the front of a desk, facing him, a cell phone held to his ear. An alarm began to blare. Jumping, Chris dropped the phone, drew a 9mm from his shoulder holster, and aimed it at him. "Zach?"

"Yes."

Swearing, he shoved the weapon back in its holster and grabbed the walkie-talkie attached to one shoulder. "Code seven. False alarm. All is well." The alarm shut off. "Damn it," he groused, "you know you have to give me some warning before you teleport in." Then he grimaced and threw up a hand to block his view. "And put some fucking clothes on. What the hell, man?"

Relaxing, Zach shrugged. "I wanted to ensure the person calling me was you and not Gershom impersonating you in an attempt to lure me and David away from his home."

"Well, it's me. Go get dressed and bring David back with you. And don't tell Seth if you run into him."

Zach frowned. "What's this about, Reordon?"

"I'll tell you when you return."

Uneasy, Zach teleported back to the bedroom he and Lisette shared at David's home.

Lisette leaned back against the pillows, her brow furrowed. "Everything okay?"

He nodded as he set the katana on the foot of the bed. "Reordon wants to see me about something. I wasn't sure it was him, so I popped over to check." He sent David a quick telepathic heads-up.

Her lips stretched in a smile. "And how did he feel about seeing so *much* of you?"

He chuckled. "Less than pleased. I'm to don some clothing before I return with David."

"Did he say what this is about?"

Zach pulled on a pair of black leather pants. "No. But I'm going to see if he can make me one of those electronic devices Seth carries around with him so fielding Seth's calls won't cause any more problems."

"Good. Seth could use a break, though he'll never admit it."

Silently, Zach agreed. If he had to kick Seth's ass to make him take some damned time off, he would. Or at least he'd try to, he amended silently. *No one* could match Seth in strength. Not even Gershom, though Seth might believe otherwise.

Leaning down, he brushed his wife's lips with a kiss. "Get some rest. I'll return as soon as I can."

She smiled as she drew her fingers down his stubbled cheek. "I love you."

"I love you, too." Straightening, he teleported to David's study.

David strode around the edge of his large desk. "Ready?"

Zach nodded. *I don't feel comfortable leaving the house unguarded,* he told him telepathically.

Over a dozen immortals slumber below.

Any elders in the mix?

Aidan and Dana are here. Aidan was a nearly three-thousand-year-old Celtic immortal who boasted powerful telepathic, telekinetic, and healing abilities. He was also an exceptional fighter with incredible speed and strength. Because he had transformed his wife himself, Dana was just as strong and fast, though she lacked his multiple gifts.

Anyone else?

Ethan and Heather.

Ethan was only a century old and not as fast or strong as the older immortals, but he'd had Aidan transform his wife Heather for him so she would be as strong as an elder.

I also called in Chaak and Imhotep, David added. *They're in the living room and will remain until we return.*

Zach nodded, though unease still taunted him. *Let's go.*

Chapter Five

AS SOON AS DAVID DREW near, Zach touched his shoulder and teleported them both to the odd round room in which Reordon waited for them.

Chris nodded. "David. Zach. Thanks for coming."

Zach surveyed the room. It was huge with a high ceiling. But there wasn't much in it to give him a clue as to where they were. A desk rested near the wall on the other side of the room, two cushioned chairs facing it. A rectangular table nearby had eight chairs on wheels pulled up to it and looked like a much shorter version of the one in Chris's boardroom at network headquarters. Not far from that, a large flat-screen television adorned the wall with some electronic devices resting on a stand beneath it.

"Where are we?" he asked.

Chris strode toward the television. "The abandoned missile silo I bought and retrofitted for our needs."

David frowned. "Why don't you want Seth to know we're here?"

Chris picked up an iPad. "Because we have a problem." When he tapped the tablet's surface, the flat-screen on the wall lit up.

Zach turned to face it and crossed his arms over his chest as he waited.

David did the same. "What kind of problem?"

"Just a second." Chris tapped the tablet a few more times.

The inside of a shop suddenly appeared in high-def on the screen. Brightly lit, it looked like a clothing store for children, one that also peddled an array of books and toys.

David's eyebrows rose. "That's Little Gifts."

Zach glanced at him. "What's Little Gifts?"

"Ami's favorite store. It's where she buys most of Adira's clothing and toys and takes her for storytime." He frowned at Chris. "You put it under surveillance?"

Chris nodded and typed something else on the tablet. A small box appeared in the upper left corner of the large monitor, offering another view of the shop's interior. "As soon as Ami started frequenting the shop, I sent a crew in to install surveillance cameras."

"Does Leah know?" David asked.

Zach looked back and forth between them. "Who is Leah?"

"The proprietress," David responded. "Leah Somerson."

Chris shook his head. "I did it after hours while she was out visiting family, then wiped all record of it from the surveillance system."

Zach eyed Chris, concern rising. "Did you have reason to believe she might be up to something?"

"No," he answered absently. "I just like to cover all bases."

David's brow furrowed. "What have you discovered? Is she is working with Gershom?"

"I've seen no evidence of that thus far."

"Nor did I when I scanned her thoughts the night I met her," David murmured.

Zach cast Chris an exasperated glance. "If you found nothing suspicious, then why are we here?"

"Because," Chris said, stepping back to stand on David's other side, "as I said, we have a problem." He tapped the tablet one last time and set the surveillance footage into motion.

Zach watched the screen. A tall, slender woman with long, straight brown hair entered from a back room, pushing a cart loaded with small garments on hangers. Rolling it to the back wall, she started distributing the clothing to the racks that peppered it. Her head began to bob to music they couldn't hear.

The video must not contain audio.

A second woman, younger than the first, danced out of the other room, bouncing on her toes as she swung her hair back and forth. When the two women started dancing together, each trying to outdo the other in silliness, David chuckled.

Zach smiled. "Seriously, Reordon, why are we here?"

"Keep watching," he murmured.

Zach sighed.

The younger woman looped a purse over her shoulder and strolled away from Leah, leaving their view. Zach's gaze went to the small box in the upper left corner that showed the interior of the store near the front door and cash registers. The woman walked into view there and exited. A moment later, on the opposite side of the glass door, she turned back and unlocked it. But she didn't open it. Instead, she walked past the front window and left the camera's sight. Seconds later, the door swung inward and Seth stepped into the shop.

Zach frowned. "Is that Gershom?"

David shook his head. "It's Seth." David knew Seth better than anyone. The two had worked together to lead the Immortal Guardians since biblical times.

Zach consulted the time stamp at the bottom of the screen. It was late, surely past closing time for such an establishment. "What's he doing there?"

"Adira left her favorite unicorn toy," David responded, no concern apparent in his voice. "Seth dropped by to retrieve it so Ami and Marcus wouldn't have to." His lips turned up in a broad smile as he watched Leah continue to dance, unaware that she was no longer alone.

But Seth didn't call attention to himself or ask the woman for the missing toy. Instead, he leaned against the nearest wall, crossed his arms, and watched Leah dance, a smile dawning.

Zach wasn't much of a lip-reader, so he didn't know what words passed between them when the woman inevitably turned around and found him watching her. She blushed and laughed and seemed to know Seth, who actually grinned as he spoke to her.

She walked toward the back room, then halted, turned back to face Seth, and...

Zach almost laughed. She must not know him very well, because she appeared to be asking Seth to dance. As if he would ever—"Holy shit!"

He and David both stiffened, arms dropping to their sides as they gaped at the screen.

Seth removed his coat and strode forward, pushing clothing racks out of the way to clear some space before he—

"Holy shit," Zach repeated as Seth began to dance with her.

Utter silence engulfed the room.

Though the music they couldn't hear seemed to have a quick tempo, something Latin he would guess, the dance the two engaged in was far different from the swing dancing Lisette and Ethan occasionally roped Zach and Heather into doing. This was… provocative. Sensual.

Very sensual.

Seth twirled the woman and drew her back against him. Zach watched in utter astonishment as Seth's eyes flared bright gold when the woman's shapely ass rubbed against his groin. Even more shocking, Seth didn't step away and end the dance. Instead, he rested a hand on the woman's flat stomach and slid it up almost to the woman's breast. He dipped his chin, breathing in her scent. He closed his eyes a moment. And when he opened them, they were dark brown again, the glow gone.

Zach nodded. So he *had* come to his senses.

After another series of steps and turns, the woman ended up pressed against Seth's back. She slipped an arm around to caress his chest… and Seth's eyes flashed golden again.

Holy shit.

David slowly moved forward, his eyes glued to the screen.

Zach tried to gauge the other immortal's response but couldn't.

When Zach looked back at the monitor, Seth and the woman were once more facing each other. Seth pulled her closer, as close as he could get while still dancing, even going so far as to insert a thigh between hers. A smile on her pretty face, she nuzzled his chest. Seth's eyes lit with golden fire once more before he closed them and forced them to return to dark brown. The fact that Seth was having difficulty keeping that part of his nature from exerting itself spoke volumes.

The dance ended in a flourish of twirls and a dramatic dip.

How the hell did Seth even know how to dance like that? The man's entire world revolved around keeping his Immortal Guardians safe and making their lives as happy as—

Oh. Right. Seth must have learned to dance for Lisette. He tended to be more protective of female Immortal Guardians, who were far more rare than the males, and had probably learned so he could dance with Lisette and lift her spirits when guilt and regret over inadvertently turning her brothers had weighed her down and Ethan hadn't been available to partner her.

But Zach knew without even asking that Seth had never danced with Lisette like *that.*

Seth chatted with the woman, smiling more than Zach had seen him do in… hell, thousands of years. And the woman laughed and talked with him as though they were old friends.

Seth took a phone call… then took another and another, his face darkening with both tension and annoyance.

Realization dawned. "That was the night we switched phones and I fielded his calls without telling Darnell first."

"Yes," Chris confirmed.

Then *this* was the woman whose scent had adorned him when Seth had returned to David's home.

Chris froze the picture when Seth left the establishment.

"Play it again," David commanded.

He did so, putting it in a loop.

Zach stared at the surveillance footage, still trying to digest it. Both Seth and Leah looked as though they wanted nothing more than to doff their clothing and spend hours exploring each other's body.

Chris turned, snaring Zach's attention as David continued to stare fixedly at the screen. "Like I said, we have a problem."

Zach nodded. "He's attracted to her." Quite an understatement.

"Yes."

Seth had shown no interest in women since the death of his wife. None at all. He had even confessed to Zach a few years ago that he still mourned her.

"There's more," Chris added grimly.

Zach shook his head. What could possibly be more earthshaking than Seth having feelings for a woman?

"She's human," David murmured.

Shit. Zach looked at the woman on the screen. The vampiric virus drove humans infected with it insane. So if she and Seth hit it off, she couldn't safely be transformed and spend the rest of eternity with him. "So was Seth's wife," Zach belatedly mentioned.

"Yes," Chris said, "Seth's wife was human, too. And we all know how that ended: enemies who wanted Seth dead brutally murdered her and their two children."

Zach frowned. "Surely you don't believe we should intercede. Seth has been alone for thousands of years. Don't you think he deserves whatever happiness he can find after all he's done and sacrificed to help not just the Immortal Guardians but humanity as a whole?"

"I do," Chris agreed, surprising him. "That's why I asked you here."

Zach glanced at the man who was closest to Seth. "David?"

David turned to face him. "You see it?" he asked, his expression unreadable.

Zach glanced at the couple on the screen, then met his gaze. "I do." The attraction the two shared was undeniable.

"We have to protect her," David said, "at all costs. We have to do everything we can to keep her safe. We *cannot* let history repeat itself."

"I agree."

"I do, too," Chris said. "That's why the day after I saw this footage, I installed a round-the-clock surveillance team in the building across the street with a dozen of my best special-ops soldiers on every shift. All are heavily armed. And all are silently alerted with a device similar to the ones Immortal Guardians carry when Seth appears, so they'll know if Gershom gets wind of her and shows up, trying to fool her into believing he's Seth. I also have the surveillance feed streamed live to the same two sites as the network's feed to ensure that Gershom can't mind-control those viewing it so they won't alert us to his visit if he does. As I said before: the bastard may be powerful, but he can't be in two places at once."

Zach frowned. He didn't like the idea of Seth's privacy being violated in such a way, or that of the woman. "I don't think—"

Chris held up a hand. "These are trusted men and women who would give their lives to protect Seth and the other Immortal Guardians. They'll keep his secrets."

It still didn't sit well, but what the hell else could they do with Gershom out there, wanting to strike at Seth in every conceivable way? "Has Seth been back to see her?"

"No," Chris said, "which poses another dilemma. I worried that Leah might be targeted by Gershom simply as a result of her association with Ami. I thought Seth pursuing a relationship with her would dramatically increase that likelihood, so—as I said—I installed the special-ops surveillance team. But it's been a couple of weeks now, and Seth hasn't returned. I wasn't sure if I should keep the crew there and wanted to ask what you thought."

Zach shook his head. "If Seth hasn't been back, it sure as hell isn't because he doesn't want to. He isn't *letting* himself go back. He hasn't taken *any* downtime since that night, hasn't had so much as a fifteen-minute break. If he were human, I'd say he was working himself into an early grave, no doubt because he's drawn the same conclusion you have: that seeing her will endanger her."

David sighed. "At least we know now why he's been so somber and withdrawn of late."

"You noticed it, too?" Zach asked.

"Of course. He's fighting his attraction to her."

Chris's gaze ping-ponged between them. "I admit I wondered if perhaps that might be for the best. I mean… she's human. Even if we keep her safe, Seth will still lose her in the end. She can't be transformed by the virus without suffering progressive brain damage and going insane. And even as powerful a healer as he is, Seth can't stop that. Look how hard he's tried with Cliff. So she'll have to remain human, and he'll inevitably lose her to old age."

The knowledge saddened Zach. He was so fortunate that Lisette had been born a *gifted one* and could spend the rest of eternity with him. "Seth can use his healing ability to extend her life. He would've done the same for his wife if he'd had the chance."

David nodded. "I did it for mine."

Surprise lit Chris's face. He must not have known that David had been married long ago.

"Their time together would still be short in the greater scheme of things," David continued, "but if he heals her every day, he can extend her life by a century and a half. Perhaps a little more."

A hundred and fifty or two hundred years instead of an eternity.

How much of that time would Seth spend dreading the inevitable?

"Well, I just..." Chris shook his head. "I didn't know which would be worse—loving Leah and losing her or never letting himself love her at all."

"Never letting himself love her at all," Zach and David responded in unison.

At last David turned away from the screen. "I still mourn my wife. I miss her every day. But I would never have given up the years I had with her."

Zach nodded. "It would be the same for me if I lost Lisette."

Chris crossed to his desk and leaned back against it. "Okay then. What do we do? How can we help him?"

Zach considered it for a minute or two. "You can start by having your tech genius make me one of those devices Seth carries around in his pocket to let immortals know I'm not Gershom. Once you do, Seth will no longer have that excuse to keep me from fielding his calls and can slow his frenetic pace."

David nodded. "Have him make one for me, too."

Chris withdrew a small notebook and a stubby pencil from his pocket and began to write. "Okay. I'll get right on it, but I'll need one of you to erase the memory of it from the technician's mind again so Gershom can't pluck the code from it."

"I'll do it," Zach volunteered, then caught David's eye. "What do you think about giving Jared one, too, and having him answer some of the emergency calls?"

David's eyebrows rose. "Really?"

Zach shrugged. "He's been at loose ends ever since he told the Others to kiss his ass." Jared had only recently joined their ranks. The rest of the ancient Others firmly believed they should not interfere in any way—no matter how miniscule—with the mortal world. They had, in fact, tortured Zach twice before he himself had defected. Once for warning Seth that his cell phone was broken and his Immortal Guardians in North Carolina were trying to reach him, then a second time just for *speaking* with Seth. "I think Jared may need something a little more challenging than hunting vampires to occupy his time. And sending him to aid Immortal Guardians who are in trouble will help integrate him into the ranks faster. At least, it did for me."

Zach had joined the Immortal Guardians at a similarly turbulent time and had fielded Seth's calls for two days when Seth had come dangerously close to collapsing, though none of his immortals would've believed such possible.

David pondered the request a moment, then nodded. "We can try it and see how he fares."

Chris scribbled some more in his notebook. "Consider it done." He looked up from the paper. "It also occurred to me that worry over an association with him endangering her may not be the only thing keeping Seth from seeing Leah again."

Zach studied him. "What do you mean?"

"After I finished cleaning up the Times Square incident, my assistant Kate made me take a weekend off."

"And?" Zach prompted when he didn't continue.

"And I haven't taken a weekend off since. I've worked every day, three hundred and sixty-five days a year, ever since Bastien came on the scene and kicked off so much crap." He grimaced and crossed his arms over his chest. "Taking time off to *relax and have fun,* as Kate put it, just felt too weird, too self-indulgent, after working nonstop for so long. I'm guessing it will be worse for Seth." He looked at David. "I know he likes spending time with Ami and Adira. But he usually only grabs whatever time he can for that between calls. When was the last time Seth actually *scheduled* time off to do something he enjoys?"

David didn't speak, apparently unable to recall such a time.

Zach hadn't thought of that. Seth had been solely responsible for the well-being and happiness of his Immortal Guardians for thousands of years, aided only by David. "So Seth will balk at taking time off and delegating."

David shrugged as he turned once more to watch Seth and Leah dance on the screen. "I'll handle his objections." He was probably the only one who could. "I'll insist he take some downtime. Then we'll see what happens. If he goes to her, we will do whatever we can to keep her safe. If he does not…"

Zach watched Seth throw his head back and laugh at something Leah said. If he did not, Seth would be sacrificing the only chance at happiness that had come along in millennia.

Zach fervently hoped his friend wouldn't turn his back on it.

"There's something else we can do. To keep Leah safe, that is. Or safe*r*."

David arched a brow.

"I can do for her what I did for Dana."

Chris stiffened. His expression darkened. "Damn it. What is it with you immortals and your love of mind control? It causes fucking brain damage!"

David held up a hand to staunch his objection and looked at Zach. "Is Chris correct in assuming you wish to mind-control Leah and — how did you describe it — plant a how-to-kick-ass manual in her brain?"

Zach nodded. "It worked well for Dana. I know Leah would be no match for Gershom. But it would give her a fighting chance against anyone else he might send her way."

David considered it a moment. "So be it."

Chris glared at Zach. "Seth will disembowel you when he finds out you tampered with her brain."

"Not if I help Zach do it," David countered in his deep, calm voice. "I can heal the damage done in real time. But it's a step we should take *only* if Seth decides to see her again."

Zach nodded. "Agreed." He hoped like hell his friend would do it.

⊷◊◊◊⊷

Leah smiled as she handed two bags and a receipt to her last customer. "Thank you. Have a nice night."

"You, too," the woman replied with a tired smile.

Leah walked her to the door and held it open. Once the woman left, Leah turned the OPEN sign to CLOSED and flipped both locks. She reached for the rod that closed the blinds but hesitated to turn it.

The sadness that had dogged her all day struck hard. Tears welled in her eyes. Blinking them back, she left the blinds open and pivoted to face the store. She had left the blinds open the night Seth had come by after hours, looking for Adira's toy unicorn. Dancing and talking with him had been so much fun. She could really use the diversion tonight and wished he would visit again. But three weeks had passed, so she didn't expect to see him.

The phone rang.

Normally after closing time she would let the machine pick up. But she really *did* need a distraction. Hurrying around the counter, she yanked up the receiver before the machine could kick in. "Little Gifts," she said as brightly as she could. Damn, she was depressed.

"Leah?" a man asked. He spoke softly, as though he didn't want anyone to overhear.

She frowned. "Yes?"

"Hi, it's Sheldon." He and his girlfriend Tracy had accompanied Ami when she brought Adira to storytime earlier.

She smiled. "Hi, Sheldon. What can I do for you?"

"I can't find Adira's little pink unicorn and I've looked everywhere. Have you seen it?"

"No, but my last customer just left and I haven't started tidying yet. Do you want to hang on a minute while I look around?"

"That would be great, thanks. I really appreciate it."

"Okay. Just a sec."

She set the receiver down and looked through the lost-and-found box first. Nothing. Rounding the counter, she bent over and scanned the floor beneath the clothing racks but didn't see anything there either.

"Brittney?" she called.

Brittney entered from the back room. "Yeah?"

"Have you seen a small pink unicorn with a key chain clip?"

"No. Is someone missing one?"

"Yes." She motioned to the phone on the counter.

"Let me help you look."

Together they scoured the store, looking more diligently beneath the clothing racks where children liked to hide and play. On the chairs. On the bookshelves. On the toy shelves.

"Aha!" Leah cried in triumph when she spotted it snuggled up to a buffalo like the one Seth had bought for Adira. If the buffalo didn't still have a tag on it, she'd wonder if perhaps that was Adira's, too.

Brittney smiled. "Cool."

"Thanks for helping me look."

"Anytime." She returned to the back room.

Leah picked up the receiver. "Sheldon?"

"Yeah?"

"I found it."

"Great!" he exclaimed with relief. Then… "Wait. Not great. Damn. I didn't realize how late it is."

Leah glanced at the clock. "We're closed for the night, but you're welcome to come by and pick it up." As usual, she had no plans. And Brittney would leave shortly. She had another big test tomorrow and needed to study for it.

"I can't. I'll have to swing by and get it tomorrow."

"Okay."

He sighed. "Seth is going to kick my butt if Adira has trouble sleeping tonight without it."

Leah's heart gave a little leap at the mention of Seth's name.

Sheldon grumbled something beneath his breath. "Oh well. I'll see you first thing in the morning. Thanks, Leah."

"You're welcome."

Brittney exited the back room, carrying a coat and purse. "Was that Ami on the phone?"

Leah shook her head and held the purse for Brittney while she donned her coat. "No. It was Sheldon."

"Ooh. Sheldon is so hot," Brittney declared.

Leah sent her a wry smile. "And he thinks Seth is going to kick his butt if Adira has trouble sleeping tonight without her favorite toy."

Shaking her head, Brittney took her purse and looped the strap over her shoulder. "I wouldn't want Seth to kick *my* butt. That man is huge." She grinned. "Of course, I wouldn't mind if he spanked me a little."

Laughing, Leah nudged her toward the door. "You just focus on your studies and get ready to ace that exam."

"I'd rather get spanked," she quipped as she let herself out of the store.

Leah chuckled and locked the door behind her, then headed into the back room. Grabbing a small black remote, she aimed it at the iPod connected to the store's speaker system and paused the music from the *Annie* soundtrack. Since children frequented the store, she always played music she thought they would like. But she also tried to choose music that wasn't so candy sweet it would make her want to pull her hair out after listening to it all day. That usually left her with movie soundtracks.

She had played the *Sing* soundtrack the night Seth had visited and put it on now, hoping it would lift her spirits. She hadn't told Brittney she had danced with Seth that night. The younger woman would've never stopped yammering about it, urging her anew to *get her cougar on*. But Leah had not been able to stop thinking about it. Or him.

Returning to the store, she began her nightly routine, closing up, tallying receipts, and preparing for another day of business. Though the same music played, her feet didn't move to it tonight, nor did her hips.

Her gaze strayed to the calendar on the wall behind the counter. Pain struck as memories surfaced and threatened to suffocate her. Damn it. Why couldn't Seth have come by tonight instead of three weeks ago?

She looked at the little unicorn toy sitting on the counter by the phone.

She *really* needed a distraction.

Unable to bear the silence, she grabbed her keys.

<hr />

David tapped his fingers on the long dining room table as he watched Zach shovel one forkful of salad after another into his mouth as though he hadn't eaten in days. "A bit hungry, are we?" he asked dryly.

Zach just nodded and ate as quickly as he could, trying to work in a meal before the next call came through.

Beside him, Lisette laughed and ate more slowly.

"I don't know how Seth does it," Zach complained around a mouthful.

"Does what?" David asked.

"Manages to eat and sleep and still field so many calls in a twenty-four-hour period."

"There have been many times, as you know, in which he couldn't." It was not unusual for Seth to go days without sleeping while he guarded his immortal flock. In the past, he had asked David to field his calls or had network heads send other elder immortals to aid those who faced lesser emergencies while Seth snuck in a few hours of sleep. But he had often abandoned that practice since they'd lost Yuri and Stanislav two years earlier.

Familiar pain settled in David's chest when he thought of the Russian immortals. Seth had taken their losses hard and seemed to believe that if he devoted even more time to the care and needs of his Immortal Guardians, he might somehow prevent similar losses in the future.

Richart grunted. "At least I'm finally getting to spend some time with my sister."

Richart d'Alençon and his wife Jenna dined at the table, too, as did his twin Étienne and his wife Krysta. Both women were now Immortal Guardians who spent their nights hunting with their husbands.

Much to David's surprise, antisocial immortal Roland Warbrook and his wife Sarah were present as well. Both had been spending more time at David's home since they had adopted Michael, Roland's orphaned descendant, who currently played downstairs with Adira under Sheldon and Tracy's supervision while Marcus and Ami trained.

"I miss my wife, damn it," Zach grumbled.

Lisette smiled and rested a hand on his arm.

"If we didn't both possess preternatural speed," he continued, "I wouldn't even have time to make love with her."

Lisette sent him a flirtatious smile. "You make me burn at any speed, darling."

"Damn it, Zach." Étienne groused. "She's my sister. Don't put those images in my head. That's way too much information."

Richart grunted. "At least you didn't teleport in and catch Lisette giving him a blow job."

Jenna flushed, having accompanied her husband on that particular occasion.

Lisette's eyes flashed bright amber. "I told you never to mention that again!"

Amusement trickled through David when Zach's lips turned up in a slight smile, his spirits visibly lightening.

Even Roland fought a smile.

Jared and Seth abruptly appeared in the kitchen. Both were

speckled with blood. Both bore heavy scowls.

The hidden devices in the younger immortals' pockets all beeped.

Seth looked at David. "All is well?"

"All is well," David assured him.

Nodding, Seth left the kitchen and strode through the dining room and adjoining living room. "I'm going to have a quick shower."

David watched him shrug off his coat as he entered the hallway that led to his bedroom. Seth's shoulders slumped with weariness. His footsteps dragged.

Our plan isn't working. Zach spoke in David's head as he met his gaze across the table.

David nodded. He had managed to coax Seth into diverting two-thirds of his emergency calls to Zach and Jared. But Seth clearly wasn't sleeping. Nor was he using the extra time allotted him to go see Leah as David had hoped. Instead, he simply dogged Jared's footsteps, claiming he wanted to see how well Jared would handle his new responsibilities.

Seth's bedroom door closed.

Jared strolled out of the kitchen, still frowning. When he opened his mouth to speak, David held up a hand, giving Seth another moment to close his bathroom door and start his shower.

Though every bedroom in the house was soundproofed now, Seth was powerful enough to still hear faintly what happened outside his door if he listened carefully. Once he was sealed inside his bathroom and the shower came on, however, he could not.

Lowering his hand, David nodded to Jared.

"How long is it going to take Seth to trust me enough to stop shadowing me every time I take a call from one of his Immortal Guardians?" the Other demanded. "Haven't I proven myself yet?"

"Give him time," David responded placidly, knowing trust wasn't the issue. "Delegating isn't easy after thousands of years of being in charge."

"He delegates to you."

"And has done so for several millennia. He just started delegating to you a week ago."

Jared snagged a napkin from the table and used it to wipe the blood from his sword. "I risked the wrath of the Others many times to aid him," he grumbled. "I think I have more than proven myself trustworthy."

Zach's eyes flashed golden with fury for a moment before they darkened to brown once more.

It was probably unwise for Jared to mention the wrath of the Others since he had doled out some of that wrath himself in the past at Zach's expense. "Just give him time," he counseled again.

Seth was clearly growing restless. David knew the powerful Immortal Guardians' leader sought any excuse he could not to sleep or relax simply because such moments left him time to think about Leah. But David maintained the hope that Seth would eventually cave and seek her out once more.

Jared's phone chirped in his pocket. Sheathing his sword, he answered. "Yes?"

"I just tranqed six vamps," Colben, an immortal stationed in Saskatoon, said. "Do you want to read their minds and see if they know anything about Gershom's immortals?"

"Yes," Jared told him. "I'm on my way."

Zach held up a hand. "Just a moment." He wiped his mouth with a napkin, then dropped it on the table and rose. "Before you go, I want to give you something."

Jared nodded. "Hurry up. I want to leave before Seth gets out of the shower."

Nodding, Zach swiftly drew back his arm and slammed his fist into Jared's face.

Jared flew backward, hit a sofa, and knocked it over as he tumbled to the floor behind it. "Son of a bitch!"

Roland and the French twins laughed heartily while their wives gaped.

Lisette sighed and rolled her eyes.

Zach shook his hand, flexed his fingers, then returned to his seat and dug into his dinner once more.

David sighed. "Damn it, Zach. How long is this going to continue?" Such had become a common occurrence.

Zach shrugged. "The bastard tortured me. I'll stop once his debt is paid."

Groaning, Jared climbed to his feet. Blood poured down his chin from his broken nose. "You don't know how much I regret that."

Zach's lips twitched. "Yes, I do."

Gingerly touching his damaged nose, Jared looked around for his phone.

David saw it on the floor nearby and used telekinesis to fling it toward him. "Catch."

"Thank you." The bones in Jared's face started to shift back into position as he teleported away.

Conversation resumed, the French siblings bantering and laughing.

A tinny version of "It's the End of the World as We Know It" interrupted them. Zach retrieved his phone. "Yes?"

"Kedron here," David heard an Immortal Guardian stationed in the UK say. "Tobey and I just tranqed five vampires. There were over a dozen in all. We had to slay the rest. None resembled the missing immortals. But you might like to peruse the thoughts of these blackguards and see what you can find before we destroy them."

Many such calls had come in since word had spread that Gershom had kidnapped and transformed a dozen *gifted ones*. All were hoping they'd come across a vampire who happened to know something since Gershom had worked with vampires in the past.

"I shall be there shortly," Zach said. After ending the call, he finished his dinner as quickly as he could.

Lisette smiled and rubbed his arm. "Poor baby. You should've eaten earlier."

Zach shook his head and rose. "Losing myself in your beautiful body was more fun." Bending, he brushed a kiss across her lips. "I'll see you later."

She smiled and stroked his cheek. "Be careful."

"You, too." He sent Richart a sharp look. "If anything happens to her, you're dead."

Lisette would be hunting with Richart and Jenna tonight since Zach was otherwise occupied.

Richart nodded. "I'm aware."

Zach kissed Lisette again.

The sound of an approaching vehicle carried to David's hypersensitive ears. When it reached the gate at the entrance to his long, long driveway, it halted.

Zach straightened and met David's gaze when no one typed a security code into the keypad by the gate. Instead, the driver just sat there with the engine idling.

It couldn't be an Immortal Guardian or one of their Seconds. They all knew the code and would already be on their way up to the house. As would Chris Reordon if he were visiting.

So who was it?

When David delved into the driver's mind, shock struck.

Zach sucked in a breath. His eyes widened. He must have read the driver's thoughts, too.

Leah waited outside the gate, questioning the wisdom of coming while she stared at the call button on the keypad.

Chapter Six

D AVID LEAPT TO HIS FEET. "Everyone out!" he shouted. The younger immortals all gaped up at him.

"What?" Sarah asked.

"Everyone out!" he ordered again. "Now! Use the escape tunnels in the basement so you won't be seen."

Zach blurred. Dishes clanked together as he began to clear the table at preternatural speeds.

Roland scowled. "Why?"

"Do not question me, Roland," David warned, "just do as I say. And hurry. Make sure none of you are seen."

Roland turned his head toward the window, finally noticing the sound of a car engine. Swearing, he rose and drew his sword. "Who *is* that? Who's coming?"

Zach finished clearing the table, then rapidly loaded the dishwasher so there would be no mess if Seth invited Leah in.

"Someone's coming?" Krysta leapt to her feet.

The other immortals all did the same and drew their swords, so distracted by David's orders that they didn't notice Zach or question why he was tidying up if an enemy was about to strike.

"Who is it?" Richart asked. "Is it Gershom?"

"No," David said, urgency driving him. He needed to get rid of them before Leah changed her mind and drove away. "Put those away, damn it!" he ordered, motioning to their weapons.

Roland shook his head. "Not until you tell us who's out there. The last time you ordered us to get the hell out, Zach hurled a couple of vampires through the front window, then dove in and knocked us all on our arses."

They had thought Zach the enemy at the time.

"We aren't being attacked," David insisted and swore when he heard Leah shift her car into reverse. Zipping over to the panel by the door, he pressed a button.

The gate began to swing open.

After a moment, she shifted back into drive and guided her car forward.

Turning back to the group by the table, he found them all staring at him in confusion.

"If we aren't under attack," Roland said, doubt written all over his ready-for-battle face, "then why do you want us to leave?"

Zach spoke in David's mind. *You're going to have to tell them.*

David sighed. "Seth has a caller."

They all exchanged puzzled glances.

"A what?" Richart asked.

"A caller," David repeated. "Seth has a caller." And probably wouldn't appreciate them knowing about it.

Étienne's brow puckered. "Like a..." He looked at his brother, his sister, then David. "Like a woman?" he asked uncertainly.

"Yes!" David declared with a hefty dose of exasperation.

Zach laughed in the kitchen.

The Immortal Guardians all viewed the much older and immensely powerful Seth as a father figure. Discovering that *daddy* might have a date seemed to have thrown them even more than the belief that Gershom might be attacking had.

Eyes widening, Roland sheathed his sword, then swept through the living room, righting the sofa and tidying up.

David didn't know why that surprised him, but it did.

Lisette's face brightened as it finally sank in. "Seth has a caller?" Clapping her hands, she practically danced in place with excitement. "Finally! Who is it? Do we know her? What's she like? Can I—?"

David pointed an imperious finger at her. "Don't do it." He looked at Étienne. "You either."

"Don't do what?" Lisette asked, all innocence.

"Don't read her thoughts," he said. "I forbid it. And do not linger once you leave and try to get a look at her or listen in."

Her expression turned disgruntled.

Zach entered. "You heard him," he told them all. "Get your asses out of here." He kissed Lisette one more time. "And be safe tonight."

"You, too, darling," she said, her smile returning.

Zach vanished.

Richart drew Jenna close, then touched Lisette's shoulder and teleported the three of them away.

Étienne took Krysta's hand. Then the two of them shot off in a blur, racing down to their basement bedroom and the hidden escape tunnel that would allow them to leave the house unseen.

Roland clasped Sarah's hand. Hope lit the antisocial immortal's usually dour face. "If there's anything I can do…"

David smiled, understanding. Roland wouldn't be sharing eternity with the woman he loved if it weren't for Seth. "I know. Thank you. Now go."

The couple dashed away at preternatural speeds.

⚯

Seth bent his head and braced his hands on the shower wall, letting hot water pound the tight muscles in his shoulders and upper back. As always, exhaustion pulled at him. His eyes burned with the need for sleep. But every time he closed them, he saw Leah… smiling up at him… winking… teasing and caressing him… rubbing up against him as she danced.

He cursed as desire flooded him and he grew hard. He hadn't had this much difficulty controlling his body in millennia. If he could just stay busy, his priorities would realign themselves and life would go back to the same old, same old. He'd aid his Immortal Guardians and battle vampires round the clock, look for the missing *gifted ones*…

He swore. The missing *immortals*.

And try to find and bury Gershom, ending this once and for all.

Seth watched water sluice down the long curtain of his hair and rain on the tile at his feet, rinsing the last of the soapsuds down the drain.

David had been watching him a little too closely of late. He clearly sensed something was troubling Seth. Something more than the usual. And for some reason, he believed giving Seth more downtime would help him sort it out.

Seth shook his head. When had *that* ever helped him? The only thing less work did was give painful memories time to resurface, along with the loneliness that had plagued him for so long.

And now thoughts of Leah bombarded him as well.

Seth, David murmured in his head.

Yes?

You're needed in the living room. We have a situation.

Is it Gershom?

No, but get here as quickly as you can.

Normally, such a request would make Seth sigh. But today he welcomed the interruption. Turning off the water, he stepped out and dried off at preternatural speeds. It took a little longer to drag a comb through his long wet hair, making him consider cutting it short like Roland's. Less than a minute later, he tugged a black T-shirt down over his chest as he left his bedroom. The hem settled over the waist of the black cargo pants he'd donned. His feet were already complaining over being stuffed into his boots again so soon.

Striding down the hallway, he tugged his hair out of his T-shirt and let if fall loosely down his back, dampening the cotton material. He hoped this wasn't about Zach's tendency to hit Jared whenever the latter least expected it. One of these days, Jared was going to get tired of it and hit back. Breaking up *that* altercation would be a pain in Seth's ass. But for now guilt still compelled Jared to take it.

David waited near the front door, his eyes bright with… mirth?

Seth glanced toward the dining room, surprised to find it empty and the table cleared. "Where is everyone?"

"I sent them away."

"Let me guess. Zach and Jared were squabbling again." He looked around. "At least they didn't break anything this time." The furniture appeared remarkably unscathed. In fact… "Is it me, or is it neater in here than when I arrived?"

David nodded. "Zach and Roland tidied up a bit."

Those two? Really? "Why?"

"Someone is coming."

Seth heard the approach of an automobile but felt no alarm. David wouldn't be so relaxed if danger lurked outside. "Who is it?" If it was Chris Reordon bringing them bad news, he didn't want to know, so he refrained from reading the driver's thoughts.

David's lips stretched in a smile. "You have a caller."

Seth stopped short. He must not have heard him right. "What?"

"You have a caller."

Certain he was still misunderstanding, Seth reached into his back pocket and drew out his cell phone to check messages.

David chuckled. "Not a call. A *caller*. Leah is here."

Seth's heartbeat picked up, something he wished he could hide. "Leah from Little Gifts?"

"Yes."

His heartbeat quickened even more. "Why is she here?" She sure as hell wasn't there to *call on him* as David had suggested.

"To see *you*."

After living for thousands of years, very little surprised Seth. But that completely flabbergasted him. "You read her mind?"

"Yes."

"She came to see me?"

"Well, she has another reason for coming but is merely using it as an excuse to see you again. She's hoping you'll be here."

Seth had no idea how to respond to that. "Why does she want to see me?"

David's deep brown eyes danced with suppressed laughter. "Perhaps because she likes your *big hands*."

Seth groaned. If David had plucked that particular memory from Leah's mind, then he most likely had seen them dancing together as well.

Chuckling, David closed the distance between them and clapped him on the shoulder. "She enjoys your company, and you enjoy hers. There's nothing wrong with that." His expression grew solemn. "But she's troubled tonight, Seth, and could use a diversion. I think she's hoping that diversion will be you."

So Leah really *had* come to see him? "How did she even know where to find me?"

"Gershom certainly didn't tell her, if that's why you're frowning."

"It is." Yet his scowl remained. Leah wanted him to be a diversion? "What kind of diversion?"

David laughed.

"Stop laughing, damn it."

"I haven't spent time alone with a woman in almost as many millennia as you, so if you're wondering what she might like to do, I'm not the best person to ask."

Seth reached out to Zach telepathically. *Zach.*

What?

What does Lisette like to do when you two have downtime together?

Make love.

Aside from that.

Dance.

Seth sure as hell wouldn't mind dancing with Leah again, but didn't trust himself to put his hands on her. Best to omit that option. *Anything else?*

Watch movies or sports.

He looked at David. "Do you think she'd like to watch a movie?"

David shrugged. "I don't know. Ask her. She's just looking for something to take her mind off what's burdening her."

The car halted.

"Do you know what's burdening her?"

"Yes."

"Will you tell me what it is?" Seth wasn't ready to delve into the significance of his not wanting to read her thoughts himself and hoped David would just assume recent difficulties had left him weary of employing his telepathy.

"No. If she wants you to know, she'll tell you herself." David gave Seth a pat on the back, then strolled toward the hallway. "I'm going to head down and spend some time with the little ones to give you two some privacy."

Seth's mind raced so rampantly that it took him a moment to realize what David had said. He turned just as the other man disappeared into the basement stairwell. "Privacy to do what?"

A laugh rumbled up the steps. "That is for you to decide."

Footsteps sounded on the front sidewalk. The doorbell rang.

Excitement set Seth's pulse to racing as he opened the front door. Sure enough, Leah stood there, as beautiful as he remembered in a pair of snug-fitting jeans and a sweater that molded itself to her full breasts and narrow waist. Over that she wore a blazer. Her long brown hair lifted and floated on a cool breeze that added some pink to her nose and cheeks.

When she saw him, her face lit up with an infectious smile, and her heartbeat increased as much as his own had. "Hi, Seth."

He smiled back. And he wondered once more why being with her always seemed to make the tension just melt right out of him. The tightness in his shoulders eased and uncertainty fled, replaced by pleasure. "Leah. What a wonderful surprise." The words left his lips before he could ponder the wisdom of speaking them.

Her own smile turned self-deprecating. "I shouldn't have dropped by like this. I'm sorry. I just..." She held up a pink unicorn. "Sheldon called earlier. He couldn't find Adira's unicorn and was worried that she wouldn't be able to sleep without it."

David's words floated back to him. *She has another reason for coming but is merely using it as an excuse to see you again.*

He took the small toy she offered, his fingers brushing hers. "You drove all this way to bring it to her? How kind of you. Come in. Please."

She stepped inside. Her hazel eyes—more green than brown tonight—widened as she looked around. "Wow. This place is *huge.*"

Chuckling, he closed the door. "May I take your jacket?"

Still staring at the living room with its multitude of sofas, love seats, and wingback chairs, then the dining room table that could seat over thirty people, she nodded absently.

Seth moved to stand behind her and helped her remove her blazer, waiting patiently as she switched her keys and purse strap from one hand to the other. He loved her scent. No perfume. Just Leah with a hint of the outdoors.

After hanging her jacket on one of the many pegs that lined the long coatrack, he turned and found her watching him.

"How many people live here?"

He smiled. "Many of the men and women who work for me either have no families of their own or have cut ties with them because their families... well..."

"Suck?" she supplied helpfully.

He chuckled. "Yes. So David and I always leave our doors open and issue a standing invitation for them to come and spend time together. Our particular line of work often includes odd hours that make socialization difficult." He motioned to the large living room and dining room. "This helps them feel less alone."

"That's so nice. I've heard of businesses that offer perks like free gyms and daycare to make their employees feel like a more close-knit group… but this takes it way above and beyond that. You open your *home* to them."

"It goes both ways. While this alleviates their loneliness, it also alleviates mine and David's." Unable to resist the urge, he touched her arm briefly. "Will you excuse me for a moment while I take this down to Adira?"

"Of course."

He gestured toward the sofas. "Please, make yourself at home." Hopefully, no Immortal Guardians would stride through the door, covered in blood, while he was gone… or worse, teleport in and abruptly appear right in front of her.

Light, swift footsteps sounded in the basement stairwell, followed by heavy boots.

Seth looked toward the hallway.

Giggles erupted as Adira and Michael emerged and ran forward.

David spoke in Seth's mind. *Adira knows Leah brought her unicorn toy. I didn't have the heart to stop them.*

Marcus and Ami's extraordinary daughter bore many special gifts they were still discovering. Since they suspected telepathy was one of them, she had likely read Leah's thoughts as soon as Leah entered the house.

Sheldon jogged out of the hallway, following the children. His face brightened when he saw Leah and the unicorn Seth held. "Hey! You brought it!" Relief and pleasure filled his features. "Wow. I can't believe you did that. Thank you, Leah. You're a lifesaver."

When it looked as though Sheldon would continue forward and sweep Leah into a hug, Seth shot him a glare. *Touch her and die.* Just the idea of the strapping young human male putting his hands on Leah sent jealousy coursing through Seth, which was totally irrational because he knew Sheldon loved Tracy.

Sheldon jerked to a halt. His face paled as his eyes widened.

Seth was dimly aware of Adira reclaiming her unicorn and saying something to Leah.

Sheldon raised an index finger to scratch his temple, glanced swiftly at Leah, then tapped his cheek below one eye, drawing Seth's attention to it.

Seth saw his reflection in it, caught the bright golden glow of his own eyes, and closed them with a silent curse. Really? Jealous fury? Over so little? How many times since he'd met Leah had he asked himself what the hell was wrong with him?

When Seth opened his eyes once more, Sheldon nodded that the glow was gone.

Leah had dropped to one knee to accept a hug from Adira and apparently hadn't caught Seth's slip. "You're very welcome, sweetie," she said with a smile.

Michael hung back, still a little shy and withdrawn around anyone he didn't see on a daily basis.

"All right, you two." Sheldon moved forward and herded the toddlers away as soon as Adira released Leah. "Let's head back down so we can hear the end of David's story. I want to find out what happens to the lion." He started back through the living room and down the hallway, a child on each side of him, holding his hands. "Thanks again, Leah," he called over his shoulder.

"You're welcome."

At the last second, Adira released Sheldon, then ran back to Seth, her arms outstretched.

Smiling, Seth picked her up and hugged her.

"Night-night, Baba."

"Night-night, poppet." He kissed her cheek, then set her down.

Adira took Leah's hand and put it in Seth's.

Seth's skin tingled as Leah wove her fingers between his own.

Satisfied, the little girl raced back to where Sheldon and Michael waited by the basement stairwell.

Sheldon stared at their clasped hands, then looked at Seth.

Tell anyone and —

You'll kick my butt, Sheldon thought, interrupting Seth's mental warning. *Got it.*

Quiet descended after the trio left.

Leah sent Seth a wry smile and gave his hand a squeeze. "It's weird that I'm here, right?"

Only because David had said she'd come to see *him*.

He shook his head. "People drop by all the time. I don't want you to feel weird about it." He tilted his head to one side. "Although I admit to being curious as to how you found us." Unwilling to break the contact just yet, he slid his thumb back and forth over her soft skin.

Did her heartbeat increase a little at the light caress?

"Sheldon signed Ami up for a year of Little Gifts Baskets," she said. "I ship one every month and try to tailor each basket to the individual subscriber, putting things in there not just for the child or children but for the mom or dad, too. He used this address when he did."

Seth tried to muster up some anger over Sheldon's having given out David's home address but couldn't. It had facilitated Leah's visit.

Looking a tad chagrined, she wrinkled her nose and shrugged. "Driving out here to return the toy seemed like a good idea at the time, but now it just feels creepy and stalkerish."

Seth laughed. "It isn't creepy and stalkerish. I enjoy your company too much for it to be."

"Really? Because I would be freaking out a little if someone did this to me."

"I'm not freaking out. It truly was a pleasant surprise."

Her lips turned up in a smile. "Remember how I said I'm a total workaholic?"

"Yes." Now *her* thumb stroked *his* hand, sending warmth all the way up his arm, through his shoulder, and into his chest.

"Well, I've been trying to ease back on that a little lately, but it's been so long that I have no idea what to do with downtime."

"I understand completely. David has been insisting I delegate more authority lately and take some time off, but..." He shrugged. "When I'm not working, I always feel like I *should* be working and find myself at loose ends."

"Exactly! This is going to sound lame, but... I don't get out much. And tonight, when the walls started closing in on me, I figured a drive in the country might be nice because I couldn't think of anything else to do. Then I got here, you opened the door, and I thought: Oh crap, he's going to think I'm a total stalker."

"Not at all." Seth raised their clasped hands and grinned. "I merely assumed you wanted to see my big hands again."

Laughing, she gave his shoulder a shove. "You're such a tease!"

His heart lightened. "Admitted without shame."

"Well, I'll forgive you," she quipped, "because you're letting me hold your hand." Drawing their clasped hands closer to her face, she cupped her free hand over them and smoothed circles over his as she assumed a comical expression of amazement. "Oooooooh. So big," she breathed.

Seth laughed.

When Leah looked past his shoulder, he turned to find David strolling up the hallway toward them.

Leah hastily released Seth's hand, looking as guilty as a little girl who had been caught sneaking a cookie right before dinnertime.

David smiled. "Good evening, Leah. What a wonderful surprise."

Smiling back, she offered him a little wave. "Hi, David."

"I apologize for interrupting, but I've been called away and need to retrieve my coat."

Seth frowned as David lifted his coat off the rack by the door. "Am I needed?"

"No." David was careful not to allow Leah to glimpse the multitude of weapons that adorned the interior of his coat as he donned it. He had removed them all before visiting her store, as had Seth. "I'll take care of it." *Bastien called. He and Cliff captured several vampires. Bastien wants me to read their minds before he turns Cliff loose on them.* He looked at Leah. "This is Seth's night off. I'm afraid he doesn't know what to do with himself in the rare instances he finds some free time, so he keeps volunteering to work."

Leah nudged Seth with her shoulder. "Him and me both."

David gave her a little bow. "Nice to see you again."

"Nice to see you, too."

The door closed behind him.

Seth looked down at Leah.

"So," she said.

He cocked a brow. "So?"

"Looks like we're just a couple of workaholics who have no clue what to do with ourselves."

"Apparently so."

"Any ideas?"

Quite a few, but they all seemed to revolve around the two of them getting naked. "No. What about you?"

She laughed. "Not a one. But I'm sure we can come up with something."

⟼⟶◦◍◦⟵⟻

Sean Linz threw a dagger that buried itself in a vampire's neck, then swung his katana at another opponent in front of him. Clangs, growls, grunts, and cries of pain disrupted the quiet college campus as he, Krysta, and Étienne fought an astoundingly large vampire crew that had descended upon UNC Chapel Hill.

There must be almost two dozen of them. If Sean's nose hadn't warned him otherwise, he would've thought they were frat boys out making mischief when he first saw them. But their bloody clothing had given them away.

As Sean sliced up the vampire in front of him, another circled around behind him and tried to hamstring him. Sean shifted at the last moment, grunting when the blade cut across his outer thigh. Decapitating the vampire in front of him with a swipe of his blade, he spun around to confront the asshole behind him.

These vamps all appeared to be newly turned. Most still retained enough of their sanity to look a little nervous when their companions began to fall beneath the Immortal Guardians' blades.

Not so confident now, are you, dipshits? Sean thought.

He spared his sister a quick glance to see how she fared.

Krysta was kicking ass as usual, thanks to her ability to see auras.

Her husband, Étienne, grunted as a gash opened on his cheek.

"Stop watching me, damn it," Krysta snapped, "and keep your eyes on your opponent."

"Watching you kick ass," Étienne gritted out, "is far more entertaining."

Both seemed to be holding their own.

The body of Sean's latest foe hit the ground and began to shrivel up at his feet.

"Sean?" Krysta called. "How you doing over there?"

"I'm good," he answered, opening the carotid artery of his next opponent.

Panic lit the vampire's glowing blue eyes as he stumbled backward, dropped his long bowie knife, and tried to stem the rapid flow of blood. One of his fellow vampires didn't move out of the way fast enough and accidently stabbed the vamp in the back.

Sean saluted him. "Thank you." He turned to face the vampire behind him.

The vampire's gray eyes lost their glow as they rolled back in his head. His bowie knives clattered to the pavement as he sank to the ground, a tranquilizer dart protruding from his chest.

Nicole. He should've known his Second would shadow them. She had minor precognitive abilities like Melanie and had warned him earlier that she *had a bad feeling* about tonight.

Something flew past Sean's left ear with a *thwit.*

He spun to find the vampire who had accidentally stabbed his friend lunging toward him with his blade raised high.

The vamp stopped short and frowned down at the dart sticking out of his chest. Then his eyes rolled back and he sank to the ground, too.

"Damn it!" Krysta shouted suddenly.

"They're running," Étienne announced with disgust, "the bloody cowards."

Sean looked around. Sure enough, seven vampires had taken off, streaking away with preternatural speed. One jerked to a halt and sank to the ground, thanks to another dart fired by Nicole. "Go," he told the couple. "I'll take care of these."

Krysta shook her head. "Seth said not to —"

"I'm not alone. Nicole is backing me up."

As if on cue, a dart struck one of the four remaining vampires in the neck.

"See? I'll be fine. Don't let those bastards get away."

Though both looked uncertain, Krysta and Étienne took off after the others, leaving his sight within seconds.

Two of the vampires who remained behind struck Sean in tandem while the third, wearing a baseball cap, hung back and bided his time. Nicole took out one of the two Sean fought with a dart before the bastard could sneak around and attack his back. Sean wounded the second, then turned and faced the third.

The vampire lifted his head, the bill of his cap revealing his features.

Shock rippled through Sean, freezing him in place. It was a woman. A slender woman who couldn't be more than twenty-two or twenty-three years old, wearing too-big clothes that concealed her sex.

Her eyes glowed green as rage darkened her pretty features.

"Oh shit," he heard Nicole whisper somewhere behind him.

The woman's hands tightened around the hilts of the deadly katanas she wielded. Her fangs gleamed in the moonlight.

Sean stared in horror. A female vampire? He had never fought a female vampire before. He'd never even seen one. Insanity usually drove male vampires to kill the human women they captured long before the women could complete the transformation. But Gershom had implanted commands in the local vampires' minds, compelling many of them to turn more humans.

If a vampire who hadn't yet surrendered to the madness had caught this woman, it was totally plausible that he had still been sane enough not to lose it and kill her before she transformed.

Sean's stomach churned. The idea of decapitating this woman sickened him.

Could she be one of the missing immortals? One of Gershom's own private army perhaps? The green eyes made that highly unlikely. All immortals had brown eyes that glowed amber. There had only been one exception in thousands of years, so—

The woman ducked to the side, dodging a tranquilizer dart. Then dodged another. And another.

He gaped. Holy shit, she was fast! No way was this woman a vampire. "Call Seth!" he ordered.

The woman tossed her katana straight up in the air, drew a dagger, and threw it. Catching the katana as it fell, she leapt forward.

Behind him, Nicole grunted.

Sean hastily raised his weapons as the woman attacked. She was incredibly fast. So fast he had to dedicate all his attention just to fending off her strikes.

A thud sounded behind him, like that caused by a body hitting the ground.

Shit! Had Nicole been hit by the dagger?

Worry rose as he deflected blow after blow of the woman's swords. "Nicole?" he called.

Silence.

One of the woman's blades carved a path across his chest as she took advantage of his distraction. Damn, she was strong. She *had* to be an immortal.

"Nicole!" he shouted, panic suffusing him when she didn't answer. Was she dead? Had this woman killed her?

His opponent landed another strike. It was like fighting an elder Immortal Guardian. How the hell was that possible? A vampire must have turned her. So—at best—she should match Sean in speed and strength and be his equal. Instead, she was kicking his ass!

He parried every blow, but the sheer power behind them slowly drove him backward. Even if she slipped and gave him an opening, he couldn't strike a killing blow. Seth wanted the missing immortals taken alive. So how the hell was he going to get out of this? He couldn't fight her and contact Seth at the same time. He wasn't telepathic and had to use a phone.

Could he hold her here until Krysta and Étienne returned?

A moan sounded behind him.

Relief rushed through him, thickening his throat. Nicole wasn't dead.

He dug in his heels, not wanting the female immortal to get any closer to wherever Nicole lay, and kept her busy so she couldn't throw another dagger.

The long blade of her katana sank into his side and stayed there.

Agony engulfed him. Sean sucked in a breath, then drew his own blade across her thigh.

She barely seemed to notice. "Immortal, my ass," she sneered. "If you bleed, you can die." She yanked her sword out.

Sean damned near sank to his knees it hurt so much.

She renewed her assault. "The other vampires all fear you." She scored another hit. "They think you're strong."

Pain lanced through him when she came damned close to severing his arm with another powerful strike. His sword fell from lax fingers, leaving him one weapon against her two.

"But you aren't. You're weak," she taunted in a voice full of hate. "Killing you will be easy."

Soft *thwits* reached his ears.

The woman danced backward as blood spurted from multiple bullet holes that opened on her chest.

The shooting stopped.

"He isn't weak, you stupid bitch," Nicole gritted.

Sean risked a glance over his shoulder.

His Second leaned against the corner of the nearest building, a dagger sticking out of her left shoulder. Blood stained her teeth and poured down one side of her face from a head wound as she aimed a 9mm equipped with a silencer and extended magazine at the woman. "He's honorable."

Grass shifted.

Sean hastily looked back at the woman.

The female immortal took a step toward him.

Nicole shot her again. Twice. "Too honorable to *hit* a woman, let alone kill her."

The female immortal growled in fury.

"Fortunately, I don't have that problem." Nicole shot her again, then again.

"Don't kill her," Sean huffed, bending over and grasping his injured arm. "Seth wants her taken alive."

No more shots ensued.

"Seth?" the woman snarled, blood spilling from her lips. Her eyes flashed even brighter as they met Sean's. "You tell that bastard I'm coming for him," she wheezed.

Sean shook his head. "Tell him yourself. I can have him here in two seconds."

Roaring in fury, she lunged forward.

Thwit, thwit, thwit.

More bullets struck home.

Staggering backward, the woman shook her head. Her weapons lowered as she fought for breath. "This isn't... over," she bit out. In the next instant, she spun around and dashed away in a blur even *he* could barely see. Her baseball cap tumbled to the ground at his feet, freeing long auburn hair.

Shit. That had not gone well.

Sean turned to face his Second. "Nicole?" He limped toward her.

She met his gaze. The hand holding the gun fell to her side. Her eyes closed. Her knees buckled.

Sean lunged forward with a growl of pain and caught her as she sank toward the ground.

Chapter Seven

L EAH SURREPTITIOUSLY STUDIED SETH FROM the corner of her eye. The two of them were slumped comfortably on the sofa in her apartment above her shop.

Seth made it feel small. Both the living room *and* the sofa. He was so big. His broad shoulders brushed hers every time he dipped his hand into the popcorn bowl between them. The muscles beneath the tight T-shirt he wore rippled as he drew out a handful of tasty kernels and carried them to his mouth. His long, equally muscular legs were crossed at the ankle, his booted feet resting beside hers on the coffee table. Her sneakers seemed almost like a child's by comparison. What size did he wear? And how hard was it for him to find shoes that large?

Really? she asked herself mentally. *That's what you're thinking about right now?*

Better that than how much she liked having him in her home.

He glanced over and caught her staring. "What?"

"Are you sure you don't want me to salt it?" Most people she knew thought popcorn that wasn't buttered, salted, or otherwise flavored tasted like paper.

He nodded. "I like it better this way."

She smiled. "Me, too." Leah returned her attention to the large flat-screen television on the wall across from them. She had stopped salting food a few years ago when her doctor had advised her to do so in an effort to bring her blood pressure down without medication. Everything had tasted blah for a few weeks when she had. Then her taste buds had adjusted and she had been surprised by how good everything she'd once thought bland had tasted.

She was glad, too, that she had begun to exercise daily at the same time, again on doctor's orders. It had helped take her mind off things and given her something to do when her apartment had grown too quiet.

The episode of *Stranger Things* they watched ended. Credits began to play.

She turned to Seth and raised her eyebrows. "What do you think?"

"I'm enjoying it."

"Me, too. Are you up for another episode?"

"Yes."

She smiled. He definitely seemed more relaxed now. As relaxed as he had been after the dance they'd shared. Good. She grabbed the remote control and negotiated the DVD menu to find the next episode. "I love that this series takes place in the eighties."

He nodded. "A time before adults and children both became obsessed with cell phones and apps and the internet."

"Exactly. There was so much more social interaction back then." Though she knew he wasn't old enough to remember that. "*And* less ugliness. Nowadays, people feel free to spout whatever nastiness springs to mind on the internet. But back then it was put up or shut up. You didn't talk shit about other people unless you knew you could beat them in a fight because it *always* got back to them and you knew they would come after you and try to kick your ass."

"True." He smiled. "What I *don't* miss are rotary phones."

She snorted. "As if you've ever used one." Despite his claims the night they'd danced, she still thought him thirty years old, tops.

"On the contrary," he countered. "I've used many. And time was often of the essence when I did, so it drove me crazy when it took so long to dial a number." Raising a hand in front of him, he mimicked dialing a rotary phone with his index finger. "*Shick*-tic-tic-tic-tic. *Shick*-tic. *Shick*-tic-tic-tic-tic-tic. *Shick*-tic."

She laughed. "And if your finger slipped, you had to start dialing all over again."

He grinned. "It took forever. So aggravating when you were in a hurry."

Leah shook her head. "You almost have me convinced you actually experienced that firsthand. But no way are you old enough."

Leaning sideways, his shoulder pressing into hers, he whispered, "I'm older than you are."

"BS. I'm forty-six."

Again, he leaned down and whispered, "I'm still older than you are."

His warm breath on her ear sent a shiver of desire coursing through her. She arched a brow, not believing him for a moment. "Then let me be the first to say holy *crap*, you look good for your age."

Seth laughed. "Thank you."

She liked seeing him like this. He really seemed to be enjoying himself. "Honestly, you look good for *any* age."

"As do you," he said, and another thrill shot through her as his gaze slowly traveled down her body. "*Very* good," he added, "which is why I don't understand why you're sitting here with me, watching television. Don't the single dads who frequent your shop hit on you all the time?"

"Some do," she admitted. "A few of the married ones do, too."

He frowned. "Really? What utter bastards."

"My sentiments exactly."

"None of the single dads appeal to you?"

She shrugged. "I'm not really looking for a relationship, so it wouldn't be fair to lead them on."

He nodded. "I'm not looking for a relationship either." Was that regret she heard in his voice? "My line of work isn't conducive to such."

"Long hours?"

"Very long."

She could sympathize.

"And too…" He spoke reluctantly, as though he felt he probably shouldn't. "I sometimes acquire enemies."

She frowned. "What kind of enemies?"

"The kind who might target those I love most in order to strike at me."

She studied him silently, the *Stranger Things* menu frozen on the screen. "You said you own a private security company. I was thinking you supplied mall cops or provided neighborhood security. But that wouldn't attract enemies. What exactly do you do?"

He pondered the question a moment. "We protect the innocent. We protect those who are targeted by... predators, for lack of a better word. Men who, for whatever reason, wish to harm or kill them. Men who delight in committing violence and terrorizing those who are weaker. And we protect these intended victims worldwide."

His company was global? Maybe he *was* older than she thought. Unless he had inherited it.

"So you're like... international bodyguards?"

"Bodyguard implies we only protect the rich and famous. We protect people from all walks of life."

"Are you mercenaries or something?" She had seen some bad stuff on the news about mercenaries. Hell, a mercenary outfit based here in North Carolina had been blown all to hell a couple of years ago by some of their own soldiers who were pissed off because their employer wouldn't help them fight criminal charges brought against them overseas.

"No. We aren't mercenaries. We don't fight other men's wars for profit. We don't train men in foreign countries to fight. We don't supply weapons as some mercenary outfits do. Our eyes are on the greater good, and we value that more than profit. We've actually forced more than one mercenary outfit engaged in nefarious activities out of business."

"That's pretty ballsy."

He shrugged.

"I can see how that might gain you some serious enemies."

"Yes."

"So you don't date or... marry... because you're afraid it might put the woman in danger?"

"In part."

The way he said it suggested he didn't want to discuss the other part. So she didn't ask, though curiosity gnawed at her. "That sucks."

"Yes, it does."

A sound reached Leah's ears.

Seth frowned and looked over his shoulder.

Skillet's "Monster" played faintly in the laundry room.

Both stood.

Leah followed Seth through her kitchen and into the laundry room where he dug his phone out of the pocket of the coat he'd hung there.

"Yes?" he answered. As he listened to whoever had called, he stiffened. His hand tightened on the phone, then lowered as he looked at her. His jaw clenched. His expression turned grim. "I have to go." Grabbing his coat, he reached for the back door's knob. "May I exit this way?"

"Yes."

He ducked outside and left without another word.

Crap. It looked like he'd gotten some really bad news.

Remembering belatedly that she had driven them here from David's place, Leah opened the door and leaned out to ask if he needed a ride... but he was already gone. Again.

Frowning, she stepped out onto the landing of the stairs that led down to the back alley.

No sign of Seth. How the hell did he do that?

Returning inside, she closed and locked the door, then set the alarm.

Quiet engulfed her, oppressive without Seth's company to dispel it.

Leah strolled slowly through the kitchen and into the living room. Kneeling before the flat-screen TV, she pressed the eject button on the DVD player and returned the DVD to the faux VHS tape case it had come in. Maybe she could talk Seth into watching the rest of it with her another time. He was good company.

Her gaze slid to the tiny memory card on which she had downloaded the security footage of Seth's last visit to her shop. Driven by impulse, she inserted it into the memory card slot of the DVD player. Rounding her coffee table, she sat in Seth's place, still warm from his body, and picked up the remote. A few seconds later, she munched what was left of the popcorn while she fast-forwarded to the dance they had shared.

She supposed she should feel embarrassed that Seth had caught her dancing by herself, but she didn't. His handsome face lit with a charming smile as he leaned against the wall and watched her. He seemed happy in that moment. Content. Considering how much stress his job appeared to dump on his shoulders, she was glad her antics had made him smile.

She watched herself lure him into joining her, and the two of them began to dance.

"Hmm." They looked good together. That surprised her. She had thought she would look too old for him, but they partnered well as they moved together.

When she had first started exercising daily, she had found it so freaking tedious that she had taken some aerobics classes. Much to her dismay, those had bored the pants off her, too. So she had signed up for dance classes in hopes of finding a more fun way to work up a good sweat and get her heart pumping.

She'd ended up liking it a lot. It had been a while though — several years, in fact — since she had traded in her dance classes for the fancy new treadmill and MaxiClimber in her apartment. But you'd never guess it by watching this.

Seth was an excellent dancer. She'd have to ask him how he'd learned the next time he —

Her breath halted. Her mind blanked as she stared at the screen.

Seth closed his eyes. When he opened them, they were dark brown.

Breathing again, she shook off the shock that had seized her. It must have been the lighting or something, because for a moment it had looked as if his —

"Oh shit," she whispered when it happened again. Seth's eyes flashed a brilliant gold as she pressed up against his back in the video and slid her hand around to caresses him. They brightened again a little later when she nuzzled his chest. But they always returned to brown before she backed away and looked up at him.

Leah's heart slammed against her ribs as she watched the footage again. And again.

Jumping up, she jogged to her apartment door, unlocked it, and hurried downstairs to her store's back room. Flipping on the overhead light, she crossed to the surveillance hub. Several taps on the keyboard with fingers that shook retrieved that night's security footage from the cloud. Leah selected the feed that had been recorded by the camera just outside the front door of the shop.

A moment later, she straightened and chewed a thumbnail as the video played.

Seth stepped outside, the little pink unicorn in his hand, and strode down the sidewalk. As soon as he was out of sight of the front windows, he halted. Leah sucked in a breath as he disappeared. He just *disappeared* in the blink of an eye.

When her knees weakened, she sat heavily, missing the rolling chair she'd shoved out of the way by a few inches.

Her ass hit the floor hard. "Shit!" Glaring at the chair, she rubbed her battered bottom, then just sat where she'd landed.

Seth's eyes glowed and he could vanish into thin air.

What the hell?

⟫⟩◈◈◈⟨⟪

Seth teleported to Ami and Marcus's bedroom.

The couple was sound asleep with little Adira snuggled between them.

A beep sounded as the device Marcus always kept with him sounded.

Marcus awoke with a start and reached for the sword he kept by the bed.

"Easy," Seth whispered, not wanting to wake the toddler.

Ami's eyes flew open and met his. She sat up. "What is it?"

"I need you. Hurry."

Throwing back the covers, she jumped to her feet.

Without another word, Seth touched her shoulder and teleported her to Sean's location.

A beep sounded. Vampire corpses in various stages of decay littered this patch of UNC's quiet campus. In the shadows of the nearest building, Sean knelt with an unconscious Nicole in his arms, a cell phone pressed to his ear.

Ami shivered. Her nightgown had thin straps that left her arms bare, and the hem stopped above her knees, providing no buffer against the chilly breeze.

Seth doffed his coat in a blur and settled it around her shoulders. "One of the missing immortals was just here. See if you can lock down on her energy signal while I help Nicole."

Nodding, Ami closed her eyes and concentrated.

Seth zipped over to Sean and sank to his haunches before the injured duo. "Where are Krysta and Étienne?"

Sean gently lowered Nicole to the ground and withdrew his touch. "Chasing half a dozen vampires who made a run for it."

Seth yanked the dagger out of Nicole's shoulder, then rested his hand on the wound. Heat rose within him and rushed down his arm into her cool form, healing the damage.

"There are too many energy signatures here," Ami murmured. "I can't figure out which one is hers."

Seth looked to Sean. "Which way did she go?"

He pointed.

"I'll heal you when I return." Crossing to Ami, Seth lifted her into his arms and took off in the direction the woman had run. This was the first time any of the missing *gifted ones* had made an appearance. He had to catch up with her, had to find her.

Some distance away, Seth stopped and waited.

Ami kept her eyes closed, tilting her head a bit.

"Anything?" he asked, trying hard to be patient.

"Maybe. There's something. But it's very faint."

Because the woman had been moving at preternatural speeds. "Can you follow it?"

"I don't know. Turn in a slow circle."

The breeze shifted as he pivoted, lifting Ami's hair back from her face.

"There." She pointed in the direction from which the breeze came just as the scent of blood reached Seth.

"Hold on." He raced forward, excitement growing now that he had a scent to follow. The woman appeared to be losing a lot of blood. He reached out to Sean telepathically. *How badly did you injure her?* Though Sean wasn't telepathic, Seth was powerful enough to read any response he thought.

Silence ensued.

Sean?

She's sporting a few cuts and multiple gunshot wounds. I'm sorry. She was kicking my ass.

Since Sean didn't carry guns, Seth guessed that Sean really *had* been getting his ass kicked and Nicole had come to his rescue. Sean simply didn't want to subject her to Seth's anger.

Have Krysta and Étienne returned yet?

Yes. Should I send them after you?

No. Sit tight.

"Wait," Ami said suddenly.

Seth skidded to a halt.

She pointed. "That way."

"Are you sure?" The scent of blood was diminishing and the damned breeze kept shifting.

"Yes."

Seth altered his direction and renewed his pursuit. Every once in a while, when the wind cooperated, he would catch the scent of blood. But the woman was smart. She changed her route frequently in an attempt to remain downwind of them.

"Her energy signal is getting fainter."

And he was losing her scent. Damn it, how had he not caught up with her yet? Although she had gotten a significant head start before he had arrived, she was newly turned. Seth was far faster and should have found her by now.

"I can't feel her anymore," Ami announced reluctantly.

Nor could Seth smell her. He halted, turning in a circle. "Anything?"

Her brow furrowed. "No."

Cursing, Seth backtracked a bit and again turned in a circle.

Ami shook her head, her emerald eyes full of regret. "Nothing."

Seth carefully lowered her until her bare feet touched the cool grass. Since she was a good twenty inches shorter than him, his coat pooled around her on the ground and provided a shield from the breeze.

Frustration battered him as he strode some distance away, tilted his head back, and drew in a deep breath. Grass. Weeds. Trees. Field mice. An owl. Opossums. A raccoon. Wood smoke from fires left burning in fireplaces. A couple of stray cats. Exhaust from the road in the distance beyond the trees. Nothing else. No hint of blood. No scent of woman. "Fuck."

Ami spoke softly behind him. "I'm sorry, Seth."

He shook his head. He had finally gotten a lead on the

whereabouts of one of the missing immortals and hadn't been able to do shit to help her.

Grass rustled as Ami approached and rested small, cold fingers on his forearm. "I think I got a fairly decent fix on her energy signal. I can help you track her like I did Cliff when he was captured."

Ami was unique in this world. He and David had rescued her from a group that had subjected her to six months of torture under the guise of *scientific study*. He hadn't learned until later that she had come to them from another planet and was the only member of her race on Earth. She was even more unique than Seth. And he loved Ami dearly.

One of the many gifts Ami had been born with was the ability to sense individual energy signals. Apparently every living thing possessed one that was as distinctive as fingerprints. It was why she could always alert him when Gershom was near. And it was how she had helped him track down Cliff and Joe when the two had been captured by mercenaries.

But that scenario had been different from this one. Since Seth had known the mercenaries were based somewhere in North Carolina, all he'd had to do was teleport Ami to locations within the boundaries of the state in ever-growing circles until she located Cliff's energy signal.

This time he couldn't narrow down the field. This time there were no boundaries. Gershom could teleport. So he could have taken the immortal woman Seth sought anywhere in the world and most likely had, rather than stationing her and the other missing immortals right in Seth's backyard where he could more easily find them.

The chill in Ami's fingers finally reached him.

Lifting her into his arms, he teleported back to Sean's side.

Nicole had regained consciousness and hovered next to Sean, who held a bag of blood to his teeth. Krysta and Étienne busied themselves with collecting the fallen vampires' weapons and clothing now that the virus that infected them had devoured them from the inside out.

Several beeps sounded at Seth and Ami's abrupt appearance.

Seth glanced down at Ami. "Can you stay a little longer in case she doubles back?"

"Of course. I'll stay as long as you need me to."

The three immortals all regarded him grimly.

Nicole rose and faced him. Fear and dread tightened her features.

Sean lowered the now-empty blood bag. "Did you find her?"

"No." Seth knelt beside Sean and placed a hand on his chest. Warmth poured from him into the younger immortal, healing his wounds. And all the while fury continued to pummel Seth.

Once more he had failed.

Clouds gathered overhead.

The immortals shared a wary look.

Seth rose. "Étienne. Krysta."

The couple crossed to his side.

Krysta had made it through the battle without a scratch, but Étienne was pretty banged up.

Seth healed Étienne's wounds as thunder began to rumble.

"Seth," Ami said softly, "it wasn't your fault."

Sean nodded as Nicole tugged him to his feet. "It was mine. I should've called you as soon as I saw her, but her eyes glowed green, so I thought she was a vampire. It caught me off guard."

Krysta frowned. "Are you sure she *wasn't* a vampire? I thought our eyes all glowed amber. Except for Seth's, Zach's, and Jared's, I mean."

Seth struggled to bring his emotions under control as the wind picked up and whipped the trees into a fury. "Sarah's eyes are hazel and glow green."

"Oh. Right," Krysta said. "I forgot."

Sean shifted. "There's something else."

"Tell me," Seth ordered.

"She may be newly turned, but she fought like an elder immortal."

Nicole nodded. "She did. She was incredibly fast."

"And strong," Sean said. "She was kicking my ass and probably would've succeeded in killing me if the bullets hadn't slowed her down."

"I shot her," Nicole blurted, wringing her hands. "A lot."

"No, she didn't." Sean stepped between her and Seth. "She's trying to cover for me. *I* shot her."

"Bullshit." Nicole moved to stand beside him. "She really *was* kicking his ass. And not just because she was stronger. Sean wouldn't take the offensive because he wasn't comfortable hitting a woman."

Étienne frowned. "*Merde.* I didn't think of that. I wouldn't feel comfortable striking a woman either."

"Well, *I* didn't have a problem with it," Nicole said. "No way in hell was I going to let her kill Sean. I shot her all to hell and would've kept it up if Sean hadn't stopped me." Straightening her shoulders, she looked Seth in the eye. "I know you want her and the others taken alive. But my first priority is to keep Sean safe, so… do whatever you have to do to punish me. I don't regret it."

"Damn it, Nicole," Sean ground out.

Seth raised a hand to halt whatever else Sean intended to say. "There will be no punishment, Nicole. You kept Sean safe, and the woman didn't die. Next time, however, call me before you begin shooting."

She relaxed a little. "I was actually reaching for my phone when the bitch threw a dagger at me. It hit me so hard I fell back into the building. The next thing I knew, I was waking up and she looked like she was about to decapitate Sean."

Frowning, Sean reached out and touched the blood that coated one side of her face. "You must have hit your head on the side of the building."

She shrugged. "I guess so."

He sighed as he turned back to Seth. "How could that woman be so strong if she's newly turned?"

Seth drew out his phone. Opening the Photos app, he scrolled past the many pictures he'd taken of Ami and Adira until he reached the ones he had snapped of the headshots Chris Reordon had assembled of the missing *gifted ones*. He held the phone out to Sean. "Which one was she?"

Sean wiped his crimson-coated hands on his pants, then swore when both came away more bloody.

"Here." Nicole turned away from him.

"Thanks." Sean wiped both hands on the back of her jacket, then took the phone. A few swipes of his finger later, he paused. "This is her." He glanced at Nicole. "Don't you think?"

She leaned in close. "Yeah. That's her." She sent Seth a look of remorse. "I'm sorry I called her a bitch. It isn't her fault Gershom is fucking with her head."

Seth took the phone and studied the picture. "Tessa Hayes." Closing his eyes, he reached out to her via that internal network of connections he shared with all *gifted ones* and immortals. The tie was usually much stronger with immortals. But once more he found only an empty void. Gershom had discovered some way to block him.

Thunder again rumbled overhead. Lightning streaked through the thickening clouds as he opened his eyes.

Nicole and the immortals all cast the sky a wary look.

Ami rested cold fingers on his arm. "Seth?"

Tucking his phone away, he touched her shoulder. "You're shivering. I need to get you home."

He teleported to her bedroom.

Marcus leaned back against the headboard while Adira slumbered beside him. He'd donned his hunting togs in their absence, ready to join them at a moment's notice if needed.

Seth gently removed his coat from Ami's shoulders. "Thank you."

She nodded. "I'm sorry I couldn't do more."

He shook his head. "The fault is mine."

Marcus rose and approached his wife.

Seth retrieved his phone and dialed a number.

"Yes?" a baritone voice answered.

"Are you alone?"

"One moment." Wind buffeted the phone. "Yes."

Seth teleported to the outskirts of Dakar, Senegal.

A beep sounded.

Imhotep stepped from the shadows, his skin as dark as the night sky above them.

"I need your postcognitive ability," Seth said.

Imhotep dipped his chin. "I am always at your service, my friend."

Seth clasped the warrior's shoulder and teleported back to the scene of Sean's battle.

Several beeps sounded. The others were still there, waiting for

Chris's cleanup crew to arrive. The network employees would swiftly make the blood that coated the sidewalk and grass disappear, then ensure that no surveillance cameras had captured footage of the paranormal fight.

The vampires Nicole had tranqed were now rapidly shriveling up. Étienne must have read their thoughts and found no information on Gershom, as well as nothing that would indicate the vamps were worth saving, then delivered them swift deaths.

Imhotep nodded a greeting to the others.

Though all nodded back, they didn't speak. None of them knew the ancient immortal well. He was currently stationed overseas and only came to North Carolina when they needed backup.

"One of Gershom's immortals attacked Sean, Krysta, and Étienne with a couple dozen vampires," Seth informed the Egyptian warrior. "The vampires were either slain or tranqed. The immortal got away. Ami helped me track her to the southeast, but I lost her scent and Ami could no longer feel her energy signal. Can you tell me where she went?"

Sheathing the long sword he held, Imhotep strolled over to a patch of blood-soaked grass.

Everyone remained silent as he walked in a slow circle, studying the ground. He closed his eyes. Seconds ticked past. He turned his head to the west, then opened his eyes and looked at Krysta. "Yours took you to the west."

Her eyes widened. "Yes."

Imhotep directed his gaze at the ground once more. Turning, he took a few steps to the southeast. He knelt and touched his fingers to the grass. "This is her blood."

Seth glanced at Sean.

He nodded. "Yes, it is."

"She fights like an elder," Imhotep murmured.

"She really does," Sean agreed.

How the hell was that possible? Gershom wasn't infected with the virus, so he couldn't have turned her himself. And immortals transformed with vampire blood were always weaker than those who came before them. Sean had only transformed a few years ago, so he and Tessa should be relative equals in terms of strength and speed.

Imhotep rose and met Seth's gaze. "Come." He raced away with preternatural speed.

Seth glanced at the others. "Go home once everything here is cleared up. No more hunting tonight." He raced after Imhotep, unsurprised to realize the Egyptian immortal was following the exact same path he and Ami had trodden earlier. Except Imhotep didn't stop where Seth and Ami had. He kept going, taking them on a zigzag route that doubled back on itself more than once.

At last he held up a hand and halted.

Seth waited quietly while Imhotep closed his eyes.

When the dark warrior lifted his lids, his brown eyes glowed amber with anger. "Gershom met her here and teleported her away."

Seth swore. He could feel no lingering tendrils of power, so no path remained for him to follow.

"She called him on her cell phone," Imhotep told him. "And it pains me to tell you, my friend, that she does not like you very much."

Pacing away, Seth ground his teeth. Thunder rumbled anew overhead. No doubt Gershom had filled her head with lies.

"How much did Sean tell you about his encounter with her?" Imhotep asked.

Sighing, Seth rubbed his forehead. "Just that she fought like an elder and was kicking his ass until Nicole shot her all to hell."

"Did he tell you she spoke to him?"

Seth faced him with a frown. "No. What did she say?"

Imhotep extended a hand. "See for yourself."

Closing the distance between them, Seth clasped his forearm and watched the battle replay in Imhotep's mind.

Seth? Tessa snarled, such contempt twisting her features. *You tell that bastard I'm coming for him.*

Lips clamping together, Seth released his friend.

"Gershom has poisoned her mind against you," Imhotep warned softly.

Seth's stomach burned as though he'd swallowed acid. "I assumed he would." But he hadn't braced himself well enough to keep her hatred from piercing him like a knife. "I'm sure he has done the same with the rest."

"You can win her over, Seth," Imhotep said with complete confidence. "Just show her your memories of Gershom being a dick."

He found a smile. "There are so many."

Imhotep chuckled.

"Thank you."

The warrior clapped him on the back. "I'm glad I could help you this time."

Using postcognitive ability was a little like investigating a crime scene. The longer the scene had to grow cold, the harder it was to see anything. And if others cluttered that scene and disturbed the evidence… Uncovering the truth could prove impossible.

When Seth and his Immortal Guardians had descended upon Shadow River's mercenary compound two years earlier, utter chaos had ensued. One of his immortals—Yuri—had been slain. It had been a wholly unexpected and devastating blow from which Seth had still been reeling when the compound's armory exploded. The battle had continued to rage. And it had been some time before he and the other immortals realized that Stanislav was gone, too, presumably taken by the blast.

Seth had searched the rubble, unwilling to believe he had lost both immortals. Though the nature of the virus that infected him would've left nothing of Stanislav's body behind to identify, they had found ragged pieces of his protective suit and his broken sword. It had been enough to convince most of the Immortal Guardians that Stanislav was dead. But Seth had refused to accept it and had called in Imhotep.

Much to his dismay, Imhotep had been unable to divine Stanislav's fate. He had seen the blast hit the Russian immortal. But thick smoke had obscured the area afterward. And between the mayhem that followed and the time that had passed, Imhotep—like the others—had only been able to guess that Stanislav had indeed died in the blast.

Seth wished that his own postcognitive abilities hadn't weakened over the millennia. He had been born with all of the abilities the other Immortal Guardians possessed combined. But those abilities were like muscles. If one didn't exercise them regularly, they weakened and withered.

For many years, Seth had focused on strengthening the gifts he thought would aid him most in defeating the Others when their fury over his defection drove them to attack. Those *and* the gifts he'd believed would best serve the Immortal Guardians he had chosen to shepherd. The rest of his gifts had diminished from disuse.

"What will you do when you find her?" Imhotep asked, returning him to the present.

"The same thing I did with Bastien when I captured him. Confine her and do whatever I can to convince her to trust me."

The quiet warrior nodded. "I will guard her for you, should you wish it."

"Thank you."

Seth just had to catch her first.

Chapter Eight

THE NEXT NIGHT, SETH PACED David's study. He had taken Ami out that afternoon to see if she could pick up Tessa's energy signature. They had started where Gershom had teleported Tessa away, then had explored ever-widening circles. That Gershom had swept Tessa far enough away to keep her out of Ami's range had come as no surprise.

But it nevertheless infuriated Seth.

According to information Chris had accumulated on Tessa during her lifetime, she was a warmhearted woman. The kind who would check on elderly neighbors to ensure they had adequate heat when temperatures dipped below freezing. The kind who would help her brother batten down the hatches for the same elderly neighbors if a hurricane threatened. The network had kept tabs on her all her life, the way they did for every *gifted one* to ensure humans wouldn't discover her special ability and try to harm or exploit her because of it. The only reason her disappearance had gone unnoticed was because her brother had been killed in a car accident right before her disappearance and she had told her employer that she needed to spend time with her parents, who were taking the loss hard.

Tessa was not the type to harbor hate. And yet she loathed Seth.

What had Gershom told her? What had he done to her? Was he hurting her?

The notion made Seth's stomach churn.

"You can try again tomorrow," David said. Elbows propped on his desk, he followed Seth's restive movements.

"How is Gershom doing it?" Seth asked for the hundredth time. "How is he keeping me from sensing where she is the way I can with Immortal Guardians?"

"I don't know. That is something even *I* cannot do." While David could conceal his own location from Seth (something he rarely did), he could not hide the location of other immortals from him.

Seth continued to pace. "Any idea how Tessa could've become as strong as an elder?"

"I am still pondering that one."

"Sean and some of the other immortals are wondering if Gershom turned her himself."

"We both know he can't." Gershom wasn't infected with the virus. His immortality had been granted him at birth.

Seth slowed to a stop and rubbed gritty eyes. "Vampire blood would not give her such strength and speed." He refused to believe any of his Immortal Guardians were working with Gershom, so how had he done it? How had Gershom made his immortals so much stronger than they should be? Because logic suggested that the other missing immortals would be as strong as Tessa when he found them.

A possible explanation teased the periphery of his thoughts, but Seth found himself reluctant to voice it. The idea both sickened him and lent him hope. And though he could do without the former, he wished to cling to the latter.

"Seth?" David prompted. "What are you thinking?"

He sighed. "You know me too well, damn it."

"I have often voiced the same complaint," David replied with a faint smile.

Seth met his gaze. "Do you think Gershom has Stanislav?"

Sadness infiltrated David's expression, bringing a faint glow to his eyes. "No."

"It would explain everything," Seth argued, desperate to keep hope alive. "It would explain why I didn't feel Stanislav's death the way I did Yuri's." Seth *always* felt the death of an immortal deep inside but had only felt Yuri's that day. "It would explain how Tessa could be as strong as an older immortal. If Gershom plucked Stanislav from the battlefield that day, he could've blocked me from sensing him all this time the way he's blocking me from sensing the stolen immortals. And Stanislav is over four centuries old. If Gershom used his blood to transform Tessa and the others, she would be stronger than Sean and fight more like an elder."

"A plausible hypothesis," David conceded softly. "But we found pieces of his protective suit." They had attacked the mercenary compound during the day, so all but the eldest immortals had worn special suits to protect them from the sunlight. Seth himself was impervious to damage from the sun. David could withstand several hours of direct sunlight before he began to suffer the effects. But the younger the immortal, the greater his or her photosensitivity. Already severely injured, Stanislav wouldn't have been able to withstand *any* sun exposure without burning, blistering, then worse.

"We found pieces of his mask," David reminded him, "torn and mangled by shrapnel. We found his sword, broken in two, so great was the blast when the armory blew. And Imhotep saw the explosion engulf him."

"Imhotep said too much chaos ensued afterward for him to see what happened next. With all the fire and smoke and the battle still raging, he could have missed seeing Gershom pop in and teleport Stanislav away."

"He didn't miss it last night when Gershom teleported Tessa away." David sighed. "I wish you were right, Seth. I do. Like you, I still grieve for Stanislav. But I think it more likely that Gershom took Aidan's blood the night he attacked him and kidnapped Dana."

Seth hadn't thought of that.

"Aidan would have no recollection of it," he continued. "I repaired the damage Gershom wrought inside his head myself. And Aidan needed a *lot* of blood to recover. At the time, we believed it was because his wounds were so severe. But Gershom could have siphoned much of Aidan's supply to use for his own purposes. Aidan is nearly three thousand years old and a *healer*, which we have come to believe is what truly imparts the greater strength. Even mixed with the blood of a vampire, his would make any *gifted one* transformed with it very strong."

His chest tight, Seth resumed his pacing. Self-recrimination bombarded him.

How many times would he fail those he had vowed to keep safe? He had failed to protect Aidan, Dana, Ethan, and Heather that night. He had failed to realize Gershom had taken Aidan's blood, something that would have forewarned him of Gershom's intention to build his own army of immortals. He had failed to protect Stanislav when they had blitzed the mercenary compound. He had failed to find Tessa, both before Gershom had transformed her and again last night. He had failed to find the other eleven missing *gifted ones* Gershom had transformed. He had even failed to keep Gershom from harming Ami, something that had traumatized little Adira.

He halted abruptly as yet another of his failures confronted him.

Dread and grief filled him as the spirit of Yuri passed through David's closed study door and strode toward him.

Seth took an involuntary step backward.

Yuri's expression darkened.

How he must hate me.

Closing his eyes, Seth teleported away.

Leah stared up at her bedroom ceiling. Sleep eluded her yet again. No big surprise. Insomnia was a frequent visitor, especially this time of year.

At least tonight the thoughts that rambled around in her head and kept her awake focused upon something new. Or rather some*one* new.

She couldn't stop thinking about Seth.

Leah hadn't heard from him since he'd left in such a hurry the previous night and hoped he was all right. Clearly he was different. The man's eyes glowed and he could disappear into thin air. But different didn't mean invincible. She had seen the look on his face before he'd left and wondered if one of those enemies he had mentioned had somehow struck at him again.

She bit her lip. *I hope he's okay.*

Thunder crashed outside, as loud as a bomb detonating.

Jumping, Leah jerked her gaze toward the nearest window while her heart did its damnedest to burst from her chest. Holy crap, that had startled her!

Bright light flashed behind the closed blinds as thunder roared again. Raindrops hit the glass, so large they clacked against it like pieces of gravel.

She frowned. There wasn't any rain in the forecast, not until next week. For months now most of the state had been burdened by a historic drought.

Throwing back the covers, she rose. Her toes curled against the chilly wood floor. While the pajama bottoms she wore kept her lower half somewhat warm, her arms and shoulders—left bare by her spaghetti strap tank top—instantly beaded with chill bumps. She always slept better when the room was cold, so she'd turned off the heater before going to bed.

Rubbing her arms, she crossed to one of the two windows her bedroom boasted. This one overlooked the street in front of her shop.

Grabbing the rod hanging beside it, she turned it until the blinds opened enough for her to peer outside. Her eyes lifted to the sky. Lightning flashed again, clawing its way through clouds that churned above as another deafening crash of thunder vibrated through her.

Sheesh. The meteorologists had really gotten it wrong this time. The oak tree beside her building bent and swayed as a strong breeze tore through it. Those large, sporadic raindrops multiplied at an insane rate, transforming into a downpour so thick she could barely see the building across from hers.

Leah looked down after a moment to see if water was already beginning to pool along the curbs… and sucked in a sharp breath. Seth stood in the middle of the street, garbed in a black T-shirt and black cargo pants, his long coat missing.

Unnerved, she ducked out of sight. What the hell? He hadn't knocked or rung the buzzer. She would've heard it.

Leaning over, she peeked through the blinds near the edge of the window.

He hadn't moved.

She frowned. Seth wasn't watching her shop. Nor was he peering up at her window like some perv trying to catch a glimpse of her naked. Instead, he just stared into the distance… and did so in a way that made her think he wasn't really seeing the road before him. His face held a faraway look. His brow was furrowed. And sadness emanated from him as rain drenched his clothing and flattened his long hair.

The unease that had set her pulse to racing vanished. He looked… lost.

She swallowed, empathy rising. How many times had she seen that same expression on her own face when she peered into a mirror?

Turning away from the window, Leah left the bedroom and grabbed her keys. Her bare feet made little sound as she unlocked her apartment door and hurried down the stairs. She jogged across the back room and through her darkened shop. Upon reaching the glass door at the front of her store, she parted the blinds.

Seth still stood there, unmoving, as though the weight of the world held him in place.

Leah unlocked the door and threw it open. More thunder rumbled as lightning flashed. Wind buffeted her. Cold rain ducked under the awning and dampened her skin. "Seth?"

He didn't react in any way.

"Seth!" she called again, louder this time so he could hear her over the storm.

Blinking, he looked toward her. Surprise lit his face for a moment before his brows drew down and he looked around as though he wasn't sure how he had come to be there.

"Are you okay?" she shouted.

"Yes," he responded but looked far from it.

Stepping back, she held the door open and waved him toward her. "Come inside."

He shook his head. "Forgive me for disturbing you, Leah. Go back to bed. I'm fine."

"Bullshit." He was *not* fine. "Get your ass in here." She narrowed her eyes. "And don't argue with me."

His lips twitched. Then some of the darkness left his countenance.

The rain let up a little as he strode toward her. Ducking, he entered her shop.

Though he brushed against her — he was so big he took up the doorway — she felt no desire for once. She was too concerned about him.

Shivering, Leah closed and locked the door. Maybe the storm heralded an early cold front blowing through.

"How did you know I was out there?" he asked softly.

"The storm. It was so loud, I couldn't resist looking out the window and saw you down in the street."

"I'm sorry."

She smiled. "It isn't *your* fault." He wasn't responsible for the weather. "Blame the meteorologists for not giving me a heads-up." With her keys clutched in one hand, she twined the fingers of her other through his and tugged him after her through the shop.

He dragged his feet. "I'm dripping water all over your floor."

She snorted. "Oh please. This floor has been drooled on, sneezed on, vomited on, peed on, and pooped on twice if you can believe that. It's also had ice cream, chocolate, fruit juice, and sticky candy crap dribbled all over it. I'm sure it can survive a little rainwater."

His expression lightening even more, he allowed her to guide him through the back room, up the stairs, and into her apartment.

Leah paused long enough to lock the door. Tossing the keys on the narrow table beside it, she reclaimed his hand. Aside from the living room, kitchen, and laundry room, the place boasted two bedrooms and two full baths. She led him to the guest bathroom and flicked on the light. Seth didn't speak. But she felt him watching her as she opened a cabinet and removed three large towels.

"Here." She shoved them at his chest. "Get out of those wet clothes and dry off."

He arched a brow.

"Don't worry," she promised with a grin. "I'm not going to take advantage of you."

He actually smiled then. "Would you be offended if I expressed disappointment?"

She laughed, relieved to see a spark of his usual playful self emerge. "No. I would question your sanity. Go ahead. Get naked. My brother plays handyman for me whenever I need one, so he keeps some spare clothes over here. I'll be back in a minute." Though she was tempted to leave the door open, she closed it behind her. Seth needed a friend, someone to talk to who could lift his spirits, not an older woman who drooled over his muscles and tried to jump his young, handsome ass every time he came around.

Lame pep talk, she criticized herself.

Her brother Ben wasn't as tall as Seth, but he was equally muscled. The sweatpants Leah found would probably be too short, but the T-shirt should fit. She didn't bother with underwear. Men in movies and TV shows always seemed to balk at borrowing other men's skivvies.

With the folded garments balanced on one hand, she left the guest room and detoured down the hallway to raise the temperature on the thermostat. She was freezing.

Seth probably was too with all that long wet hair.

She tapped on the bathroom door. "Ready for clothes?"

The door swung inward.

Leah stared. "Holy crap." Seth was naked, save for a towel he had wrapped around his hips. And his body was pure perfection. His arms and legs both bore beautiful, thick muscle. But not too thick like some of the bodybuilders she'd seen whose arms and legs were so bulky they couldn't rest their arms against their sides and seemed to walk bowlegged. Seth was built more like a professional basketball player. Broad shoulders. A well-developed chest. Even his abs rippled with muscle and begged to be touched.

Realizing she had been staring—aka drooling—she looked up at him. "Seriously, how are you still single?"

But Seth wasn't looking at her face. His eyes were fastened on her body.

Her breath caught when a faint golden glow illuminated his dark brown irises.

"I was going to ask you the same thing," he murmured, his voice deeper than usual and husky with what she thought might be desire.

A thrill rippling through her, Leah glanced down. Her eyes widened.

The rain that had found its way past the awning out front had plastered her pajamas to her skin. Her white tank top had been rendered transparent, clearly defining her breasts and hard pink nipples. It had also ridden up when she'd retrieved the towels, exposing a strip of bare flesh at her waist. Her striped pants weren't quite as transparent but hung low on her hips, clung to her thighs, and showed a shadow of the dark curls at their juncture.

"Oh shit." Heat crept up her neck into her cheeks. She shoved the clothing at him. "Here. I'll be back." Hurrying up the hallway, she ducked into her bedroom and closed the door.

He might as well have seen her naked!

Leah didn't know why that unnerved her more than his glowing eyes, but it did. Perhaps because no man had seen her naked in over a decade.

It only took her a couple of minutes to shuck her wet pj's and pull on panties, a matching bra, a pair of her favorite black yoga pants, and a red V-neck T-shirt. Unbraiding her hair, she dragged a brush through it.

Wait. She paused as a thought occurred to her. Did Seth's eyes glow when he was turned on? Is that what that meant? They had glowed whenever she had touched him or rubbed against him in the video of them dancing. And they had glowed just now as he'd studied her body. Had he wanted to—?

Get your mind out of the gutter, she admonished herself with a frown. *The man is hurting, not trolling for an easy lay.*

Right. She couldn't let herself forget how he had appeared when she had first seen him out there, standing alone in the rain.

And don't pester him with questions about his eyes. If he wanted you to know his eyes glowed, he wouldn't have tried to hide it from you.

Right again. Seth had been nothing but courteous and friendly and fun since she'd met him. She wasn't going to start fearing him or treating him like a freak just because he was different. She'd seen too many people pull that shit with Ben and her father.

Quiet curled around her. She glanced toward the windows, then tilted her head to listen.

No thunder. No pitter-patter of raindrops. The storm must have already passed. Crazy-ass weather.

Hanging on to the hairbrush, she wadded her pj's into a damp ball and left her bedroom.

The bathroom door opened. Seth stepped out, garbed in the T-shirt and sweats.

She smiled. "Not bad. I knew the pants would be a little short."

Ben was six foot two to Seth's — what — six foot eight? "But other than that, they fit you well. The T-shirt, too." The soft cotton shirt hugged his lovely muscles but didn't appear uncomfortably tight.

"Thank you."

Hoping to make him smile again, she glanced down at his bare feet, then winked up at him. "Big hands *and* big feet. Oh my."

He laughed.

"Where are your clothes, handsome? I'll toss them in the wash."

"That's not necessary. I don't wish to trouble you further."

"It's no trouble. I have a really good washer-dryer combo, so it won't take long."

His brow furrowed as he handed her the wet clothes. "Shouldn't you go back to bed? Your store opens early in the morning, doesn't it?"

"Yes." She wrinkled her nose. "But I was having trouble sleeping anyway. Insomnia. It happens from time to time." She led him toward the kitchen and nodded at the table in the breakfast nook. "Have a seat."

After putting the clothes in the wash, she returned to the kitchen. "Would you like some tea or hot chocolate? And before you decide, the tea is decaf."

"Tea, please, though I really don't wish to trouble you."

"It's no trouble." She put the kettle on, then settled herself in the seat across from him at the small table. "Remember? I told you anytime you need to de-stress or decompress, you're welcome to drop by."

"You're very kind."

She wasn't kind. She just enjoyed his company. "So," she said softly as she studied him. His eyes were dark again and full of pain or grief or something else she couldn't identify. "What happened tonight?"

He lowered those soulful eyes to the table. Rubbing one index finger on the surface, he remained silent.

Leah frowned. "Before you tell me… Are you on duty tonight?"

He looked up. "What?"

"Are you working? Is your phone going to start ringing off the hook again?" Because that was the last thing he needed right now.

"Yes, I'm on duty. And yes, most likely it will."

"May I see it?"

"My phone?" he asked with some surprise.

"Yes, please."

Reaching into one of the sweatpants pockets, he drew out the phone.

Leah took it from him and slid her thumb across the screen. It instantly lit up with an adorable picture of Ami and Adira, no passcode necessary. She tapped the phone icon at the bottom of the screen. "Am I right in guessing David is your right-hand man or second-in-command? Or would that be Zach?"

"It's David," he said, watching her curiously.

She opened Contacts. *Sheesh.* There were a *lot* of numbers stored on his phone. "Did you store his number under his first name or his last name?"

"First."

It looked as though he stored *everyone's* number under a first name. There were several Davids. All but one had a foreign country listed by his name in parentheses. "Is this him?" She pointed to the one that didn't have a country designation.

"Yes."

"Thank you." She tapped Call and placed the phone to her ear.

It only rang once before David's warm baritone voice carried over the line. "Seth? Are you all right?" He sounded concerned.

"David?" she said. "Hi, this is Leah from Little Gifts." She glanced at Seth, surprised he wasn't stopping her.

Seth watched her as though he couldn't figure out what in the world she was doing.

A slight pause ensued. "Leah. You're calling me from Seth's phone. Is he all right?"

"He's fine," she assured him. "But I was wondering if maybe you could field his calls for the next couple of hours." That was the phrase Seth had used when he'd referred to Zach, wasn't it? Fielding his calls? "I know it's last minute, but—"

"Of course," he agreed easily. "I would be happy to."

"Really? Thanks."

Seth spoke up. "Have Zach or Jared do it. I don't want to leave Ami and the others unguarded."

Unguarded? Were they in danger? "Seth asked you to have Zach or Jared do it instead," she relayed, "so Ami and the others won't be left unguarded."

"Of course. I shall see to it at once."

"Thank you."

"You're very welcome, Leah."

She ended the call and slid Seth's phone across the table.

He studied the picture of Ami and Adira for a moment before he tucked the device back into his pocket.

"I'm surprised you let me do that."

"I am, too," he admitted. "But then, the past twenty-four hours have been full of surprises." Unpleasant ones, judging by his expression.

"Do you want to talk about it?" she asked gently.

He stared down at his hands. "Not much purpose really. It won't change anything." A weary sigh escaped him as he drew a hand down over his face. "It never does."

"I don't know about that." Reaching across the smooth wood surface, she covered one of his hands with her own. "What happened tonight? What drove you to stand out there, alone, in the middle of a rainstorm?"

Though he sank into silence, his thumb stroked the back of her hand.

"You looked lost, Seth."

Turning his hand over, he clasped hers. "Not lost," he corrected, his voice as quiet as hers. "Just… haunted by old ghosts."

She swallowed as sorrow suffused her. "I know what that's like."

He met her gaze. "Do you?"

She nodded. Her attention strayed to the calendar on the wall. "You know how I just dropped by your place out of the blue last night?"

"Yes."

Now *she* stared down at their clasped hands. "I didn't do it because I was trying to break my workaholic ways or because I really thought Adira wouldn't be able to sleep without her toy. I did it because I needed a distraction." Her throat thickened as a familiar lump rose in it. She had to clear it twice to find her voice again. "This month is always hard for me to get through because I lost my husband and our baby twelve years ago this week."

His hold on her hand tightened. Leaning forward, he covered their entwined fingers with his free hand. "I'm so sorry, Leah."

Her eyes began to burn with unshed tears. She blinked them back impatiently and shook her head. "It was a car accident. It was bad. I can't say anything more than that because I still bawl my eyes out whenever I think about it. I just told you because when I saw you standing out there in the rain…" Shrugging, she sent him a sad smile. "You looked like I've felt for the past twelve years."

Propping his elbows on the table, Seth closed his eyes, raised their clasped hands, and rested his forehead against them.

Leah's heart ached for him. Unable to resist the urge, she leaned across the table and drew her free hand over his wet hair in a brief caress, then rested her hand on the nape of his neck, a quiet gesture to let him know she was there for him.

Seth squeezed Leah's hand tighter. She had lost her husband and baby and was still struggling to get through her own grief. Yet here she sat in the middle of the night, holding his hand and trying to comfort him.

She didn't need him dumping his problems on her. She didn't need him burdening her with his own grief. Particularly since he feared every minute he spent with her would put her more at risk of getting caught up in Gershom's sick games. And yet…

"There are so many people under my protection," he found himself confiding. "So many I care about. And I keep failing them." He thought of Yuri and Stanislav. Yuri was dead because of Seth. And for hundreds of years, Yuri had loved Stanislav like a kid brother. He must be doubly furious that Seth had failed to keep Stanislav safe.

Seth just couldn't face that on top of everything else tonight.

He saw again the hate on Tessa's face when she had spoken to Sean. And worse, as he catalogued yet again his failures, he relived the moment Gershom had nearly killed Ami.

"I keep failing them all," he whispered. And these weren't minor failures. They were monumental ones for which he would never forgive himself.

The teapot began to whistle.

Leah's chair scraped the floor as she pushed it back and rose. But she didn't withdraw her hands. Instead she pressed a kiss to the top of his head and stroked the back of his neck. "Give me a minute to fix our tea, then we'll go sit on the sofa. Okay?"

He shouldn't. He should leave and have Darnell return Leah's brother's clothing tomorrow. But selfishness drove him to nod. He needed her close tonight. Just this once, he needed to do what he *wanted* to do instead of what he *should* do. Then he would let Leah return to her regular life, safer without him in it.

A couple of minutes later, she handed him a warm mug and guided him over to the sofa where they sank down to sip their tea.

"I hope it isn't too sweet. I added a little stevia."

He gave it a taste. "It's perfect. Thank you."

Both were quiet for a time.

Eventually, Leah leaned toward the coffee table and set her mug on a coaster. "Talk to me, Seth," she entreated gently as she settled back against the cushions. "You can tell me anything. I promise it will go no further."

He wanted so badly to share his troubles with her but would have to couch it in terms that wouldn't reveal what he was. "You once said I treat my employees like family."

She nodded.

"Well, I think of them that way, too." He lowered his mug to the second coaster. Why the hell was he doing this? "I was married once, like you."

Surprise lit her curious gaze.

"We had two children—a son and a daughter. And both were slain alongside my wife."

Dismay rippled across her pretty features. "By whom?"

He shook his head. "Madmen." Madmen who had learned the truth of what Seth was, then had felt his wrath when he'd discovered what they had done.

Again she took his hand. "I'm so sorry, Seth."

He nodded. "My employees are my family now, my brethren. They're good, strong, honorable men and women. Though there are a lot of them, we're a close unit. I love them all and only want to keep them safe and do whatever I can to facilitate their happiness. But as I told you, there are people who would exploit my attachment to them."

"The enemies you mentioned."

"Yes." He sighed. "There is an enemy plaguing me now who continues to elude me, one I can't seem to eliminate no matter how hard I try. And he has cost me dearly."

She scooted closer, as though sensing his need for comfort, and leaned into his side. "Tell me."

"This enemy was working with a mercenary group that grew very dangerous. Not just to us, but also to the country and — though it may seem an exaggeration — to mankind as a whole. Stopping the mercenary group in their tracks and ensuring they would never be able to implement their plans was a nasty business. Two of my brethren were slain for their efforts on my behalf."

She covered their clasped hands and rested them on her thigh.

"One was killed in battle. An explosion took the other." He shook his head. "But we were never able to recover his body, so I can't seem to abandon the hope that…"

"That he might have somehow survived?" she finished for him.

"Yes. Everyone else is certain he's gone." He shrugged helplessly. "I just don't want to believe it."

"I understand."

"Last year the same enemy targeted me personally and nearly killed Ami because he knows how much she means to me."

"Oh no," she breathed.

"He fatally wounded her right in front of Adira. That's why you rarely see Adira without her mother. Most days she's still afraid to let Ami out of her sight."

"Poor baby. How is Ami doing? She always seems fine when she comes in the store."

"She's doing well. And we're doing what we can to help Adira get past it. But my enemy eluded me yet again. He started kidnapping men and women who were loosely tied to me."

"Shit."

"Some of them he killed. Most we were able to rescue. But a dozen are still missing. We've been searching for them for months, but could find no trail to follow until last night. I left so precipitously because I got a call that one of the missing women had been spotted."

"Did you find her?"

He shook his head. "I tracked her as far as I could before I lost all traces of her. So she's still out there somewhere, at the mercy of this monster." Again he drew a hand down his face, trying to rub the weariness away. "Even if I'd found her tonight, Tessa wouldn't have come with me willingly. One of my men spoke with her briefly and… my enemy has poisoned her mind. He has convinced her that *I* am the villain."

"Tessa is the woman's name?"

"Yes."

Quiet settled upon them. A clock nearby ticked off the seconds.

"I'm so sorry, Seth," she whispered. "That response seems woefully inadequate considering what you're up against, but I am. I wish I could help."

He squeezed her hand. "You are." Just by being there for him and not repudiating him.

"Can't the authorities help? I mean, kidnapping is a felony. If your enemy crossed state lines, then it's a federal crime, too. Can't the feds help you? I would think dozens of people being taken would've drawn their notice."

"We remain in contact with several federal bureaus and agencies." Chris Reordon did, anyway. He had contacts and operatives in all of them, rendering whatever aid they could. "We've even worked with the military on occasion." Seth and his Immortal Guardians had raced to the army's aid when Gershom had driven vampire mercenaries to attack an army base.

"Well, it sounds like you're doing everything you can to get this guy."

"It isn't enough."

"I think you're being too hard on yourself."

"Because I'm responsible." He combed his fingers through his damp hair. "He has turned this into some sort of personal vendetta. He hates me. But I don't know why."

"Some people don't need a reason to hate. They'll use any lame excuse that comes along and see nothing wrong with it."

He shook his head. "I've put them all in danger. I'm placing *you* in danger just by being here."

"Well, you can't just cut yourself off from everyone and live in a box." She patted his hand. "And I appreciate your concern, but don't worry about me. I can take care of myself."

"Not against him, you can't."

"Don't be so sure. With or without weapons, I can take down an attacker. Multiple attackers, if you want to know the truth."

"How can you be so sure?" Fury rose. "Did someone try to hurt you, Leah?" Had she been attacked in the past?

If so, he would demand the bastard's name and —

"No." Her lips twitched. "And I'm going to deviate from the subject here for a moment and say you are freaking *hot* when you turn into Mr. Tough Protective Guy."

Seth shook his head as his anger drained away. "How is it you can always make me smile?"

She shrugged. "I don't know. I guess I'm just good at entertaining men." Her eyes widened. "Wait. That came out wrong."

Seth laughed. "You're such a treasure, Leah."

"Nah," she protested. "I'm nobody special."

But she was.

"Anyway..." She shrugged. "My dad signed me up for every martial arts class he could, beginning at an early age. He wanted me to be able to protect myself."

"Your father sounds like a good man."

"He's actually my stepfather. My birth father ran out on us when I was so young that all I can remember about him was that he made my mother cry a lot. But then Mom met a truly wonderful man a couple of years later, fell madly in love, and married him. My stepfather has raised me and loved me as if I were his own ever since. And he's *very* protective. He knew the statistics — that one in three women in the US will be sexually assaulted during their lifetime — and he wanted to make damned sure that if any man tried to touch me without my consent, I could kill him with my bare hands."

Seth nodded his approval. He, Marcus, Ami, and David had already begun discussing when to start training Adira in self-defense. "I like your stepfather. He's a wise man."

She smiled. "Yeah. Dad's the best. I love him to pieces."

"Even so..." Seth covered their hands. "I shouldn't be here with you, Leah. I fear it will endanger you." He held up a hand to forestall her argument. "This man—my enemy—is like no other you have fought. All your martial arts instructors working together could not defeat him."

"Then I'll shoot his ass full of bullets. I'm not only good at hand-to-hand combat. I'm good with weapons, too. And I'm not afraid to use them."

Bullets would only piss Gershom off, but Seth couldn't tell her that. "It's too great a risk."

"Why? It's not like we're dating. We've already admitted that neither one of us is looking for a relationship. There's no harm in two friends hanging out and sharing popcorn or pizza while we watch a movie, is there?"

"If he misconstrues it, yes. There is great harm. Or rather great risk."

"Well, since the risk is mine, don't you think I should be the one to decide whether or not it's a risk worth taking?"

Not when she had no clear understanding of who and what Gershom was. She still thought a well-placed hit or kick or even a few bullets would stop him.

That wouldn't even slow his ass down.

"Look," she said, sitting up straighter and turning to face him. "I'm going to level with you, Seth. Aside from my dad and my brother, you're the first man I've been able to hold a conversation with in years who didn't spend nearly the whole time staring at a phone while mumbling a word or two periodically or who didn't make me glance longingly at the clock while I fantasized about the sprinkler system malfunctioning or someone clearing the room with one long, loud—and I mean *really* loud—fart."

Seth burst out laughing.

"I'm serious!" she exclaimed. "I enjoy your company. You're a fun guy. I like talking with you. I like laughing with you. I like dancing with you. I don't want some asshat with a grudge to get in the way of us having a good time together. We both lead stressful lives. You more than I, clearly. We're both self-proclaimed workaholics. And, if you'll forgive me for saying it, we both desperately need an escape."

He was tempted to let her talk him into it. He was so drawn to Leah. And it wasn't just physical. He liked her and enjoyed her company. He would've never guessed while standing out in rain spawned by his own grief and guilt that he could be laughing twenty minutes later. But Leah seemed to have that effect on him.

"If you're worried about how it will look," she continued, "then bring Adira to storytime twice a week. The three of us can hang out up here afterward while Brittney, Mandy, or Tiana—you haven't met her, but she's great—mind the store. And you can carry a bag when the two of you leave so it will look like you came for the story and stayed to shop. It'll be in the afternoon, so no one would believe it was a date or put any kind of romantic spin on it."

Was that plausible, or did he simply *want* it to be?

"Or what about a playdate? My brother and sister-in-law have been worried that my nephew isn't getting adequate socialization. He's about Adira's age. You and I could meet at the park and hang out while they play."

That was doubly tempting, because it would certainly appear innocent. "Would you object to my bringing Adira's cousin Michael, too?" Why was he even considering this?

Her lips twitched. "Is Michael the one with the glowering British papa who grumbles a lot and scares Sheldon nearly as much as you do?"

Seth laughed. "I take it you've met Roland?"

"He and his wife have come to the store with Ami and Marcus a few times. You're welcome to bring Michael. I think Aaron would like it. How about Tuesday afternoon, one o'clock?"

"Actually, I didn't say I would—"

"Excellent," she interrupted with a bright smile. "Tuesday it is." Giving his hand a pat, she released him and clapped her hands on her knees. "Now. I'm wide awake and won't be able to sleep anytime soon. You need to wait for your clothes to dry. So... what do you think? Pizza and a movie?"

"I really think it best if I—"

"Pizza and a movie it is." When she stood, her gaze strayed to the top of his head. "If you stop arguing with me and let me choose the movie, I'll brush your hair for you so it'll dry faster."

He stared at her. "Really?" Just imagining Leah brushing his long hair made some of the tension that knotted him up inside ease.

"Sure." She winked. "I won't even make you paint my toenails afterward." Spinning away, she headed into the kitchen and removed a pizza from the freezer.

And damned if Seth didn't feel another smile tug at his lips.

———◊◊◊———

Tessa stared at the back of Little Gifts. She and Gershom stood atop a three-story apartment building a few blocks over. But her preternaturally sharp eyesight, aided by the moon in the cloudless sky above them, allowed her to see it clearly once she found an angle unobscured by trees.

Cold wind buffeted her, but the virus that infected her enabled her to control her body temperature, eliminating the discomfort autumn temperatures ordinarily would have imparted. She didn't wear the long black coat favored by the Immortal Guardians she despised so much. She didn't need one. The baggy clothes she wore hid not only her gender but also the multitude of weapons strapped to her slender body.

The back door of the apartment above Little Gifts opened.

Seth stepped out.

Fury rose as it always did when she saw him, almost painful in its intensity.

Gershom rested a hand on her shoulder and gave it a gentle squeeze. *Easy,* he cautioned telepathically.

She took comfort in his presence beside her. He was the only reason she still breathed. And he was her only comfort, her source of strength.

A woman appeared in the doorway. Holding the door open, she tilted her head back and spoke to Seth.

Both smiled. Then Seth threw his head back and laughed.

It only made Tessa's hatred burn brighter.

Smiling, the woman ducked back inside and closed the door. Then Seth teleported away.

"He took what you loved," Gershom murmured softly.

She nodded, furious tears burning the backs of her eyes. "So I'll take what *he* loves."

Gershom nodded. "*Everything* he loves." He wrapped an arm

around her shoulders. "Together we will finally succeed where in the past I have failed."

She looked up at him. He was so tall that her head barely reached his armpit. "Thank you for helping me."

He smiled. "Thank *you* for helping *me,* child." He glanced over at the door through which Seth had exited. His eyes narrowed. "Seth will pay for all he has wrought."

Chapter Nine

T HE NEXT SEVERAL DAYS PASSED in a blur. Though Seth and Ami spent a few hours each afternoon searching for Tessa, they did not succeed in locating her. Tessa also had made no more appearances at night. Nor had any of the other missing immortals.

Seth had hoped that the incident with Tessa would herald the appearance of the rest, that they too had begun to hunt with vampires in the area and would show themselves to his Immortal Guardians. But none had.

Frustration burned his belly as Seth strolled through the front doors of network headquarters. The building's exterior was unassuming. None could possibly guess its purpose by looking at it. Nor would it inspire any interest should someone inadvertently stumble upon it.

Parked in a meadow surrounded by forest, it lay many miles away from any towns or cities. No houses or other businesses resided nearby. Only uninterrupted nature. A long slab of parking lot sprinkled with trees preceded it. No windows or ornamentation of any kind adorned the one-story structure. The bland brick exterior reminded Seth a bit of a warehouse for a package delivery service. The building even looked rather tired and worn, though it wasn't even a decade old. Chris had merely made it appear much older to dissuade ne'er-do-wells out to make mischief.

Once inside, Seth found himself enclosed in a glass vestibule that would no doubt withstand a strike by a bunker-busting missile. Beyond the clear walls on one side lay a waiting area for guests. Gray sofas clustered together in a U shape while potted plants that thrived in low light conditions interrupted the monochrome decor with splashes of color. Straight ahead, several armed human males sat behind a granite counter that concealed numerous surveillance monitors. All wore black shirts and black cargo pants rather than the standard security uniforms many businesses insisted upon. Behind them, more humans armed with automatic weapons manned two elevators.

One of the guards behind the counter rose and approached the glass enclosure. "Sir."

Seth nodded. "Good evening, John."

John Wendleck swiped a card in the keypad beside the door and punched in a code. A buzz sounded, then the door opened. "Good to see you again."

Seth smiled. "I take it Chris's gadget alerted you to my presence before I even entered."

"Yes, sir."

"Is he in his office?"

"Yes, sir."

"Thank you." Seth strode past the front counter. He nodded at the men behind it, then nodded again to the soldiers who manned the elevators.

All stood straighter as he passed. Those who hadn't encountered him before stared in open amazement, excited to finally see the Immortal Guardians' ancient and powerful leader in person.

"Thank you all for your service," he said, sincerely grateful to each and every one of them.

"Thank you for yours, sir," one man said. His companions all nodded.

Seth passed the elevators and headed down a hallway beyond them. At the end of it, a dozen soldiers — all as heavily armed as the others — guarded the entrance to the reception room outside Chris Reordon's office.

Seth frowned. Had something happened? Guards were very rarely posted there.

They straightened, abandoning their relaxed stances as he approached.

Seth nodded to them. "Gentlemen."

They nodded back with a chorus of *sirs*.

Seth entered the reception room.

An array of comfortable chairs on one side provided ample seating for anyone who had to wait to see the man in charge. Guards now occupied most of them. Additional guards stood sentry at the door to Chris's office.

The other side of the room boasted a wall full of file cabinets and a large desk, behind which sat an attractive brunette garbed in a formfitting business jacket and skirt. The buttons on the front of her jacket were unfastened, allowing him to glimpse the holstered weapon she wore under one arm.

When she looked up and saw him, her eyes widened and an expression of dismay flashed across her pretty features before she carefully schooled them into a polite mask of friendliness. "Hi, Seth."

"Hello, Kate. It's good to see you." What was going on?

She wrinkled her nose. "It still feels weird to call you by your first name. You're my boss's boss and the most powerful man on the planet. I feel like I should at least put a mister in front of it."

He smiled. "I assure you, no mister is necessary. Is our boy in?"

"Yes, he is," she admitted, her reluctance evident. "But now might not be the best time to see him."

"I just need to speak with him for a moment. It'll be quick."

She hesitated, then reached for the intercom. "Mr. Reordon? Seth is here to see you."

A muttered expletive carried across the line.

She shot Seth a quick glance.

He arched a brow.

"Okay. Send him in," Chris ordered.

Kate straightened. "He can see you now."

"Thank you." Seth headed for the door, his curiosity rising.

One of the guards opened it for him, then closed it after Seth strode inside.

Chris rounded his big desk and met him halfway across the spacious office. "Hi, Seth. I have a conference call coming up in a few, so I apologize in advance if we're interrupted. What can I do for you?"

Seth had a sneaking suspicion the conference call was bullshit and Chris just wanted to get rid of him. "What's with the guards?"

Sighing, Chris leaned against the back of a chair. It wasn't until then that Seth realized Chris's long sofa was missing. "There was an incident earlier with the vampires."

That caught and held Seth's attention. "Did Cliff have another psychotic break?"

"No. Stewart did. His third in as many months." Stewart was another of the seven vampires who had surrendered to the Immortal Guardians, hoping to avoid insanity.

"Was anyone hurt?"

"Not really. Melanie and Bastien seemed to sense something was up and opted to stay here today instead of sleeping at David's place. Melanie was in the lab with Stewart. Bastien was up here with me."

That surprised Seth. Chris's one and only fault thus far had been a tendency to hold grudges. And he'd held one against Bastien—who had harmed dozens of guards here at the network during his darker days—for years.

"What happened?"

"Stewart lost it. Melanie said she didn't know what triggered it, but she had to physically overpower and subdue him to keep him from attacking the guards. Cliff saw them struggling. Stewart got in a couple of lucky shots because Melanie was trying not to hurt him. Cliff thought Stewart was trying to kill Melanie and just... tore into him."

"Of course he did," Seth said grimly. Cliff loved Melanie like a sister. He would kill anyone who threatened her.

"Melanie managed to sedate them both before Bastien reached them. Stewart went down instantly. But the madness has progressed enough in Cliff that one dose of the tranquilizer won't knock him out."

"And two doses can be dangerous." Two doses could—and often did—prove fatal for vampires.

"Yeah. Cliff's okay though. We managed to calm him down without hurting him. But everyone is a little on edge."

"Understandable."

"So what can I do for you?"

"May we speak in the conference room?" That particular room

was so heavily soundproofed that even Seth couldn't hear what happened inside it. And he wanted no one but Chris to hear what he had to say.

Chris glanced at the conference room. "You know what? It's a mess in there right now. Why don't we just step into the bathroom instead?" It too was soundproofed. All bathrooms at network headquarters were so the vampires who lived five levels belowground wouldn't complain about having to listen to employees relieve themselves twenty-four hours a day.

The bathroom would've been fine, but Seth shook his head. "I prefer the conference room. I don't mind a little clutter." And he wanted to know what the hell was in there that Chris didn't want him to see.

Chris snorted. "Says the man who turned up his nose and looked like he couldn't leave fast enough when a little clutter in my home aggravated his OCD."

Seth almost laughed. "That wasn't a *little* clutter. That was a mess the likes of which the CDC would've quarantined if they'd seen it."

"Oh, ha ha ha. Well, my bathroom here is pristinely clean, so…" He motioned to the open door on one side of his office.

Seth shook his head and motioned to the other. "We'll talk in the conference room."

"Why?"

"Because I'm curious to see what you're trying to hide from me."

Chris stared at him for a long moment, then swore. "Fine. But just this once I'm going to say you suck for not letting me get away with it."

Unoffended, Seth followed the blond man to the door of the conference room and entered behind him. No clutter adorned the long, gleaming table around which sleek, modern rolling chairs gathered. But Seth did notice a new addition beyond it.

Chris closed the door.

Seth knew now why Chris's sofa had been absent. He had dragged it in here and installed it at the opposite end of the room. Clothing littered the floor in front of it, having been hastily removed by the attractive couple that slumbered upon it beneath a blanket.

The woman was beautiful with smooth skin the color of milk chocolate. Her raven hair was drawn back from her pretty face in a series of intricate braids that ended about the same place Adira wore headbands. There it blossomed into an Afro that looked as soft as a cotton ball. Her features were relaxed, her narrow shoulders bare.

Cliff was spooned up behind her, his skin a bit darker, his hair twisted into a mass of thin dreadlocks. He showed no hint of the peace his lover had found in sleep. His bare arm lay atop the covers, wrapped around her and clutching her tightly. Every visible muscle was tense. His brows drew down in a deep V. His lips tightened. A muscle in his jaw twitched as he clenched and unclenched his teeth. The eyes behind his closed lids moved rapidly back and forth.

Sadness suffused Seth. Cliff was a good man, honorable to his core. He deserved better than to suffer the brain damage the virus would continue to spawn until he became a monster. "You called Emma," he said softly. "When the first tranquilizer dose didn't render him unconscious, this is how you calmed him."

Chris regarded him grimly. "Yes."

Silence reigned. Seth crossed to the couple. Cliff held the woman so tightly he would probably leave bruises. But Seth knew she wouldn't complain. He touched a fingertip to Cliff's temple. The vampire's thoughts were so chaotic and filled with violence—his dream so nightmarish—that it took Seth several minutes to infuse Cliff with tranquility and steer his dreams toward happier times.

Cliff sighed in his sleep and loosened his hold on Emma. Snuggling closer, he buried his nose in her hair.

Seth rested a hand on Emma's shoulder. Cliff hadn't harmed her. He had been rough and aggressive when they'd made love, but he hadn't frightened or injured her. She loved Cliff and didn't mind when his touch acquired a desperate edge. She just feared losing him.

Seth sent healing warmth into her to take care of the few bruises that were beginning to form where Cliff had held her too tightly. The same healing warmth filtered from her into Cliff where they touched, further calming him.

He straightened.

"You knew," Chris said.

Strolling back toward him, Seth nodded. "I've known for quite some time that they've been seeing each other."

"I admit I'm a little surprised you didn't call a halt to it."

"Surprised and relieved?"

Chris stared at the couple. "Yeah."

"They're adults. They love each other. And both are aware of the risks involved in being together. If Emma believes them worth it, I won't stand in the way of whatever happiness they can find together."

Chris studied Seth. "Even though she's a *gifted one?*"

"Even so." He cast Chris a mildly censorious look. "You didn't need to hide it from me."

The human sighed and shook his head. "I didn't want to, but I know how protective you are of *gifted ones.* I figured you'd want to spare her the heartache."

"I wish I could." Seth thought of Chris's assistant and found a smile. "Kate looked like a deer caught in the headlights when I strolled into her office."

Chris laughed. "Yeah. She likes Cliff and is really rooting for him. What did you want to see me about anyway?"

"Something that I wish to go no farther than this room."

"Okay. What's up?"

Seth shifted. The problems he dealt with on a daily basis usually revolved around immortals, *gifted ones,* and vampires. Aside from certain issues that had arisen with regards to Ami, the problems he brought Chris were never of a personal nature. So he suddenly found himself fighting an absurd urge to fidget. "I need you to covertly provide additional security for a location."

Chris drew a small notebook and a stubby pencil from his front pocket. "Okay. What's the address?"

"It's Little Gifts."

"Leah Somerson's store?"

"Yes."

"Done."

"You can secure it without her knowing?"

"I already have."

Seth stared at him. "What?"

"Remember how I told you I looked into Leah's background as soon as Ami started taking Adira there?"

"Yes."

"Well, I also hacked into her surveillance system to see how good her security was, then improved it by installing some of my own equipment while she was off premises. I like to cover all bases and wanted to have eyes on the place in case Gershom decided to pop in and try to nab Ami or the baby."

"You didn't mention it before."

Chris shrugged. "Beefing up security anywhere Ami goes became standard procedure as soon as Gershom came on the scene."

Of course it had. Chris always went the extra mile for them, often without asking. "Does that security include Leah's apartment?"

"Yes."

Seth studied him. Then Chris must already know that Seth had been spending time with her. "Who monitors the feed?"

"A select group of men and women I would trust with my life. The same ones who monitor the security feed here. They watch it in real time from two different locations. And they report directly to me, so I'm the only person who knows what they see."

Seth wasn't sure how to respond to that. Just how much *had* they seen? If they monitored the back door of her apartment, then they would've seen him leave quite late the other night and might've assumed he and Leah were lovers.

Chris returned his pencil and notebook to his pocket, then slowly backed away a few steps. "In the interest of full disclosure, I should also tell you…"

Seth frowned. "What?"

"I viewed some of the footage myself. And after seeing the two of you dance together, I installed a special-ops team in the building across from hers that remains in position round the clock. They're heavily armed. They all carry the same device Immortal Guardians do. And they monitor the feeds as well. But *their* feeds include the interior of her apartment."

Anger instantly ignited within Seth. When he had asked Chris to provide additional security for her shop and apartment, he'd meant the *exterior,* not the *interior!* Men had been surveilling Leah in her home? They had been watching her during private moments? Did they watch her in her bedroom? In her bathroom? Had they seen her unclothed?

He took a menacing step forward.

Chris hastily backed away another pace and threw up his hands. "Don't kill me! Hear me out!"

"You watch her in her home?" he growled, stalking Chris around the boardroom table. "*They* watch her in her home? Your men? Are there cameras in her bedroom? In her bathroom?"

"*Hell* no!" Chris quickly replied. "The cameras only show the apartment's front and back doors and her living room. Bathrooms and bedrooms are off-limits."

Seth recalled the way Leah's wet tank top and pajama pants had clung to her, revealing the beautiful body beneath almost as clearly as fucking plastic wrap.

"Okay," Chris said, "your eyes are really bright, so clearly you're pissed. But damn it, Seth, I'm just trying to keep her safe. That's why you came by today, isn't it? You were going to ask me to help you keep her safe?"

Halting, Seth drew in a deep breath. He closed his eyes and fought down his anger. Chris was a good guy. He was just trying to help. "I don't want men watching Leah when she's in the privacy of her home."

"I don't either." Some of the tension left Chris's voice. "That's why only female operatives are allowed to view the interior feeds of both the store and her apartment. The men view the exterior feeds."

Seth glowered at him. "Are you saying you're a woman? Because you just told me you saw the footage of us dancing yourself!"

Chris winced. "If the female operatives see something they believe is important, they bring it to my attention. Everyone knows Gershom is striking at you through those you care about. And it was clear from the moment you danced with her that Leah means something to you. They thought I should know you two—"

"We're just friends. We aren't lovers."

Sighing, Chris rubbed his eyes as if he were suddenly weary. "I'd ask you why, but already know the answer." Lowering his hand, he shook his head. "You and I are the same in so many ways, Seth. We both have thousands of men and women under our command. We both feel wholly responsible for the health, happiness, and welfare of every single one of them. And we've both lost people we care about in this war with Gershom." His shoulders rose and fell in a helpless shrug. "I don't want to lose any more. So I took measures I thought would reduce the chances of that even though I knew it might result in you beating the shit out of me when you found out."

Seth's anger receded, replaced by regret that such steps were even necessary. "Thank you."

"I'm always on your side, Seth."

"I know that. I'm just…"

"Feeling possessive and protective."

"Yes, damn it, though I shouldn't." Such emotions indicated a far greater attachment to Leah than he should allow himself.

"We're fighting a never-ending battle here," Chris said softly, "trying to keep the vampires in check, trying to keep humanity from finding out about *gifted ones* and immortals. I've been doing this for thirty years. You've been doing it for thousands. Thousands of years of always putting the needs of others before your own, Seth. Forgive me for being blunt, but I think it's high time you had something for yourself. It's time you had some*one* for yourself. Someone who can ease the loneliness and the shitload of pain you carry around inside you every day. Even if it's just friendship, even if you never take it further than that, I think you should explore whatever this is you've found with Leah. Because I *have* seen the footage. I've seen how you are with her, how much you laugh and enjoy her company. You shouldn't deny yourself that. I mean, how often does that come along?"

It had come along only once before in Seth's long life. That's what scared him. He wasn't sure he could keep a relationship with Leah restrained to friendship. "Now isn't a good time."

Chris snorted. "When *is* a good time? There is *never* a good time for men like you and me. And you have it much worse than I do. I'm only responsible for the East Coast. You're responsible for the whole fucking planet."

Seth sometimes forgot that this battle to protect humans was often as hard on the Seconds and other humans who aided them as it was on the immortals. "Is that why you don't date? Is that why you haven't pursued a relationship with Kate?"

Chris looked toward the closed conference room door as if he could see his assistant through it. "Yeah. That's it in a nutshell. I wouldn't be good for her. I wouldn't be good for *any* woman." He met Seth's gaze once more. "But you *would* be good for Leah—as good for her as she is for you. She's suffered losses of her own and is due some happiness."

"You looked into her background."

"Yes."

"She said she lost her husband and baby in a car accident."

"Yes. Twelve years ago."

"She said it was bad."

Chris nodded, his face grim. "It was. Did you see it in her memories?"

"I've not been reading her mind," Seth reluctantly confessed. Perhaps Chris wouldn't realize the significance of that, but David would if he knew. Seth hadn't read his wife's mind either, not unless she'd asked him to.

"Leah and her husband were on their way home from visiting his parents in Danville," Chris said. "She was eight months pregnant. It was late at night. A truck driver fell asleep at the wheel, came around a curve, and hit them head-on. It not only totaled their car, it pushed them off the road and into the trees."

Seth stared at him. "Are you saying—?"

Chris nodded. "You know how people are, always driving with their heads down, staring at their damn phones. It took over an hour for someone to notice the skid marks on the road and the taillights almost hidden by the trees. The truck driver was thrown through the windshield of his truck and ended up wedged halfway through *their* windshield between Leah and her husband. He died instantly. The front of the car was totaled and looked like a fucking accordion. My contacts were able to pull up pictures of the accident scene for me. Leah's husband was severely injured and crushed against the steering wheel. Leah suffered multiple broken bones and was pinned against the dash. Her water broke, but she experienced no contractions. Neither she nor her husband could move, so they couldn't find their cell phones and call for help. Her husband lost consciousness pretty quickly. Leah was trapped in that car for over an hour — not knowing if her husband was alive or dead, not knowing if her baby was either — before rescue teams arrived. Firefighters had to use the Jaws of Life to extract them both from the vehicle. Not only had her water broken, Leah was also bleeding and paramedics had difficulty detecting a fetal heartbeat."

Seth swore.

"Doctors weren't able to save the baby but managed to save Leah. Her husband lingered for three days, then died of complications from his injuries. And if that isn't fucked up enough, he died within hours of being told they'd lost the baby."

Seth's heart ached for her.

"Leah never got to hold her daughter. She wasn't able to attend her baby's funeral. Nor could she attend her husband's. She didn't even get to tell him goodbye because she was in such bad shape herself."

No wonder she'd said the whole week was tough for her to get through.

"You've both suffered losses, Seth," Chris concluded. "And you both deserve happiness. Which is why I plan to do whatever I can to keep Leah safe, even if it pisses you off because you think it crosses a line. You've done a hell of a lot for me. I want you to be happy." His attention strayed to the sofa.

Seth glanced over his shoulder.

Cliff shifted in his sleep. His brow furrowed as he tightened his hold on Emma.

Crossing to him, Seth again touched Cliff's forehead, infusing him with calm and guiding his dreams away from nightmarish violence. He then retraced his steps and stopped before Chris. "With Gershom out there —"

"There's never going to be a good time, Seth. It sucks, but there you have it. Just look at the immortals who have fallen in love in recent years. When Roland found Sarah, Bastien was doing his damnedest to kill him and take down all Immortal Guardians.

When Marcus found Ami, that jackass who crowned himself vampire king was raising his own army. When Bastien found Melanie, fucking mercenaries started hunting immortals and bombed the shit out of—"

Seth held up a hand. "I get it. You've made your point. But Gershom is a far more formidable foe than those we've fought in the past. And you're forgetting one thing."

"What?"

"Leah is human. I, on the other hand, am immortal and possess abilities that—"

"—would make most men shit their shorts. I know. Believe me, I know."

Seth shook his head. "But Leah *doesn't* know."

Chris waved off his concern. "I'm not worried about that. I think you'll find Leah is good with different."

Seth frowned. "What makes you think so?"

"Let's just call it gut instinct," he said in lieu of a true answer. "And don't be an ass and read my thoughts. Just take my word for it." Only Chris Reordon would dare say such to Seth.

Jealousy rose. "Has Leah dated a *gifted one* in the past?"

"No." Chris pointed at him with a knowing look. "And that right there—that overtly jealous gleam in your eyes—confirms that I'm right. You care about her. So go spend time with her, damn it."

He wanted to. Badly. "I fear we won't be able to keep her safe. It wouldn't be fair to her."

A female voice spoke softly behind him. "Let her decide."

Seth turned.

Emma had awoken and lay watching them, Cliff still curled around her.

"What?"

"Let *her* decide if seeing you is worth the risk," she repeated. "If that decision had been taken from me, I would've been denied Cliff's love." She freed an arm from the covers and rested it atop Cliff's, twining her fingers through his. "And his love is well worth the difficulties we face." Moisture glimmered in her eyes. "Even if I lose him, I will not regret a moment of the time we've had together. I'm so grateful to him for letting me decide. You should do the same for the woman you care about."

Seth considered her words. "You knew what Cliff was when you met him. You knew exactly what you were getting into."

"Yes. Cliff made sure I did. He even made me watch surveillance footage of one of his psychotic breaks once he realized Mr. Reordon knew about us and could provide him with it. But it didn't change my mind. I love him and want to spend every minute I can with him, even if Dr. Lipton is unable to halt the brain damage and prevent him from going insane. I plan to be with Cliff until the end."

Seth could hear in her voice and see in her eyes that she had lost hope that there would be a positive ending for them. "I'm sorry I haven't been able to help him."

She shook her head. "Don't apologize. You could've killed him the day you met him, but you didn't. You're the reason he's alive and holding me right now. So do what Cliff did. Tell this woman what you are. Warn her of the danger she faces. If she wants to cut ties with you, honor her wishes. If she wants to keep seeing you, then spend what time you can with her and do whatever you can to protect her. But don't just make the decision for her."

Seth didn't know if her words swayed him because she was right or because it was what he wanted to hear. And what Leah herself had asked of him. But he nodded.

Emma looked down at her wrist. "If things work out, you might want to get her one of these."

Seth looked at the device. "A watch?"

She nodded. "Aidan gave it to me. It's a smartwatch that's also a phone and is voice activated. If there should ever come a time when I believe Cliff might harm me, all I have to do is say two words. The watch will dial Aidan's cell phone, and he'll teleport directly to my side."

Chris moved to stand next to Seth. "Actually, that's not a bad idea. I can give you a second cell phone, Seth, one that's just for emergency calls from Leah, then program the watch for her. That way if it rings, you won't even have to answer it to know she's in danger and can teleport to her instantly."

That sounded good. Even if Gershom teleported away with her, Seth would reach the place he'd abducted her so fast that he would have no difficulty following the energy trail left behind.

"Do it," he told Chris, then looked at Emma. "Thank you."

"Thank *you* for taking such good care of Cliff."

He smiled. "You're doing far more for him than I ever could. I'm glad he found you."

Chapter Ten

L EAH SMILED AS SHE WATCHED Aaron dig in the sandbox. The playground around them was deserted. She'd like to think it was because it was a school day and most children were in school. But this playground was often deserted. She didn't know if parents were simply too busy working long hours to bring their children, too tired from the same, if they didn't want to be bothered with it, or if the children would simply rather stay inside, playing with electronic devices or watching television. But she thought all of the above pretty sad.

When she was a little girl, every child in the neighborhood had wanted to play outside as long as they could. Playgrounds like this one had been active every weekday after school and all day on weekends. Neighborhood streets had become the sites of street hockey games. Sidewalks had become roller-skating thoroughfares and giant canvases for chalk art. And children had been so reluctant to see the fun end that when the sun went down, parents had to practically drag them inside.

She glanced behind her at the empty swing set and the large climbing/sliding apparatus beyond. The park in her neighborhood hadn't boasted nearly this many features. Yet children had still enjoyed playing in it.

"Look."

She turned back to Aaron and smiled as he proudly displayed the hill he had constructed. "Oh, that's a nice hill. Who do you think should live on it?"

"Lion."

Leah reached into the backpack she'd brought and removed a large mesh bag full of toy animals. "I think there's a lion in here somewhere." She dumped them all out into the sandbox just as her cell phone rang.

Digging it out of the backpack, she saw it was her brother calling and sighed. "Yes?"

"Is he there?"

"No. Not yet."

"Maybe he isn't coming."

She rolled her eyes. "Don't sound so relieved. He's coming."

"I just don't think this is a good idea."

"You told me last week that you were worried Aaron wasn't getting enough playtime in with other children. Adira is a sweetheart. They're going to have a lot of fun together."

"What about the boy?"

"I've only met Michael a couple of times. He's pretty shy, but he's always well-behaved at the store."

Ben was silent for a moment. "I don't think this is a good idea. I think I should be there."

"You're being paranoid."

"I'm being cautious. Can you blame me?"

Leah watched Aaron plunk the lion on top of the hill. "No. But you're forgetting I used to take *you* to the park when you were Aaron's age. And nothing bad happened, right?"

"Right." Another moment passed. "Maybe I'm just looking for an excuse to come check out this guy you're seeing."

She smiled, knowing he must be dying of curiosity. "I told you, he's just a friend."

"Uh-huh," he said, his tone conveying patent disbelief.

"He's like sixteen years younger than me, Ben. He's even younger than you."

"So what? You *look* sixteen years younger."

"Flattery won't make you less annoying, you know."

He laughed.

A sleek black vehicle turned onto the street. Slowing, it parked at the curb behind her gray subcompact car. The driver's door opened. Seth emerged, wearing jeans, a black T-shirt, and dark sunglasses.

Smiling, she waved.

His lips stretched in a grin as he waved back.

Her heart gave a little flutter. The man was just too damned attractive. "He's here. I gotta go."

"I still think I should —"

Ending the call, she tucked the phone in her pack and watched Seth close his door.

Her eyes widened as both back doors opened into falcon wings, revealing two toddlers strapped into car seats. Wow. That was a cool-ass car. And so quiet. Was that the Tesla Model X her brother had been drooling over?

Adira chattered as Seth removed his sunglasses and ducked inside to unlatch Michael. Seth smiled as he spoke to her, then pointed at Leah and Aaron.

Adira looked around. As soon as she saw Leah, her face lit up with a grin and she began to bounce in her seat and kick her feet.

Laughing, Leah waved again.

<hr/>

Seth chuckled as Adira bounced and kicked her feet in excitement, eager to get out onto the playground. As he helped Michael out of the car, he caught Adira's eye. "Just a minute, sweetheart. Let me come around to the other side. Okay?"

"Okay."

He closed the door, took Michael's hand, and walked him around the back of the car to the other side. Michael hovered close as Seth leaned in to free Adira.

The little girl scrambled clumsily out of the car and waited impatiently as he pressed the button on his key fob to close the door. "Baba," she urged, tugging on his pants.

"All right. Let's go see Miss Leah and her nephew." Tucking the key fob in the pocket of his jeans, he took each child's hand and strolled onto the playground. Adira hurried along in front of him, pulling on his fingers and trying to make him go faster. Michael hovered close, squeezing his hand tight.

Seth didn't know if Michael had been shy before he'd lost his mother or if it was a result of the abrupt change in his circumstances. His mother had been one of the *gifted ones* Gershom had killed. She had also been a descendant of Roland, who—along with his wife Sarah—had been more than happy to adopt Michael. But the boy tended to be quiet around strangers.

"It's all right, Michael. You're going to have a lot of fun today."

Leah rose, smiling as she watched them approach.

A little boy about Michael's age and size played in the large sandbox. Turning, he eyed them curiously, his hands falling still as they approached. His skin was browner than Leah's, and he bore a short, neat black Afro.

As they neared the sandbox, Adira released Seth's hand and ran forward, holding her arms up.

Laughing, Leah bent and picked her up. "Hi there, sweetie. Don't you look pretty today?"

Adira hugged her, then pointed at the sandbox.

Leah set her down.

"Hello," Seth greeted her. "I think we're a little late. My apologies. I have a new respect for parents who manage to get their little ones to places on time. I had no idea taking two toddlers to the park required so much gear or that it was so difficult to get them to sit still long enough to fasten them into their car seats."

She laughed. "Yeah. The first time I volunteered to babysit my nephew, I'm pretty sure my jaw dropped at all the stuff my brother and sister-in-law brought over with him." She motioned to Aaron, who had abandoned his sand hill and stared at the other two children curiously. "Speaking of whom, this is Aaron, my nephew. Aaron, this is Mr. Seth."

Seth smiled at the boy and motioned to his two. "Nice to meet you Aaron. This is Adira and Michael."

Adira climbed over the thick plastic edge of the sandbox. "Hi."

"Hi," Aaron said.

Michael leaned into Seth's side.

Seth smiled at Leah. "He's a little shy."

Leah didn't seem to mind. She smiled. "Hi, Michael. It's nice to see you again. We brought lots of toys with us. You're welcome to play with them."

Adira plunked herself down next to Aaron and began to bury her fingers in the sand.

Leah sat down on the sandbox edge. "Is it okay if Aaron calls you Mr. Seth? I didn't ask how you'd like him to address you."

"That's fine." Rounding the sandbox, he seated himself on the edge kitty-corner to Leah.

Adira twisted around, looking for her *cousin*. "Micuh." She held her hand out to him.

Michael climbed into the sandbox and quietly settled next to her. When Aaron offered him a plastic shovel, Michael took it and began to dig.

Aaron grabbed another shovel and handed it to Adira.

"Say thank you," Seth reminded them softly.

"Thank you," Adira and Michael chorused.

Leah's smile widened. "They're so cute."

He chuckled. "So is your nephew."

She pushed some plastic animal figures closer to the children. "He looks exactly like my brother did at that age, except Ben was lighter." She turned her attention to Seth. "My stepdad is black."

He nodded. "I thought so when I saw Aaron. Either him or your sister-in-law."

"My sister-in-law is black, too. I didn't think it would bother you since you and David are so close."

"It doesn't."

Her face brightening, Leah *oohed* over a shovelful of sand Aaron held up for her inspection. "I've also met Darnell and know he's a friend of yours. He comes to the store with Ami sometimes. He's nice." She sent him a teasing glance. "And handsome. I'm beginning to think everyone in your surrogate family is stunningly attractive."

Seth straightened his back, puffed out his chest, and arched a brow in feigned jealousy. "Darnell may be handsome, but I'm taller."

She winked. "And have bigger hands and feet."

He laughed, relaxing once more.

"Careful, Aaron." She rested a hand atop his when he flung sand into the air to watch it drift on the wind. "You don't want to get sand in Adira's and Michael's eyes."

He looked at the other children.

Adira and Michael both squinted and blinked rapidly, but both seemed fine.

Aaron abandoned the shovel and started sorting through the animals Leah had brought. He handed a tiger to Michael. Adira examined Michael's new treasure while Aaron went back to digging through his pile of toys. His brow furrowed, then cleared as he spotted a lioness near Leah's foot. He reached a hand toward it. The toy began to slide across the sand to him.

Leah hastily grabbed it and handed it to him. "Here you go, sweetie."

Chris's words came back to Seth. *I think you'll find Leah is good with different.*

Of course she was, because her nephew was a *gifted one*. Seth acquainted himself with all *gifted ones*, beginning at their births. But babies changed so quickly that he hadn't recognized little Aaron.

"Are you kidding me?" Leah muttered, her tone rife with aggravation.

Seth glanced at her, noted her frown, and followed her gaze to a man who was crossing the street toward them.

He was tall, approximately six foot two, with light brown skin and a muscular build. His black hair was short and cut into a fade at the temples. Seth had little difficulty recognizing him, having checked up on him periodically during his lifetime. Like Aaron, Ben was a *gifted one*. Seth just hadn't realized he was Leah's half brother.

Seth looked at Leah. That must be why she had seemed so familiar when he'd had that first dream. He must have seen her one of the times he had looked in on Ben to ensure he was well.

"I'm really sorry about this," she murmured. "That's my brother."

"The one whose clothing I borrowed?"

"Yes, but I'd appreciate it if you wouldn't mention that. It'll just make him wonder what you were doing at my apartment and why you had no clothes."

Seth grinned. "A bit protective of you, is he?"

She rolled her eyes. "Very. You'd think *he* was the older sibling instead of the other way around."

"Is he here to ensure *you* are safe or his son?" he asked curiously.

"I'm guessing both. Again, I'm really sorry."

"Stop apologizing. It's all right. I don't blame him for wanting to protect you. We live in a dangerous world." Seth knew that better than anyone. He rose as the man drew closer.

Leah did, too.

Nodding a greeting, Seth offered his hand. "You must be Leah's brother. I'm Seth. Good to meet you."

Ben gave his hand a firm shake. "Nice to meet you. I'm Ben."

Leah gave her brother a comically exasperated look. "What are you doing here?"

His expression all innocence, Ben looked around. "It's a beautiful day. I finished work early." He shrugged. "A nice, quiet afternoon at the park sounded too good to resist."

Leah quirked a brow. "Does your boss know you finished work early?"

He grinned. "No. But I'm indispensable, so he isn't going to complain."

Seth smiled. The company for which Ben worked was actually one of many owned by the network. Though he didn't know it, Ben was one of Chris's tech geniuses.

Ben looked at the children. Adira and Michael had placed their animals on top of the sand hill next to Aaron's lion. All three children were now pouring sand on them. Seth couldn't tell if they were trying to bury the animals or make the hill bigger, but they all seemed to have the same intent and were enjoying themselves.

He motioned to Adira, then Michael. "This is my granddaughter Adira and her cousin Michael."

Ben's eyebrows flew up. "Granddaughter?"

Seth shrugged. "I'm older than I look."

Leah snorted. "You can say that as much as you want, Seth. I'm never going to believe it."

He looked down at her and arched a brow. "I don't know why. You're older than *you* look."

Laughing, she gave his shoulder a playful shove. "Don't say that!"

"Why?" he asked with a smile. "Isn't that a good thing?"

"Yes, but when you say it like that, it makes me feel old."

That certainly had not been his intention. "How was I supposed to say it?"

"Instead of saying I'm *older* than I look" — she narrowed her eyes in mock anger, then assumed a sweet, innocent expression and lightened her voice—"you're supposed to say I look as young and fresh as a daisy."

Schooling his features into a somber mask, Seth bowed. "Forgive me, Leah. I misspoke. I meant to say you look as young and fresh as a daisy, though no daisy could compare to your immense beauty."

"Much better." Winking, she nudged him with her shoulder. "Flatterer."

He grinned. "I'm a fast learner."

They turned back to Ben, who stared at them.

Leah frowned. "What?"

He blinked. "Nothing." Stepping into the sandbox, he sat on the edge near his son.

Seth waited for Leah to retake her seat, then sat kitty-corner to her once more. "Adira's mother isn't actually my daughter," he told Ben. "I just think of her as such. When she lost her own family, I welcomed her into mine and love her as if she truly *were* my daughter."

"Are you married then?" Ben asked casually.

Leah glowered at him.

"No," Seth responded, unperturbed. "Over the years I've formed close ties with men and women I consider family. Adira's mother is one of them."

Ben nodded, then smiled at his son. "Whatcha working on there, sport?"

Aaron smiled at his father, then reached toward the pile of toys again. A black bear began to skid toward him.

Ben swiftly clasped the toy and guided it through the pile toward Aaron. "What about this one? You think he'd like to join the fun?" He cast Seth a quick look.

Seth smiled and nodded at the growing pyramid of sand. "I can't decide if the children are trying to bury the toys or build them a castle."

Ben relaxed. A quick peek into his thoughts revealed relief as he assumed Seth hadn't caught his son's slip. Like many other *gifted ones*, he knew how dangerous it would be for others to realize his son bore special abilities.

Michael gradually relaxed, too, Seth was happy to see. The three children diligently dug holes and increased the mass of their pyramid while the adults casually conversed and offered aid to the little builders.

Seth and Leah engaged in their usual banter while Ben observed them and tried not to be too obvious about it. He was a good guy, easy to talk to.

Every time Aaron compelled a toy to come to him, Ben was quick to grab it and did an admirable job of making it appear as though he had moved the toy himself. He even rested one of his feet amid the pile of toys so he could make it look as if his foot had instigated the movement. But the quick glances he sent Seth each time gave him away. Aaron's telekinetic abilities were remarkably strong for a new generation *gifted one*. Some *gifted ones* born in the current century bore bloodlines that had been so diluted by human DNA over the millennia that they didn't even realize they *had* special abilities.

Seth glanced at Leah after the sixth or seventh time and found her watching him.

She knew he'd noticed her nephew's special ability. He saw it in her eyes. But unlike her brother, she seemed fine with it.

The next time a toy moved, it damned near flew across the sandbox.

Ben fumbled to catch the lion cub sailing toward the pyramid and sent Leah a panicked look. "I think Aaron may be getting tired. We should probably leave soon."

Seth shook his head. "It's all right. That time it wasn't Aaron. It was Michael."

Ben froze. "What?"

"That was Michael's doing, not Aaron's." Leaning down, he patted Michael on the back. "Did you want the lion cub, Michael?"

He nodded, his eyes on the toy Ben held.

Stunned, Ben handed it to him.

"Thank you." Michael added it to the pyramid. Then he looked at a second lion cub that was over by Leah.

The toy slid across the sand and into his little hand.

Leah looked at Seth with delight. "Michael is different? He has telekinetic abilities?"

He smiled. "Yes. He knows he isn't supposed to use his gifts outside the home, but he thought it was okay after Aaron used his several times without being cautioned."

Ben said nothing. He just kept staring at Seth as though he wasn't sure whether or not to believe him. The toy could've just as easily been moved by Aaron to help his new friend.

"It's all right," Seth assured Ben, knowing how deeply the man feared his son's gifts coming to light. He looked at Leah. "I hadn't planned on telling you this way, but I'm different, too."

"Different how?" Ben asked before Leah could respond.

Seth glanced around, ensuring the playground—along with the sidewalks and streets that surrounded it—were deserted. He closed his eyes and touched upon the minds in all the houses within view.

No humans were peeking out their windows at them.

Turning back to face the sandbox, he whispered, "Adira, would you like me to make you a castle?"

She nodded, her face brightening with a grin.

The sand pyramid the children had formed began to shift and move as Seth exercised his own telekinetic gift. Drawing moist sand up from the bottom of the sandbox, he mixed it with the dry, molding it into an impressively large, multitiered medieval castle with an animal perched atop each tower.

Ben and Leah gaped.

The children giggled and grinned and bounced on their bottoms, excited by the display.

"That is *awesome!*" Leah declared with a wide grin. Then she slapped him on the arm. "Why didn't you tell me you could do that? I could've put you to work in my shop, hanging up clothes for me while I sat back with my feet propped up and ate pizza."

He laughed, relieved that she wasn't upset because he'd kept it from her.

Her brother didn't seem amused. "Who *are* you, Seth?"

"Just someone born with gifts like you and your son were. I don't ordinarily share that but could tell you were concerned about Aaron." Leaning down, he spoke softly to the toddlers. "Now, children, I only did that because no one was around to see it. It's very important that you not use your special gifts when others are around. It might frighten them."

"Okay, Baba," Adira chirped, well aware of the rules.

Michael nodded.

Aaron did, too.

All three went back to playing with their new sand castle.

Ben still seemed worried.

"I wish you no harm, Ben. I vow it. I *protect* those who are different. I don't persecute them or seek to use them for my own gain. I'm sorry if my display made you uneasy. I was merely attempting to show you that your secret is safe with me."

Leah nodded at her brother. "It is. Seth won't betray you."

Ben considered him a moment. "Did you know my son and I have special abilities before you started spending time with my sister?" The implication was clear. He worried that Seth might have nefarious plans and had used his sister to get to them.

"Ben!" Leah protested.

"No," Seth answered honestly. "I did not. I trust you will keep my secret, too?" He could not stop a dark edge from entering his voice when he continued. "I take all threats to my family seriously and would *not* react well to your sharing this knowledge or endangering Adira and Michael."

Leah began to look uneasy.

But the sharp warning seemed to put her brother's mind at ease because he nodded. "Your secret's safe with me."

Seth smiled. "Then we're good. Would you be averse to these three having another playdate in the future? Adira and Michael's parents have been worrying about them not getting enough socialization. Taking them to the playground has become more tricky — if not risky — since their abilities have begun to manifest themselves."

Ben responded with a slow shake of his head. "As long as the kids get along, I think that would be okay."

Seth addressed the toddlers again. "Children, would you like to play together again soon?"

Michael and Aaron both nodded.

Adira pushed herself to her feet. Sand coated her shoes, clothing, and hands as she moved around Michael and crossed to Seth. Reaching over, she took Leah's hand and put it in his.

Leah laughed and scooted a little closer so he could rest their entwined fingers on his knee. "I'll take that as a yes."

While Adira rejoined the boys, Ben stared at Seth's and Leah's clasped hands. "Yeah. Another playdate sounds good."

<hr />

When the playdate ended, Seth wanted to follow Leah home and confirm she truly wasn't angry with him for hiding he was different from her. But calls began to come in as soon as he returned Adira and Michael to David's place.

Vampire numbers continued to increase at an alarming rate. It was almost as if Gershom had mind-controlled every damned vampire on the planet and instructed them to turn as many humans as they could. That meant more vampires went out trolling for victims each night. More battles ensued between immortals and vampires. More serious wounds required Seth to heal them when two immortals took on a dozen vampires. More missing person cases inundated the network and had to be dealt with to keep authorities from finding out vampires had nabbed the missing man or woman. More vampire victims' deaths required creative camouflaging by the network so they would be labeled accidents, muggings, or the like. And when some crime scenes made vampire attacks impossible to conceal through other means, Seth had to telepathically alter memories.

He also worried that more vampire activity would increase the chances that another *gifted one* would be transformed, not necessarily at Gershom's instigation but by sheer happenstance. If such occurred, Seth would need to reach him or her before Gershom could get wind of it and increase his private army.

Seth teleported from country to country, problem solving, aiding Immortal Guardians overwhelmed by sheer numbers, *and* reading the minds of every vampire he could. None provided even a hint of where he might find Gershom or the missing immortals.

When night fell in North Carolina, Seth waited until Leah's shop closed, then asked Zach to field his calls long enough for him to go see her. He wasn't like younger men today. He didn't want to text her or talk to her over the phone. He wanted to see her in person and watch every minute change in her facial expression so he could determine how she really felt about him being different.

The blinds on the shop's windows were all closed, but light shone behind them. No music played. Nor did conversation carry to his sensitive ears.

Drawing in a deep breath, he rapped on the locked door.

Brittney opened it. "Hi, Seth. Are you here to see Leah?"

"Yes."

"Cool. She's in the back room." She stepped outside. "I was just leaving."

He offered her a brief bow. "Then I bid you good night."

"Good night," she said with a smile. "Go on in. I'll lock the door behind you."

Seth did as requested and listened as she locked both locks. The heels of her pumps clicked on the sidewalk as she walked away.

Silence descended.

He couldn't help but feel a little anxious. Leah had seemed fine with his being different while at the playground. But some of that could have been a friendly facade donned for her brother's benefit.

"Well?" Leah called after a minute. "What are you waiting for? Get your handsome ass in here."

He grinned, relieved. Her tone was teasing, not angry.

Opting to keep his coat on, he strolled through the store to the back room.

Leah sat at a desk, staring at a computer screen that displayed a spreadsheet of some sort. "Give me two minutes," she mumbled, her tone distracted, "then I'll be done."

Seth leaned against the wall and crossed his arms. She wore glasses tonight. He had never seen her do so before and wondered if she needed them for reading and close-up work the way many humans did once they reached their forties. The frames were black, reminding him of those that had been popular in the sixties. Her long hair was pulled back in a slightly disheveled bun. The jeans and blazer she'd apparently changed into before going back to work hugged her beautiful figure.

She had, as Sheldon would say, a real sexy-librarian thing going on that heated Seth's blood. The longer he watched her, the more he wanted to touch her, to peel that blazer off, loosen her hair, and —

"Finally," she announced with a sigh. Closing the file, she removed her glasses and spun the chair around to face him. When she looked at him, her eyebrows flew up. "Hi."

"Hello."

She studied him for a moment. "Something on your mind?"

Aside from a deep desire to strip her naked? "You aren't angry."

She tilted her head to one side. "Why would I be angry?"

"Because I hid that I was different from you."

Smiling, she rose. "I have news for you, Seth. You didn't hide it very well."

He straightened, staring at her in surprise. "You already knew?"

She chuckled. "Yes, I already knew. It was pretty obvious."

"How?" He'd been so careful.

Closing the distance between them, she took his hand. "Hold that thought."

A now-familiar tingle raced up his arm as Seth twined his fingers through hers, happy for any excuse to feel her skin against his.

Leah activated the alarm system, then led him over to the stairs.

He tried very hard not to stare at her perfect ass or notice the alluring sway of her hips on the way up but failed miserably. Damn, that was tempting.

Fucking Gershom. If it weren't for him and the threat he posed, Seth would kick caution to the wind, lift Leah into his arms, and take her to bed. *If* they made it that far. Her sofa was closer. It was way too short for him, but he could make it work.

Once inside her apartment, she led him through the living room. Seth stared longingly at the sofa as he imagined the many ways he could take her on it. Or hell, the many ways she could take *him* on it. He wouldn't have to worry about it being too short for him if he were sitting down and she straddled him.

Tearing his thoughts away from *that* delectable image, he followed her down the hallway and into the guest bathroom.

Once there, she faced him and looked up at him expectantly.

She seemed to be waiting for something.

Seth shifted. "What?"

Her full lips quirking in amusement, she released his hand, gripped his biceps, and turned him to face the mirror.

Seth looked at his reflection. "Oh shit." His eyes bore a bright golden glow.

She laughed. "You look a little panicked."

Closing his eyes, he tried to darken them. Unfortunately, when he opened them again, his eyes were still as bright as could be. "I'm sorry. I thought I had more control than this." He usually did, but it seemed to abandon him whenever he was with Leah. He slid her a glance and found her still smiling. "How long have you known I'm different?" How long had he been inadvertently dropping his guard around her? David would understand the significance of that as well. Seth had *married* the last human woman around whom he'd dropped his guard.

"Since the night you left so abruptly when Tessa was spotted."

That long?

His emotions *had* been running high that night. But he was old and powerful enough to maintain control when in the company of mortals. At least, he had been until he'd met Leah. He motioned to his face. "This doesn't unnerve you?"

"No." Stepping closer, she stared up into his eyes. His pulse leapt when she pressed a soft hand to his cheek. "One, because I think they're beautiful." A statement that—accompanied by her touch—only increased his desire to drag her into his arms and finally find out what those tantalizing lips of hers tasted like, something that no doubt made his eyes glow brighter. "And two," she continued, "because Ben and Aaron aren't the only members of my family who are different. My dad and *his* dad are, too. Or at least Grandpa was before he died. So I've been around people who are different ever since I was a child."

"Your stepfather is a *gifted one*." Seth mentally traced her brother's lineage back to her grandfather.

"Yes. Aaron inherited his telekinetic abilities from Dad. Ben has telekinetic abilities, too, but his are different. I don't know how to explain it other than to say he can... manipulate matter, I guess, is the way to describe it. He can change things, reshape them." Which was why Ben was one of Chris's tech geniuses. "And my grandpa could dreamwalk." She smiled. "After we moved to North Carolina, he used to find me in my dreams all the way from Denver. I thought it was the coolest thing ever... until I met you."

Seth smiled. "You're good with different."

"Yes, I am." Stepping back, she took his hand again and led him to the kitchen. "I like that you call them *gifted ones*." Once there, she spun him away from her and tugged his coat off his shoulders.

"The term seemed appropriate," Seth murmured, glad he had removed the weapons he normally stashed in his coat before coming. When her fingers brushed the back of his neck, more of that delightful tingling awareness shot through him. He silently cursed himself. As long as she kept touching him, even casually, there was no way he'd be able to get his eyes to stop glowing.

Leah hadn't caught on that desire was most often the cause of the glow when they were together, had she?

She hung his coat up in the laundry room. "Would you like something to eat?"

"No, thank you."

"Good." Her lovely face brightened with barely leashed excitement. "Okay. Since you apparently aren't going to mention it, I will. How do you disappear into thin air the way you do? Curiosity has been killing me!"

Seth gaped at her. "What?"

"The disappearing thing. How do you do it?"

Astonishment rippled through him. "You know I can teleport?"

"Is that what you call it? Teleporting? Like in sci-fi movies?"

"Yes," he answered weakly.

"Then yes, I want to know how you teleport."

Was there anything he *hadn't* inadvertently revealed to her? Shit! How could he have been so careless? "I just picture where I want to go and…" He shook his head. "I go. I don't really know how it works. It just does. I can also follow phone signals, tracing them back to their origin and teleporting directly to whoever calls me."

"That is *so* cool." Curling her fingers around his biceps, she tugged on his arm. "Show me—show me!"

He grinned, amusement eating away at his dismay. She was so damned adorable. "All right. But you'll have to release me."

She did.

Seth teleported away.

Chapter Eleven

L EAH GASPED. ONE MOMENT SETH stood in front of her. The next he was gone.

She waved her hands back and forth through the air where he had stood, searching for... well, she didn't know what. But he was actually gone!

He reappeared in the next breath.

She let out a little squeak of surprise, then laughed in delight. His hair, shoulders, and thick eyelashes were dusted with fat snowflakes. In his arms, he cradled a white rabbit.

"That is so freaking cool!" she practically shouted.

Laughing, he handed her the bunny.

Leah cuddled the soft little creature close. "Is it wild?"

He nodded. "I startled him with my sudden appearance."

She stroked the pretty creature's fur. "He doesn't seem scared at all."

"I calmed him. I'm an empath, too." His smile grew. "Would you like to come with me when I return him home?"

"Really?"

He nodded.

"Hell yes!"

Grinning, he looped an arm around her waist and drew her close.

Her pulse leapt at the feel of his strong, muscled body pressed against hers.

"You might find this a little disconcerting." It was the only warning he issued before everything went black.

Leah felt a momentary weightlessness, like that she sometimes felt in an elevator. Then bright light exploded around them. Her shoes sank into snow until it reached her knees. A frigid breeze blew fat snowflakes into her face and frosted her breath.

Shivering, she stared at her surroundings in awe. The sun shone overhead, battling clouds and bathing breathtakingly beautiful mountains in patches of golden light. She didn't know where they were, but the thin air told her they were high above sea level.

The rabbit in her arms squirmed.

Leah set him on the snow as her teeth began to chatter.

Instead of racing away in fear, it hopped toward the snow-coated trees nearby as though nothing had happened.

Seth wrapped his arms around her, warmth radiating from him like a furnace.

"How can you b-be so warm when I'm f-freezing my ass off?" she asked, snuggling closer.

"I can control my body temperature."

Damn. What *couldn't* the man do?

Darkness engulfed them once more. Leah gripped the front of his shirt and squeezed her eyes shut as that odd weightlessness swept over her. Heat replaced the cold at her back. The sound of ocean waves accompanied it.

Opening her eyes, she turned her head. She and Seth now stood on a lovely beach. Pristine white sands. Water so clear you could see the bottom far beyond the point water lapped against the shore. No tourists were in sight. Nor were structures of any kind. Just palm trees and a few seabirds trolling for tasty morsels along the water's edge.

Tilting her head back, she stared up at the powerful man who held her. "I know I said this once before. But wow, Seth. You're my new best friend."

He laughed.

The snow that coated them swiftly melted, dampening their clothing and hair.

Leah stepped back and turned toward the ocean. Taking his hand, she strolled along the water's edge. "I don't know how you can be so stressed when you can come to places like this anytime you want to," she murmured with a smile.

He shook his head. "The enemy I now face is a formidable one."

Neither protested when waves crept over their shoes.

"Speaking of which…"

Leah looked up at him, squinting against the bright sunlight. He didn't speak for a long moment as he seemed to wage internal war with himself.

"Yes?" she prompted gently.

He looked out over the ocean, then shook his head and stared down at his boots.

"You can tell me anything, Seth," she reminded him.

He met her gaze. "I want to spend more time with you."

Her heart began to beat faster within her breast. "I want to spend more time with you, too."

His pensive expression softened a bit. "Your friendship has come to mean a lot to me."

Despite what she'd told her brother, Leah wasn't sure friendship was all she wanted from Seth now. She thought about him all the time, loved his company, and couldn't seem to keep herself from imagining him running his hands all over her body.

"But my enemy poses a serious threat to you."

"I know," she said softly. He had made that very clear.

"There are other things you should know before you decide whether or not you wish to continue seeing me."

She couldn't imagine him telling her anything that would change her mind. "Okay."

"Let me take you home first."

"Why?"

He forced a smile. "So you can boot me out the door if it proves to be too much."

Leah wanted to say something light to ease his worry, but those somber dark eyes of his warned her he was going to drop a serious bombshell. "Okay."

Seconds later, they stood beside the sofa in her apartment.

"You should remove your wet shoes," he murmured.

"Okay." She toed off her running shoes. "You should, too."

"They're waterproof."

"Oh." Bending, she removed her wet socks, then carried both her shoes and socks into the laundry room. When she returned,

Seth motioned to the sofa.

"Have a seat," he said, a request rather than a demand.

She did, feeling a little twinge of anxiety. This was going to be big, wasn't it?

When Seth didn't join her, she patted the cushion next to her. "Sit with me. You're making me nervous."

Seth sat beside her but didn't take her hand.

Leah took his instead, needing the contact. He was really starting to worry her. He looked grim as hell.

"Tell me what you think I need to know," she encouraged him gently.

He stared down at their hands for a moment. "Forgive me if I bungle this. I'm fairly certain I will."

"Okay."

"You know I'm different."

"Yes."

"But you don't know *how* different."

Nervous butterflies fluttered in her belly. "How different are you, Seth?"

"Teleportation, empathic, and telekinetic abilities aren't the only gifts I bear."

She was fine with that. "What else can you do?"

He shook his head. "The list is a long one. My gifts are numerous. Some are remarkably strong, and some are weak from disuse."

"Like what? Can you dreamwalk like Gramps?"

"Yes. I'm also telepathic and bear healing, precognitive, postcognitive, and psychometric abilities, to name a few."

She stared at him. "A few? You mean there are more?"

"Yes." But he seemed reluctant to tell her.

Carefully schooling her features into what she hoped was a blank mask that hid her shock, she gave his hand a squeeze. "Keep going. Tell me all of it." Then she ruined it by frowning. "Wait. You're telepathic?"

"Yes."

Dread filled her. "You've been reading my thoughts all this time?" If he had, then he knew she had been mentally undressing him and weaving some wicked sexual fantasies about him ever since they'd met.

"No," he corrected hastily. "I haven't read them at all. Not once. Unlike younger telepaths, I don't hear other people's thoughts unless I choose to. And I have never explored yours."

He'd know she wanted to be more than friends if he did. "You said younger telepaths. Do your gifts or powers strengthen as you get older or something?"

He shook his head. "*Gifted ones* are born with special abilities because their DNA is more advanced and complex than that of ordinary humans."

"What?" Ben and her dad had advanced DNA? "Why?"

"*Gifted ones* have existed since biblical times. But over thousands of years, as they procreated with ordinary humans, that DNA became diluted. A little more with each generation. Most *gifted ones* today are born with only one gift. And sometimes that gift is so weak they don't even realize they possess it and mistake it for good instincts or the like."

"I don't understand," she said. "If *gifted ones* today usually only have one gift, why do you have so many? And why are yours so strong?"

One corner of his lips turned up in a smile that conveyed sadness rather than amusement. "Because I'm older than I look."

Leah studied him. For the first time, she believed it. "How much older?"

He seemed to brace himself before answering. "Thousands of years, I'm afraid."

Her heart began to slam against her rib cage. "That's not possible."

"Yes, it is. My body has extraordinary regenerative capabilities." Glancing at her coffee table, he reached over and picked up the pencil she had been using to do a crossword puzzle. "I'm sure there is a better way to show you this, but..." Tugging his hand from hers, he rested it on his knee, fingers splayed. Then he raised the hand with the pencil and drove the sharp point down with a hard thrust.

Leah cried out as the pencil punctured the center of his hand. "Oh shit!" Tucking her feet up under her, she knelt on the cushion and gaped down at the damage. Only half the pencil was visible.

So the rest of it must have gone straight through his hand and into his knee.

Seth yanked the pencil out. A muscle in his jaw jumped as he set the bloody writing tool on the coffee table.

"Are you fucking crazy?" she shouted and grabbed his hand. A hole mangled both sides of it. His pants now bore a similar hole in the knee. Trembling, she tucked his hand against her stomach and tried to wrap the base of her shirt around it to staunch the flow of blood.

Seth had stabbed himself in the hand. He had *stabbed himself* in the *hand! And* the knee! She had to call 911. She had to—

Seth held up his free hand. "Easy." He spoke softly, evincing none of the anxiety that was freaking her the hell out. "It's okay." He nodded at his injured hand. "Look."

Leah looked down at the hand hidden by her shirt.

"Forget about the blood and examine the wound."

Fingers shaking, she unwrapped his injured hand and did as he instructed. Her breath caught. The wound had already ceased bleeding. Her heart began to beat even faster as the edges of the ragged hole drew together and sealed shut, his hand healing on both sides. She glanced at his knee. Touching the hole in his pants, she reluctantly tucked a pinky finger inside. Though his skin was wet with blood, she could find no wound.

"Holy crap," she whispered. "How is that possible?"

"My body can heal itself of any injury save decapitation. It remains, in fact, in a constant state of regeneration—even when I'm not injured—so..." One of his shoulders lifted and fell in a faint shrug. "I don't age."

Leah struggled to process it all. "You're thousands of years older than me?"

"Yes." And he looked as though he expected her to strike a blow. Not a physical one but an emotional one. By repudiating him, perhaps?

As always, the need to put him at ease and see him smile overrode all else. "Well," she said, striving for a normal tone of voice, "on the upside, apparently *I'm* not the one robbing the cradle here."

A startled laugh escaped him. "I suppose not."

Leah shook her head. She had worried about the age difference between them being too great when she had thought herself sixteen or eighteen years older than him. Now Seth was *thousands* of years older than *her.* "Why are you even here?" she blurted.

His smile vanished as his brow furrowed. "I thought the decision to continue our friendship should be yours and that you should know more about me before you—"

"No," she interrupted. "I mean why are you *here?* With *me?* You're thousands of years old, Seth. I must seem so young to you, like a child!" She was only twenty-one years older than Brittney, and sometimes Brittney seemed like a teenager to her.

"Not at all," he quickly assured her. "Ben is ten years younger than you. Does he seem like a child to you or an adult?"

She hesitated. "An adult."

"Do you enjoy spending time with him?"

"Yes."

"Did you enjoy spending time with me when you thought I was thirty years old?"

"Yes, damn it," she grumbled. She had enjoyed it a lot. More than she had thought she should.

"Then why would you think it any different for me?"

She eyed him uncertainly.

"You see the irony, don't you?"

She nodded. In the space of a few minutes, she had gone from believing she shouldn't want to be with Seth because she was older than he was to believing he shouldn't want to be with her because she was so much younger. But the wisdom he must have accrued during those millennia of living... She must seem embarrassingly ignorant by comparison. "I'm just so much younger than you," she said, trying to reconcile it in her mind.

His lips turned up in a wry smile as he squeezed her hand. "*Everyone* is much younger than me." He frowned. "Well, except for David and a few others."

Her jaw dropped. "David is thousands of years old, too?"

"Yes. I probably shouldn't have told you that. That was his secret to share, not mine."

She fought to find order amid the chaos of her thoughts. Seth was thousands of years old and apparently he wasn't the only one.

How many of those he considered his brethren were as well? "So you don't age, can teleport, are telekinetic, telepathic, empathic, precognitive, postcognitive—"

"I'm afraid those last two aren't my strongest talents anymore."

"You can heal any wounds you receive."

"And wounds on others. I can heal with my hands."

She clamped her lips shut.

"What?"

"You can heal with your hands?"

"Yes."

"So if I were injured, you could heal me?"

"Yes."

Leah eyed the bloody pencil on the coffee table.

"Don't you dare," Seth commanded with a scowl. "I won't let you injure yourself so you can watch me prove that particular talent. You'll just have to take my word for it."

She sighed. "I probably wouldn't have had the guts to do it anyway."

His expression lightened with what she thought was affection. Reclaiming her hand, he smoothed his thumb across the back of it. "I'm not so sure. You're still sitting here with me after my revelations. That shows great courage."

She didn't feel very courageous at the moment. More like shocked beyond belief. If she hadn't grown up around Ben, her stepdad, and Gramps, she feared she would have long since bolted for the door. "What else?"

"I'm faster and stronger than ordinary men."

"How fast and how strong?"

When he started to rise, she tightened her fingers around his. "No. You don't have to show me. Just tell me. Your being close is sort of what's keeping me grounded."

Nodding, he relaxed back beside her. "When I run at top speeds, I move so quickly the human eye just sees a faint blur of motion."

Un-befreaking-lievable. "So... you're like the Flash?"

"Yes."

That was actually pretty awesome. She would love to be that fast. She might actually be able to get in a solid eight hours of sleep a night if she were. "How strong are you?"

"Strong enough to lift an eighteen-wheeler over my head as easily as you would that pencil."

She gaped.

"I'm also strong enough to jump from street level to the top of a ten-story building."

"Seriously?"

"Yes."

"If you tell me you can fly, too, I'm going to—"

"I can fly, too."

She stared at him. Long minutes passed.

"Leah?" He shifted, unease creeping into his expression. "Should I not have—?"

She held up a finger to stop him. "First, you are *so* taking me flying once I wrap my mind around all of this."

There was no mistaking the relief that entered his handsome features.

"Second... is that all of it?" she asked. "Is that everything you can do?" Because that was a hell of a lot.

His face creased with sort of a half grimace she thought cute as hell. "Nnnnooo," he admitted reluctantly. "I have other abilities, many of which I rarely use anymore. I thought it best, over the years, to focus on strengthening those that would aid me most in keeping my brethren safe. But there *is* one I've not mentioned yet because I fear it will throw you even more than the others."

"Seriously? More than teleportation, not aging, and being able to fly?"

"Yes. I would be tempted not to mention it at all, but it's one you need to be aware of in order to understand the true extent of the danger my enemy poses." Judging by his expression, he feared it would be the proverbial straw that broke the camel's back.

"What is it?"

He sighed. "I can shape-shift."

Leah blinked and tried very hard not to gape again. That was definitely a doozy. "Like a werewolf?"

"Yes. But it's entirely voluntary and has nothing to do with the moon. I can also shift into the shape of any living creature I wish to, not just that of a wolf, though the smaller the creature, the more difficult the task is. And I'm still me," he hastened to assure her, "when I take an animal's form. I don't start thinking like an animal or anything like that."

She stared at him.

"Leah?"

"Yeah. You're going to have to show me that one."

He released her hand. "Is there any animal in particular you'd like me to change into?"

She shook her head. "Just… something that won't make me pee my pants."

He laughed and seemed surprised that he could do so. "You are so damned appealing." In the next instant, his form shifted, shrank, and sprouted fur.

Leah gawked at the adorable, plump, fuzzy lion cub that now sat on its haunches beside her. *"What?"*

Rising on all fours, it crept toward her. Slowly. Its brown eyes holding hers. Not making any quick movements. One of its big paws came to rest on her knee. When she didn't protest, the cub crawled into her lap and leaned against her chest.

Stunned, Leah wrapped her arms around the soft feline and cuddled it close.

Seth could shape-shift.

The cub began to purr as she stroked its soft fur, low rumbles she could feel like vibrations where it leaned against her. She drew a hand over its head, petting it as it peered up at her with orangish-brown eyes.

"Are you sure you're still in there?" she asked. She'd seen too many movies and read too many books in which shape-shifting men lost their humanity as soon as they changed forms and started behaving like wild animals.

It rested a soft paw on her chest above her collarbone.

Was that a yes? "Do something to prove you're still you when you're in this form."

The cub immediately withdrew its paw, ducked its head, and nuzzled her breasts.

She laughed. "Flirt." Leah hugged the cub to her. "Let me hold you a little longer while I gather my thoughts. It's calming me."

The cub settled more comfortably in her lap and leaned against her, its head pillowed by her breasts. The rumbling purrs continued while she caressed it for several long minutes. She could see why doctors said people with pets tended to live longer. This was definitely soothing her and lowering her blood pressure as she tried to process everything she'd learned.

Seth could shape-shift.

He was right. That *had* thrown her more than anything else. Ben, her dad, and her grandfather might have all been born with special gifts, but those gifts hadn't altered their physical appearance in any way.

She glanced down at the cub. At least Seth was still Seth when he changed forms.

She frowned as she continued to draw her hand down over the cub's silky fur. "Wait. If you're still you when you're an animal, you won't get turned on if I stroke you like this, will you? Because that would hit a little too high on my weird-o-meter."

Damned if the cub didn't make a sound that came close to a chuckle as it ducked out of her hold and backed off her lap. A second later, it grew and shifted back into Seth's form, clothes and all. The only difference she noticed was that his hair was now loose instead of drawn back with a tie.

⇒◈◈◈⇐

As soon as he regained his form, Seth laughed and shook his head. "No, it won't turn me on. Though I confess I did enjoy nuzzling your lovely breasts."

"Flirt," she accused once more with a grin.

"Only with you." As soon as he said it, he clamped his lips shut. Dismay shot through him, accompanied by several curses. "I'm sorry. I didn't mean to say that out loud."

He heard Leah's heartbeat increase. "It's okay." Instead of pressing him about the inadvertent admission, she motioned to his clothing. "What happens to your clothes when you shape-shift?"

"I move them out of the way as I shift."

"I didn't see you do that."

"Because by moving them out of the way, I meant I teleported them into a pile behind the sofa as I became the cub. Then I teleported them back onto my body when I resumed my ordinary form."

Leah motioned to his body with a wry smile. "I have news for you, Seth. This form is far from ordinary."

He grinned. The fact that she still found him attractive was a good thing, right?

"So you can do that?" she asked. "You can send objects to other locations without accompanying them?"

"Yes. I'm far more powerful than my younger brethren who can teleport. They can only teleport themselves and whomever they happen to be touching at the time. I can teleport objects that I'm *not* touching." He shrugged. "I couldn't do it at first but worked over many years to develop and strengthen the talent."

"To help you protect your brethren."

"Yes." It had aided him many times in rapidly cleaning up battle scenes before humans could catch sight of them.

Her brow furrowed. "If your enemy is as dangerous as you say, why don't you just teleport him into a prison cell?"

Sighing, he slumped back against the cushions and dragged a hand through his hair. "I wish it were that simple."

"Why isn't it?"

"Because I have come to believe that he may match me in strength and power."

"He can do all the things you can do?"

"Many of them, yes."

"So he could just teleport out of the cell."

"Yes. But there is more to it than that." How could he explain it? "There are eleven more ancients like myself who—to hide the source of their age and power—call themselves Others. And we've all lived long enough and seen enough to understand that a delicate balance must be maintained in the world at all times."

"What kind of balance?"

"The kind that—when irrevocably altered in the past—resulted in utter devastation."

"And by utter devastation, you mean…?"

"Humanity almost didn't survive it." He shook his head. "The events that unfolded when that balance was shattered were so horrific that they've been edited out of some religious scripture."

"Then how do *you* know about it?"

"I'm afraid I can't tell you that." Regret filled him. He now knew how Zach felt. There were things about his past and his very existence that Zach had been unable to share with Lisette because he couldn't risk one of the other telepaths plucking the information from her thoughts. Seth didn't like having to hold anything back from Leah either. If he was going to share his world with her, he wanted to share it *all* with her. But he couldn't.

Leah's brow furrowed as she bit her lip. "Because you don't trust me?"

Shaking his head, he reclaimed her hand. "Because I don't trust those around you."

"I wouldn't tell anyone."

"I vowed long ago that I would never expose all my secrets again. Doing so always results in bloodshed."

Her fingers tightened around his. "Is that how you lost your wife and children? Did someone learn your secrets?"

It didn't surprise him that she had drawn the correct conclusion. "Yes."

"How long ago was that?"

"Before the Great Pyramids were built."

Her lips parted. "That was thousands of years ago."

"Yes." And the pain of those losses had not diminished over the years.

"Did you remarry?"

He shook his head. "There have been no women in my life since then."

Her throat moved in a swallow. "So you've been alone all this time?"

"I've had my brethren."

"But no lovers?"

"None."

Releasing his hand, she reached up and drew him into a hug.

Surprised, he closed his arms around her.

"I am so sorry for your loss, Seth," she murmured.

"And I'm sorry for yours."

They held each other for several minutes before she released him and sat back against the cushions. "Tell me more about this balance. Help me to understand."

"*Gifted ones* and immortals must keep things on an even keel.

They mustn't ever gain too much power over humanity."

"I can sort of see why. I mean, with as many things as you can do, you alone could conquer the world and force humanity to do your bidding."

"Yes. So — though my brethren and I all possess special gifts — when we battle others, we must do it on their level. When we fight mercenaries, for example, we fight with weapons."

"Instead of using telekinesis to fling them around or teleportation to dump them all in the arctic?"

He smiled. "Exactly. Sometimes our gifts do come into play. If the mortals greatly outnumber us in battle, we feel freer to use whatever gifts we must to even the odds. But we must never skew the odds too much in our favor. Such would disrupt the balance and — "

"Bloodshed would follow."

"It always does."

She pondered that for a long moment.

Seth anxiously awaited her response, worried that she wouldn't be able to accept his need to keep certain secrets from her.

"You're telling me all this so I'll understand how great a threat your enemy poses." She shook her head. "I see what you mean when you say I couldn't hold my own against him in a fight."

"Yes." Withdrawing his hand, he gave hers a pat. "I'll be back in a moment. I have to fetch something from my coat." He sped over to the laundry room where she had hung up his coat. Opening it, he rifled through his inner pockets until he found the items Chris Reordon had given him earlier. He would've just teleported them into his hands, but that actually took more energy than teleporting *himself* would have, most likely because that wasn't how that particular gift was supposed to work. It had taken him quite a while to learn to twist and warp it in such a way.

He sped back to Leah's side.

She yelped at his sudden reappearance, then laughed. "Sorry. I know you said you were fast, but that still startled me."

He shook his head and held out the box. "Forgive me. This is for you."

She took it with a smile and studied it curiously. "This is one of those smartwatches that does everything but your laundry, right?"

He laughed. "Yes. It's also a voice-activated phone with my number programmed into it."

Her smile dimmed somewhat. "So I can call you in an emergency."

"Yes. If you wish to speak with me for any nonemergency reason" — he handed her a second box — "please use the number on *this* phone."

"I already have a phone."

"This one is secure. Yours isn't."

She studied him somberly. "If I have a secure phone, why would I need the watch for emergencies?"

"With the watch, all you have to do is say *Call Seth* and it will dial a number linked only to this phone." He held up the third item he had retrieved — the phone Chris had programmed to receive emergency calls from Leah. "I will keep it on me at all times. No one else has the number. No one else can call it. So the moment it rings, I'll know you're in danger and will teleport instantly to your side."

"You think your enemy will come after me if you keep spending time with me."

"Yes."

"Can you show me a picture of him? If I knew what he looked like, maybe I could keep an eye out for him and — "

"He can shape-shift."

She quieted.

"And he can make himself look like me."

Her throat moved in a hard swallow. "Shit."

"Exactly."

"How will I know he's *not* you?"

"That's what this is for." He gave her his final offering, a tiny device exactly like the ones his Immortal Guardians and their Seconds carried with them. "Keep this on you at all times. And I mean *all* times, even if you have to tape it to your watch to ensure you don't forget it. Whenever I draw near you, it will beep."

"You're near me now and it isn't beeping."

"It only beeps once. Watch." He teleported a mile away, then teleported back. A beep sounded. "If you ever see me and don't hear this beep, say *Call Seth* so I can come to you immediately."

"He can look that much like you?"

"Yes. He fooled one of my brethren into believing he was me not long ago and nearly killed him."

"Crap. What does he look like when he doesn't turn into your twin?"

Rising, Seth shape-shifted into Gershom's form, taking on every aspect of the Other's normal appearance from his bare chest to his huge, dark, semitranslucent wings. He even teleported on a pair of black leather pants.

Leah gaped up at him. "That's what he looks like?"

"Yes."

"You know I want to ask about the wings, right?"

"Yes."

"But if I do, you can't answer me."

"I'm sorry. I would if I could." He shifted back into himself and his usual black T-shirt and cargo pants. "But I can't."

Leah stared down at the electronic devices in her hands. "We're just friends. You really think he poses a danger to me?"

"Yes." More so if Gershom suspected even for a moment that Seth was developing stronger feelings for her. "If you don't wish to see me anymore, Leah, I understand. To reduce the risk to you, I can also ask Ami not to bring Adira to your store anymore. When I first learned of her connection to you, minor though it may be, I worried even *that* would endanger you."

After a moment, she shook her head. "I'm so sorry, Seth."

His heart sank. And the pain that cut through him—actual pain, not disappointment—left him unable to deny he wanted more than friendship with Leah. "It's all right. I understand. I shall leave at once." He rose.

Setting the phone aside, she grabbed his forearm and tugged him back down next to her. "No. I mean I'm so sorry you have to deal with this, that you can't even be friends with someone without worrying it will make them a target because some asshole is out to get you."

He mustered a weak smile. "I am, too." He covered her hand on his arm. "But the danger is very real, Leah. You *must* take it seriously."

"I do. I will." Removing the watch from the box, she strapped it to her wrist. A tiny sticky note clung to the band. Leah typed in the four-digit passcode written upon it, then said, "Call Seth."

Seth's new phone rang.

She nodded. "Okay. Looks like we're set. I have you on verbal speed dial. And I promise I won't use it to con you into bringing me ice cream."

He smiled. Reaching out, he brushed her hair back from her face and tucked it behind her ear.

She caught his hand as he lowered it and twined her fingers through his. "You seem both worried and relieved."

He shook his head. "I'll never forgive myself if you're harmed."

"Well, you'd damned well better," she countered with a frown. "Because it will be your enemy's fault, not yours, Seth. If something happens to me, place the blame where it belongs: on *his* sorry ass, not your hot one."

As usual, she made him smile. "You think my ass is hot?"

"Hell yes," she said without hesitation. "Now, why are you relieved? Did you think I wouldn't want to see you anymore because you're different?"

"Yes," he confessed.

She tilted her head to one side. "I'm good with different."

His smile broadened. "So I noticed."

She winked. "And I want to finish watching *Stranger Things* with you. Are you up for a couple of more episodes?"

He regarded her with surprise. "Tonight?"

"Sure."

"You don't need time alone to think things over?"

"No."

Damn, that was tempting, particularly since he no longer had to worry about revealing his true nature to her. "I can only stay for an episode or two, then I need to get back to work."

"Okay. You pop in the DVD while I get us some snacks."

Seth smiled as she headed into the kitchen. After everything he'd revealed to her, she still wanted to see him.

Rising, he retrieved the *Stranger Things* DVD case... and hoped like hell Leah wouldn't come to regret it.

Chapter Twelve

CRISP AUTUMN LEAVES CRUNCHED BENEATH Seth's boots as he strode through dense forest. Those that still clung to the trees around him bore brilliant gold, orange, and red coloring, though some stubbornly remained green. Branches clacked together as wind weaved its way through them, plucking more leaves from their perches and letting them float to the ground like feathers.

The pink and peach hues of sunset gave way to gray as the sun disappeared over the horizon. The sky began to darken, revealing the moon's bright glow. Night sounds arose, competing for Seth's attention as he walked. Dusk-loving insects buzzed busily, as though they knew their time was limited. Frogs began to croak and peep and twang. Field mice scampered through the detritus, remaining out of sight and out of his path as the wings of predatory birds seeking a meal flapped above him.

Three small, fluffy brown shapes darted across Seth's path— rabbits out foraging for food. He smiled, remembering Leah's delight when he had handed her the arctic hare.

The trees thinned. Leaving the forest, Seth crossed what used to be a paved road. It had not seen regular traffic since the night they had lost Yuri and Stanislav two and a half years ago. It was a little amazing to witness the changes nature could manifest in so little time.

He could spy no concrete. Weeds had staked their claim and completely overgrown the road, urged on by the nutrient-rich sediment a nearby river had deposited there when a hurricane had driven it to overflow its banks. The only hint one could find now that the lush vegetation hid an old thoroughfare was the long, straight stretch of land that bore a uniform width. But saplings had also rooted themselves in the new soil atop the pavement and would swiftly eradicate even that hint. So too would they hide the twisted remains of the chain-link fence that marked the border of the mercenary compound the Immortal Guardians had destroyed, if the kudzu vines didn't accomplish it first.

On the opposite side of the hidden road he traversed, the fence's large gate folded outward in a permanent bow. Seth himself had tossed the grenades that had blown it open. More kudzu vines crept their way up and over it, seeming almost to pull it down closer to the ground. Seth passed between the two gates. Though the place shouted of neglect, he couldn't help but notice that the NO TRESPASSING signs each gate bore remained clean and unobscured. There had been very few incidents of curiosity seekers nosing about since Chris Reordon had purchased the place, but network guards still monitored the compound via hidden surveillance cameras.

Strolling onto the grounds, Seth eyed the remains of the buildings. Not much to see really. Dense vines worked determinedly to hide the scorch marks and jagged holes in the walls and ventured into broken windows to claim new territory.

They were welcome to it. This place bore only painful memories for Seth.

Yet he often felt compelled to visit it when troubled.

His feet carried him to the center of a slab of blackened concrete where an armory had once stood. He wondered absently why nature hadn't hidden *this* as it had so much of the rest. Did Chris Reordon keep the vines at bay?

Such would not surprise him. Since guards monitored the place, Chris must know how often Seth visited. He probably sent a maintenance crew out once a month to cut back weeds and vines and keep it clear enough for Seth to find. Not that Seth needed any help with that. He had lost Yuri and Stanislav on this patch of pavement. He would know it even if ten feet of soil covered it.

Sighing, he closed his eyes. Despite their efforts, the vampire population continued to grow. He had been working his ass off trying to locate Gershom, but that wily bastard continued to elude him. No matter where Seth had taken Ami, she had been unable to sense either Gershom or Tessa, and no vampires knew his whereabouts.

Seth struggled to clear his mind, a task that seemed to grow more difficult by the day. He used to be able to accomplish such in seconds. Now it took many long minutes. Unless he was with Leah. She alone could make him forget for a time the heavy responsibilities he bore, the grief each new loss compounded, the anger and guilt that constantly pecked at him.

No matter how dark his mood, she could make him laugh or smile with just a look.

And heat his blood with the same.

Shaking his head, he focused on Tessa. Though many Immortal Guardians were unaware, there were three things Seth always felt internally: the birth of a *gifted one,* the transformation of a *gifted one* into an immortal, and the death of an immortal. Once a *gifted one* was born, an intangible link formed between that infant and Seth. Should he ever wish to find him or her, he need only focus on that link and trace it back to them. But Gershom had somehow found a way to bury that link, or mute it, or perhaps sever it altogether.

Frustration swam through Seth when he could find no trace of Tessa. He focused on the next missing *gifted one*-turned-immortal and again met with no success. He steadfastly continued, hoping he might at last stumble upon one that Gershom could not conceal as well. Or perhaps one who had escaped Gershom and sought freedom.

Nothing.

He sighed. Opening his eyes, he stared at the scorched pavement where the armory had once stood. Thoughts of Yuri bombarded him. Seth would never forgive himself for that loss. He had been so focused on finding the leaders of the mercenary group during that battle that he had neglected to watch over his immortals as assiduously as he usually did.

Now Yuri's spirit haunted David's home.

But Stanislav's didn't. It was one of the reasons Seth couldn't quite bring himself to believe Stanislav was really gone, that he had died that day mere moments after Yuri. Yuri and Stanislav had been inseparable, as close as brothers. Seth had always stationed them together in the same city or town, knowing they were best friends and staved off each other's loneliness. So it seemed odd to him that Stanislav would've crossed over and abandoned this plane of existence while Yuri remained.

Wouldn't he have at least said goodbye? To Yuri? To his Second, Alexei?

Alexei had been devastated by Stanislav's death. Every human Second was tasked with guarding his immortal's back. Alexei believed he had failed that day. Like Seth, he blamed himself and didn't want to accept that his friend was dead. Alexei even continued to carry his and Stanislav's gear around in his car, though he thought no one knew it.

How would either of them get past this?

A field mouse scurried across one corner of the pavement.

Was Seth's inability to abandon hope making it harder for everyone else to come to grips with the loss? He knew Lisette still wept for Stanislav on occasion. Zach had told him as much... and had known without asking that Seth did, too.

Sighing, Seth rubbed his gritty eyes. He was exhausted and had nothing to show for it. Tessa and the other new immortals were still missing. His Immortal Guardians were getting cut the hell up every night, fighting larger and larger packs of vampires that he was certain Gershom was throwing at them as a diversion.

Seth knew that with everything going on he shouldn't be spending time with Leah, but he couldn't seem to find the strength to stay away from her. He took Adira and Michael on playdates with her and Aaron a couple of afternoons a week and sometimes even took them to storytime. Every once in a while, he teleported directly into her apartment after hours to park his ass on her sofa and watch TV shows or movies with her. Or hang out and chat as they cooked dinner together. Or keep her company while she did inventory. Anything to snag a few minutes or even hours of what he'd been missing for so damned long.

Every day he seemed to crave her company more. Her touch too, though she continued to keep things on a friendship level. Or perhaps he was the one who did? The idea of the latter made him want to kick his own ass, because damn, she made his body burn. But Seth had subverted his own needs for so long that it felt wrong to give in to them now. It felt... selfish. Decadent. And Seth didn't do decadent. Too many lives depended upon him.

Once more he shook his head and told himself to suck it up and mentally search for Stanislav. He'd saved Stan for last because every time he failed to find him, Seth felt the loss anew and hope diminished a little more.

Closing his eyes, he quieted his thoughts and concentrated.

He sucked in a sharp breath. For the first time in two and a half years, he felt something. It was weak... barely there... like the last slender tendril of smoke rising from a candle's extinguished flame. But it was there.

Seth's heart began to pound as he focused harder. He definitely felt something. Greatly muted. Difficult to lock onto. A link to Stanislav's spirit perhaps? Seth still felt a link to Yuri's spirit on occasion. Had Stanislav not crossed over when he'd died?

The link was so faint it took Seth several minutes to trace it to its source, some distance away right here in North Carolina. As soon as he did, he teleported to it.

Bright light blinded him—headlights from an SUV parked haphazardly on a lawn. Another SUV was parked a few yards away, its lights trained on a small frame house to Seth's left. Trees formed dense forest to his right. He heard several heartbeats but could see nothing because the damned high beams blinded him.

Gunshots split the night, both automatic and semiautomatic, some silenced, some not. The strong scent of blood carried to him on the breeze.

What the hell?

"Seth!"

Gasping, he spun around.

His heart stopped as he stared in astonishment.

Stanislav stood several yards away. Not his spirit but *Stanislav*. Alive and riddled with bullet wounds. Blood poured from the younger immortal's mouth and down his chin. Wrapping his arms around an injured woman, he began to limp with her toward the back of the house.

Seth growled.

Stanislav was alive. And these bastards were trying to kill him.

Well, fuck that.

Bullets slammed into Seth's back, fueling his fury.

Thunder split the night like an explosion. Lightning streaked across the sky, its skeletal fingers clawing through rapidly gathering clouds. Seth swung back around and teleported directly into the shooters' midst.

Two men lay on the ground, unconscious and bleeding from gunshot wounds. Two more panicked when he appeared right in front of them. Yelping, they tried to turn their weapons his way. Seth yanked the rifles from their hands and tossed them toward the back of the house. A swift search of their minds confirmed these fuckers had shot both Stanislav and the woman.

Seth palmed two daggers in a blink. Screams erupted as he repaid them wound for wound. When they crumpled to the ground beside their comrades, Seth turned to confront the rest. One fell before he could reach him, taken down by bullets fired by Alexei, who was there too. Seth viciously attacked the villains who remained, inflicting pain and injuries that would incapacitate them but leave them breathing. Though he dearly wanted to kill them all, he needed to find out what the hell was going on and couldn't do that if they died.

Alexei's gun fell silent as he let Seth work.

A minute later, the brief battle ended. Sheathing his bloody daggers, Seth teleported directly to Stanislav's side.

Stanislav stood behind the house, both arms still clutching the injured woman, his face buried in her hair. Barely managing to remain on her feet, the woman jumped at Seth's sudden appearance, then moaned at the agony the sharp movement spawned.

Stanislav lifted his head.

Seth stared at him, almost afraid to believe it.

Stanislav's eyes glowed bright amber. The scent of his and the woman's blood suffused the air. What Seth could see of the younger immortal's shirt was saturated with the ruby liquid and bore numerous holes. The woman's was soaked, too, and bore a ragged hole in the back.

Stanislav's breath wheezed in and out of lungs that had clearly been damaged by a barrage of bullets. But he was alive. Stanislav was alive!

Lightning flashed above them again. Raindrops began to fall with a pitter-patter that swiftly coalesced into a downpour, reflecting the intense emotion that buffeted Seth.

"Stanislav," he whispered hoarsely past the thick lump that lodged itself in his throat. "I thought you were dead." Moisture burned the backs of his eyes as he shook his head. "I reached out to you so many times but couldn't feel you. Not until tonight."

Stanislav nodded. A muscle twitched in his jaw as he clenched his teeth and tightened his hold on the woman. "D-Don't let me drop her," he choked out, blood painting his teeth.

"Of course." Leaping forward, Seth gently took the woman from him and lifted her into his arms.

When the woman cast Stanislav a frantic look, the younger immortal limped forward and brushed a bloody hand over her hair. "It's okay," he wheezed. "I trust him... with my life."

Alexei jogged around the far corner of the house and approached them, his boots splashing in the water that rapidly pooled on the lawn and rolled downhill. Eyelashes spiked by the large drops, he told Stanislav, "All of them are down. Three dead. Six unconscious." Then he smiled up at Seth. "You showed up just in time."

Just in time for what? What the hell was going on? Where had Stanislav been all this time? Why hadn't he reached out to Seth? Who were those men who had been trying to kill the three of them? Were they in any way related to Gershom? Had Gershom held Stanislav captive all this time? Were these men trying to kill him because he had escaped?

The many questions bombarding him would have to wait.

Stanislav wavered on his feet.

Seth glanced at Alexei. "Help him inside."

Alexei looped his rifle strap over his shoulder and quickly moved forward to offer Stanislav support.

Did Alexei's presence here mean he had known all this time that Stanislav was alive?

No. As soon as the thought arose, Seth dismissed it. Alexei had grieved as deeply as Seth over Stanislav's loss. He must've just found out.

Seth turned toward the back of the house. Careful not to jostle the woman in his arms, he carried her up the steps and across a long deck. The body of a man—another of their attackers, he assumed—sprawled on the wood and propped the back door open for him.

Seth strode inside.

"I can't remember the last time I saw you with so many wounds," Alexei told Stanislav outside. "You're off your game."

Stanislav laughed, then grunted in pain. "Yeah. A little bit."

Seth lowered the woman to the sofa. Blood saturated the front of her shirt, pouring from a ragged wound a bullet had carved through her chest, damaging organs. Her coloring was bad. She could barely breathe. And Seth was stunned to realize he recognized her.

Susan Meyer. She was a *gifted one* who had nearly been abducted in California several years earlier. Men had found out she was telepathic and had intended to send her to the same facility in which they had held and tortured Ami for six months. Though Susan didn't know it, Seth and David had thwarted the attackers from whom she had escaped and prevented them from finding her when she had fled to North Carolina. He hadn't seen her in years.

How had she and Stanislav ended up here together with men trying to kill them both?

Seth rested a hand over her wound. Warm healing energy raced through him and into Susan. He stifled a curse as he realized the full extent of the damage. If he had arrived just a few minutes later, she would've died.

His hand began to glow as flesh knitted itself back together and organs healed.

Her breathing grew smoother. The lines of pain in her face receded. A little color returned to her pallid features. But her teeth chattered, both as a result of blood loss and from the rain that had soaked her amid the cool autumn temperatures.

Seth flooded her with warmth. He'd seen a fireplace when he'd entered. Glancing at it, he ignited the carefully stacked logs within it to raise the temperature in the room and make her more comfortable.

Stanislav and Alexei entered.

Seth's hand ceased glowing as he withdrew his touch.

Susan stared at him with wide eyes, then tentatively tucked bloody fingers into the neckline of her shirt and lifted it a few inches. Tilting her chin down, she peered at the flesh that should have borne an ugly bullet wound but now was completely healed. Her lips parted as she released her shirt and looked over at Stanislav. "That's amazing."

Stanislav mustered a smile that was part grimace. "Susan, this is Seth... the eldest and most... powerful amongst us."

Seth's preternatural hearing allowed him to hear the blood rattling in Stanislav's lungs. Rising, he closed the distance between them.

Alexei made sure Stanislav could stand on his own, then stepped back.

Stanislav exhibited no anger as he transferred his smile to Seth. "I'm afraid I'm too... weary to explain it all," he wheezed. "Just... read it in my mind."

Seth gripped Stanislav's shoulder and felt the hard muscle beneath his shirt. *He really is alive.* Overcome with joy, Seth blinked back new tears and pressed his free hand to Stanislav's chest.

Stanislav shivered with cold, a testament to how weak his wounds had left him. All Immortal Guardians could control their body temperature with a thought unless severely wounded.

Energy swept through Seth as he filled Stanislav with soothing warmth, then set about healing the younger immortal's wounds. There were so many of them. Several bullets that hadn't passed through him worked their way out of the holes they'd carved and fell to the floor with a clatter. As Seth wove the ragged flesh back together, he combed through Stanislav's memories.

Pain struck as he witnessed Yuri's decapitation through Stanislav's eyes, felt the devastating grief that had propelled Stanislav toward his friend's body amid the chaotic mercenary battle and had driven him to inadvertently deflect a grenade hurled at him into the armory.

Stanislav hadn't died in the blast, but he had come damned close. Vampire mercenaries had stolen him away in the ensuing chaos and buried him in the basement of one vampire's house. Believing them responsible for Yuri's death, Stanislav had used his empathic gift to warp the vampire's emotions into anger and distrust and tricked them into killing each other. Then he had lost consciousness and slipped into the odd stasis or involuntary state of hibernation that gripped immortals when their blood supply dipped too low.

No wonder Seth hadn't felt him. No wonder he'd lost his connection to him. Stanislav had remained in stasis, buried in that basement, for two and a half years until Susan had bought the house and found him. He had only been awake for a few days.

"You were weakened before the battle even began tonight," Seth pronounced, his voice rough with emotion as he healed the younger immortal's wounds. "You should have called me." The muscles in the shoulder Seth gripped relaxed as Stanislav's breathing grew easy again and the pain dwindled.

Stanislav shook his head. "I didn't remember you until minutes before the attack. I didn't remember *any* of my past."

Seth saw as much in his thoughts. Stanislav had awoken with no memory of who or what he was. He hadn't remembered until this evening after blood infusions and a long healing sleep.

As soon as he finished mending all of Stanislav's wounds, Seth dragged him into a tight hug. Emotion choked him when Stanislav hugged him back. Joy. Grief. Guilt. And half a dozen others.

"We lost Yuri," Seth choked out.

Stanislav nodded and clutched him tighter.

"I thought I'd lost you, too." Shame and self-loathing writhed within Seth as it always did when he thought of that day. "I failed you both."

"No," Stanislav insisted, his voice thick with tears, "you didn't." Loosening his hold, he stepped back.

Seth didn't want to release him but forced himself to let go.

"Why couldn't I remember you?" Stanislav asked with a baffled shake of his head. "Was it brain damage caused by the explosion?"

"No." When his voice once more emerged hoarse, Seth cleared his throat and tried again. "No. It was a consequence of the stasis." He drew a hand down his face, erasing the tears that mingled with the moisture rain had left on his cheeks. "Even *I'm* not clear on how the odd state of hibernation immortals can slip into affects the various portions of the brain. But I have learned over the millennia that the longer an immortal remains in stasis, the more likely he is to forget his past. It all depends on how long he sleeps. Sometimes the memory loss is partial. Sometimes it's total. Or near total, as it was with you."

Stanislav nodded. "I remembered what a *gifted one* was, but not what an immortal was. I remembered how to shield my thoughts from telepaths but couldn't remember any telepaths. And I kept seeing flashes of the battle."

"It has been centuries since an immortal remained in stasis longer than a day or two," Seth told him. "Such has rarely happened since I began assigning you all Seconds to watch over you and keep track of you." It was yet another reason he had begun to do so. It was hard as hell to find an immortal who lay in stasis. Having a human Second who could narrow down his or her immortal's location had aided Seth immensely. "But thus far, the memory loss has never been permanent, even for those who slept longer than you. With more blood infusions, you would've regained your memory faster."

Alexei spoke up. "Is the stasis the reason you couldn't feel him? Couldn't locate him?"

"Yes. Until the immortal heals and regains his memory, he remains off my radar, so to speak. I don't know why." That and death were usually the only two things that would keep him from locating immortals. It was why Gershom's newfound ability to block Seth and keep him from locating the missing immortals puzzled him so. Tessa was proof that Gershom wasn't keeping them locked in stasis, yet Seth still couldn't feel them.

Stanislav moved closer to Susan. Reaching out, he took her hand. In the few days the two had spent together, he clearly had developed deep feelings for her.

When Susan tried to rise, she reeled dizzily and sank back down. Though her wounds were healed, she remained pale. Or paler than usual, based on what he read in Stanislav's thoughts. And Seth could hear her heart beating too quickly.

Stanislav cast him a look of concern. "Is she okay?"

Alexei spoke before Seth could. "She needs a transfusion. You do, too, Stan."

Seth nodded, kicking himself for not having already taken care of it. "Forgive me. We shall see to it now. Do you wish to go to

David's place or to the network?"

Both had state-of-the-art infirmaries and kept blood on hand.

"David's," Stanislav said. He bent over the sofa.

Seth touched his shoulder. "Let me." Having healed him, he knew how weak Stanislav's wounds had left him.

Stanislav stubbornly shook his head. "I'll do it."

Privy to the strong emotion Stanislav bore for Susan, Seth offered no protest.

Stanislav smiled and lifted Susan into his arms. But as he cradled her against his chest, his smile slipped away and his brow furrowed.

A peek into his thoughts revealed regret over the violence he'd introduced to Susan's world. This apparently had not been the first time men had tried to capture him since Susan had found him. His thoughts now ran along the same lines as Seth's did for Leah. Stanislav believed the kindest thing he could do would be to get Susan the medical care she needed, then return her to her life and walk away. But like Seth, he didn't know if he could find the strength to do it.

Susan curled her arms around his neck. "Don't you dare even try," she whispered. "I don't *want* you to do it."

Stanislav closed his eyes and pressed his forehead to Susan's. He swayed dizzily. Eyes flying open, he struggled to right himself as he listed to one side.

Seth and Alexei both clamped hands onto his shoulders to steady him.

"Easy there," Alexei cautioned.

"Let's get you home," Seth murmured and teleported them to the bright, modern infirmary in David's large home.

"Darnell!" he called.

"What just happened?" Susan blurted.

Footsteps sounded in the hallway as Darnell approached.

"Seth teleported us to David's home," Stanislav explained. "David is his second-in-command and—"

"Holy shit," Darnell whispered as he stopped short in the doorway. His eyes widened. "Stanislav?" His brown, cleanly shaven head gleamed in the overhead lights. "We thought you were dead."

"Not quite," Stanislav responded with a smile.

"Darnell," Seth said, drawing his attention, "Stanislav needs blood and Susan needs a transfusion."

"Right. I'll, uh… I'll need her blood type." Shaking off his shock, Darnell crossed to the adjacent storage room and opened the large refrigerator therein.

Alexei guided Stanislav toward one of the beds in the recovery room portion of the infirmary.

Stanislav lowered Susan onto the closest bed. "Do you know your blood type?"

"No. I'm sorry."

Seth drew a phone from his back pocket and dialed Chris's number.

"Reordon," he answered curtly.

"I need to know the blood type of Susan Meyer."

"Susan Meyer?" Chris parroted, surprise entering his voice. "From California?"

"Yes."

"Just a sec."

Darnell returned, carrying several bags of blood he held out to Stanislav.

"Thank you." Stanislav took the bags, then lowered himself to the mattress beside Susan.

Darnell smiled and clapped him gently on the shoulder. "It's good to have you back."

Stanislav offered him a weary smile. "It's good to *be* back."

Chris spoke. "Looks like she's A negative."

"Excellent," Seth replied. "Thank you." Pocketing his phone, he turned to Darnell. "She's A negative."

Susan stared at him. "Do I even want to know how you know that?"

Darnell snorted. "Are you kidding?" He jerked a thumb toward Seth. "This guy knows everything."

"Smart-ass," Seth grumbled as Darnell moved away. But he kept his eyes on Stanislav, still finding it hard to believe he was back.

Out of sight, the front door slammed open.

"Seth!" David called, the word infused with concern.

Stanislav grinned upon hearing it.

David's boots clomped as he strode up the hallway and entered the room, his brow furrowed. "I felt your turmoil and — " Catching sight of Stanislav, he stopped short and gaped. "Stanislav?"

Stanislav nodded. "It's good to see you, David."

An amber glow lit David's eyes as moisture glimmered in them. Racing forward, he swept Stanislav into a tight hug. "We searched for you," he uttered hoarsely. "We feared you hadn't survived but couldn't give up hoping…"

Stanislav clapped him on the back. "I'm sorry. I would've contacted you if I'd remembered you sooner."

David released him and stepped back with a frown.

"He's been in stasis," Seth informed him.

Did Gershom have him? David asked Seth telepathically.

No. Now that he had calmed a bit, Seth reviewed both the thoughts he'd read from the men who attacked Stanislav and the thoughts he'd plucked from Stanislav's mind.

It would seem the vampires who had nabbed Stanislav had hoped to use him to find a cure for the progressive brain damage that afflicted humans infected with the vampiric virus. Their colleagues, on the other hand, had known about Stanislav's immortality and had wanted get their hands on him so they could study him and use him to create a fountain-of-youth serum they could sell to multimillionaires and billionaires.

David was silent for a moment as he combed through Stanislav's memories. "No wonder Seth couldn't feel you." He turned his gaze upon Susan. "I'm David. It's a pleasure to meet you, Susan. Welcome to my home."

She offered him a shy smile. "Thank you. It's a pleasure to meet you, too."

David looked to Seth. "Do the others know?"

"Not yet. We've only been here a minute or two."

Moving to stand beside Seth, David rested a hand on his shoulder. "You were right. We didn't lose him."

Seth nodded, a lump once more lodging itself in his throat. "I'm afraid to take my eyes off him," he admitted as he forced a smile.

David squeezed his shoulder. "Me, too."

They returned their attention to the couple.

"Stop procrastinating and do it," Susan ordered softly.

Stanislav eyed her warily. "Do what?"

She looked pointedly at the bags of blood in his lap.

He hesitated.

Seth didn't blame him. Susan hadn't discovered what exactly Stanislav was or that he needed regular blood infusions until the previous day.

She sighed. "After all the weird things I've witnessed since I met you, do you really think your drinking blood out of a bag is going to scare me away?"

"Maybe."

She rolled her eyes. "You stopped an *SUV* with your *fist*, Stanislav, then threw it over my head like a freaking basketball. *This*" — she pointed to the bags of red liquid — "is nothing."

Seth bit back a laugh. The two had been through a lot during the past few days. And they had weathered it well together.

Until tonight.

He sobered.

David met his gaze, his own eyes dark with regret.

After two and a half years of suffering, Stanislav had only just regained his memory and returned home. Now he and the woman he loved would be dragged into this damned war with Gershom.

David squeezed Seth's shoulder. *We'll keep them safe.*

Seth nodded, hoping like hell he was right. "I think it's time we talk to Roland and Sarah."

Nodding, David gave his shoulder a last pat. "We shall do it tonight after Stanislav and Susan are settled in."

Chapter Thirteen

S ETH CAUGHT ROLAND AND SARAH as they left for the night's hunt. He would've given all the immortals the night off so they could continue to celebrate the return of their brother, but Stanislav and Susan needed rest and vampires were no doubt already trolling for human victims. "Roland. Sarah."

The two looked at him, a question entering their expressions.

"I need a moment of your time."

Sarah smiled. "Okay."

Roland nodded.

Since the two were already holding hands, Seth rested a hand on Roland's shoulder and teleported them away from David's place.

Sarah grinned up at her husband when they arrived at their destination. "I wish I could teleport," she whispered. "We would have so much fun."

Roland's dour expression lightened with a smile. "And would get no work done whilst you talked me into gallivanting around the globe with you."

She laughed. "True."

He glanced around the sparse, circular room. "Where are we?"

Seth moved to stand beside David, who waited for them near the desk. "Nine stories underground in the abandoned missile silo Chris purchased and retrofitted for the network."

Sarah examined the space curiously. "Do any vampires live here?"

"No. Though there are holding cells a few floors above us, none

~ 203 ~

are currently occupied." Any vampires the immortals tranqed who hadn't yet descended into madness were temporarily installed in those cells. Once the drugs wore off, Seth offered them each the opportunity to remain with the Immortal Guardians so network doctors could try to end their compulsion to prey upon humans. But none of the vampires turned at Gershom's direction had yet exhibited any interest in doing the right thing, which compelled *Seth* to do the right thing and kill them before they could harm more innocents.

"So why are we here?" Roland asked. The notoriously antisocial immortal might be gruff with others, but he almost always held Sarah's hand and tenderly stroked it with his thumb as though he couldn't resist touching her.

"You're here," Seth told them, "because we need weapons in our arsenal that Gershom will not expect."

Both stared at him blankly.

David cleared his throat, drawing their attention. "We would like *you*, Roland, to become one of those weapons."

"All right," Roland agreed without hesitation. "What do you have in mind?"

His willingness to aid them didn't surprise Seth. "There is something that only a select few immortals know. David is one. Marcus is another. Aidan knows too, and a couple of other ancient immortals who are imbued with the healing gift."

Roland frowned. "Marcus isn't a healer."

"No," Seth said, "but he was close enough to Alyssa to have divined what I'm about to tell you."

Sarah curled her free hand around Roland's arm and looked up at him. "Who is Alyssa? That name sounds familiar."

"When Marcus was a boy, he served as Lord Robert's squire," Roland reminded her. "Robert was the younger brother of Lord Dillon, Earl of Westcott, who was one of the most powerful men in England at the time. Lord Dillon rather scandalously married his wisewoman, Alyssa."

"Who was a healer and seer," she finished. "Right. I remember now."

"*Gifted ones* and immortals," Seth told them, "who can heal with their hands are different in ways we don't entirely comprehend."

Roland tilted his head to one side. "Because when immortal healers transform *gifted ones,* they end up being as strong as we are instead of weaker, as is the norm?"

"That is one way, yes."

"You heal faster, too," Sarah mentioned. "Even when you were mortal, you healed faster."

Seth nodded. "Healers are naturally imbued with greater regenerative properties. Even Jenna, whose bloodline has been so diluted by ordinary human DNA that she didn't realize she had a gift, healed so quickly as a mortal that she never became ill before her transformation. But those are not the only differences."

Roland frowned. "They aren't?"

"No." Seth strolled toward them. "What I'm about to tell you must remain between us."

"All right," Roland agreed.

"Okay," Sarah seconded.

Seth dipped his head in acknowledgment. "When *gifted ones* or immortals who can heal with a touch are *themselves* healed by another in the same manner, they can acquire new gifts."

Silence fell as the couple shared a look.

Roland shook his head. "You and David have both healed me many times, Seth, and I never acquired new gifts."

"Because we both have found a way to protect you from such when we heal you. What did Marcus tell you about Alyssa the year Lord Dillon fell in love with her?"

Roland shrugged. "Not much really."

"You know she nearly died twice."

"Yes. I accompanied you when you gathered the *gifted ones* in her family together and showed them how to combine their gifts *and* mine to heal her so they would be able to do so when you weren't around."

"Do you remember what happened afterward?"

Roland's brow furrowed as he pondered it. If he didn't remember, Seth wouldn't be surprised. The events had taken place in the twelfth century. Roland had just lost his granddaughter and had been grieving deeply.

Roland's forehead smoothed out as surprise lit his features. "Marcus told me she acquired new gifts."

David nodded. "Because you and the others did not know how to prevent her from siphoning some of your own."

"Siphoning?"

One of David's shoulders lifted and fell. "However you choose to describe it. We believe it is similar to what happens when you heal someone else's wound."

"He takes it into himself," Sarah said.

Roland continued to frown. "My gifts didn't weaken after I healed her. Wouldn't I have noticed if she had taken something from me?"

Seth shook his head. "Not necessarily. I freely admit we don't know how it works, if healers actually siphon the gift or perhaps they absorb something that stimulates dormant DNA that provides them with the new gift. But after you all healed her, Alyssa possessed gifts she did not have before."

"That's amazing," Sarah said.

"What we *do* know," Seth continued, "is that if David and I do not withhold our gifts—for lack of a better way of explaining it— when we heal a fellow healer, that healer will change. And we cannot predict which of our gifts he or she will acquire."

Sarah looked from Seth to David. "Have you done that before? Have you healed without restraining your power or however you want to put it?"

"Yes," Seth answered.

David spoke up. "I was not born with the ability to shape-shift. I acquired it after Seth healed me."

"That is so cool," Sarah said with a smile.

David's returning smile held a wry twist. "It didn't seem so at the time. Seth is very powerful and boasts many more gifts than the rest of you. All of that unrestrained power flowing into you can hurt like hell."

Roland nodded slowly. "Right. I remember that, too, now. Marcus said Alyssa appeared to be very ill after we healed her."

"As was David," Seth admitted, casting his friend a penitent look. "He was so ill I thought he would not survive."

"But I did," David said simply, "and am stronger because of it. I have no regrets."

Seth clapped him on the back. "The same happened when I

healed Aidan the first time," he admitted. "Aidan didn't have telekinetic abilities until then."

"When we realized that only healers were thusly affected," David said, "we quickly learned to harness our gifts while healing others and have done so ever since. Aidan does, too."

Roland frowned. "*I* don't."

Seth arched a brow. "How many healers have you ministered to?" Before he'd met Sarah, Roland had led a very reclusive existence.

Roland thought about it. "Good point. I think Alyssa was the only one."

"You also," David pointed out, "are a great deal younger than we are."

Sarah nodded, her face acquiring a humorously somber expression. "He is. Roland is only nine hundred and fifty years old, give or take a decade. A mere babe in the woods."

Chuckling, Roland pressed a kiss to the top of her head.

Seth smiled. "We, on the other hand, have lived thousands of years, as has Aidan. Because you're so much younger, Roland, you only possess two gifts—healing and telekinesis. And your telekinetic abilities aren't nearly as strong as an ancient's."

"True," Roland conceded. "Apparently they aren't strong enough to pass along, otherwise Jenna would likely have gained that ability."

"Oh," Sarah said. "Right." Her brow furrowed as she looked at Seth and David. "*Did* she acquire that ability?"

"No. We noticed no changes after Roland transformed her."

Roland shared a look with his wife. "Could you be mistaken then in believing healers can gain new abilities?"

Seth shook his head. "I think it more likely that a mere blood exchange does not spark the change. You didn't heal Jenna, Roland. You drained her blood then infused her with your own."

"But," David added, "it has been long enough that I thought we should test our theory and confirm it still held true. So we did."

Roland raised his brows. "And?"

Seth turned to his second-in-command. "Show them."

David offered them a brief bow, then vanished.

Sarah's mouth dropped open as she looked around the room.

"Is he moving so quickly that I can't see him or did he just teleport away?"

David reappeared on the other side of the room with a neatly folded pile of clothing in his hands. Bright white snowflakes now dusted his dreadlocks.

Sarah jumped, startled by his sudden reappearance. "Well, that answers that," she said with a laugh.

Roland's eyes widened. "You can teleport?"

David smiled. "I can now." Until a few months ago, he had lacked that ability.

"Which brings us," Seth said, "to the answer to your question, Roland: why you are here. I would like you to become one of those weapons I mentioned that Gershom will not expect. With your permission—and only if Sarah agrees—I would like to fatally wound you, then heal you without harnessing my gifts."

Sarah blanched.

Roland turned to face her and cupped her face in his hands. "You know I have to do this."

Swallowing hard, she curled her hands around his wrists and clung. "David is a lot older than you. What if that's what enabled him to survive it?"

He brushed his thumbs across her pale cheeks. "Alyssa was born a century after I was, and she survived it."

Sarah shook her head. "She was healed by you and her family, not by Seth." Her hazel eyes clouded with worry as they met Seth's. "Can you guarantee he'll survive?"

"Yes," he replied. "It will be painful, both the wound I will inflict and what he will experience in the days that follow. But he will survive and, at the end of it, be stronger."

"The gifts he already possesses," David said, "will be more powerful. And he will acquire others that he can hone and use in battle as I have."

Sarah stared into her husband's eyes. "I'm scared."

"I know, sweetling. But Gershom seems to be well versed in all of our individual gifts. Our strengths. Our weaknesses. This would be a hell of a surprise to spring on him, one we could use to our advantage."

Face still pale, she nodded. "Okay. I love you."

Roland kissed her. "I love you, too." He turned to Seth. "Shall we do it now?"

"Yes. That's why David has brought you a change of clothing. We'll take you to David's home afterward so he can watch over you as you recover, and we don't want Michael to be frightened by the blood." Seth looked at Sarah. "Roland will be bedridden for a few days. You'll have to cover for him if Marcus and the others ask why he's not around. When you both remain out of sight, they will assume you are either hunting or spending time alone. But when they see you without him multiple times, they'll begin to wonder. He tends to stick pretty closely to you."

Roland wrapped an arm around her. "Just tell them being around so many people all the time was starting to aggravate me, so I'm doing my hermit thing. Since they already think I'm antisocial, they'll accept that readily enough. Even Marcus will, because he routinely asks me how I'm holding up now that we practically live at David's."

She drew in a deep breath and forced a smile. "Okay. I'll tell them you're taking a break from all the family hoopla. And if I have to ask Ami, Marcus, or Sheldon to watch Michael for us, I'll tell them I've tied you to the bed and plan to spend a few hours doing wicked things to you."

Roland laughed. "Either answer will swiftly silence their questions." He pressed another kiss to her lips, then turned to Seth. "All right. Let's do this."

Seth drew a long dagger.

Roland gently eased Sarah away from him.

Dread pooling in his stomach, Seth closed the distance between them. "I'd say this is going to hurt me more than it will you, but..."

"You'd be talking out of your arse," Roland said with a smile. "Just do it and get it over with."

"So be it." Lunging forward, Seth drove the dagger deep into Roland's chest and gave the blade a sharp twist.

Roland grunted, pain tightening his features.

Beside him, Sarah cried out.

David appeared behind her and wrapped an arm around her waist, preventing her from leaping forward.

Roland staggered and braced a hand on Seth's shoulder. His

breathing grew labored as blood painted his teeth. "You call that... a wound?" He wheezed and shook his head. "Give me all you've got... you pansy."

David chuckled.

Seth would have, too, if he hadn't felt Roland's body already hurrying to heal the wound. Even the fact that the blade had pierced his lung and nicked his heart wouldn't prove fatal to an immortal healer Roland's age. Seth would have to inflict more damage.

Steeling himself, he yanked the blade out, drew it across Roland's throat, then buried it in his stomach, severing the abdominal aorta and damaging organs.

Sarah began to weep.

Roland's knees buckled as he gripped his abdomen.

Yanking the dagger out, Seth dropped it and wrapped his arms around Roland. He gently lowered him until the immortal lay on the floor. "Forgive me, my friend."

Roland managed to shake his head, his eyes telling Seth not to worry about it, that he trusted him. And trust did not come easily to Roland.

The British immortal raised a shaking hand and tapped his temple with one bloody finger.

What is it? Seth asked him telepathically.

I can take more damage, just do it quickly for Sarah's sake.

No. This should suffice. Because the virus was rushing to repair the damaged organs and struggling to keep Roland's heart beating, it couldn't stem the flow of blood.

The more I'm wounded, the more healing energy you have to pour into me, right? Roland thought.

Yes.

Then fuck me up some more before you heal me. Just don't let me die.

Lips tightening, Seth retrieved his blade. *As you wish.*

⋖───⊙⊙⊙───⊱

Leah's cell phone rang. Abandoning the box she was cutting open, she glanced at the display. Her heart began to pound as she answered. "Hi, Seth."

"What are you up to tonight?" He had the most delicious voice, so deep and resonant.

"Work, as usual," she admitted with a grimace. "What about you?"

"The same," he said, but there was something in his voice that roused concern.

She leaned back against her desk. "You sound kinda down. Is everything okay?"

"Yes."

"Are you sure? You don't *sound* okay."

A long pause ensued. "It's been an... eventful night. A rather difficult one, frankly. But I'm fine."

No, he wasn't. She could hear it in his voice. "Why don't you take a break and come over for a bit?"

More silence carried over the line.

"Seth?"

"Such would be unwise."

He worried about endangering her and still sometimes avoided coming over after hours. The store was closed for the night. Brittney had already gone home. Anyone watching would know he wasn't there to shop, but...

"Playing hard to get, huh? What if I told you I have my dancing shoes on?"

"Do you?" he asked, a smile entering his voice.

She glanced down at her feet. "Only if scuffed sneakers qualify as dancing shoes."

He laughed.

"I'm wearing my dancing clothes, too."

"And by dancing clothes you mean..."

"Bike shorts and a tank top." She had snuck in a run on the treadmill after Brittney left.

"Damn, that's tempting. You don't play fair, do you?"

"Nope. Never said I would." Picking up a small remote, she aimed it at the iPod connected to the store's speaker system and cycled through the playlists on it until she found the one she wanted. "Bamboleo" began to play. "You hear that?"

"I do."

"My feet are beginning to move."

"Do tell." He was definitely smiling now.

"My hips are moving, too."

"That I'd like to see."

"I could sure use a dance partner right about now."

"Look at your front door."

Surprised, Leah took a few steps back and peered into her shop. The lights inside it fell upon Seth, who stood just inside the front door, his phone pressed to his ear.

She grinned as she approached him. "Hi, handsome."

Smiling, he pocketed the phone. "Hi yourself, beautiful."

Excitement skittered through her as it always did in his presence. "I admit I'm surprised you came." Surprised and pleased. She loved spending time with him. "I thought it would take a little more arm twisting."

"Well… the idea of seeing you dance in bike shorts and a tank top prompted me to haul ass and teleport over here."

She laughed. Holding her arms up, she assumed a playful pose and turned in a slow circle. "Was it worth the rush?"

A golden glow entered his eyes as they skimmed her form. "Hell yes, it was."

"Then take off your coat and dance with me." She couldn't wait to feel his arms around her.

"Yes, ma'am," he responded with a charming grin.

This was what she liked to see: Seth smiling and lighthearted, no more weariness weighing down his words, the burdens he usually bore no longer leaving his face somber.

As soon as he finished hanging up his coat, he started pushing clothing racks aside to clear the floor. Leah followed him as he worked. And when he turned to face her, she held out her hands.

Seth took them, carried them to his lips for a kiss, and began to dance with her.

Yet again, she marveled at how fluidly he moved and how good it felt when he touched her. His big hand on the small of her back urged her closer as they moved to the music. Her pulse quickened as her breasts brushed against his chest. He had not wavered from his intention to remain friends. He never kissed her. He never touched her when they were outside her shop, or hell, even when they were *inside* her shop during business hours unless it was to kiss her hand in greeting or farewell or when Adira coaxed them into holding hands.

But when they danced...

His arm tightened around her, pressing her fully against his hard body as he slipped a thigh between hers. Her body heated when she felt the erection constrained by his cargo pants. His hand slipped lower, those long fingers of his brushing the upper curve of her ass.

When they danced, some of that control he clung to slipped.

He dipped his head, nuzzled her neck for a few heartbeats, then spun her away from him.

This wasn't the first time he had become aroused by her touch, by the sensual roll of her hips against his. But he always spun her away before she tempted him into doing more than just nuzzle her neck.

"Tease!" she accused with a grin, her own body burning.

He laughed, his brown eyes bearing that fascinating golden glow she had come to associate with desire, and twirled her around behind him. Well, two could play that game. Leah pressed her front to his back and wrapped an arm around him. Splaying her fingers on his chest, she slid her hand down his rock-hard abs until it rested just above the waistband of his cargo pants.

He sucked in a sharp breath. "Now who's teasing?" he called over the music.

Smiling, she let him take her hand and step away, then turn to face her. He was so much fun to be around. She really regretted agreeing to keep things platonic. He made her want him, crave him, need him. With a look. With the most innocent of touches. And the less innocent touches their dancing prompted.

But no matter how strongly his body responded to her, he remained determined to keep things casual. And he had so much on his plate right now that she didn't want to add to his troubles by pushing him to change the rules of the game. Rules they had both agreed upon.

The song ended. Drums replaced the brief silence that followed, tapping out a beat that made her feet want to move again. Trumpets began to blare.

Seth smiled. "'Sing, Sing, Sing.' Benny Goodman."

She nodded. She had programmed a new dance playlist for

them. Knowing he would make her body burn with the Latin dances and even some of the pop-rock ones, she had thought it a good idea to add some big band music to put space between them or at least make their dancing less intimate. "Do you know how to swing dance?"

Nodding, he held out a hand. Leah took it and was surprised anew by how well he moved. He danced as though he had spent every spare moment he could find in the forties swing dancing in the jazz clubs.

And perhaps he had, she realized with surprise, still struggling to reconcile his true age with his youthful appearance.

Her heart began to thump even faster, not from his nearness or his touch this time, but from the physical exertion of the dance. She laughed when Seth picked her up and effortlessly slung her around his back, catching her on the other side, never missing a beat. Thanks to the building's old construction and the high ceilings of her shop, he was even able to flip her over his shoulder. He grinned, looking even younger than he usually did.

Leah soon forgot everything except how much fun it was to dance with him. He was so strong. Lifting her and supporting her while she did a backflip over his arm was easy for him. And she loved the way his deep laughter rang out as he swung her around and made her gasp.

She was out of breath by the time the song ended. "Whew! You are *good!*"

He grinned. "So are you. I love dancing with you."

A slow song came on. She was a little worried about how he might react to this one. "Unforgettable," sung by Nat King Cole. It always made her think of Seth now.

Smiling, he took her hand and drew her close, sliding his other arm around her waist. "I love this song."

"I do, too."

"And it will give us a chance to catch our breath."

She nodded. Though her own breath came quickly and perspiration added a shimmer to her skin, Seth seemed fine. He must be in really great cardiovascular shape. "You never told me how you came to be such a good dancer."

"A friend of mine—one of my brethren—loves to dance," he

said as they moved in slow circles. "She became involved with a man who enjoys it, too. They used to dance together every minute they could on weekends. But when she realized he cared for her more than she cared for him — that he was falling in love with her — she broke things off."

Unease blossomed within her. "I take it she didn't love him back?"

"Only as a friend. She didn't think it fair to keep seeing him when she couldn't return his deeper feelings. But he had been her best friend for a long time, and she missed him afterward."

"Even though she was the one who ended it."

He nodded. "I knew her spirits were low. She already had a lot weighing her down as it was. So I started taking her dancing whenever time would allow to cheer her up."

Leah thought it a bad sign when jealousy slithered through her.

Seth's lips turned up in a wry smile. "I never danced with her the way I dance with you though."

That helped. "You didn't?"

"She's more like a baby sister to me. Or another daughter. I never held her as closely as I do you and certainly never danced so..."

"Provocatively?" she suggested.

"Yes."

Leah wasn't one for mincing words, particularly with Seth, so she went ahead and asked what she probably shouldn't. "Is that story true, or was it a cautionary tale told for my benefit?"

His eyebrows rose. "What?"

She shrugged. "We agreed we would keep things on a friendship level. So I thought maybe you were using the story to warn me not to develop deeper feelings for you."

The surprise that lit his handsome features appeared genuine. "No. It's true, Leah. I vow it. You asked me how I came to dance. And I learned to dance in an attempt to lift Lisette's spirits. I didn't like seeing her so unhappy."

"Oh." She wrinkled her nose. "Sorry about that."

He shook his head. "Lisette wanted to keep things casual with Ethan because she knew she couldn't love him the way he loved her. I'm keeping things casual with you because pursuing anything more would endanger you."

Her heart leapt. Did that mean he felt something deeper than desire for her and was just afraid to explore it because of his enemy?

That really sucked.

"And because I know you aren't looking for a relationship," he added.

She wished now she hadn't told him that.

Another slow song replaced "Unforgettable."

"How did *you* learn to dance?" he asked.

She grimaced. "I didn't do so well after the accident. Once I completed my physical therapy, I just sort of stopped taking care of myself."

"Grief can do that to a person."

"It sure as hell did to me," she muttered. "I didn't eat well, at first because I had no appetite and then because cooking for one just depressed me and made the losses harder to bear. I ate a lot of takeout, didn't exercise, and didn't sleep hardly at all. I went into debt opening this business to try to keep myself occupied. It was stressful as hell. But I needed to block out the silence. I just couldn't take it anymore."

He nodded. "That's why I spend so much time with David and the others. The silence was suffocating after my wife and children were slain. I complain about being busy all the time, but..."

"It's what's kept you sane?"

"Yes."

"Yeah. I worked crazy long hours getting my shop going and building my clientele. It all inevitably began to take a toll." She shrugged. "You saw how protective Ben is."

His lips twitched. "I did."

"Well, my whole family grew concerned about my health and made me go for a checkup."

"Judging by your expression, the news wasn't good."

"My blood pressure was frighteningly high. My cholesterol was high, too. I had packed on quite a few pounds." She shook her head. "My doctor pretty much bitch-slapped me with what I could expect if I didn't dig my way out of my grief and start taking better care of myself. It was scary. But my parents' and my brother's reactions were what really shook me up."

"They feared losing you."

"Yes. So I started eating healthier and cut back a little on my work hours so I could get more sleep. I also started exercising daily. When that bored the pants off me, I looked into alternative ways to get some aerobic exercise that might be more fun."

"And settled upon dancing."

She nodded. "Turns out it's a great stress reliever for me."

He gave her hand a squeeze and drew her closer. "For me as well."

They danced in silence for a time.

"So…," she said after a time. "Do you want to talk about it?"

"About what?"

"Your day. When you called, it sounded as though you'd had a tough one."

He nodded. "I did." His lips stretched in a smile. "But it wasn't *all* bad. Do you remember the man I told you about, the one who died in the explosion but whose body we never recovered?"

"Yes."

He flashed her a grin. "Turns out we couldn't recover his body because he wasn't dead. Stanislav is alive, Leah. I found him tonight."

"Oh my gosh!" Joy for him rushed through her. "Is he okay?"

He nodded. "He was badly injured when I found him. It's a long story. But I healed him, and he's at David's house now, resting."

"That's fantastic!" She hugged him tight. "I'm so glad, Seth."

Hugging her back, he rested his cheek on top of her head. "I am, too. I wanted to tell you as soon as I found out. But I still had work to do and…"

That work had been unpleasant, judging by the way he'd sounded when he had called. Surprised that he wasn't pulling away, Leah squeezed him tighter.

"Thank you for dancing with me tonight," he murmured.

She nodded against his chest. "As I said, anytime you want to de-stress, you're welcome to come by, Seth." Perhaps in time she could convince him to seek other, more intimate ways to de-stress with her.

Chapter Fourteen

B ASTIEN WATCHED THE VAMPIRES DO their damnedest to burn out the engines of the specially designed treadmills in the lab on sublevel five of network headquarters. Five of the vamps, those who had surrendered to the Immortal Guardians most recently, razzed each other and cracked frequent jokes. But he knew it was a facade assumed for the benefit of the other two vampires in their midst.

Cliff and Stewart ran side by side, their faces grim, their eyes glowing with the madness that threatened to consume them. Though Stewart had only been infected with the vampiric virus for three and a half years, the progressive brain damage it caused was rapidly eroding his impulse control and filling his head with a need to commit violence. He fought it. Hard. But he had suffered three psychotic breaks in recent months.

Born with empathic abilities, Bastien could feel the young vampire's emotions every time he touched him. Stewart was scared shitless that he wasn't going to make it until Melanie and the other doctors could find either a cure or a way to reverse the brain damage.

Bastien shifted his gaze to Cliff and felt his throat thicken. He loved Cliff like a brother. They had been close friends ever since Bastien had found Cliff shortly after his transformation. Cliff had been amongst the first to join the army of vampires Bastien had amassed to help him destroy the Immortal Guardians. Six years, give or take, had passed since then. And Cliff was the only member of that vampire army who still lived.

That Cliff had managed to suppress and hold off the insanity growing within him for so many years was unheard of. He had waged a truly heroic battle, clinging desperately to his humanity long after others would've succumbed to it or even embraced it wholly. Seth had done what he could for Cliff. David had, too. But brain damage was tricky to heal. And this virus behaved like no other on the planet. Seth could only slow the progression of the brain damage it spawned. He couldn't halt it altogether.

Bastien glanced at his wife. Melanie was furious with herself because she had not yet found a cure. She, too, did what she could for Cliff. As did Aidan. The ancient Celtic immortal had become a good friend since Seth had transferred him to North Carolina two or three years ago. Aidan was a powerful healer and could teleport. Almost every day, he took Cliff into the sunlight, something he had discovered silenced the voices in Cliff's head, and healed the damage the sun inflicted on the young vampire in real time.

Bastien played his part as well, wanting desperately to save his friend. Bastien's dark past had not made his entry into the Immortal Guardians' world an easy one... or a pleasant one. Seth had basically *forced* him to join the ranks. But Bastien had ultimately sucked it up and played nice, both for Melanie's sake—so Reordon wouldn't fire her for associating with him—and for Cliff's sake. Playing nice had enabled Bastien to convince Seth to let him take Cliff vampire hunting with him, which had given his friend a much-needed outlet for his ever-strengthening violent impulses.

He returned his attention to the vampires when Melanie ducked into a supply closet.

No one, however, had helped Cliff more than Emma had. Bastien would love that woman for the rest of her mortal life and would always be grateful to her for bringing happiness into his friend's life. Cliff adored her. Bastien knew Cliff frequently felt guilt and regret over bringing such turmoil into her life. If Emma told Cliff tomorrow that it had become too much, that she couldn't be with him anymore, he knew Cliff would walk away without a backward glance, no matter how much it tore him up inside to do it. But Bastien hoped like hell she wouldn't.

She was the only reason Cliff still lived.

The desperate hope that Melanie and her colleagues would miraculously find a way to cure Cliff and restore his mental faculties so he could spend the rest of his life as an ordinary man with Emma was all that kept Cliff going. That one desperate hope prevented Cliff from either ending it himself or asking Bastien to do it for him.

Pain struck. Cliff wouldn't be the first vampire friend to ask Bastien to kill him. Vince's death would forever haunt Bastien.

"Honey, would you help me with this please?"

Bastien glanced over as Melanie exited the supply closet. Her arms were full of white boxes of medical paraphernalia. Since she was immortal, the weight of them didn't bother her. But the fact that she could barely see over the top of them made carrying them awkward.

Straightening, he closed the distance between them and took the boxes from her. "Where are you taking them?"

"The clinic on sublevel one."

Bastien nodded at the vampires. "We'll be back in a minute."

The younger vamps offered him cheerful salutes. Cliff and Stewart kept running.

Bastien accompanied Melanie down the hallway to the elevators. He nodded to Todd and the other dozen or so guards stationed there.

All nodded back and engaged in light conversation with Melanie.

Bastien had noticed a distinct change in their attitude toward him during past year and a half. The guards who used to hate him for the havoc he had wrought there during his first couple of years with the Immortal Guardians had treated him cordially ever since Gershom had made an appearance at the network. Bastien had sustained quite a bit of damage protecting the guards topside from grenades Gershom had hurled their way, then had gone on to battle the dozens of vampires that had swarmed inside afterward, intent on killing everyone on-site.

Though he doubted they would ever be friends, the guards at least were no longer openly hostile toward him and treated him with respect now.

The elevator ride up to sublevel one was quiet. When Melanie's shoulder brushed his, anxiety flooded him through the light touch, enough to make him suspect this little excursion had nothing to do with carting medical supplies.

Melanie gave nothing away either verbally or visually while they delivered supplies to the lighter-duty clinic. As they walked back to the elevators, however, she suddenly grabbed Bastien's arm and tugged him into the men's restroom.

Two network employees standing at the urinals gaped at her.

"Sorry," she blurted as soon as the door swung shut. Closing her eyes, she hastily gave them her back.

Bastien smiled at them over her head and winked. "Just looking for a bit of privacy. You don't mind, do you, boys?"

The two finished, zipped up, and hurried out of the bathroom without washing their hands, giving Bastien a wide berth as they did so.

The door closed, sealing them inside the soundproof room.

"What is it?" he asked, smoothing his hands up and down Melanie's biceps in a gentle caress. "I can feel your anxiety."

Opening her eyes, she looked up at him. "You need to take Cliff hunting."

He nodded. "I know. He's struggling. We can go as soon as—"

"It's more than that," she said, interrupting him.

When moisture welled in her eyes, dread settled heavily in his stomach. "Has he said something to you?"

"No, but..."

"What?"

A tear spilled over her lashes. "I've been getting that feeling."

Bastien bit back a curse. Melanie had minor precognitive abilities. She didn't see the future unfold in bold, dramatic visions. But he had rapidly come to understand that when she got a bad feeling, something fucked up was about to go down. "Could it be Gershom?"

She shook her head. "I think it's Cliff. Every time I've gone near him tonight, I've gotten this feeling. And I'm worried that... I'm afraid it might mean..." Biting her lip, she shook her head. Another tear trailed down her cheek.

"You think that if he can't bring the voices under control, tonight might be his last?"

She nodded and leaned into him, burying her face in his chest.

Bastien wrapped his arms around her and rested his chin on her head. "We'll take him hunting. See if that will help."

"I can't go with you. I need to stay here and keep working," she said, voice breaking. "And you can't go alone. Seth will be furious."

True. "I'd ask Aidan, but he spent most of the day with Cliff, taking him into the sun. So he could probably use a rest."

She nodded. "I wish he didn't have to take the pain and wounds into himself when he does that. He's really gone above and beyond for Cliff."

He had. Bastien thought Aidan would be as crushed as he and Melanie would be if they couldn't save their friend. "I'd ask Richart, but Jenna would accompany us and…" Richart's wife was such a sweetheart. Bastien was reluctant to let her see just how vicious Cliff could be while hunting.

He was actually reluctant to let *most* of his immortal brethren see how vicious Cliff could be now. He feared some of them might object to Bastien's continuing to take him beyond the secure walls of network headquarters if they did.

"What about Sean?" she suggested. "He's been bouncing from one hunting partner to the next lately."

Bastien nodded. "Good idea. Sean has spent a lot of time here at the network, studying medicine when he isn't hunting. He's also been here more than once when Cliff and Stewart had psychotic breaks and handled it well. Cliff likes him. And since Sean is younger, Cliff doesn't view him as a threat."

She squeezed him tight. "Just be careful."

"I will."

Tilting her head back, she rose onto her toes and pressed a tender kiss his lips. "I love you."

Bastien stole another, longer kiss. "I love you, too."

⊰◈◈◈⊱

Crash!

Leah jerked awake. Her heart slammed against her rib cage as she jackknifed up in bed, unsure what had awakened her.

Whatever it was had been loud. Had a couple of cars collided out front or something?

Her home alarm began to blare.

Oh shit! Fear seized her.

Heavy footsteps thumped on her wood floors as bodies poured through her apartment's back door.

Adrenaline surging through her veins, she rolled out of bed and yanked open the top drawer of the bedside table. Two 9mms with seventeen-round magazines rested inside, along with four spare magazines. She had taken Seth's warning seriously and stocked up.

Palming the weapons, she spun and faced the doorway just as a dark figure filled it. A thin man about her height paused there, his face in shadows. But his eyes glowed bright blue.

"Call Seth!" she yelled belatedly and fired.

Blood spurted from the man's chest. Roaring in fury, he lunged toward her.

Leah ducked as soon as he blurred. Driving her shoulder forward, she hit him in his abdomen and pushed up with all of her strength, then fired at another man who darted through her doorway.

The first man sailed over her shoulder, hitting the wall behind her with a crash. The second man cried out and stumbled backward into two more who tried to breach the room.

"Call Seth! Call Seth!" she yelled again when he didn't miraculously appear.

Her guns continued to spit bullets, striking every man who barreled toward her. In the neck. In the femoral artery. In the abdominal aorta. In the brachial artery. She didn't know why the hell she was targeting those particular areas—she had always been told to aim for the head and chest—but couldn't seem to correct the impulse.

Some of the men's eyes glowed green. Some glowed blue. Some silver. When ambient light from the streetlights outside struck their faces, Leah's fear multiplied.

They all bore what appeared to be very real, very sharp fangs.

Seth's enemies are freaking vampires?

She would've discounted the notion out of hand and assumed these guys belonged to one of those weird vampire-wannabe clubs or some crap, but they moved so fast they blurred whenever they had the space to do so. And they were taking a hell of a lot of damage without going down.

Where the hell was Seth?

"Call Seth!"

The vampire behind her clambered to his feet.

Leah delivered a roundhouse kick to his head and continued to fire at the three in front of her. The vampire behind her grunted and hit the wall again. When another vampire tried to race around the bed to reach her, she spun and caught him in the throat with a push kick, then shot him in the carotid artery when he fell back against her dresser. She resumed firing at the three in front of her as they lunged forward. She would have to change magazines soon and feared that would be it for her. No way would these guys just halt and calmly wait for her to reload.

"Call Seth!" she practically shrieked.

One of the vampires in front of her stumbled backward as blood spurted from his arm and snarled, "Who the hell is she talking to?"

A smaller vampire entered. This one was female. And her eyes glowed amber. "Who cares?" she called over the din. "Just don't kill her."

"Fuck you," he spat out. "She shot me. That bitch is dead."

"Fuck you!" the female retorted irritably. "She's mine. I need her to take down Seth."

Was this Tessa, the missing woman whose mind had been poisoned by Seth's enemy? He hadn't mentioned her being a vampire, but why else would she be gunning for Seth and wanting to use Leah as bait?

Glass shattered, spraying inside the room from the bedroom windows. The men in front of Leah began to jerk and dance backward as blood spurted from holes in their chests.

What the hell? Someone outside was shooting them? Was it Seth? Why didn't he just teleport in and —

Strong arms wrapped around Leah from behind.

For a second she felt relief, thinking Seth had arrived.

But those arms locked *hers* at her sides as an unfamiliar male voice growled, "Gotcha now, bitch."

Fear consuming her once more, Leah bent her wrists to reposition her weapons. As the man behind her ducked his head and placed his lips on her neck, she fired several times.

His legs buckled. Howling in rage and pain, he released her and stumbled backward. His injured legs collapsed, taking him down.

More vampires filled the room. More bullets sailed through the window.

Leah swiftly ejected now-empty mags and replaced them with full ones, advancing the first bullets into the chambers.

Bodies hit the floor. Blood spattered the walls. Bullets zipped past her like bees, but none struck her.

Leah looked frantically around for the woman. "Tessa?" she shouted over the cries of pain that filled the room.

The woman's head whipped around. Her brows drew down in a deep V. "How do you know my name?"

The vampire between Tessa and the window crumpled.

Blood spurted from a wound in Tessa's shoulder as a bullet struck her.

"No! Don't shoot her!" Leah yelled. Scrambling onto the bed between them, she dove forward.

Tessa's eyes widened just before Leah tackled her.

Pain erupted in Leah's shoulder as they hit the floor, hard.

Tessa pushed Leah off her and rolled over onto her knees, staying behind the bed so she wouldn't be in the sights of the shooter or shooters. Everyone else in the room was down, either dead or dying.

At least Leah *thought* they were dying. Did bullets kill vampires?

She didn't know and couldn't see much from where she lay, pain burning through her chest. It grew weirdly hard to breathe.

"Why did you do that?" Tessa demanded, staring down at her.

Reaching toward her, Leah bit back a moan and rested a hand on the younger woman's arm. "Seth has been so worried about you, Tessa." Was her voice weak, or did it just seem like it because her ears were ringing from all the gunshots? "I couldn't let them hurt you." A coppery taste filled her mouth. She must have bitten her damn tongue when she hit the floor. "He's going to be so glad you're okay."

Tessa slowly withdrew from the touch and shook her head. "Seth wants me dead. He—"

"No," Leah interrupted. "He doesn't. He wants to protect you." When she struggled to sit up, pain lanced through her. "Shit!" She lay back down, clenching her teeth. "I think I b-broke a rib or something when I tackled you."

Tessa's hands curled around the daggers she held. Biting her lip, she rubbed those fists up and down the fronts of her thighs. Her glowing amber eyes filled with confusion and indecision. "You didn't break a rib. You've been shot."

"I have?" Leah asked in surprise.

"Yes."

Looking down, Leah saw blood spreading across her T-shirt in a large stain. "Shit."

"Leah?" Seth roared from the living room.

Finally!

"Yeah!" she called back, then clenched her teeth. Damn, that hurt.

What sounded like a sword fight of all things erupted in the living room.

Tessa dropped her daggers and leaned forward. Placing her hands on Leah's chest, she applied pressure to the wound.

Leah nearly passed out as agony burrowed into her.

"Don't lie to me," Tessa urged. "Tell me why you really did it. Were you just trying to keep me here until Seth could arrive and kill me?"

"No." Leah swallowed hard when dizziness made the room tilt and whirl. She covered Tessa's hand with her own. "He j-just wants you safe." She found enough strength to squeeze the woman's hand. "I do, too."

A vampire darted into the room.

More glass burst from the window, glittering like fairy dust as bullets slammed into his chest.

His body hit the floor beside Leah with a thud.

—————◦◦◦◦————

Seth's heart pounded as he swung his katanas. Blood sprayed from a vampire's neck as the vamp stumbled backward and tripped over the body of one of his fallen comrades.

Panic rode Seth hard. That and fury. There must be two dozen damned vampires in Leah's apartment. "Leah!" he bellowed.

"Yeah!" she called back.

He felt only marginal relief when he heard her voice. She sounded shaken. Scared. Because two dozen fucking vampires had attacked her!

But Chris had assured him that members of his special-ops team were keeping the vampires from injuring her.

Even as Seth cut down a couple more vampires, a third raced into the bedroom.

The vampire jerked to a halt just inside the doorway, grunted several times, then sank to the floor. Either Leah or the soldiers Chris had installed across the street must have shot him.

Dropping his swords, Seth drew daggers and flung them at the vampires still standing as he strode toward the bedroom. One blade after another found a home in major arteries with preternatural speed. Thuds sounded as the vampires all crumpled to the floor.

Seth shot forward in a blur.

Several vampires sprawled around Leah's bedroom in various stages of decay.

Leah lay on the floor near the closet.

The figure looming over her leapt back in a blur and rose to face him.

Tessa.

She drew two sais.

Seth's gaze zeroed in on the blood that coated her hands. He looked at Leah, down on the floor with blood staining her chest.

Fury crashed through him. A low rumble sounded as the floor began to vibrate.

Tessa glanced down, then back up at him. Her hands tightened on the hilts of her weapons as fear and anger fused in her glowing amber eyes.

"*You hurt her?*" Seth bellowed.

Tessa tilted her chin up as she faced him with grim determination. "Payback's a bitch, isn't it?"

Seth waved a hand.

Her weapons leapt from her hands and flew out the window.

Somewhere outside a man swore and yelled, "Heads up!"

Tessa's eyes widened, but hatred still glinted in them. Clamping her lips together, she darted forward in a blur.

Seth deflected the blow aimed at him and pressed a hand to her forehead. "Sleep."

She closed her eyes. Her body went limp.

Catching her, he lowered her to the floor, then swung toward Leah.

Blood stained the front of her tank top as well as the pale skin of her chest, neck, and one shoulder. A tear in the fabric revealed a jagged hole in her chest.

"Leah," he whispered. Heart slamming against his ribs, he knelt beside her.

"Y-you okay?" she asked, her breath choppy. Blood painted her straight white teeth.

Unable to speak, he nodded and rested a hand over her wound. Energy and warmth built inside him, racing down his arm and into her wound.

She glanced down at his hand on her breast. "C-cradle robber," she accused with a faint smile.

His breath huffed out in the closest thing he could muster to a laugh.

"If I'd kn-known this was all I had to do to get you to feel me up, I w-would've gotten shot sooner."

He shook his head. As soon as her flesh was healed, he lifted her against his chest and hugged her as tightly as he could without cutting off her breath.

Leah wrapped her arms around him and buried her face in his neck.

Chris's special-ops team entered the apartment through the back door. Seth could hear them moving around in the living room and hallway, checking for survivors and beginning the cleanup. One muttered to Chris over either a cell phone or walkie, offering a verbal report.

Seth didn't join them, nor did he call out to them. Shifting, he sat cross-legged on the floor and settled Leah in his lap, never lessening his hold.

She had nearly died tonight. Because of him.

Long minutes passed.

"Are you sure you're okay?" she asked tentatively, her voice stronger now.

"I'm so sorry," he whispered hoarsely. "This was my fault."

She stroked his back. "No, it wasn't. It was your enemy's."

He shook his head. "I put you in his sights."

"For all you know, I've been in his sights ever since Ami visited my shop for the first time. Stop blaming yourself and focus on the good."

He raised his head and studied her in disbelief. "What good?"

She pressed a palm to his cheek. "We found Tessa."

Renewed anger rose as he glanced at the unconscious woman. "She hurt you." It was something he hadn't even considered. He had worried *Gershom* would hurt Leah. Or perhaps vampires acting on Gershom's behalf would. But he hadn't considered that the missing *immortals* would target her.

"No, she didn't."

Seth shook his head. "Don't protect her. I'll read it in her thoughts. Your blood is on her hands and she was leaning over you when I came in."

"I'm not lying to protect her. It's true. She didn't hurt me. I…" Her features twisted into a grimace. "When I realized who she was, I sort of… threw myself in front of her to keep whoever was outside from shooting her."

Seth stared at her. "You *what?*" he nearly bellowed.

"I was just trying to take her down to the floor and hold her there until you got here," she said hastily, "and accidentally got shot in the process."

Leah couldn't have held Tessa down. The fact that she had even managed to tackle her was astonishing. She must've really caught Tessa off guard.

"Don't ever do that shit again," he ordered.

Leah gave his cheek a little pat. "Help me up."

He would've pushed her to give her word, but could feel her trembling and knew what a shock this had been. The last thing she needed was for him to bitch at her for risking her life when *he* was the one who had put it in danger in the first place.

Rising, he drew her up with him.

Leah glanced around the room, took in the vampires—whose bodies were rapidly shriveling up—then eyed him with disbelief. "Vampires? Seriously? What the hell, Seth?"

Now *he* winced. "I... might have left out a few things when I told you about my enemy."

"Ya *think?*" She peered down at the decaying figures. "Why are they shriveling up like that?"

"They're infected with a virus."

"Viruses don't do that."

"This one does. It's a very rare symbiotic virus that behaves like no other on the planet."

"Sounds like something some dumb ass created in a lab," she said irritably.

"I honestly don't know its origins. But the virus can't live without its host. So the virus is... consuming them, for lack of a better explanation, in an attempt to continue living."

Her expression turned uneasy. "Is this virus contagious?"

"It's not airborne, if that's what worries you. It's blood-borne."

"Of course. Because they're vampires." Turning away, she stepped over two corpses. "Un-befreaking-lievable," she muttered as she grabbed the watch he had given her off the bedside table. The charging cord attached to it fell to the floor as she held it up to her mouth. "Call Seth, damn it!" she shouted at the thing.

Nothing happened.

Seth scowled as he moved closer. "It isn't working?"

"No." She sounded as pissed as he felt. "At least, I don't think it is. Did you get a call from me and just couldn't get here sooner?"

"No." The call he had received had come from Chris's special-ops team across the street, not from Leah.

"Then it doesn't work," she grumbled. "I told it to call you at least half a dozen times."

Seth took the watch and turned it over. "What the hell? I'm going to kick Reordon's ass for this."

A throat cleared.

He looked toward the doorway.

A woman garbed all in black and sporting a vest, helmet, and numerous firearms, leaned in. "Sorry. I couldn't help but overhear, sir." She motioned to the watch. "She has to be wearing it for it to work."

Seth shifted his frown to Leah. "Why aren't you wearing it? I thought I told you to wear it at all times."

"I had to charge it," she replied. When she fastened it to her wrist, the screen lit up. Leah tapped it four times, entering a passcode. "Call Seth."

The emergency phone in Seth's pocket rang.

She sighed. "Figures."

The network soldier spoke once more. "I'll order a second watch from Mr. Reordon when I make my report and have it delivered later today. That way she can wear one while the other is charging and will never be without it again."

"Thank you..." He raised his brows.

"Cynthia McCoy."

"Thank you, Cynthia. I would appreciate that."

Skillet's "Monster" broke the silence. Seth dug his phone out of his pocket and answered it. "What?"

"I'll have a new watch ready for her when you get here," Chris said without preamble.

Seth frowned. *How had he known...?*

Anger began to bubble up inside him once more as he glanced up at the ceiling. "Did you install surveillance cameras in Leah's bedroom?" he nearly roared.

Leah's mouth fell open. *"What?"*

"No," Chris replied calmly. "I got the call that Leah was being attacked the same time you did and have been monitoring things via network soldiers' helmet cams."

Seth glanced at Cynthia. "There's a camera in your helmet?"

Nodding, she touched a small dark circle on the front of it.

"Oh." He returned his attention to Leah, who looked furious, appalled, and dismayed. "There are no cameras in here."

"There damn well had better not be," she retorted, "or I'm going to kick somebody's ass."

If Seth weren't so angry, he would've smiled.

"What are you going to do with Tessa?" Chris asked.

Seth studied the unconscious woman. When he had captured Bastien, he had basically incarcerated him in Seth's castle in England with David, Darnell, and Ami for company.

Ami had been new to their world at the time and recovering from months of torture. Seth had thought the isolation would benefit both her and Bastien. And too, he'd thought Ami's presence would make Bastien feel less like a prisoner, less threatened.

He thought it unwise, however, to allow Tessa near Ami while Tessa still thought him the enemy.

"I know you want her to be comfortable while you help her understand that you're the good guy," Chris said, "but I don't think she should stay at David's."

"Nor do I," Seth admitted. Tessa had attacked Leah with two dozen vampires. As much as he would like to, he just couldn't trust her around his family.

"As soon as you told me Gershom had transformed a dozen of the kidnapped *gifted ones,* I took the liberty of expanding and turning a few of the holding rooms here at network headquarters into studio apartments. Why don't you bring her here? She'll be comfortable, well taken care of, heavily guarded, and the alarm will alert us immediately if Gershom teleports in to steal her away."

Not a bad idea, but... "I think the missile silo would be better." It was more isolated and had fewer employees who might get caught in the crossfire if violence erupted.

"I disagree. She has preternaturally sharp hearing. If we confine her to one of the studio apartments on sublevel five, she'll be able to hear everything that happens in the building and will grow to doubt whatever bullshit Gershom has been feeding her much faster. No one who listens to the many conversations that take place here on a daily basis can deny that we're the good guys, Seth."

"It would put network employees at risk."

"That's my call to make, not yours."

After a moment, Seth nodded. "So be it. Tell Melanie we're on our way. And send a cleanup crew here."

"The crew is already en route."

Of course it was. Pocketing his phone, Seth met Leah's gaze. "Can you call Brittney and have her open the shop for you in the morning?"

Her mouth fell open. "I can't open my store today. Look at this place! It's shot all to hell and there's blood every-freaking-where!"

"The damage — including the back door and broken windows — will be repaired and the blood cleaned up within a couple of hours."

She closed her mouth and looked around the room, doubt written clearly upon her pallid features. "Really?"

"Yes."

"Will it be safe? I mean, I don't want to put Mandy or Brittney in danger."

"Mandy is the one who is always here during storytime?"

"Yes. She works mornings most days."

He shook his head. "Gershom isn't interested in them. He's only interested in you."

"Gershom is the asshat who wants to make you suffer?"

Choked laughter erupted from several of the network soldiers in the hallway.

Seth smiled wryly. "Yes."

"You don't think he'll go after my employees?"

"No."

"Okay then. I'll have Mandy open for me and call Tiana in to help her. Brittney has classes in the morning."

"Grab your phone."

As Leah turned back to the bedside table, Seth moved to stand over Tessa.

She looked so young and innocent. Crouching on his haunches, he slipped one arm under her shoulders and one beneath her knees. When he rose with her in his arms, her head rolled and settled against his chest. One arm dangled loosely over his.

"Is she okay?" Leah asked softly.

He nodded. "I put her to sleep."

"You can do that? With just a touch?"

"A touch and a command, yes. Although it's more of a compulsion than a command."

She tilted her head to one side. "Would you be offended if I asked you to do that to me the next time my insomnia kicks in?"

Surprise flitted through him. "You would trust me to?"

"Yes."

"As you will."

She smiled. "I love the way you talk."

Seth, too, found a smile. "Come closer and wrap your arm around me."

It meant a lot that she complied without asking the whys of it.
He turned to the doorway and found it empty. "Cynthia?"
She poked her head in. "Yes, sir?"
"We're leaving."
"Yes, sir. Don't worry. We have everything under control here."
"Thank you." In the next instant, he teleported to the infirmary at network headquarters.

Chapter Fifteen

B ASTIEN AND MELANIE WERE WAITING for them when Seth, Leah, and Tessa arrived in the infirmary.

Leah swore and weaved a bit on her feet as bright light surrounded them.

Eyes widening, Bastien leapt forward to steady her. "Whoa. You okay?"

Frowning, Seth studied her.

"I'm fine," she said, but one of her hands fisted in the back of Seth's coat as she reached out with the other and gripped Bastien's arm. "Just a little light-headed." She mustered a smile. "Sorry about that."

Seth didn't know if she was apologizing for being light-headed or for having to hang on to Bastien. Because she wasn't releasing him. He shot Melanie a concerned look.

Melanie offered Leah a bright smile and moved forward. "Hi. I'm Dr. Melanie Lipton. This is my husband, Sebastien Newcombe."

"Leah Somerson. Nice to meet you."

Melanie looked up at her husband. "Bastien, honey, why don't you help Seth while I find a place for Leah to lie down and give her a quick exam?"

"I'm fine," Leah protested. "Seth healed me."

"Seth can heal wounds," Melanie responded gently, "but he can't replace the blood you've lost. I can tell by your pallor, your rapid breathing, and the moisture on your skin that you've lost quite a bit. Let's get an IV going so you'll feel better."

Leah glanced around. "Is this a hospital?"

Seth spoke before Melanie could. "It's the infirmary at my business, Leah. Dr. Lipton and the other medical professionals here provide both nonemergency and emergency healthcare to my employees and their families."

"Oh." Leah nodded at Melanie. "Okay. Thank you."

Melanie smiled at Bastien as she took his place in supporting Leah. "I've got her."

Nodding, Bastien pressed a kiss to his wife's forehead. "I'll help Seth get Tessa settled."

"Would you draw some blood for me while you're at it?" Melanie asked. "The kit's over there."

Nodding, he grabbed a tray with a needle, some tubes, and other paraphernalia on it, then preceded Seth through the doorway.

Out in the hallway, Seth looked toward the elevators. A dozen men bearing automatic weapons clustered around a desk, facing him. More guards were spaced in twos on both sides of most of the doors the hallway boasted. At least half a dozen of the doors— those on the opposite side that were closed—led to luxury apartments. The vampires who inhabited them all battled on some level the insanity the virus brewed, residing at network headquarters full-time while Melanie and the other doctors tried to help them. None but Cliff was allowed to venture outside the building. And Cliff only did so under the supervision of Bastien or Aidan.

Since Seth saw no sign of the vamps, he assumed Chris had ordered them to their apartments as soon as he learned Seth would be bringing Leah to the network.

A *ding* broke the silence.

The elevator doors parted.

Chris Reordon exited and strode toward them. "How's Leah?"

Seth appreciated Chris's coming down to check on her personally. "She could use a blood transfusion."

He nodded. "I already sent Dr. Lipton Leah's blood type." His gaze lowered to the unconscious woman Seth held. "How's Tessa?"

"Your special-ops team shot her once, but she's already healing." No condemnation colored Seth's voice. If Chris's team hadn't shot Tessa, she might have killed Leah. "I put her to sleep so she wouldn't fight us while we get her settled."

"Good." Chris continued past Seth and led him to an unmanned door. Facing the electronic keypad beside it, he swiped a card, then typed in a security code. A *thunk* sounded. Gripping the handle, Chris swung the door—as thick and heavy as that on a bank vault—open and stepped inside.

Seth entered behind him and looked around.

The last time he had seen this room, it had been a small, barren holding cell decorated with only a table near the door, a cot against the opposite wall, and heavy titanium chains that ended in manacles. Chris had since expanded it, nearly tripling it in size, and converted it into a very nice studio apartment complete with wood floors, a queen-sized bed, a plush love seat, a small bathroom, and a kitchenette that included a bar with two stools.

"Will this do?" Chris asked.

"Quite well," Seth told him. It hadn't even occurred to him to ask Chris to prepare something nice like this for the missing immortals. "Thank you." The man really did seem to think of everything.

Chris shrugged. "I figured making them feel like criminals in a jail cell wouldn't aid you in swaying them to your side." Crossing to the bed, he drew back the covers.

Seth lowered Tessa to the soft mattress.

Bastien set his supplies on the bedside table. "How much longer will she sleep?"

"As long as I want her to," Seth answered.

Bastien didn't bother to don protective gloves. Immortals were immune to every illness save the virus that infected them. Vampires were, too. He did, however, swab the bend of Tessa's arm when the time came to insert the needle, presumably to ensure the sample wasn't contaminated in any way. "Once Melanie has seen to Leah, she can bathe the blood from Tessa and put her in some clean clothes." His lips turned up slightly as he released the rubber tourniquet on Tessa's arm. "I assume you don't want me to do it."

"You assume correctly," Seth confirmed with a smile. "I'll have her sleep another three or four hours." As soon as Bastien moved out of the way, Seth leaned forward and touched Tessa's forehead, extending the sleep compulsion.

Chris spoke. "If you're good here, I'm going to head back up to my office so I can monitor the cleanup."

"Go ahead," Seth told him.

Chris headed out the door. "Let me know if you need anything." His boots echoed in the hallway as he returned to the elevators.

Seth eyed Bastien. "You're wearing your coat. Did you just return from hunting?" The fabric bore no bloodstains as far as he could tell.

Bastien shook his head. "I'm waiting for Sean. He and I are taking Cliff hunting tonight." He tidied his tray, which now bore three tubes of blood. "Reordon said Tessa and a couple dozen vampires attacked Leah. Was it random or did Gershom target her?"

"Gershom targeted her."

The immortal black sheep frowned. "Why? Is she a network employee? Or maybe a *gifted one* he hoped to add to his collection?"

"Neither." Seth hesitated. "She's a friend of mine."

Bastien sent him a sharp look.

"And of Ami's," he added, hoping it would stave off further questions.

It didn't.

"Is she *the* friend?" Bastien asked, curiosity entering his brown eyes. "The one who came calling at David's place?"

Seth almost groaned. "Yes." He couldn't help the irritation that entered his voice. "Is everyone talking about it?"

Bastien's lips twitched. "Only the immortals stationed here in North Carolina."

"All of them?"

"Yes."

Seth did groan then. "It would've been nice if those who were present when she arrived had kept that information to themselves."

Bastien laughed. "They tried to. But there are a lot of telepaths here. And you know how nosy they can be. They were bound to find it in *somebody's* thoughts... and did." He picked up the tray.

"We're just friends," Seth said softly so his voice wouldn't carry to Leah and the human guards as he followed Bastien to the open door.

The younger immortal stopped and lowered his voice as well. "Melanie and I started out as friends, too. For what it's worth, I hope whatever you have with her will deepen into love, Seth. It's time you found some happiness of your own."

"Such would put her in danger."

"And friendship hasn't?" Bastien clapped him on the back. "There's never a *good* time for one of our ilk. That doesn't mean it isn't time. I fought my feelings for Melanie for as long as I could. You know how much the rest of the Immortal Guardians hated my ass. I worried that would spill over onto her or, at the very least, that being with me would end her career. Hell, it nearly ended her life. But... look how things turned out."

Seth smiled. "They turned out very well for you."

"They can turn out well for you, too. I know — more than anyone save David — the burden you carry. I know the toll being a leader takes, how much you give of yourself, how much you sacrifice."

There had been over a hundred vampires in the army Bastien had raised. He had tried to save every one of them, yet only Cliff remained. Seth knew that ate at him.

Bastien continued, "Find what happiness you can. The rest of us will help you guard and protect her. And together we'll defeat Gershom's sorry ass while we do it."

Seth shook his head and ceased whispering. "Melanie has been a good influence on you."

Bastien frowned. "Ah hell. I'm doing it again, aren't I?"

"Doing what?"

"Being nice."

"Yes."

Bastien raised his voice, though he didn't need to. "See what you've done to me, woman?"

"I'll do a lot more to you," she retorted, a smile in her voice, "if you'll bring your gorgeous ass back in here."

Bastien grinned. "Damn, I love her."

As soon as Leah felt better, Seth teleported her to his bedroom in

David's home.

"Teleporting is awesome!" she exclaimed with a big grin. "And I didn't get dizzy this time. Not as much, anyway. Can you teleport anywhere in the world?"

"Just about."

"When all the hubbub dies down, will you teleport me to the Great Pyramids of Giza? I've always wanted to go there but couldn't afford to."

"Absolutely," he promised with a smile. He was so damned relieved to see her looking hale and hearty again.

Grinning, she wrapped her arms around him and gave him an exuberant hug. "Thank you!"

Seth hugged her back, relishing her nearness after he had come so close to losing her.

"Where are we?" Her face lit with curiosity as she stepped away. "What is this place?" Turning, she began to meander around the room.

An enormous bed, specially designed to accommodate his height, dominated one side of the room. A long sofa, ottoman, and flat-screen television resided on the other. Though Seth normally had little to no downtime, David had insisted he have a nice bedroom suite in which to enjoy some solitude whenever he could. Two doors adorned the wall beyond the bed. One led to a closet full of standard black hunting togs with a few pairs of jeans and a suit thrown in. (He'd had to add the latter when immortals in the area began to marry.) The other door led to a large bathroom.

"This is beautiful." Leah set her phone down on the ottoman. "It's like one of those fancy hotel rooms I've seen on TV that costs thousands of dollars per night."

He smiled. "It's the room I stay in when I visit David's home."

She cast him a speculative look. "This is *your* room?"

He nodded. "It's the safest place I could think of to bring you."

Her gaze skipped to the bed. "And that's your bed?"

"Yes."

"It's a big bed."

"Yes, it is."

She tilted her head to one side. "Will you be staying here with me?"

He slid his hands into his pockets. "Would you like me to?" He held his breath, awaiting her answer.

Her pretty face sobered. "Yes. I'm trying not to show it because this all seems pretty par for the course for you, but tonight scared the hell out of me, Seth."

Regret and self-recrimination battered him. "I'm so sor—"

She held up a hand. "Don't apologize again. None of this is your fault. It really isn't." With slow steps, she moved to stand before him. "I know I teased you earlier about trying to rob the cradle and cop a feel. I don't want you to think I'm trying to use this as an excuse to pressure you into a more serious relationship. That's not what I'm asking for right now. I'm just... shaken. I don't want to be alone. And I can't think of anyone I would rather have hold my hand tonight while I try to pull myself back together. Okay?"

Reaching out, he twined his fingers through hers. "Okay."

"I'll take the sofa..." She grinned as she motioned to it. "Because holy crap, that's a huge sofa! It's like a freaking queen-sized bed."

He laughed. "I have long legs."

"I do, too, so I'm going to love it."

"I would rather you take the bed while I take the sofa."

"That's not necessary, Seth. I don't think I'm going to be able to sleep tonight anyway, so I'll probably just sit and watch TV until the sun rises." She glanced down. "Can I use your shower first though? I'm all bloody and gross."

"Of course." Still holding her hand, he led her into the bathroom and flipped on the light.

"Wow. You guys are loaded, aren't you?" she asked as she looked around.

Again he laughed. "We're very comfortable financially, yes."

"Seriously, I could *swim* in that tub," she said, admiring it. "I mean, I could lie down in the bottom of it, reach my arms above my head, and would barely be able to touch both ends."

He shrugged. "David wanted to ensure I could stretch out in it comfortably."

She turned her attention to the shower. "Ooh! Look how high the showerhead is. Awesome! I won't have to duck down to rinse the shampoo out of my hair like I do in mine. Someone really short must have lived there before me."

He grinned, loving how much *she* was loving his bathroom.

"And look." Opening the shower door, she drew him in after her. The glass walls that enclosed them left plenty of elbow room. "It's big enough for two," she said with a wink.

He shook his head as his damned body responded to the image of the two of them naked in the shower. "Don't tempt me."

She wrinkled her nose. "Sorry. I said I wasn't going to do that, didn't I? Something about you just really brings out the flirt in me." She led him out of the shower.

"Just me?" he couldn't resist asking. Imagining her flirting with other men brought on an acidic surge of jealousy.

"Just you," she confirmed, then leaned closer to whisper, "which is why I'm filing away the big-enough-for-two shower-and-tub thing for future reference."

He laughed. Giving her hand a squeeze, he released it and crossed to a cabinet. "Here are some fresh towels." He took two down, one for her lovely body and one for her hair. "Soap, shampoo, and conditioner are already in the shower. There's more by the bath if you would rather have a nice long soak."

"Any chance I could talk you into keeping me company for that soak?" she asked with a smile, then frowned. "Damn it. I did it again. Sorry. Forget I asked that. I'm just... out of sorts and really don't want to be alone."

Seth hesitated. If he stayed while she bathed, there was no way in hell he'd be able to keep his hands off her.

"I'll just take a quick shower." She bit her lip. "There *is* one problem though. I didn't bring any clothes with me."

Seth partially closed the bathroom door, allowing her to see the long garment that hung on the back of it. "You can borrow my robe. If you like, I can call Chris and have one of the women on his crew collect some of your clothing and deliver it when they're finished."

"That would be great. Maybe he could ask Cynthia to do it? She seemed nice."

"I'll see to it now."

"Thank you. Now hurry up and leave before I blurt out another flirty response."

Chuckling, he headed into the bedroom and closed the door.

Much like the network, every bathroom in David's home was

soundproofed, so he couldn't hear Leah's movements within.

Well, since he was so old and powerful, he could if he really strained to hear her. But Seth didn't think that wise considering how much he wanted to get naked and join her. He was having a hard time quelling the desire that pumped through him at just the thought of her taking her clothes off.

A quick call to Reordon ensured Cynthia would pack a bag for Leah and deliver it in the morning. Seth felt a moment's guilt. David always kept a substantial wardrobe on hand for both males and females in a variety of sizes for any immortals or Seconds who dropped by and wanted to change out of bloody clothing. There was bound to be something that would fit Leah, but...

He wanted to see her in his robe. It was the closest he could get to doing what he really wanted to do: wrap himself around her and never let her go. He was feeling very protective. Very possessive. Leah was *his*. He'd nearly lost her tonight. And he didn't want to leave this room.

But he would have to eventually. Duty always called.

He frowned, surprised that duty hadn't already done so.

Reaching into his pocket, he drew out his cell phone and stared at it intently. *David*, he called telepathically.

Yes?

Why isn't my phone ringing?

I told Darnell to redirect your calls to Zach and Jared. How is Leah?

He glanced at the bathroom door. *I healed her wounds and Melanie gave her a transfusion. She's shaken up but handling it well.*

She's strong.

Yes, she is.

Seconds passed. *What troubles you?* David knew him better than anyone.

Seth hesitated, aware of how much his next words would reveal. *I don't want to leave her.*

Then stay with her, David replied, unruffled. *Zach, Jared, and I can field your calls.*

Seth stared down at his toes, unaccustomed to shirking his duties.

Open your door.

Crossing to the door, he opened it.

David stood outside. In his arms, he held three large bags of chips and several bottles of tea and club soda. *Here.*

Surprised, Seth tucked his phone away and took the goodies. *Where did you get these?*

David's lips twitched. *Sheldon walked by, carrying them. He and Tracy are enjoying a movie night while they keep tabs on Richart, Jenna, and Lisette.*

Did he object to your confiscating his snacks?

No. That boy is always offering others food.

Seth smiled. *He's a good kid. He didn't even ask who they were for, did he?*

*No. Now stop worrying. And stop feeling guilty. It's time you had something — and some*one — *of your own Seth.*

That meant a great deal coming from David... and damned near precisely parroted Bastien's and Chris's words. *Thank you. Do the others know Leah is here?*

No. They know you *are because the devices they carry beeped, but they think you're alone.*

Thank you again.

Nodding, David reached in and pulled the door closed for him.

Seth set everything down on the sofa, then shrugged out of his coat and hung it up. He had just finished arranging the chips and drinks on the ottoman when the bathroom door opened.

Steam poured out, preceding Leah.

As soon as she stepped into the bedroom, Seth's breath caught.

Her brown hair looked black when wet and was slicked back from her beautiful face. Her pale skin still bore a glimmer of moisture from the steam and provided stark contrast to the black robe she wore. *His* robe, which swallowed her, the sleeves falling past her fingertips, the hem dragging on the floor.

His gaze fell to her long legs. Because the robe trailed behind her, it parted above the knees every time she took a step. Leah had worn pants every time he had seen her with one exception—the time he'd called after fatally wounding Roland and she'd invited him over to dance. Those long, lovely legs of hers had been bare then too, her tempting ass covered by tight bike shorts.

Well, nothing covered her ass now underneath that robe. Knowing she was bare beneath it made his pulse pound and his body harden. His hands curled into fists as she approached. He didn't realize until she stood right in front of him—close enough to touch, close enough to feel her warmth—that she had been speaking to him.

He raised his gaze from the cleavage he desperately wanted to bury his lips in and met her gaze. "I'm sorry. Could you repeat that?"

Smiling, she reached up and pressed a palm to his cheek. "Your eyes are glowing."

Damn it. Of course they were. He hadn't had so much difficulty suppressing that particular trait in millennia.

She gave the stubble on his jaw a little pat. "Go shower. Then we'll watch a movie together. How does that sound?"

The only thing that would sound better would be her joining him in the shower. "I'll be quick," he promised. And the shower would be a very cold one. Striding over to the closet, he drew out clean clothes, then headed into the bathroom and closed the door.

An hour later, Leah munched another chip as she watched a couple on-screen race madly away from men with guns who were intent on killing them. She and Seth sat shoulder to shoulder on the sofa, both slumped down until they were practically lying on their backs. Seth had pulled the matching ottoman up against the sofa, so it really did feel as if they were lying in bed together, watching a movie.

She slid him a covert glance.

He had donned black cargo pants and a black T-shirt after his shower but had left his big feet bare. He had also left his hair loose. It now spilled over the back of the sofa in a glossy curtain, the thick wavy tresses still drying.

He chuckled at something the male protagonist said.

Leah smiled. She loved seeing him laugh. She didn't think he did so as often as he should.

Every once in a while, she noticed his gaze would slide to her legs. Her feet were propped on the ottoman close to his. The robe she had borrowed had parted just above her knees and fallen back, leaving most of her legs bare. And that pale flesh repeatedly drew

Seth's attention.

She held the bag of chips out to him.

Smiling, unaware that the faint golden light of desire illuminated his eyes, he poked his hand in and drew out a couple of chips.

She smiled back, then returned her attention to the screen.

The protagonists had at last made it to safety. They checked each other over for wounds, something both had miraculously escaped incurring in true Hollywood fashion. Then they fell into each other's arms, finally giving in to the lust that had sparked between them ever since their first contentious meeting.

Leah sighed as she watched them peel each other's clothes off with eager hands. It made her want to do the same with Seth. Her body even began to respond as her imagination kicked in. "I miss sex." The words were out of her mouth before she could question the wisdom of speaking them.

"I do, too," Seth confessed.

She glanced over at him and found his eyes glued to the screen. *More so since I met you.*

Her eyes widened when his voice sounded in her head. "Really?"

"Yes." The actors on-screen fell naked onto the bed and began to simulate sex, their moans and groans and cries of passion filling the room. "It's natural to miss it," he said matter-of-factly. "Nothing to feel guilty about."

"No. I mean, you really miss it more since you met me?"

He froze. A look of dismay crossed his features as he cut her a glance. "I said that out loud?"

"No. I heard it in my head."

Shit.

She grinned. "I heard that, too."

Fuck.

She laughed. "Stop cursing."

He grimaced. "Forgive me. It's just... I seem to be inadvertently letting my guard down more and more around you."

"I like it when you let your guard down around me." Her words appeared to do little to alleviate his concern though. "Is that so unusual? Don't you let your guard down around your brethren?"

He shook his head. "I have always spoken freely with David. Ami too, sometimes. But I've never broadcast my thoughts to either of them without meaning to. I haven't done that since —" He broke off, seeming disinclined to continue.

"Since your wife?" she asked gently.

He nodded.

That was telling.

He watched her uncertainly.

Did he worry she would freak out over his mentioning the wife he'd lost?

He hadn't freaked out when she had mentioned the husband *she'd* lost.

"Whatever thoughts you send my way I won't betray," she promised.

Thank you.

She grinned when his baritone voice once more filled in her head. "That is so cool. You aren't reading my thoughts, are you?"

"No."

"Good."

His lips curled up in a slow smile. "Why? What would I find if I did? What are you thinking?"

She swallowed. Did she dare tell him? "This may sound weird, but hearing your voice in my head totally turns me on." Beneath the robe, her nipples had hardened. Other parts of her tingled. Her pulse raced. "And I'm sort of fixating on the fact that you've been missing sex more since you met me. Because I've been missing sex a *lot* more since I met you."

The golden light in his eyes grew brighter as a low rumbling sound filled her head. Seeming almost to vibrate through her, it set her body aflame.

"Oh shit," she whispered. "That's so hot."

"What is?" he murmured.

"You just made this sort of low, growly sound in my head." And it had affected her as much as stroking all of her erogenous zones at once would have.

"I didn't mean to."

"That just makes it even hotter." Grabbing the remote, Leah aimed it at the television long enough to pause the movie, then tossed it onto the ottoman. She hoped she wasn't about to totally blow their friendship but couldn't prevent herself from sitting up and turning to face him. "Seth, I like being friends with you."

"I do, too." His gaze fell to her lap when the robe parted more at her movement.

"I'm also very attracted to you."

His eyes rose and met hers.

"The only reason I haven't acted on that was because I thought I was a lot older than you and—"

"You aren't older than me."

"I know that now. Does the fact that you're a lot older than me bother you?"

"No."

Taking a chance, she rose to her knees and slung a leg over his.

He sucked in a breath and gripped her hips as she settled herself on his lap.

"Then what the hell are we doing?" she asked softly. "What are we waiting for? I want you. You want me." She glanced down at the erection his pants did little to conceal and scooted forward to rub against him. When pleasure shot through her, she released a shaky breath. "Let's take a chance. Let's take this to the next level."

His hands slid around to grip her ass and press her more firmly against him. "Take care, Leah," he whispered. "I don't think I can resist you tonight." *I came too close to losing you.*

Her heart melted at the involuntary words he spoke in her head. "Then don't. I know you aren't looking for a relationship, but—"

"I only said that because I was trying to protect you. I thought if I kept things casual between us, it would keep you safe."

"But it didn't. Tonight made that clear. Was that the only thing holding you back—a desire to protect me?" She held her breath, hoping he wouldn't say he still mourned his wife too much to pursue anything romantic with her.

"Yes," he admitted hoarsely. "That was it."

"Good. Because I've been wanting to do this for a very long time." Leaning forward, she cupped his face in her hands and pressed her lips to his.

Leah wasn't sure what she had expected. Another protest? Another warning? A reluctant capitulation? A first tentative kiss?

All of the above?

Instead, Seth shocked the hell out of her by clasping the back of her head in one strong hand and holding her to him while he opened his lips beneath hers and slid his tongue inside to stroke her own. Her breath caught as he devoured her, kissing her as though they had just spent the past hour grinding on each other while they danced.

Holy shit, he could kiss! Her whole body went up in flames and began to pulse with need.

He reached between them with his free hand and tugged at the robe's sash. As soon as it loosened, he parted the soft material and pushed the thick robe off her shoulders.

Leah felt a moment's qualm and drew back. Unease took the edge off her desire. The accident that had cost her so much had also left her scarred. Seth, on the other hand, was perfect in every way. She didn't like feeling self-conscious about her flaws but couldn't help it.

Seth's eyes, however, weren't on the scars that marred her abdomen. They were on her breasts. Leaning forward, he drew a taut nipple into his mouth and sucked hard.

Her head fell back as heat seared her, melting away uncertainty. "Yes." Spearing her fingers into his thick hair, she urged him closer.

He growled and nipped the sensitive bud.

Leah moaned, wishing he were as naked as she was.

One big hand palmed her other breast, kneading and teasing and tweaking her nipple. He slid his other hand down her bare back, over her ass, and squeezed, urging her to rock against him. She did so eagerly, already close to coming.

"Seth," she breathed.

Those long fingers of his continued down and slipped beneath her to find her entrance. "You're so wet for me," he murmured against her breast.

"Yes."

He slipped a long finger inside her. "So tight."

She moaned. "Yes." Every time she rocked her hips forward, her clit slid against his hard cock, still constrained by his pants. Every time she rocked backward, his finger thrust deeper. His lips and teeth and tongue continued to tease and torment her breast. His growls of pleasure rolled through her like thunder.

He slid another finger inside her, stretching her and stroking her. Her breath came in gasps as the pleasure built and built until an orgasm crashed through her. So good. The ripples of ecstasy went on and on until she collapsed against him, her heart slamming against her ribs.

Chapter Sixteen

SETH BURIED HIS FACE IN Leah's hair as need rapidly eroded what little remained of his self-control. She felt so good against him, her body tight and wet and warm around his fingers, squeezing him with every rhythmic pulse of her climax.

He desperately wanted to unfasten his pants, free his erection, and plunge inside her. Every muscle was tight and tense as he eased his fingers from her warm passage and cradled her close. His breath came nearly as quickly as hers. His heart pounded in his chest.

Leah straightened in his arms. When her eyes met his, he could see the brilliant glow of his own reflected in them. Reaching down between them, she began to tug at the hem of his shirt.

"Take it off," she demanded.

Hell yes. He wanted to feel her bare breasts against his chest.

She smiled. "I heard that."

Seth shook his head. "You rob me of all control, Leah."

"Good." She dragged the soft T-shirt over his head and took a minute to untangle his long hair from it. "Now the pants," she said as she slid a hand down his stomach and began to stroke his shaft through the thick cotton material. Leaning forward, she kissed him. "I want more." She teased his lower lip with her teeth. "I want you inside me."

Swearing, he drew her into his arms, stood, and strode to the bed, barely stopping himself from using preternatural speed. He telepathically sent the covers hurtling backward, most falling to the floor. As soon as he lowered Leah to the sheets, Seth reached for the button on his pants.

Leah scooted over to the center of the big bed and rested her hands on her lightly muscled abs as she watched him with hungry eyes. She was so damned beautiful and had felt so good coming apart in his arms as her inner muscles had clenched around his fingers.

Seth ditched his pants.

Her eyes widened.

"Don't say it," he warned as he knelt on the edge of the bed.

"Don't say what?" she asked, still staring at the hard length that strained toward her.

Grasping her delicate ankles, he eased her legs apart. "Big hands, big feet..."

Her lips twitched as she met his gaze. "Fine. I'll just think it." Her heartbeat picked up, matching his as he moved forward. "Lucky me. Come here, handsome." Bending her knees, she planted her feet on either side of his hips.

Seth stretched out above her, letting her take some of his weight. She sucked in a breath when he slid his cock against her clit.

Supporting his upper body on his elbows, Seth dipped his head and nuzzled her neck. He loved her scent. Would never get enough of it.

Leah wound her arms around him and slid her hands across his back.

Palming one of her full breasts, he drew a thumb across the tight peak as he rubbed his hard cock against her clit again. Her skin was soft as silk, her body wonderfully responsive.

Moaning, she caressed a path down to his ass and arched up against him. "I mean it. I want you inside me, Seth. Please."

He wanted to do more. He wanted to taste her first. Everywhere. To use his lips, teeth, and tongue to drive her to another orgasm. He wanted to draw out their first time together and make it perfect. But his whole body shook with need after thousands of years of celibacy and restraint.

Reaching between them, he positioned his cock at her entrance. "Look at me," he murmured.

Her eyes met his, glinting with desire.

He pressed forward, entering her damp heat.

She bit her lip, pleasure flushing her cheeks.

He groaned, muscles tense. She was so tight. So hot.

Seth withdrew, then thrust deeper, stretching her a little more. Withdrew, then thrust deeper, withdrew, then thrust deeper, giving her body time to adjust until he was finally buried to the hilt.

Both moaned as he ground against her.

Her fingernails dug into his ass. "You feel so good," she whispered. Then she circled her hips and squeezed her inner muscles around him.

Seth swore. Withdrawing all the way to the crown, he plunged inside her again.

"Yes," she moaned. "Harder. Don't hold back."

He couldn't, not anymore, not with her body squeezing him tight, not with her hands stroking him and her legs wrapping around him, urging him on as she stared up at him, her face flushed with passion. Propping his weight on his hands, he drove inside her with deep, powerful strokes, making sure he hit all the right places to enhance her pleasure.

"More," she moaned as her hands on his ass urged him on.

"Leah," he whispered. He needed her so much his body shook with it. Or maybe it was the bed rocking from his thrusts and slamming into the wall. Or the ground itself. Seth didn't know and didn't care. He was too busy losing himself in her beautiful body as Leah arched up to meet him thrust for thrust, tantalizing cries escaping her, passion rising, muscles tightening until an orgasm crashed through them both, the pleasure so sharp it stole Seth's breath, going on and on until both collapsed.

Rolling onto his back, he brought Leah with him and settled her atop him—their bodies still joined. His heart raced as madly as hers. Little ripples of lingering pleasure continued to tease him as her tight sheath delivered light squeezes in the aftermath of her orgasm.

"Wow," Leah exclaimed breathlessly as her body went limp atop his. "That was amazing."

Seth smoothed his hands up and down her back, then hugged her tightly. "Yes, it was."

The doorbell rang.

Seth loosed the foulest curse Leah had ever heard him use.

Frowning, she lifted her head. "Is that someone at the front door?" It had sounded as if the bell had rung inside the room with them, not out in the living room or hallway.

"No," he grumbled as he reached up to rub his eyes. "It's someone at *this* door." He sounded pissed. Looked it, too.

When he started to sit up, Leah planted a hand on his chest and used her position on top of him to push him back down again. "Ignore it."

"I can't." Easing her off him and over to his side, he sat up again. "They'll kick the door in if I do."

Rising to her knees, Leah straddled him once more and pushed him back down. "No they won't." The two of them had just shared something amazing, something Seth had both needed and enjoyed. She wasn't about to let whoever was ringing the doorbell drag him off to work. He deserved some time to himself, damn it.

And with her core resting atop his length, she could feel him already hardening again beneath her. So the quicker she sent the intruder on his or her way, the quicker Seth could make love to her again. "Don't worry. I'll handle it."

Some of the irritation left his face as he arched a brow. "You will?"

Smiling, she scooted down to the foot of the bed and hopped off. "You think I can't?"

"I think I won't let you if you plan to do it naked."

She blushed as his heated gaze swept over her.

The doorbell rang again.

Grabbing Seth's black T-shirt off the floor, Leah pulled it over her head. The neckline was too big, exposing one shoulder. But her breasts were covered and the hem reached halfway down her thighs. "You see? No longer naked."

His eyes flashed brighter with desire.

Leah drew her hands down her body. "You like seeing me in your shirt, don't you?"

"Hell yes, I do. It makes we want to peel it off and—"

She pointed at him. "Hold that thought." Crossing to the door, she swung it open... and looked up. At least a dozen or so males—all with black hair, brown eyes, broad shoulders, and a lot of muscle—were crowded into the hallway outside. And not one of them stood less than six feet tall.

"Wow. He wasn't kidding," she murmured, remembering David's words the night he and Seth had come to her store for the first time. "You guys *are* tall."

For some reason, her words made them tense.

"Who was right? Gershom?" Roland demanded. He and Marcus were closest. "What are you doing here, Leah? Where is Seth?"

Leah was a bit surprised he remembered her name from the store but gave it little thought. Every one of the men appeared tense and held weapons. Swords. Short swords. Daggers. Sais.

What exactly did they think the two of them had been doing in here?

The thought made her smile. "Seth is unavailable at the moment. May I take a message?"

If anything, the polite words made Roland's brows draw down farther. "Not good enough. Let us see him."

Leah glanced at Seth, who lounged—gloriously naked—on the bed, beyond their sight. She faced the men once more. "I don't think so."

"I'm afraid I'm going to have to insist," he retorted. When he would've moved forward and pushed his way inside, Marcus grabbed his arm.

"Roland," he cautioned.

Roland turned on him. "The ground was shaking just moments ago, Marcus, and you know that only happens when Seth is pissed."

The ground really *had* shook? "I knew it!" she exclaimed in triumph. "I knew I felt the earth move! I just didn't want to say anything because it sounded so cliché." Then she frowned. "Wait." Roland thought that only happened when Seth was pissed? "What exactly do you think has happened?"

"I think you've harmed Seth," Roland declared furiously.

Leah stared at him in astonishment, then motioned to herself. "I'm naked under this shirt!" What the hell harm could she do to Seth while in the nude?

Roland's face darkened. "And my wife was naked when she stabbed me in the heart with a dagger. Step aside."

Leah gaped at him. "Sarah stabbed you in the heart with a dagger?" She had only met the woman a few times in her store but had liked her.

"No. My first wife did."

"Oh. Did you cheat on her or something?"

"No. She cheated on me."

Leah frowned. "*She* cheated on *you*, then stabbed you in the heart? What a total bitch!"

The statement seemed to take him by surprise.

"You see?" Sarah called from somewhere out of sight. "I told you your first wife was a bitch!"

Marcus leaned forward and caught Leah's eye. "We all know Seth is here. We all know he's in that room. A minute ago the ground was shaking and it was storming so badly outside that the wind nearly peeled the shingles off the roof. The fact that Seth didn't answer the door himself has only heightened our concern. Please, step aside and let us see him."

Sighing, Leah looked over at Seth. "Well, I guess you'd better cover up, buttercup," she said with resignation. "We have company."

But Seth no longer seemed annoyed. In fact, he seemed amused as he dragged a corner of the sheet over his lap.

Backing up a step, she swung the door all the way open.

The men in the hallway tensed as though readying for battle.

Several gasped, eyes widening as they noted the scattered clothing, comforter, and pillows on the floor, then located Seth's long, muscled form reclining on the bed. Though the sheet covered his goods, it left his chest, arms, and one leg bare. His long hair was mussed from her fingers. A fine sheen of perspiration glistened on his bare skin. He looked sated and relaxed. Only a complete imbecile would fail to guess what they had been doing.

Stunned silence engulfed them.

Leah shifted her weight as she waited for someone to break it. Seth looked positively edible, sprawled out before her like a banquet, and she was eager to partake again.

When the quiet stretched, she tilted her head to one side and met

Seth's gaze. "It storms when you make love?"

His eyes still held a golden glow as he sent her a sheepish smile. "Apparently. I think because it's been so long."

After thousands of years of celibacy—and considering how powerful the man was—she supposed it shouldn't surprise her that he had rocked the very earth and sparked a storm when he had finally unleashed his passion.

Turning back to the large warriors in the hallway, Leah flashed them all a grin. "Well then, boys, you'd better put your rain boots on. Because monsoon season is coming."

Their mouths dropped open just before she shut the door in their faces.

Seth burst out laughing.

Skipping over to the bed, she hopped up onto it.

"I can't believe you said that."

Chuckling, she knelt beside him. "I know. Did you see their expressions?"

That sparked another round of laughter.

Leah swung a leg across his hips and straddled him once more.

Seth smiled up at her as he settled his hands on her hips. "You're such a delight."

"I like to see you smile," she told him softly.

His smile turned tender. "No one makes me feel the way you do, Leah."

Her heart leapt.

"No one makes me so happy." He slid his hands down her thighs to her knees, then back up to her hips in a caress that heated her blood. He tugged the T-shirt over her head, then settled his hands at her waist. His thumbs slid across her stomach in a caress. When they encountered the thick scars that marred it, she casually brushed his hands aside and brought one to her lips for a kiss.

His brow furrowed. "What's wrong?"

"Nothing." Nothing she wanted to talk about anyway.

"Don't lie to me," he implored gently. "I felt the change in your emotions and want you to be able to speak freely with me when something upsets you."

Silently, she swore. She had forgotten about his empathic ability and all it probably revealed to him.

"Please, Leah."

Unable to deny him, she nodded, though she felt—for the first time with Seth—a reluctance to talk. "I don't like you touching them," she admitted, having to force the words past her lips.

"Your scars?"

Again she nodded. The backs of her eyes began to burn.

His gaze fell to the ridges on her abdomen, then the ones on her knees. "Do they hurt?"

Swallowing hard, she shook her head.

"Then why does it bother you when I touch them?"

Unwanted tears welled. "Because they're ugly." And Seth was perfect from head to toe.

He frowned. "They're a part of you, Leah. Nothing that is a part of you could ever be ugly to me." He settled his hands on her hips once more. "May I?"

She nodded but couldn't help but cringe inside when he smoothed his thumbs over the scars. Leah fought the desire to curse when she couldn't stop a tear from spilling over her lashes. "I wanted to have a plastic surgeon do whatever she could to remove them or reduce the appearance of them." Seeing them every time she went to the bathroom or changed her clothes or showered or bathed had made it harder for her to put her life back together after the accident. "But I couldn't afford it and insurance doesn't cover it. It's considered cosmetic surgery."

He met her gaze. "You want them gone?"

"Yes," she choked out. "I don't need a visual reminder of what I lost."

"Because that loss is always with you."

She nodded, unsurprised that he understood, having suffered such a loss himself. Leah bit back an instinctive protest when he splayed a hand over her stomach. She hated those scars, both seeing and touching them, and couldn't bring herself to believe that—

Heat suffused her where his hand covered her. Her skin began to tingle.

When she looked down, her eyes widened.

Was Seth's hand glowing?

Yes, it was. The warm light emanating from it was faint but

definitely there.

Then the glow faded, his skin tone returned to normal, and the heat receded.

He slid his hand back over to her hip.

Leah gasped. The scars were gone. Only smooth, pale skin remained.

She drew shaking fingers over her stomach, then met Seth's gaze.

"Do not mistake my reason for removing them," he ordered softly. "I meant what I said. Nothing that is a part of you could ever be ugly to me, Leah. I only removed them because they caused you pain and I wanted to make you happy."

Leaning down, she pressed a kiss to his lips, then hugged him tight. "Thank you."

He wrapped his arms around her. "Anything for you."

Raising her head, she again pressed her lips to his. "I'm going to tell you something, and I don't want you to confuse it with gratitude. Okay? It isn't. I would've said the same thing before you erased my scars."

"Okay."

She brushed his long hair back and studied his ruggedly beautiful face. "I'm falling in love with you, Seth."

Golden light flared amid the dark brown in his irises. Cupping her face in his big hands, he stared up at her for a long moment. "I've been falling in love with you ever since I held your hand the night we met."

Her heart soared.

"Lisette once told me that before she met Zach it seemed as if she were just sleepwalking and going through the motions. Then Zach woke her up and made her feel again." Taking one of her hands, he pressed a kiss to it, then placed it on his chest above his heart. "That's what you've done for me, Leah. I was sleepwalking... for thousands of years. Then you came along and woke me up. Now I'm feeling things I never thought I would again."

Emotion choked her. She had been alone for twelve years. Seth had been alone for thousands. More tears welled as elation battled with despair.

He brushed the tears away. "This makes you unhappy?"

"No." She swallowed hard. "There's something else, something I should've told you before we made love."

"Tell me now," he said, no concern evident.

Regret twisted her stomach into knots as she sat up. "The scars you healed aren't the only ones I carry."

His gaze slid to her knees on either side of him. Cupping a hand over each, he healed those too, erasing the marks as if they had never existed.

"Those aren't either."

He studied her a moment. "You refer to the emotional scars you bear?"

She shook her head, swallowing hard. "I can't have children." Another tear spilled over her lashes. "There was too much damage from the accident. The doctors I consulted all told me the same thing, that I have no chance of ever getting pregnant again, even with in vitro fertilization."

Brow furrowing, Seth smoothed a palm over her abdomen and stared at it. After a moment, he lifted his gaze to hers. "They didn't perform a hysterectomy."

She shook her head. "But my uterus and—"

"Do you want children, Leah?" he asked, interrupting her.

"Yes," she answered, silently adding *with you.*

His hand heated.

"Seth," she whispered. She knew he wanted to help, but the doctors had been very clear.

His gaze fell to her stomach, a look of concentration sweeping over his visage. "Had they removed your uterus, ovaries, and fallopian tubes, I would be unable to help you. My healing gift is not so great that I can enable someone to regrow a limb or an organ that was removed. But damage and scarring..." His hand cooled. "That I can heal." His eyes met hers. "All is restored, Leah. You can have children."

She held her breath, afraid to believe it. "I'm forty-six years old."

"And now have the reproductive system of a thirty-year-old."

Glancing down, she slid her hands over her stomach. "I can really have babies?"

"Yes."

She didn't know whether to laugh or cry or shower Seth with kisses.

She opted for the latter and leaned down to brush her lips against his. She meant the kiss to be tender, to convey the multitude of feelings she bore for him. But Seth cupped the back of her head in one large hand and took control, deepening the contact and teasing her with his tongue until both were breathless.

Rolling her onto her back, he settled himself between her thighs. Leah hummed her approval when he slid one hand down to grip her ass and urged her to wrap her leg around his waist. He palmed her breast, kneading it, then tweaking the taut peak. She moaned when he abandoned her lips to take that tight, sensitive bud in his hot mouth and tease it with his tongue and teeth.

His hard shaft slid against her clit.

Sensation shot through her. "Yes." Wrapping her arms around him, she grasped fistfuls of his long, thick hair and urged him closer. She loved the way he felt against her. His mouth on her breast. His cock teasing her center. He was so hard and made her body burn. "Seth," she gasped. "Take me. I want you inside me again."

But he shook his head. "I'm doing it right this time."

She moaned a protest when his lips left her breast. "If you had done it any more right the first time, my head would've exploded."

He laughed.

And she sucked in a breath when it made his cock jump against her. "Seth, please. I really want you."

Smiling, his golden eyes mesmerizing, he shook his head and winked. "You'll want me more by the time I'm finished."

So saying, he lowered his head to her other breast.

Leah gripped his back, still holding fistfuls of his long, loose hair. She'd never been with a man who had long hair before. It was so soft and beautiful and somehow managed to tickle her with little brushes against her bare skin and tantalize her all at the same time.

He shifted, slipping lower on the bed.

She squirmed when his lips left her breast and trailed kisses down her stomach. Though the lust thrumming through her did not lessen, tears welled anew when his lips caressed her newly scar-free skin. Seth had done that for her. He had healed her.

Then his soft lips brushed her mound and she sucked in a sharp breath, forgetting everything else. He drew his warm, wet tongue over her clit.

Moaning, Leah threw her head back and dropped her hands to the bed. So good.

Another long lick followed.

Her fingers curled into fists, clutching the sheets.

That oh-so-talented mouth. That wicked tongue. Stroking and flicking and sucking, driving the pleasure higher and higher. She arched up against him, wanting more.

He rested a hand on her stomach to hold her in place, then slid the other up to cup her breast. She cried out when he pinched her nipple at the same time his tongue stroked her. Her breath grew short, emerging in pants and gasps as she writhed beneath him. "Seth."

Just when she thought she would die if he didn't make her come soon, his tongue vibrated against her and sent her careening over the edge.

Leah screamed his name and arched up against him.

But Seth didn't stop, his mouth and hands continuing to torment her, drawing the orgasm out for so long she damned near couldn't breathe.

At last she collapsed against the covers.

As she lay there, panting, she became aware of a rumbling. The bed shook beneath her.

She glanced around. *Everything* shook.

She looked up at Seth as he rose above her and lost what breath she had managed to regain.

His golden eyes shone as brightly as hundred-watt bulbs. His face was hard with need as he settled himself between her thighs once more.

She gasped when he entered her with one hard thrust.

Both moaned. It felt so good. And Leah loved looking up at Seth, seeing his muscles ripple as he withdrew almost to the crown and drove inside her again. His long hair fell down around them like a curtain, some pooling on her breasts and teasing her with light touches.

Again he nearly withdrew, then slid home, grinding against her clit and sparking another moan.

Leah wrapped her arms around him. "More," she begged.

A muscle in his jaw clenched. "I don't want to hurt you."

She slid her hands down to grip his ass and arched up against him. "I can take it."

The bed shook harder. Or was it the ground?

Seth left her no time to decide as he ducked his head and took her lips with a voracious kiss.

She closed her eyes. Her hands tightened on his ass, urging him on as he drove inside her deep and hard, over and over, touching all the right spots. The scent of fresh rain suddenly filled the air, as strong as Seth's own tantalizing aroma.

His mouth left hers and trailed down her neck.

Leah opened her eyes... and gasped. Huge dark wings now adorned Seth's back. The semitranslucent feathers they bore were the same color as his tanned skin at their base, then darkened to black at their tips.

"Seth," she breathed, staring up at him in awe.

Seth told himself to slow down, to ease his hold a bit and take more care, but he couldn't seem to bring his body under control. Leah felt so good beneath him. Her hands gripping his ass. Her hips arching up to meet him, thrust for thrust. Her warm, wet body clutching him tightly as he drove inside her, squeezing him and pushing the pleasure higher and higher.

She whispered his name.

It only made him more frantic to claim her, to make her *his*, to make her come for him again. He never wanted it to stop. He tried to tell himself to be gentler. Feared he would leave bruises on her pale skin if he wasn't. But he couldn't hold back. He had wanted her since the day he had met her. And she tasted so good. Smelled so good. Felt so good beneath him. Was so responsive to his touch.

"Seth, please," she begged.

He gave her what she wanted, what he needed most. Her tight, hot sheathe clamped down around him as she threw her head back and cried out in ecstasy. Seth shouted her name as he finally succumbed and let an orgasm rip through him. On and on it went.

By the time the pleasure ended, both breathed heavily, their skin coated with a fine sheen of perspiration.

Bracing his weight on his elbows, Seth burrowed his hands beneath Leah and hugged her to him as he rested his head beside hers on the pillow. Her heart raced madly. As madly as his. He closed his eyes, embracing the happiness and contentment she brought him.

How he needed this.

How he needed *her*.

Her hands left his ass and caressed a path up his back. Another shiver of pleasure shot through him as she lightly drew her fingertips across his wings.

Smiling, he sighed in satisfaction... then stiffened. His eyes flew open. "Oh shit."

"Yep," she said, still breathless from their vigorous lovemaking. "Looks like you forgot to mention something else."

Ducking his head, he lightly bumped his forehead against her shoulder, wishing instead that he could bang it against the wall in dismay. "It would seem I have no control at all when I'm with you," he murmured. And could keep few secrets. Raising his head, he eyed her warily.

Her brow furrowed. "Is it a shape-shifting thing?" Her slender fingers gently explored his wings. "Were you afraid it would scare me if you added the wings?"

He should say yes and leave it at that. But his heart wouldn't let him lie to her. "No." Carefully withdrawing from her warm body, he eased away. "I didn't hurt you, did I?" He rested a hand on her hip where he had gripped her so tightly. "Was I too rough?"

"No. It was wonderful." Raising a hand, she positioned her index finger half an inch from her thumb as if she held a small marble. "You came *this* close to actually making my head explode."

Relieved, he found a smile.

Red crept up her neck and entered her cheeks. "And I'm pretty sure I've never screamed like that before."

Grinning, he shook his head and moved to sit on his heels down by her knees. "Being immortal does have its perks."

"No kidding," she said with a faint smile. Drawing her legs together, she rested her hands on her stomach and studied him with a faint question in her hazel eyes—more brown than green tonight.

Seth motioned to his body. "This is the real me, Leah." He stretched his wings out as far as he could, a wall restricting the movement on one side. "This is who I am."

Face sober, she sat up.

"I only kept it from you because I knew it would raise questions I couldn't answer without endangering you and everyone else I love."

She bit her lip. "You think I would betray your confidence?"

"No. I trust you implicitly. But the telepaths would read it in your thoughts. I can command them to stay out of your head while they're awake. But the younger ones lose control over their gift when they sleep and may find the answers in your dreams."

She was silent for a moment as her gaze wandered over him. "You were born like this?"

"Yes."

"And they don't know? All those guys in the hallway—they don't know this is the real you?"

"They don't know," he confirmed. "I've never shared this with them. David, Zach, Lisette, and Jared know. Zach and Jared are like me. Lisette is Zach's wife, so she knows he's like me. But she doesn't know *why* we're like this. Only David knows, because he's been my closest friend for thousands of years and *no one* can read his thoughts."

She remained silent for a long moment.

"There's something else," he added reluctantly.

"Okay." She drew in a deep breath as though bracing herself, then nodded.

"Melanie explained the virus to you when we were at network headquarters, didn't she?"

"The virus that infects all vampires and Immortal Guardians? Yes."

"Well... I'm not infected with it."

She blinked. "You're not?"

"No. I'm a *gifted one*."

"I don't understand. Melanie said the virus is what transforms mortal *gifted ones* and gives them immortality."

"It's a conundrum, I know. I wish I could explain it to you."

"What is it you fear will happen if the rest of your brethren find out?"

He shook his head. "Sooner or later, someone will share the information with someone they shouldn't. They'll trust someone they shouldn't. And when they do, violence and death will follow. It always does."

She frowned. "You've told someone before?"

"Yes. My wife and our children. Our son and daughter both fell in love and married humans we trusted. I loved my son-in-law and daughter-in-law as though my wife had birthed them. I loved them as much as I do Ami and Adira. But..." He shook his head. "My daughter-in-law shared the secret with someone she shouldn't have. She told her sister. And her sister betrayed her, betrayed us all. When word of what I am traveled, a plan was hatched. A man lured me away to heal his dying child, and his coconspirators slaughtered my wife and children in my absence."

She touched her fingers to her lips, then reached out to him. "Oh, Seth."

He refused to let her console him. Best to tell her all of it. "I lost it, Leah. When I saw what they'd done... When I saw how my wife had suffered... the violent deaths our children had been dealt..." He shook his head. "I lost it."

"Of course you did," she declared gently, no condemnation in her voice. "You—"

"I killed them all," he told her, steeling himself for her response. "Every man and woman who had plotted against us. Every teenager who had eagerly joined in, their minds already corrupted by hate. And I didn't stop there. I swept through the city, slaying every man and woman who *hadn't* plotted against us but who had hoped those who did would succeed. Every man and woman who had embraced that darkness fell beneath my sword. I razed most of the city, burned it to the ground. And I know people today like to believe that there were only tiny, primitive villages back then, but it was a large, thriving city, Leah. And I destroyed most of it. Had David not found me and intervened, I would've continued on to the next city. And the next. And the one after that, determined to wipe out every hateful heart that would've risen against those I loved had they been given the chance. I—"

Rising to her knees, Leah surged forward and wrapped him up in a hug. "Shhhh. It's okay."

Seth held her close and buried his face in her neck.

"It's okay, Seth. It's okay."

"No it isn't," he whispered, still tormented by the memories. "Do you know how many children I orphaned that day? How many lives I destroyed?" He tightened his hold on her. "I can't let that happen again, Leah. I can't."

"Is that why you've worked so hard to keep everyone from finding out about *gifted ones* and immortals? You fear history will repeat itself?"

"Yes."

Loosening her hold, she leaned back and clasped his face in her soft hands.

Seth met her gaze, expecting to find disappointment, disapproval, horror perhaps, but found only love and understanding.

"Keep whatever secrets you must, Seth, to prevent that from happening. I trust you."

He shook his head. "It isn't fair."

"I know. But I understand the reasons for it and can live with that as long as it means I can have you. I want you to be happy." Her lips turned up in a half smile. "*I* want to be happy." She brushed her lips against his in a tender kiss that touched him deeply. "And you make me happier than I ever thought I could be again. Can you erase your wings from my memory or make that knowledge disappear?"

He offered her a rueful smile. "I could, but I fear such would prove futile. I seem to have no control when I'm with you, so they're bound to make more appearances when we make love."

She grinned. "Good. I like them." She stroked the feathers, then met his gaze. "They're soft. And beautiful."

He drew his wings in and closed them around her, cocooning her inside. "Hopefully," he suggested, "if any of the telepaths wander into your dreams and see them, they'll assume I shape-shifted."

"You see? Problem solved."

Sighing, he pressed his forehead to hers. "I wish I could share everything with you, Leah."

"I do, too." Her look turned mischievous. "You've shared so much of yourself already. Soooooo much." She glanced down at his body, making him harden once more. "You are a *fantastic* lover."

Sliding his hands down to her tempting ass, he lifted her and settled her on his lap.

Her eyes widened at the feel of his long, hard length.

He grinned. "Why don't we put that to the test, shall we?"

Desire flaring in her hazel eyes, she wiggled against him. "Hell yes."

Chapter Seventeen

T ESSA CAME AWAKE SLOWLY. RAISING her arms above her head, she gave a leisurely stretch and sighed. For once, no nightmares had plagued her. They had besieged her on a nightly basis for so long that she had forgotten what it felt like to enjoy a peaceful night's sleep.

Smiling, she opened her eyes... then stiffened. Her heart began to slam against her ribs as she took in the unfamiliar room around her. She was in what appeared to be an upscale studio apartment. Aside from the queen-sized bed that supported her, it boasted a very comfortable-looking love seat, a huge flat-screen television, a kitchenette with a bar and two stools, and a bathroom. She couldn't tell if it was a full or half bath from her position, but the tile she glimpsed was of the pricey variety.

Two walls in the main living space bore windows that displayed a sunny meadow rife with wildflowers outside. The brightly colored blossoms danced on a breeze, the grass around it rippling like ocean waves.

Rolling out of bed, Tessa hurried over to the windows, eager to identify where the hell she was and make her escape.

Disappointment struck when she realized they weren't actually windows but flat-screen digital displays made to *look* like windows.

Where the hell was she?

Voices filtered through the walls and ceiling, reaching her hypersensitive ears. There must be hundreds of them. Conversations blended together until she concentrated and tried to sort through them all, seeking as much information as she could gather. Most were of the mundane, daily routine variety. Others belonged to guards.

Guards? Guards where? And whom were they guarding? Her?

She caught the word *vampires* more than once. Not *vampire* singular. *Vampires* plural. Perhaps she wasn't the only one the Immortal Guardians had caught. There had been two dozen with her when she had invaded Leah's apartment. But the guards spoke as if Tessa was the only new vampire in the mix.

The last thing Tessa remembered was trying to attack Seth after he'd rid her of her weapons even though she'd known she wouldn't survive it.

She glanced around. Apparently she had. Why hadn't he killed her? Seth and his so-called immortals bore no love for vampires. They slew them all, willy-nilly, with no care or compassion. So she didn't understand why she still lived and found it hard to believe there were other vampires here. Wherever *here* was.

Perhaps Seth had let her live so he could torture information about Gershom out of her.

She frowned when she heard the guards again reference *the vampires.*

"How long do you think she'll sleep?" a woman asked.

Tessa zeroed in on that voice, because it seemed closer to her than the others.

"I don't know," a male responded, his words colored with a Scottish accent. "I admit to being surprised she's slept this long."

"Did you read her thoughts?" another male asked. His voice carried a British accent.

"Yes," the Scot replied grimly. "Gershom did an excellent job of turning her against Seth."

"What did he do?" the woman asked. She sounded American.

"He assumed Seth's form," the Scot told them, "and killed her twin."

Bitterness invaded Tessa as memories bombarded her. For the thousandth time, she saw Seth gutting her brother—*Seth*, not Gershom—and hated herself for failing to slay the bastard.

"Oh no," the woman said softly with dismay that was surely feigned.

"He killed the boy right in front of her and did it damned slowly," the Scot went on. "Then he cut Tessa up."

The Brit swore.

Blinking back tears, Tessa began to look for another way out of the swanky apartment.

"Does she not know that Gershom can shape-shift?" the woman asked.

Tessa snorted. Shape-shifting? Really? *That* was how they were going to malign Gershom's name and try to clear Seth's? By trying to convince her that Gershom had somehow morphed into Seth and done the fucked-up deed?

Utter bullshit.

"No," the Scot replied. "Gershom has not revealed that particular talent to her. She thinks it impossible."

"More impossible than teleporting," the Brit asked, "moving things with his hands, healing with his hands, reading her thoughts, *manipulating* those thoughts — ?"

"Aye. He played her well," the Scot interrupted with regret. "She thinks Gershom saved her. She thinks him her friend."

A loud sigh ensued. "Well," the Brit said sadly, "who the hell am I to criticize? I thought Roland responsible for killing my sister for two damned centuries before I came to understand that my best friend had done it instead."

"Bastien, honey," the woman said softly, "I wish you'd stop beating yourself up about that. It wasn't your fault. Blaise was your best friend. You loved him like a brother and had no reason to doubt him. Of course you trusted him when he told you Roland killed her."

"I protected that bastard for years," he countered. "Blaise killed Catherine with their babe still in her belly, and I fucking protected him. I raised a damned army of vampires to help me kill Roland and take down the Immortal Guardians because I believed that bastard, only to discover that Roland — the man I had viciously hated and hunted for so long — was instead the one who had brought my sister's killer to justice."

"Well," the woman said helplessly, "maybe it would be better if *you* speak to Tessa then. You've actually been in her position. You once believed Seth and the Immortal Guardians were the enemy.

Seth captured you instead of killing you. He wanted to save you, just like he wants to save her. Who better to help her see the truth?"

Tessa's heart thudded heavily in her breast. It was bullshit, right? They knew she was awake and hoped to manipulate her into believing they were the good guys and Gershom—who had saved her and helped her in so many ways—was the bad guy?

Gershom, who had tried to save her brother's life.

Gershom, who had saved her own, enabling her to live and seek revenge.

She shook her head. It was bullshit. Gershom had told her they would try to fuck with her head if they ever got their hands on her. Just as they had Veronica.

Fury and sadness flooded her.

The Immortal Guardians had kidnapped Veronica Becker's son and attempted to use him to gain her cooperation in their hunt for Gershom. And even though one of the immortals had deceived her, Veronica had gone to them.

Tessa hadn't blamed her. She would've done the same thing to save her brother. But whatever information Veronica had given the Immortal Guardians hadn't been enough. Gershom had found her body three days after she went missing. And he had blamed himself for her death.

"Shite," the Scotsman spat.

"Aidan?" the woman asked. "What is it?"

The Scot's name was Aidan? *The* Aidan? The one who had kidnapped Veronica?

"Gershom told her we killed Veronica," Aidan disclosed.

"Veronica Becker?" Bastien asked in surprise.

"Yes."

Dismay struck. Was Aidan reading her mind?

"Veronica was Roland's descendant!" Bastien exclaimed. "His relative. We would never have harmed her."

"Hell, look what happened when Roland thought *I* had harmed her," Aidan said. "He tried to kill me even though he knew Seth doesn't like fighting amongst the ranks and would be furious."

"Seth *was* furious," the woman reminded them wryly. "Poor Roland. He took Veronica's murder hard. Is there any way we can prove to Tessa that Gershom killed her, not you or Seth?"

"I don't see how," Aidan replied.

"We could tell her about Michael," Bastien said.

Tessa gasped. Michael was Veronica's son.

"Perhaps," Bastien continued, "once she knows Roland and Sarah adopted him and how well they've been caring for him, she'll begin to question the lies Gershom fed her."

Michael was alive? Gershom had told her he'd died alongside his mother.

Aidan swore. "That bastard Gershom told her Seth killed Michael, too."

Because Seth *had* killed Michael.

"Well, that's easy enough to disprove," the woman said. "We'll just show her Michael."

"You know damned well," Bastien retorted, "that Roland isn't going to let Michael anywhere near Tessa. Not while her mind is still chock-full of lies. He won't risk her harming him."

As if she'd harm a toddler! That was such bullshit! All of this was! Empty words. Nothing more. No proof.

"She wants proof," Aidan stated.

That's right, asshole, Tessa thought. *Put up or shut up.*

"Is she awake?" the woman asked with surprise.

"Aye."

"Aidan!" she reprimanded. A chair scraped the floor. "Why didn't you tell me? She's probably hungry. Let me get her something to eat and introduce myself."

"No, Melanie," Bastien said softly. "Let Aidan do it. She's dangerous."

"More dangerous than the vampires who live across the hallway?" Melanie retorted. "I can handle her."

"No," Aidan said. "I'll do it. I may have a way to clear things up for her."

Bring it on, asshole, Tessa thought. Clearing her mind, she began to sing a song in her head to keep him from reading her intent. Then, crossing to the kitchen, she appropriated every weapon she could find.

———◦◦◦———

Seth lay in bed with Leah pressed up against his side, her head resting on his shoulder while he toyed with her hair.

"Do you feel guilty?" she asked softly.

"No," he responded and was a little surprised by that. "Do you?"

"No." She was quiet for a moment. "I thought I would. I thought I would feel like… I don't know… I was being disloyal to my husband or something."

"I thought the same thing, even though David assured me my wife wouldn't want me to remain alone for the rest of my life." He stared up at the ceiling. "I think I *would* have felt guilty if I had slept with someone else, someone who meant nothing to me."

"Me, too." She drew circles on his chest with one finger. "Is it weird that I asked?"

"No. I was lying here wondering if *you* felt any guilt or regret."

"I don't."

He pressed a kiss to her hair. "Good."

Shifting, she propped her chin on his chest and looked up at him.

Amusement rose as he stared at her. "Something else on your mind?"

"Yes." She wrinkled her nose. "But I'm afraid to ask you. It seems a little morbid."

"Go ahead. You can ask me anything."

She bit her lip. "Do I remind you of your wife?"

He chuckled. "Afraid you might look like her and that's what attracted me to you?"

"Only maybe one-half of one percent of me. The one-half of one percent who has seen too many made-for-TV movies in which men seduced women, then tried to convince them to dye their hair and wear different clothes so they'd look just like their dead wives."

He laughed. "Aside from being close in height, you look nothing like her."

She smiled. "Good to know."

"I'd ask if I look like your husband, but I saw the pictures in your home." Her husband had been several inches shorter than Seth with closely cropped dark blond hair and blue eyes.

Skillet's "Monster" disrupted the quiet.

Seth frowned at the cell phone he'd left on the bedside table, then reluctantly reached for it. "Yes?" he answered, wincing a little at the resignation in his tone.

"I would've spoken to you telepathically," Zach said, his deep voice tinged with mirth, "but I thought it unwise considering what you might be doing in there."

Seth sighed. "I assume you heard what happened earlier?"

"Yes, and laughed my ass off."

"Of course you did."

"I thought you should know that Tessa is awake and Aidan has something he wishes to discuss with you."

Voices carried over the line. *Many* voices. "Where are you?"

"In David's living room."

"Is everyone still here at the house?" He had felt the sun set a couple of hours ago and would've thought they'd all be out hunting by now.

"Yes. Your little immortal family isn't quite sure how to react to daddy's romantic escapade and are reluctant to leave until you make an appearance."

"Seriously?"

"Seriously," Zach said around a chuckle.

"You're loving this, aren't you?" Seth asked balefully.

"Hell yes, I am."

"Fine. Tell them we shall see them shortly."

"Feel free to make them wait," Zach taunted before he ended the call.

"What's up?" Leah asked. "You're all tense now."

"It looks like I'm going to have to share you with my brethren earlier than I'd hoped."

"You mean those guys from the hallway?"

"Yes. Them, their wives, their Seconds, and more."

"Second what?"

Right. He hadn't told her about Seconds yet. "I'll explain that while we dress."

A soft thump sounded.

Seth looked toward the door. A neat pile of clothing now rested on the floor in front of it, teleported in by Zach, no doubt.

"Did that just appear out of thin air?" Leah asked.

"Yes."

"What is it?"

"Fresh clothing for you would be my guess."

Rolling off the bed, Leah crossed to the neat bundle and picked it up. Seth admired her lovely bare body as she inspected the garments.

"Cool," she declared with a grin. "They're all my size."

Zach had better not have plucked those sizes from her thoughts.

Seth rose. "Let's take a quick shower before we dress."

"Okay."

The shower ended up not being so quick. Once Seth watched water cascade over Leah's beautiful breasts and started running his soapy hands over her delicious curves... Well, who could blame him for giving in to the desire that struck and taking her against the wall?

"You did it again," she declared breathlessly as he lowered her feet to the tile floor. "You made the earth move."

He shook his head with a wince. "Sorry about that." It had probably stormed outside again, too. How long would that keep happening when they made love? It hadn't done that thousands of years ago. But he was far stronger now than he had been then, *and* he could manipulate the weather now, something that—since he'd grown in strength—tended to slip out of control when his emotions ran high.

"Don't apologize. I enjoyed it immensely." She sent him a teasing smile. "But we should probably hurry and get dressed before those guys from the hallway come busting in here to see if you're okay."

Seth shook his head. "So humiliating. What you must think of me..."

Rising onto her toes, she pressed a quick kiss to his lips. "I think you're an amazing lover." Her hazel eyes twinkled with merriment beneath eyelashes spiked from the water's spray. "And now that I know making love with you could end the drought that has stricken the area, I think it my solemn duty to nail you as often as I can."

He laughed. "You'll hear no objections from me."

Leah didn't seem nervous at all about meeting his Immortal Guardians. Seth found that a relief. After what had happened earlier, he wasn't sure what to expect. He still couldn't believe they'd thought Leah had harmed him in some way. Roland, he could understand. But everyone else? Really?

The clothing Zach had provided fit Leah like a glove. Black cargo pants. Black T-shirt with a V-neck that taunted Seth with glimpses of cleavage. Black socks and black boots. Seth assumed Lisette had chosen the underwear, because it wasn't the generic, plain white fare David kept on hand for any immortals or Seconds who might arrive coated in blood and in need of a change of clothes. No. Both the panties and the bra were tiny, black, and lacy. It just made Seth want to drag Leah back to bed again. But then, so did seeing her garbed like an immortal warrior.

Leah grinned as she finished tying her bootlaces and stood. "I'd ask how I look, but your eyes say it all."

"You're so beautiful."

"And you're gorgeous. Now tuck all of those delicious desires of yours away so you won't walk out of here hard."

Seth glanced down and sighed.

She laughed. "Wouldn't want to shock your guys any more than you already have."

At least she had a sense of humor about it.

As soon as Seth reined in his desire, he escorted Leah out of the bedroom, down the hallway, and into the living room.

Almost every immortal currently stationed in the area appeared to be present. David. Zach and Lisette. Roland and Sarah. Bastien and Melanie. Richart and Jenna. Étienne and Krysta. Ethan and Heather. Aidan and Dana. Sean, Imhotep, Chaak, and Marcus. Their Seconds were also present, as were Ami and Adira. Even Stanislav and Susan were there.

Where's Jared? Seth asked Zach telepathically.

Guarding network headquarters.

All conversation ceased when Seth and Leah stepped into view. Everyone stood and faced them, clustering together.

"This is Leah Somerson," Seth announced, resting a hand on her lower back.

Leah smiled and offered them a friendly wave. "Hello."

Before they could respond, Seth scowled and decreed sternly, "Do *not* read her mind, telepaths. I expressly forbid it. Zach, you and David may read Leah's mind *only* in the case of a dire emergency. The rest of you may not. Do so against my wishes and you will suffer my wrath."

Leah nodded somberly. "Seth told me that many of you view him as something of a father figure." Leaning into his side, she gave his chest a little pat. "Trust me when I say you do *not* want to read my mind and see the kinky shit daddy does in bed."

Eyes widened as over a dozen mouths fell open.

Seth threw back his head and laughed as Zach burst into guffaws.

Curling his arm around Leah, Seth hugged her close. "She's teasing you," he told their stunned audience, then looked down at her. "Tell them you're teasing. Quickly. I'm already starting to pick up on some freaky guesses they're mentally broadcasting."

Leah grinned. "I'm just teasing."

Everyone laughed and parted to allow David passage.

David shook his head as he approached Leah, his deep brown eyes alight with laugher. "Well done."

"I couldn't resist," she told him with a laugh.

Taking her hand, he pressed a kiss to it. "I'm happy to see you well and recovered from your injuries. I've been assured that your home has already been cleaned and put back in order. All repairs are complete. And your employees are running the shop well."

"Thank you."

"Thank *you* for holding Tessa for us. She probably would have escaped us yet again if you hadn't distracted her."

Leah sobered. "How is she?"

"Confused." David met Seth's eyes. "That's why Aidan wishes to speak with you."

Aidan stepped forward. "Sorry about that, Seth. I didn't realize you were with Leah when I told Zach and David I needed to talk to you."

"Don't worry about it."

Aidan smiled and offered Leah his hand. "I'm Aidan. It's a pleasure to meet you."

She smiled. "Nice to meet you, too." When Aidan kissed the back of her hand instead of shaking it, she sent Seth a glance. "You guys are all so gallant."

"Because we're so old," he returned with a rueful smile.

"Hi, Leah!"

Seth looked over the heads of the others. Sheldon and Tracy stood in the entrance of the kitchen, waving.

Leah waved back. "Hi, Sheldon. Hi, Tracy."

Darnell stepped into the doorway behind them.

"Hi, Darnell."

Smiling, he waved back.

Leah looked up at Seth. "Seriously, who *doesn't* live here?"

He laughed. "Usually it's only David, Darnell, Ami, Marcus, Adira, and me. But Roland and Sarah have been staying here since they adopted Michael. And everyone else has been sticking close to keep them all safe while my enemy is at large."

"That's so sweet." Leaving him, she moved forward to stand among the immortal males, every one of whom smiled down at her and studied her curiously. "And look," she said with a broad grin as she tilted her head back to look up at the warriors. "I'm shorter than all of them."

David chuckled. "I told you you'd love our family."

"You were right. I feel positively dainty."

Ami and Sarah stepped up beside Leah, both barely five feet tall.

"Hi, Leah."

"Hi, Leah."

Leah sent Seth a wry smile. "Well, I *did* feel dainty."

He grinned.

Ami surprised Seth by giving Leah a hug. She was usually painfully shy around men and women she didn't know well, a holdover from the torture she had endured.

Leah hugged her back.

"I'm so glad you're okay," Ami told her. "Were you badly injured?"

"No." Leah waved it off the way one might a paper cut. "It was nothing."

"It was *not* nothing," Seth countered, his amusement dying. "She was shot in the back and the bullet tore through her chest."

Silence fell. Expressions darkened as everyone stared at her.

Leah shot the men around her a disgruntled look. "What? It was an accident. I didn't do it on purpose."

Ami touched her arm. "They aren't angry at you for getting hurt. They're angry that someone hurt you."

"Oh."

"How did it happen?" Roland asked, stepping up behind Sarah and resting his hands on her hips.

Seth answered before Leah could. "She took a bullet for Tessa."

Sean moved forward. "The missing immortal I fought?"

"Yes. Tessa led the vampires that attacked Leah in her home last night. Leah guessed who she was and took a bullet to save her."

Leah frowned. "Don't say it like that. You make it sound like I saw the bullet coming and dove in front of it like action heroes do in movies. That's not what happened."

Seth arched a brow. "You saw a bullet strike her, knew more would follow, and dove between her and the shooter, tackling her and taking her to the ground. How exactly is that different?"

"Dude," Sheldon said. "That was badass."

"Yes, it was," Seth acknowledged, then frowned at Leah. "Don't do it again."

Instead of getting offended or expressing anger at the order, Leah smiled and closed the distance between them. "I've said it before, and I'll say it again," she quipped lightly. "You are *hot* when you turn into Mr. Tough Protective Guy."

He shook his head. "You think you're going to wrap me around your little finger, don't you?"

"Not really." She winked. "But I'm going to have a lot of fun trying."

Curling an arm around her, he pulled her up against his side once more.

"Speaking of having fun," Sheldon said. "I'm sure you two have worked up quite an appetite, so I—"

Tracy elbowed him in the ribs. "Sheldon!"

"Ow! What? I counted at least four or five thunderstorms and earthquakes. Who wouldn't be hungry after that?"

Rather than being appalled at having her sex life discussed so openly, Leah laughed. "Actually, I *am* pretty hungry."

"I am, too," Seth added and felt guilty that he hadn't offered her more than chips before now.

"Excellent," Sheldon replied with a grin. "Anybody else

hungry?"

Many voiced an affirmative.

"That's what I figured, which is why Tracy and I have spent the past few hours working our butts off to cook you dinner. Who wants to set the table?"

Krysta, Étienne, and Sean all darted forward in a blur. Place settings appeared on the long table in the adjoining dining room as if by magic as the three zipped back and forth from the kitchen.

Leah smiled up at Seth. "That is awesome! I'm totally going to borrow some of your guys the next time I do inventory in my store."

Everyone laughed and began to migrate toward the table.

Aidan hung back.

"What did you wish to speak to me about?" Seth asked.

The ancient Celtic immortal's face acquired a grim look. "I read Tessa's mind. Gershom did an excellent job of making her want you dead."

"Tell me." He had been too concerned about Leah to delve into Tessa's thoughts earlier.

"He took your form and slaughtered her twin brother."

Leah gasped.

"And he did it right in front of Tessa, dragging out the pain to make him suffer. Then he damned near gutted Tessa, too."

"That poor girl," Leah said softly.

Aidan nodded. "Before she could bleed out, he stopped, looked over his shoulder as if he heard something, then sped away in a blur."

Fury filled Seth. "Let me guess."

"As soon as he was out of sight, Gershom shifted back into his own form, cleaned up in seconds, and raced back to Tessa's side. Because he came from the opposite direction, it looked to her as if he was hunting you and you were fleeing him. He made himself the hero, healing her wounds and burying her brother. And he's given her no reason to suspect otherwise. She doesn't know he can shape-shift. She thinks such impossible. Gershom even convinced her that *we* killed Veronica. The two women saw each other briefly right after he *rescued* Tessa." A muscle jumped in Aidan's cheek, betraying his anger. "I fear Veronica could not tell the difference between Gershom and me when he took my form and kidnapped her, so Tessa heard her expressing confusion over why I had done it. She, too, thought Gershom had rescued her... from me. Gershom separated them before she could say more, then later told Tessa that we killed Veronica when we got our hands on her again and weren't satisfied with the information she gave us, then killed her son."

Payback's a bitch, isn't it?

The words Tessa had spoken when he had accused her of hurting Leah resurfaced in Seth's memory. Such bitterness had infused them. She thought he had tortured and killed her twin. And she wanted to bring him the same pain by harming those he loved most.

No wonder she had attacked Leah. Gershom must have already divined that Seth was seeing her.

"Did you speak with Tessa?" he asked Aidan.

"No. She heard me talking with Bastien and Melanie. Nothing we said swayed her though, so I thought..."

"What?"

"I wanted to ask your permission to take the children to see her."

"Hell no!" Roland roared from the dining room.

Seth held up a hand, forestalling further refusals. "Does she even know what Michael looks like?"

"Yes. Tessa looked Veronica up on social media after Gershom gave her a cell phone to call him in case of an emergency when she started hunting immortals."

Leah made a thoughtful *hmmm* sound.

"What?" Seth asked her.

"Well, I think that's a good sign, don't you? Why would she look Veronica up on social media if she thought the woman was dead? It sounds as if she wasn't sure, despite Gershom's words, and wanted to see if Veronica had posted anything recently that would indicate she still lived."

Aidan nodded. "I thought the same."

Roland joined them, scowling up at Seth. "You can't actually be considering it—letting him take Michael and Adira to see her at the network. She attacked Leah. She's dangerous."

Seth shook his head. "I won't let him take Adira and Michael to the network."

Roland relaxed.

"I'll bring Tessa here instead."

Once more, the room fell silent.

"What?" Roland and Marcus both barked.

"I'm going to bring Tessa here," Seth repeated. "She will be joining us for dinner."

Krysta ducked into the kitchen to fetch another place setting.

Roland looked furious, Marcus worried.

Seth shrugged. "There are over a dozen immortals present and at least half a dozen Seconds. Tessa couldn't harm Adira and Michael if she tried. And if she *does* try," he added, catching every immortal's eye, "incapacitate her if you must, but do *not* kill her. Understood?"

"Understood," most chorused. He didn't blame Roland for refraining.

"As long as she thinks us monsters, she will remain loyal to Gershom," Seth told them. "So let her see us as we are—a loving family and protectors of innocents."

It took a moment, but activity resumed as immortals helped Tracy and Sheldon carry trays bearing three large turkeys to the table along with bowl after bowl of side dishes.

Seth clapped Roland on the back. "Relax. I won't let Tessa hurt them. I vow it."

Drawing in a deep breath, Roland released it in a long sigh. "I know you won't."

Leah looked around. "Where *are* the children?"

Roland nodded to two sofas that had been pushed together—facing each other—to form a huge crib of sorts. "Napping on the sofa." His lips twitched as he met Seth's gaze. "The tremors and storms unnerved them a bit, so they wanted to stay up here with everyone else."

Damned if Seth didn't feel heat creep into his cheeks.

Leah bit her lip. "I don't know what's worse: the dismay I feel that everyone knows exactly how many times we made love, regret over possibly frightening the children, or fear that you aren't going to touch me anymore, Seth."

Roland chuckled. "Don't worry about the children. We

managed to convince them that the ground shaking was like a fun carnival ride."

Leah grinned. "It sure as hell was for me."

Laughter erupted throughout the room.

Even Seth joined in.

Two little heads poked up from behind the sofa's back.

Adira's eyes brightened when she saw Leah. Squealing with glee, she stood and started to climb over the back of the sofa.

Marcus zipped past and caught her before she could fall. Roland did the same for Michael when the little boy opted to follow her.

As soon as their feet touched the floor, the toddlers raced over to Leah, who knelt and accepted warm hugs.

R.E.M.'s "It's the End of the World as We Know It" filtered faintly through the conversations that arose. Across the room, Zach answered his phone. "Yes?"

"Riley and I are badly outnumbered and could use some help," Quinn, an immortal stationed in Ireland said. "Shite!"

Zach teleported away.

Guilt suffused Seth.

"Don't," David said softly enough to prevent Leah from hearing him.

Seth sent him a penitent look. Zach, David, and Jared had been fielding his calls for hours while he lolled in bed and explored Leah's beautiful body. "You shouldn't have had to field my calls for so long. I should have—"

"Done exactly what you did and taken the time you needed. You'll hear no complaints from us, Seth. Immortals around the world are becoming accustomed to their calls being answered by Zach and Jared. They all have devices that confirm Zach and Jared aren't Gershom. And both are fine with taking on additional responsibilities." He patted Seth on the back. "The fact that you *can* shoulder all of the burden yourself doesn't mean that you should."

Seth smiled. "I haven't shouldered all of the burden myself in thousands of years. You've taken much of it off my shoulders."

"Zach and Jared will take even more." David's smile broadened. "Jared is loving it, by the way. He's been bored for millennia. This gives him something useful to do and will save us a lot of headaches by keeping him too busy to date."

Seth chuckled and shook his head. "That's going to be a nightmare."

"Such was my thought."

The Mills Brothers began to sing rhythmic *dos* to the accompaniment of piano and drums in the tune "I've Got My Love to Keep Me Warm."

David palmed his cell. "Yes?"

"David," a Finnish immortal named Leena said breathlessly. "Joakim is down. We've defeated the vampires, but he nearly lost an arm and could use a healer."

"Call the network and have them send a medic and a cleaning crew to you. I'll be there as soon as I can." Pocketing the phone, he sent Seth a smile. *I'm so glad I can teleport now,* he told him telepathically.

Seth was, too. Only Sarah, Roland, and Zach knew it, however. So David left through the front door and flew away in the form of a hawk on the off chance Gershom might be watching from far enough away that Ami couldn't detect him. Once David had flown a few miles, he would seek the cover of forest, retake his form, teleport somewhere discreet near Leena, then fly to her side.

They would let no one else learn that particular secret until their final confrontation with Gershom.

Chapter Eighteen

T ESSA PACED THE LENGTH OF the studio apartment. Her stomach
growled.

Aidan hadn't made an appearance with a dinner tray. She had
dared him to come to her, dared him to try to convince her that
Gershom had lied. But he hadn't.

"Coward," she muttered furiously, resting a hand on the butter
knife she'd tucked into a pocket. One didn't need a sharp blade to
penetrate flesh when one had preternatural strength. Tessa
planned to pierce the Scot's heart as soon as he made an
appearance, then fight her way out of… whatever the hell this
building was.

"*You're* the coward," a male growled in response.

She jumped. It was the same man she'd heard arguing with
himself and saying some truly scary stuff. It had not taken her long
to determine he wasn't right in the head. "What?"

"*You're* the coward," he repeated. "Too afraid to see what's right
in front of your fucking face," he grumbled. "Too afraid to admit
you've placed your trust in the hands of a monster."

"You're one to call someone else a monster," she challenged.

"At least I have an excuse," he retorted without pause, offering
no denial. "I'm a vampire."

"So?"

The deep laugh he released carried a maniacal lilt. "Did
Gershom keep you so clueless about the virus that infects you that
you don't even know it causes brain damage in humans?"

She frowned. "Bullshit. I'm human. And all it's done is make me stronger."

"Really?" he countered. "Did *he* tell you that? Did *Gershom* tell you you're human? No big fucking surprise there. Well, news flash. You aren't human. You're a *gifted one*."

He thought she wasn't human? What did he think she was—an alien or something? "You're insane."

"No shit. I've been fighting the madness this fucking virus spawns for six years. Even Seth hasn't been able to stop it. But that doesn't change the fact that you're a *gifted one*... as in someone who is born with gifts others don't possess. Haven't you ever wondered why you can do the things you do? How you can do things no one else you know can do?"

She stilled. How did he know she was different?

"It's because you were born with advanced DNA. All *gifted ones* are. It's why Gershom chose you. It's why he kidnapped you. He knew he could transform you without you going insane. You aren't a vampire. You're an immortal." He loosed another growl and something crashed to the floor somewhere. "I wish to hell I were, too." He sounded tormented.

"Is that why you're a prisoner here? Because you're a vampire?"

"*I'm not a fucking prisoner!*" he bellowed.

Even though Tessa couldn't see him, her heart began to beat faster with fear as more crashes sounded. She patted the pocket that held the butter knife, terrified the man might burst through the wall and try to kill her with his bare hands.

Quiet descended.

"Shit," he said. "I'm sorry. I'm sorry. That was... That was the virus. I'm sorry. I... *Fuck!* I can't think straight tonight!"

"Cliff?" another male said softly. "You hanging in there?"

A choked laugh full of despair carried to her. "I'm hanging on by a thread, Stewart," the insane man—Cliff—replied. "Clinging to the edge by my fucking fingertips."

"You want me to call Bastien? Or Aidan?"

"No. They've done enough babysitting for the day."

Tessa cleared her throat. "Who are *you*?" she asked the second speaker.

"Stewart," he replied. "I'm a vampire, too. You should listen to Cliff. He's known the Immortal Guardians longer than I have."

"You don't sound insane."

"No," he acknowledged somberly, "but I've been struggling a lot lately. I'm having psychotic breaks now. Like one a month. But the immortals who are usually on hand—Melanie and Bastien—make sure I don't hurt anyone. That's why we're here—me, Cliff, and the other vampires. We don't want to hurt anyone. The immortals are doing everything they can to help us and to keep us from completely losing it and killing innocents."

Tessa sank down on the comfy love seat. "Help you how?"

Cliff answered. "I surrendered to the immortals not long after my transformation when I realized they were the good guys. Their doctors have been trying to find a way to help us. To help *all* humans who turn vampire. They're trying to find a cure for the virus, or at least find a way to keep us from going insane."

It didn't sound as if they were succeeding. "If what you're saying is true—"

"*Of course it's fucking true!*" he raged. "You think I'm *lying?*" Another crash sounded. "You think I *want* to be insane?" Crash. "You think I *want* to turn into someone whose thoughts would've fucking made me vomit eight years ago?" Crash. "This isn't who I am!" Crash. "This *isn't* who I *am!*" Crash. Crash.

Silence.

He swore. "I'm sorry. I'm sorry. I'm sorry…" He kept repeating it over and over, his voice getting softer and more controlled with each apology. "I'm sorry. It's…" He sighed. "I'm sorry. It's not your fault you doubt us. Gershom has been fucking with your head as much as this virus is fucking with mine."

"Cliff," Stewart said, "let me call Aidan."

"No. It's okay. I'm… I'm okay."

He wasn't. He really wasn't. Tessa thought Cliff would've killed her if he had been in the same room with her.

"Tessa," Cliff said, no anger lingering his voice, "from what I've heard, you were hunting with vampires for at least a few weeks before you attacked Leah."

The fact that he sounded completely calm now unnerved her as much as his violent outbursts had. "So?"

"So, haven't you ever encountered vampires who *weren't* newly turned? Vampires who weren't quite right or who seemed unnaturally eager to kill just for the sake of killing? Vampires who maybe weren't as clean-cut as the ones Gershom had you hunt with? Vampires who didn't bathe or wash the blood from their clothing after a kill? Vampires who were so clueless in regard to right and wrong that you worried they might attack *you* — the only female in the group?"

Yes, she had. And they had totally creeped her out. But she had just chalked it up to their having been sick bastards before they'd been turned. If not all humans were good people, she had reasoned, then not all vampires would be either.

"I'll take your silence as a yes," Cliff said. "*Those* vampires — the ones who get off on terrifying and torturing — are the vampires Immortal Guardians hunt. Newly turned vampires like I was when I met them and like Stewart and the others here were when they met them, are given the option of joining the immortals and seeking medical help."

"Yeah," Stewart said. "Like he said, Immortal Guardians are the good guys. They don't get off on hurting people the way Gershom does. I really lost it one time when I was badly injured and accidentally hurt Dr. Lipton. I thought the immortals would kill me for it, but they didn't. They continued to help me. And Melanie has never held it against me."

"I know it sucks," Cliff added, "to discover that everything you thought was truth is actually a lie, but that whole *ignorance is bliss* thing is bullshit. Ignorance isn't bliss. Ignorance just makes it easier for other people to manipulate you. And Gershom has been manipulating the hell out of you to get you to do bad shit to good people. Seth and the others just want to help you."

As if summoned by his name, Seth abruptly appeared inside the apartment.

Tessa lunged to her feet.

Standing near the door, he offered her a slight bow. "Good evening, Tessa." His stance remained relaxed, unthreatening, as she eased around the coffee table and braced herself for a fight.

Cliff and Stewart grew quiet.

"You won't be needing those," Seth said and waved a hand.

The butter knife, vegetable peeler, pointy bottle opener, pencils, pens, and other *weapons* she had amassed leapt out of her pockets and deposited themselves in the sink. "I've come to take you to dinner."

Tessa fought the fear that inundated her. How had he known about the weapons? He had filched every single one of them!

"I knew about them because I'm reading your thoughts," he replied as though she had spoken the question aloud. "Gershom can do the same. It is how he has managed to control and mislead you for so long, quashing every doubt as soon as you think it."

Damn it. She didn't want to doubt Gershom. He had helped her. He had saved her. And he had tried to save her brother and been so crushed when he couldn't.

Seth's lips tightened. "I know you won't believe me or think me sincere when I say this, but I'm sorry I couldn't find you sooner. I've been searching ever since I learned you and the other *gifted ones* had been taken. But even I have my limits. And I am so sorry for your loss. The police report indicated that William was killed in a traffic accident while the two of you were visiting your parents in New York. I had no idea Gershom was involved."

As usual, grief swamped her at the mention of her brother's name. But so did anger. She couldn't trust this man after seeing what he had done.

Seth approached her slowly, raising his hands in a take-it-easy gesture that showed no weapons. But he hadn't needed a weapon to plunge her into unconsciousness.

"I apologize for that," he said, "but Leah was injured and bleeding profusely. I couldn't heal her as long as you persisted in attacking me."

Tessa's thoughts shifted to the woman she had meant to use as bait to entrap Seth. The woman who had taken a bullet for her and tackled her to the floor to remove her from the shooters' line of sight. "How is she?" she asked, angered by the guilt the inquiry sparked. Gershom wouldn't want her to feel sorry for Leah.

Uncertainty rose as she questioned that for the first time.

"You're questioning it because Gershom isn't present to feed your fury and need for vengeance."

Could Gershom really do that? Because without it... "Did Leah survive?" she asked.

He smiled. "Yes, and she's worried about you. She will be

dining with us."

She would?

When Seth reached out and touched her shoulder, Tessa flinched and brought her hands up. The room went dark and that weird weightlessness struck as he teleported her away. A moment later, bright light erupted around her. Multiple *beeps* sounded.

Breaking Seth's hold, she backed away and took in her new surroundings.

Not a holding cell. Not a torture chamber. But a huge living room with high ceilings and multiple sofas, love seats, wingback chairs, and coffee tables. She frowned. Coffee tables with small foam cushions attached to every corner. The kind she had seen a friend use while baby proofing her home. Which was weird, because atop some of those coffee tables lay sheathed swords and daggers.

"The children know not to touch the weapons," Seth told her as he pulled a cell phone out of his pocket.

Children? What children?

He dialed a number, then pressed the phone to his ear.

"Reordon," a man answered.

Her preternaturally enhanced hearing enabled her to hear both sides of the conversation. And this man's voice was one Tessa had heard often since awakening in that studio apartment. She had quickly concluded that he was one of the higher-ups at whatever facility had held her.

"Just letting you know we've left," Seth said. "You can turn the network's alarm back on."

"Will do."

The network. That's what everyone seemed to call that place. But the name didn't tell her diddly-squat about it.

Seth nodded as he tucked his phone away. "That's why we call it the network. If an employee slips and mentions it in public, no one will have any idea what we do there."

Lunging forward, Tessa grabbed a sword off the closest coffee table, discarded the sheath, and held the blade up between her and Seth. It pissed her off when he didn't even tense. She knew he could yank this weapon out of her hands as swiftly as he had the others but still felt better holding it.

"Which is why I'm letting you," he remarked softly.

Movement behind him drew her gaze to what appeared to be a dining room table. Well over a dozen men and women—all wearing black clothing—stood around it, staring back at her.

Immortal Guardians. Her heart began to race as ice filled her veins and her fear multiplied. There were so many of them!

"Easy," Seth said. "We are not your enemy, Tessa."

Despite the things Cliff and Stewart had told her, she couldn't bring herself to believe it.

A man stepped up to Seth's side. Seth was at least six foot eight inches tall. This man was six foot four or thereabouts and offered her a nod of greeting. "I apologize for not having brought you a meal earlier. I wanted to speak with Seth first," he said with a Scottish accent. "I'm Aidan."

This was Aidan? This was the man who had kidnapped Veronica and so many of the other women?

"You son of a bitch!" Tessa sped forward, raising the sword.

A blurred form passed between them and grabbed her arms before she could finish swinging the blade.

Straining to free herself, she stared up at the warrior who held her wrists above her head.

He wasn't quite as tall as Aidan but bore piercing brown eyes and an air of menace that unnerved her. "It's all right," he crooned in a British accent. With slow, careful movements, he extracted the sword from her fingers and released his hold.

Tessa stumbled backward.

"Aidan didn't harm Veronica," he said.

"Bullshit. After Gershom rescued her, she told me Aidan was the one who kidnapped her."

He shook his head. "I thought Aidan guilty, too, at first. I'm Roland Warbrook. Veronica Becker was my descendant."

Tessa shook her head. "She would've mentioned it if she had an immortal relative."

"She didn't know about me. I'm nearly a thousand years old, Tessa."

What?

"I watch over my descendants, but don't introduce myself." He shrugged, his ruggedly handsome features tinged with sadness. "I don't age, so I can't be part of their lives without raising questions that are best left unanswered." Bending, he picked up the discarded sheath, slid the sword home, then returned it to the coffee table. "And I admit getting close to them, then losing them, generation after generation, was taking too great a toll on me."

She stared, not knowing what to think.

"When Gershom made it appear as though Aidan had abducted Veronica," he continued, "I wanted Aidan dead."

She shook her head. "Veronica was certain it was Aidan."

Roland looked to the Immortal Guardians' leader. "Seth, show her how he did it."

She returned her attention to Seth.

Seth sighed. "Gershom can shape-shift."

She laughed. Did they think her a simpleton? No one could —

Shock stole her breath when Seth's form began to change. His long hair shortened. His height did, too, by a few inches. Then his features and build transmogrified in swift, small increments until she found herself staring at Aidan's twin.

She backed away a step. Then another.

"Gershom can shape-shift," Seth said again, only this time he sounded exactly like Aidan. "It's how he convinced Veronica and so many of the others that Aidan took them." His form changed again, growing taller, his hair changing length again, his features altering until Gershom stood before her. "It's also how he convinced you I killed your brother." He looked and sounded just like Gershom, except he now wore no shirt and bore huge dark wings with translucent feathers.

"Gershom doesn't have wings," she choked out.

Seth-Gershom tilted his head to one side. "He's never showed them to you?"

She shook her head.

The wings vanished as a dark shirt enveloped Seth's arms and covered his chest. "Is this more like it?"

She nodded numbly as her world began to crumble.

Seth once more spoke in his own voice. "Gershom killed your brother, Tessa, after assuming my appearance. He injured you, then sped away before you could bleed out. As soon as he left your sight, he shape-shifted back into himself and returned, valiantly playing the hero to win your trust." Seth shifted back into his own form.

She shook her head.

"I protect *gifted ones*." He took a step closer. "I watch over you all, as best I can, from the moment of your birth." His form changed again.

Tears welled in her eyes as Tessa stared up at her brother, who—despite being her twin—had been half a foot taller than her own five foot six.

"I would never have harmed William," he said in her brother's voice. Moisture glimmered in his brown eyes, which were lighter now. "I would never harm any *gifted one*." His Adam's apple rose and fell with a swallow. "I'm so sorry I wasn't there to save him."

A sob caught in her throat as she slowly moved forward and raised a hand to touch his face. "Will," she whispered. He looked exactly like him. He even sounded like him.

How many times had she wished her brother were standing before her once more? How many times had she wished she could tell him she loved him and say goodbye?

Wrapping her arms around him in a tight hug, she burst into tears. She knew it wasn't really Will. She knew it wasn't her brother. But the chance to hold him again… to feel one of his big bear hugs…

She just couldn't resist it.

Deep wracking sobs erupted as her heart broke. She missed him so much.

He rested his cheek on her hair and wrapped his arms around her in a bear hug, which only made her cry harder. He even *felt* like Will.

Someone pressed some tissues into one of her hands. Tessa just balled them up, unwilling to release the brother whose loss had left such a gaping hole inside her. She didn't know how long she clung to him, soaking his shirt with her tears. But she reluctantly loosened her hold when her nose began to run.

Stepping back, she scrubbed at her tears and blew her nose.

Leah now stood beside them. Her smile was gentle as she held up a small stainless steel wastebasket with one hand and offered Leah more tissue with the other.

"Thank you," Tessa said, her voice hoarse.

Leah nodded, then looked at Will. "Maybe you should go back to being you now."

Tessa fought back a protest when William shifted back into Seth's form. More tears welled. Frustrated, she scrubbed them away with more tissues.

No one spoke.

Well, *almost* no one. Over in the dining area, someone with a British accent said softly, as though speaking to a child, "No, no, sweetie. Stay here with Daddy. She's okay. She's just sad."

Everyone watched Tessa with concern and sympathy that just did not seem feigned.

"I don't know what to think," she admitted. In that moment, she felt as shattered mentally as Cliff had sounded when he had spoken to her earlier. If all this was true... and it felt horribly, horribly true... then she had been fighting for the man who had slain her brother. The man who had tortured Will and reveled in his agony. She had been doing his bidding and helping him hurt more people and...

"I can't believe it," she whispered. "I don't *want* to believe it."

"I didn't either," another Brit said. That voice she recognized as Bastien's. And when he stepped up beside Roland, she could put a face to the voice. "I've been where you are." Bastien shook his head grimly. "For two hundred years I thought this one" — he jerked a thumb in Roland's direction — "had killed my sister and her husband Blaise, who was my best friend. And for two hundred years I plotted Roland's demise, determined to avenge their deaths. I vowed to slay every Immortal Guardian on the planet and even raised an army of vampires, much the way Gershom is now, to accomplish that feat."

Tessa glanced at Roland, then back at Bastien. "I take it you failed?"

Bastien smiled. "Yes, and I'm thankful I did." His expression darkened. "Come to find out, Catherine was slain by her husband." He shook his head. "You don't know how much it continues to torment me that I protected my sister's killer after her death."

"I do," Melanie said as she joined them and leaned into his side. "And I wish it wouldn't. It wasn't your fault, honey." She looked at Tessa. "And it isn't your fault that you trusted Gershom."

"I never once questioned him," Tessa admitted, self-loathing consuming her.

Seth recaptured her attention. "Because he was manipulating your emotions." When she opened her mouth to protest, he held up a hand. "I mean he was *literally* manipulating your emotions."

Calm immediately suffused Tessa, erasing all her grief and sadness and loosening the muscles in her shoulders.

"To keep you from questioning him," Seth continued, "he fueled your anger, suppressed any doubt or guilt that attempted to rise, and filled you with hate and a lust for vengeance."

In the next instant, rage consumed her, quickened her breath, and drove her to dive for the sword again.

Before she could touch it, the rage vanished, replaced by calm.

Shaken, Tessa stared at Seth with wide eyes. "Oh shit." Had he done that? Had Seth made her feel all that?

"Yes," he answered. "Like Gershom, I possess empathic abilities. A few of the other immortals present do as well."

Bastien nodded. "I do. But I can't manipulate emotions. I can only read them with a touch."

Melanie pursed her lips. "Something I still wish you would've told me sooner." She cast Tessa a self-deprecating smile. "He knew I was lusting after him *way* before I knew he was lusting after me."

They all seemed to take such miraculous abilities in stride.

The only gifts Gershom had revealed to Tessa were his ability to teleport and his ability to heal with his hands. And Tessa and her brother had only been able to manipulate plants, making them flourish with a touch.

She looked at Seth, a tiny part of her still trying to rationalize it and make the things Seth told her a lie instead of the months she had spent with Gershom.

Seth looked over his shoulder. "Marcus, bring Adira here, please."

The men and women watching from the dining room parted. A handsome man strode forward with a toddler on his hip. The pretty little redhead studied Tessa somberly as her — *father?* — frowned up at Seth.

Seth smiled at Adira and took one of her hands. Pressing a kiss to it, he said softly, "Adira, sweetheart, I want you to show Miss Tessa what Gershom did to Mommy."

"No," Marcus instantly growled. Cupping a protective hand around the child's head, he pressed her cheek to his chest. "*Hell* no. I don't want her reliving that."

Seth released Adira's hand and held up his own in a calming gesture. "I wouldn't ask her to do it if I thought it might make the nightmares return."

"If she thinks about that evening, you know damned well the nightmares will return."

Dread filled Tessa's stomach as she watched them. This did not feel like an act or a show put on for her benefit.

"She thinks about it every time her mother leaves her sight, Marcus," Seth said.

Marcus looked pained by the revelation.

"You know how much I adore Adira," Seth went on. "I would never do anything that would cause her harm."

Marcus swallowed.

"Everyone here can understand why Tessa might be reluctant to take our word. But I don't think anyone—even Tessa—could believe Adira would show her anything but the truth. She's too young and innocent to harbor a deceptive agenda."

A full minute ticked past as Marcus visibly battled his need to protect his daughter. "Fine."

Seth patted his shoulder. "Thank you. Let Tessa hold her, please."

"Hell no. Adira can show her while *I* hold her."

Seth shook his head. "I don't want any of us touching Adira while she shows her. It would give Tessa an excuse to doubt the veracity of what she sees."

"Ami?" Marcus called.

A short redheaded woman who closely resembled Adira joined him. "Go ahead." Taking the toddler from Marcus, she transferred her to Tessa's arms. "Please don't hurt her."

Tessa met Ami's green eyes. "I would never hurt a child."

Adira seemed perfectly content in Tessa's hold. Leaning into her chest, she stared up at Tessa with somber emerald eyes identical to her mother's.

"Adira," Seth repeated softly, "show Miss Tessa what Gershom did to Mommy."

Reaching up, the toddler touched a tiny hand to Tessa's cheek.

Tessa sucked in a breath when the living room vanished, replaced by a large front lawn as the child's memories became her own. The scenery blurred. Wind whipped her. Tessa saw everything from the point of view of the toddler. Ami held her as Marcus carried them both in his arms, racing for the safety of the trees. She could feel Ami's anxiety and fear. Panic built inside her when the bad man—Gershom—teleported in front of them and thwarted them time and time again as they tried to get away. Marcus finally stopped. Setting Ami down, he placed himself between them and Gershom. Ami cradled her close and pressed a kiss to the top of her head. She heard Gershom warn human males bearing weapons that if they fired, he would send every bullet into Ami. When an immortal tried to help Marcus, Gershom flung out a hand and hurled him at least thirty feet into a tree. Bones cracked audibly.

Tessa's fear spiked, making it harder to breathe.

"Easy," she heard Seth say from somewhere out of sight, distracting her. "What you're feeling is what Adira felt in that moment. It's all part of the memory she's sharing with you."

The memory blurred, letting the living room bleed in for a moment, then sharpened again.

Fear returned and grew at an incredible rate as she watched Seth and his Immortal Guardians fight Gershom. She hugged Ami tight, clutching the front of her shirt as the battle raged. A roar of fury suddenly filled the air. She whimpered.

Then Gershom vanished and reappeared behind Ami. Smiling savagely, he drew a blade across Ami's throat. Warm red liquid poured forth, soaking her clothing as Ami tightened her hold and began to fall.

"No!" Tessa cried.

Adira withdrew her hand. The vision vanished, returning Tessa to the living room.

Adira stared up at her, her pretty face solemn.

Ami took the child from Tessa's arms and cuddled her close.

Tessa began to shake uncontrollably as she stared at them.

Ami's brow furrowed with concern. "Tessa? Are you all right?"

Tessa couldn't speak. She could barely breathe.

Seth frowned. "She needs air. Clear the way." Gently curling a hand around her upper arm, he guided her toward the front door.

Another immortal opened it as they approached.

As soon as she and Seth stepped outside into fresh air, Tessa shook off his hold. He voiced no protest when she kept walking, placing a good twenty yards between herself and the house. Bending over, she braced her hands on her knees, closed her eyes, and drew in one deep breath after another. Such chaos reigned in her head that she couldn't seem to focus upon a single thought.

Seth said nothing.

After several minutes, her heart didn't slam quite so painfully against her ribs. Her breathing began to slow. And she stopped trembling.

Releasing a long sigh, Tessa straightened and opened her eyes.

Moonlight filtered down from a cloudless sky, illuminating the large front lawn and the forest that bordered it.

Her stomach sank. It was the yard from Adira's memories.

Turning, she faced Seth and was surprised that the door behind him had closed, leaving the two of them alone. "This is where it happened?"

"Yes." He strolled toward her.

She stared up at him helplessly as he drew near. "I can't think straight."

"I know. I did not wish to cause you such distress, but could find no way to help you see the truth without it."

She looked around, thinking the peaceful night a painful contrast to the turmoil deep inside her. "I don't know what to do."

He nodded, nothing but concern reflected in his handsome features.

"Don't you hate me?" She had attacked Leah. And Leah had nearly died. She had helped Gershom. And Gershom had slit Ami's throat.

"No," he responded simply. "I only want for you what I want for all *gifted ones* and immortals. I want you to be happy and safe and well."

She couldn't seem to digest that.

"None of this was your fault, Tessa." He looked away, his brow furrowing. "It was my fault for failing to keep you safe in the first place."

She heard swears erupt inside the house, followed by muted conversation.

"Gershom is *my* enemy," Seth said. "And he knew he could use you to strike at me."

Before Tessa could respond, the front door flung open.

Leah marched toward them. "That's bullshit!" she yelled.

Eyebrows rising, Seth swung around to face her. "What?"

"I said that's bullshit." She frowned as she joined them. "None of this is your fault, Seth."

Now *he* frowned. "How did you even hear what I was saying?"

"I didn't." She waved a hand at the house behind her. "*They* told me. And they think it's bullshit, too." The anger left her features as she turned to Tessa. "I know this has come as a shock to you. I'm actually still trying to process it myself. Are you all right?"

Tessa slowly wagged her head back and forth. "Not by a long shot."

Smiling, Leah stunned her by pulling her into a hug. "That's okay. We're all here for you, Tessa, and will help you through it."

Tessa hugged her back. "I'm so sorry I attacked you."

Leah shrugged. "It's okay. We both came through it unscathed." Stepping back, she produced a smile. "Aside from having our minds blown, that is. But like I said, we'll get through it together." She turned to Seth. "And *you*..." Moving forward, she wrapped her arms around his waist and leaned into him. "You need to stop beating yourself up over things you can't control." When Seth slid his arms around her waist, she reached up and pressed a palm to his cheek. "You can't be everywhere at once, Seth. I know how hard you've been searching for Tessa. I saw how torn up you were after she made that first appearance and you weren't able to find her and bring her to safety."

Tessa stared at him. Really?

"And I know you've been killing yourself trying to find the rest of the missing *gifted ones*."

"Immortals," he corrected softly.

She smiled. "That's going to take me a while to get used to."

Ducking his head, Seth rested his forehead against hers.

"You'll find them," she told him with complete confidence. "You'll find the other immortals and you'll stop Gershom."

He sighed. "I'm sorry I brought you into all this."

"You didn't. If memory serves," she countered, her voice acquiring a teasing note, "*I* was the one who asked *you* to dance."

His eyes acquired a faint golden glow. "I should have refused."

She winked. "If you had, I would've missed out on an awesome carnival ride."

He grinned.

Laughter erupted inside the house.

Leah rose onto her toes and pressed a kiss to his lips, then turned back to Tessa. "So?" She held out her hand. "I'm really hungry, and — by the looks of it — Sheldon and Tracy have prepared enough food for at least fifty people. Are you ready to join us?"

Tessa stared at her, knowing Leah wasn't just asking her to join them for dinner.

Reaching out, she took the woman's hand. "Yeah. I'm ready."

Scared as hell, but ready.

Chapter Nineteen

SETH LEFT THE CHAIR AT the head of the table vacant for David and claimed the one at the foot of it. He seated Leah on his right, then seated Tessa on his left before sitting down himself. His stomach growled.

Several immortal males chuckled.

Seth just smiled and shook his head. He really *had* worked up an appetite.

Ami sat beside Leah and held Adira on her lap while Marcus attached a hook-on high chair seat to the table next to her. As soon as it was secure, he lifted his daughter, blew raspberries in her chubby neck rolls to spark giggles, then tucked her into the clever chair and claimed the seat on the other side. Roland sat beside Marcus after installing Michael in a similar hook-on chair between him and Sarah.

Tessa gasped when she saw Michael.

Roland looked over at her.

"That's Veronica's son," she said softly. "I recognize him from the pictures on Veronica's social media pages."

Roland nodded. "My wife and I adopted him."

The rest of the immortals and their Seconds found seats around the long table. They had added yet another leaf when Stanislav had rejoined their ranks, bringing Susan with him. Susan seemed to be fitting in well.

Seth slid the lovely woman at his side a glance. Leah was, too. She and Ami were already chatting as though they were longtime friends. And she had a unique talent for making the rest of the immortals and Seconds smile and laugh. She really *was* good with different.

How he wished she were different, too, capable of transforming without descending into madness.

He frowned. Speaking of madness...

He looked down the table and caught Bastien's eye. "Bastien, Cliff is struggling."

Bastien's brow furrowed. "I know he was earlier, but he seemed okay when I left." He glanced at his wife. "Are you still getting that feeling?"

Melanie nodded, her face grim.

Much to Seth's surprise, Tessa spoke. "Stewart is worried about him and wanted to call you, but Cliff told him not to."

Bastien studied her. "You spoke to them?"

The room quieted.

Tessa nodded. "Cliff was trying to help me understand that Immortal Guardians are the good guys and Gershom is the villain. When I was reluctant to believe him..." She cast everyone at the table a quick, apologetic glance. "He kept erupting into rages. It sounded like he was tearing up his apartment or whatever room he was in."

Bastien sent Seth a panicked look. "Cliff's apartment is always scrupulously neat. He said keeping it that way helps distract him."

Seth nodded, even more concerned now that he knew Melanie's mild prophetic gift was warning her something bad was about to happen. "As soon as you've eaten, you and Aidan should take him hunting."

Aidan rose. "We'll do it now."

Bastien agreed.

Sheldon jumped up. "Hang on a sec, guys." He jogged into the kitchen while Bastien and Aidan kissed their wives.

Melanie frowned. "Do you want us to come, too?"

Dana nodded. "We can come with you."

Aidan shook his head. "Stay and enjoy your dinner, get to know Tessa."

Bastien nodded. "We'll be fine."

Seth knew neither warrior wanted the women to see the ferocity with which Cliff tore his vampire opponents apart now.

Sheldon returned, carrying a large cloth grocery bag that zipped at the top. "Here."

Bastien took the bag. "What is it?"

"Foot-long sandwiches, chips, and bottles of tea. Enough for all three of you."

Aidan smiled, though it didn't reach his eyes. He and Bastien were both close to Cliff and knew his days were numbered. "Thank you."

Seth called Reordon and alerted him to the incoming immortals.

A moment later, Aidan grabbed Bastien's shoulder and teleported him away.

Somber silence took the room.

Tessa looked around uneasily. "You guys seem to really like Cliff."

"We do," Seth acknowledged. "He's a brilliant, honorable man who has been a good friend and ally to us."

Sheldon, Richart, and Étienne began to carve the turkeys and dole out portions.

"What will happen if you can't cure him?" she asked hesitantly.

Melanie answered, her eyes sparkling with tears. "He'll die, either by his own hand or by ours. He doesn't want to become a monster like the one who turned him. If we can't halt or reverse the damage, at some point he'll—" Her voice cracked, halting her words.

Tessa took in the grim faces around the table. "Are there any vampires *here?*"

Seth shook his head. "Only immortals, humans, and *gifted ones.* Immortals, raise your hands and introduce yourselves."

Several hands rose in the air.

"Now the humans."

The human Seconds present did the same.

"Now the *gifted ones.*"

Darnell, Nicole, and Susan raised their hands and introduced themselves.

Susan smiled at Tessa. "I'm new to all this, too. I had no idea vampires and immortals even existed until I found Stanislav buried in my basement."

Tessa's eyebrows flew up. "He was buried in your basement?"

Nodding, Susan gave Tessa a quick rundown on how she'd met Stanislav and tumbled into the Immortal Guardians' world. Seth liked Susan. She was funny and told a good story, entertaining them all and bringing smiles to their faces. In a very short time, she had everyone laughing as they dined.

Seth tucked into his own food, then devoured additional helpings.

Leah grinned and leaned in close. "Keep it up. You burned a hell of a lot of calories today."

He laughed.

So did several immortals.

Seth was pleased with how the dinner progressed. He, Zach, and David took turns responding to calls from immortals in the field. Tessa gradually relaxed enough to eat something. Seth knew it would take her some time to adjust to the new reality, but she'd made a good start. And he was happy to have her amongst them.

As the meal wound down, he took Leah's hand and brought it to his lips. "I need to speak with Roland privately. Will you be all right if I leave you alone with this lot?"

She smiled as she glanced at the men and women seated around the table. "Sure. I like your family."

He hoped one day it would be her family, too.

Rising, he rounded the table.

Roland was already standing when Seth reached him. Seth caught Zach's eye. *Follow me.*

Nodding, Zach lowered his fork and stood.

Seth palmed his phone and made a quick call. Then he teleported Roland to the soundproof room in Chris's redesigned missile silo. Zach appeared a moment later. Seth spoke into the phone again. "We're here."

"Yes, sir," Brian responded. He was the highest-ranked network employee on-site when Chris wasn't around. "The alarm's back on."

Seth pocketed the phone and stared at Roland. "So? How are you?"

"I'm good," he said with a nod.

"You seem to have come through the healing all right. I apologize for not looking in on you more often."

Roland waved off the apology. "You've got enough on your plate, Seth. You don't need to play nursemaid to me on top of that." And Roland wasn't the type who would want anyone fussing over him regardless of how sick he was.

"Have you noticed any new abilities? I poured a hell of a lot of energy into you." More than he had Aidan.

"Stop looking so guilty when you say that," Roland ordered. "I told you to do it. And yes, I *have* noticed new abilities." Giving them a very un-Roland-like grin, he said, "Check this out." He vanished.

An alarm sounded.

Swearing, Seth called Brian. "Sorry about that. That was us. Turn the alarm off until further notice, please."

"Yes, sir."

"Looks like he can teleport now," Zach commented. "That's a plus."

So it was.

A long minute passed.

Zach arched a brow. "Do you think he's having trouble finding his way back?"

Seth frowned. "Possibly." Teleportation could be a tricky skill to master. If your mind wandered even a little bit, you could end up somewhere you didn't intend to.

Roland reappeared, his hair and clothing soaking wet. "It's raining in Miami," he said on a laugh.

Seth grinned. "Excellent."

"Good job," Zach said. "Have you mastered it enough to always end up at your chosen destination?"

"Yes. I've been practicing every time Sarah and I go out hunting."

Seth frowned. "Do you leave her alone or take her with you?"

"I started out by teleporting to the other side of campus whenever we patrolled Duke or UNC or one of the others to ensure I could do it and so she wouldn't be left alone. But once I mastered that, I started taking her with me, going a little farther each time."

"And how did that go?" Seth asked.

Roland grimaced. "There were a few mishaps. I forgot the time difference more than once and teleported us into direct sunlight."

"Ouch," Zach said with a wince.

"Exactly. I also startled the hell out of a hunter once. But he'd been drinking heavily and was already questioning what he saw as I teleported us away again."

If the hunter had mentioned it online, network employees who monitored such would've taken care of it.

"Any other new abilities?" Seth asked. For whatever reason, the most common abilities that seemed to transfer over during a healing were the three *t*'s: teleportation, telekinesis, and telepathy.

"My telekinetic abilities have strengthened," Roland said. Everything in the room that wasn't nailed down and didn't breathe suddenly leapt into the air.

Seth nodded. "Excellent. I want you to spar with David every other day and practice using those telekinetic skills in battle."

"I'll begin tomorrow."

"Anything else?"

Roland nodded and closed his eyes. His brow furrowed with concentration. Seconds later his clothing tore and fell away as he shape-shifted into a lion.

Seth's eyebrows flew up. "Unbelievable," he murmured. Shape-shifting was one of the most complex gifts one could possess. Because Roland was so much younger than himself, Seth hadn't expected him to acquire it.

Strolling forward to examine the creature, he touched the thick mane and found it as coarse as a lion's. "Can you roar?"

The lion shook his head, then gave it a try, releasing something that sounded more like one of Roland's growls of fury than a lion's roar.

Zach laughed.

Seth did, too. "Try again."

After several more tries, Roland managed to come a little closer.

"Now shift back."

The lion transformed back into Roland.

A naked Roland.

Zach grimaced and threw up a hand to block his view.

Looking down, Roland swore and cast Seth an exasperated look. "How do you always manage to have your clothes on when you shift back into your normal form?"

"I teleport them on. Have you tried that yet?"

"No."

"Teleporting objects you aren't touching can be tricky, but you should eventually be able to master it with small items." Seth thought of the extensive wardrobe at David's place.

A pile of clothing abruptly appeared at Roland's feet. Smiling, he bent and began to tug on a pair of pants. "Thank you."

Zach lowered his hand. "Does Sarah know you can shape-shift?"

"No. I only told her about the teleporting. I practice the shape-shifting and telekinesis while she sleeps." He eyed both men. "I thought the fewer people who knew, the fewer minds from which Gershom can pluck the information if he has the time. Sarah won't mind my keeping it from her. She wants me to do anything and everything I can to keep Michael safe and help you defeat Gershom. I wouldn't have told her about the teleporting, but I didn't want to leave her alone while I practiced."

"I understand." Seth looked at Zach. "So we've one more weapon in our arsenal that Gershom won't expect."

Zach turned back to Roland. "Practice shape-shifting into other people. Sarah. Ami. Sheldon. Anyone Gershom won't view as a threat."

Seth nodded. "Sheldon or Chris would be good, as would other human males about your size who won't necessitate a change of clothing and whom Gershom will assume weak."

"Good idea," Zach said. "Choose males. That way you won't have to worry about altering your voice much either. One of the trickiest parts of shape-shifting is sounding right. Can you speak with an American accent?"

"Yes, I can speak with an American accent," Roland replied, losing his British accent, "among others."

"Good. Then practice assuming other male forms." Zach glanced at Seth, then hesitated. "If he takes on Ami or Sarah's form, his clothing will swallow them, but... it wouldn't be quite as bad if he took on Leah's form. She's almost six feet tall."

Seth wasn't sure what emotion filled him then, but it didn't sit well. "She's half my weight, her shoulders aren't nearly as broad, and she has a tiny waist."

"But the pants will only be maybe three inches too long and her breasts and hips will help fill out the shirt and hold up the pants."

Roland spoke. "Give me a set of clothing in her size. I'll practice shape-shifting into her form and see if I can't master teleporting on the clothing as well."

Seth started to shake his head.

Finished dressing, Roland took a step toward him. "Seth, let me do this for you. We all know Gershom is going to target her because you care about her. If he pops in while I'm there, I can assume her appearance and—"

"He'll read it in your thoughts."

"But he'll have to take the time to do that. Even a few seconds can make a big difference when battling him."

"Do it," Zach said.

"Very well," Seth agreed. "I'll get you the clothing later tonight." He gripped Roland's shoulder. "Zach, remain here for a moment. I wish to speak with you."

"Okay."

Seth teleported Roland home to David's, then returned to the missile silo.

"I know," Zach said, holding up his hands. "You don't like the idea of anyone mimicking Leah. If someone took on Lisette's form, it would freak me the hell out, but—"

Seth smiled. "That isn't why I asked you to stay."

"Oh." He lowered his hands. "Is it that you're pissed because I know Leah's clothing sizes?"

He fought a laugh. "No."

Zach shifted his weight from one foot to the other... and began to get that look. The kind that filled Seth with both frustration and foreboding—his patented *there's a slight chance I might have done something that will make you want to kill me* look.

"Ah, hell. What have you done now?"

Zach's expression turned innocent. "What makes you think I—?"

"Zach."

"Fine." He paused. "Have you by any chance been reading Leah's mind?"

"No."

Zach's eyebrows rose. "You haven't?"

"No."

"Not at all?"

"No."

"Then I didn't do anything."

"Zach!"

He grimaced. "All right, all right. I knew you were seeing Leah and assumed it would place a giant target on her back, so I... did the whole plant-a-how-to-kick-ass-manual-in-her-head thing."

Fury rose. Seth took a menacing step forward. "You mind-controlled her?"

Zach held up his hands. "I was only trying to protect her the way I did Dana. But I didn't actually have to do much because she already *knew* how to kick ass." He offered Seth a smile. "She's taken a *lot* of martial arts classes."

"Her father wanted her to be safe."

"Good man. All I really had to do was tweak things a little here or there—have her aim for the major arteries when firing a gun instead of the head or chest, have her make her defensive moves and counterattacks earlier than she ordinarily would since vampires move so damned quickly, that sort of thing."

"How much damage did it do?" Mind control and erasing memories always caused brain damage. The less altered, the less damage inflicted, sometimes effecting no change in the person's health at all. But anything that took a lot of time—

"None. She came through it fine. Don't be pissed, but David was there with me, healing the damage—*minimal* damage—in real time."

Seth wanted to cling to his anger but trusted David implicitly and had come to trust Zach almost as much since they had renewed their friendship. "Thank you." Those minor tweaks had likely kept Leah alive when Tessa and the vampires had attacked.

"You're welcome."

"Stay the fuck out of her head from now on."

"I will," he vowed solemnly, "because I don't want to see the kinky shit you do in bed."

Seth laughed. "I did *not* expect her to say that. Did you see their expressions?"

Zach grinned. "Priceless."

Seth teleported his favorite katanas into his hands. "Now draw your swords."

"Why?"

"I want to spar with you."

Surprise lit Zach's features. "Really?" Then he frowned. "Wait. Are you saying I need practice?"

"No. I do."

Zach snorted. Though the two of them were roughly the same age, Seth had spent thousands of years building and strengthening his gifts and fighting skills. Both knew who would win if the two of them ever fought in earnest.

Yet Seth shrugged. "I *do*. I want to try something new."

"Like what?" Zach drew two swords.

Seth arched a brow. "I wouldn't want to spoil the surprise."

"That sounds interesting." Smiling in anticipation, Zach adopted a fighting stance. "Let's do this." He attacked in the next instant.

Seth grinned. There were few immortals on the planet who could provide him with a real challenge. David could. Though Gershom and the rest of the ancient Others might think David posed no threat to them, Seth's second-in-command had been sparring with him for thousands of years and could kick most of their asses. Aidan was a strong, fierce fighter and had trained with David, so he too could hold his own well in a sparring session with Seth. But Seth had come to believe that Zach would eventually become his equal if he continued to train as he had since falling in love with Lisette.

Neither man spoke as they fought. Neither held back either, only avoiding attempted decapitation. Should one accidentally sever the limb of the other, both were powerful enough healers to reattach it.

Seth had to admit it was exhilarating but didn't let that distract him from the task he had assigned himself.

Minutes passed as metal struck metal and occasionally slipped into flesh. Those slips were few at first. Then Zach's brow furrowed. Sweat began to bead on his forehead and trailed down one temple. Seth's blade slashed a deep furrow into Zach's side.

Grunting, Zach redoubled his efforts to fend off Seth's blows. But he took the offensive less and less, instead defending himself more and more. He swore as Seth began to drive him backward. Seth scored another hit. Then another.

"What's happening?" Zach huffed as he staggered beneath Seth's latest blow.

Seth said nothing, just kept hammering away at him. One of Zach's swords went flying.

Swearing, Zach staggered.

Seth scored another hit, making sure this time that it was shallow. He felt Zach try to teleport... and fail.

"What the hell?" Zach rasped just before Seth swept his other sword from his hand.

Zach stumbled and nearly fell to one knee. He thrust a hand out toward Seth, trying to yank Seth's weapons away with telekinesis.

Nothing happened.

He tried again to teleport.

Nothing happened.

Seth smiled in triumph as he pointed the tip of one sword at Zach's throat, then tapped the underside of his chin.

Zach shook his head and sank to his knees. "What did you do?" Leaning forward, he braced his hands on the floor. His head hung low. "I couldn't teleport. I couldn't use my telekinetic ability." He paused a moment to draw in a couple of rasping breaths. "I'm so weak I can barely move."

Seth crouched on his haunches in front of him and waited until Zach raised his head. "I drained you of your energy, every ounce that I could."

Zach gaped at him. "But you weren't touching me." Seth had drained Zach of his powers once before and then left him for the Others to deal with when he had believed Zach betrayed him. But he had had to touch Zach to do it.

"I don't have to now. I found a way to do it *without* touching you."

Utter astonishment entered his friend's weary features. "That's fucking brilliant."

Seth grinned.

"How the hell did you learn to do that?"

He shrugged. "I've been trying to figure it out for a few years now and redoubled my efforts after Gershom hurt Ami. I finally managed to do it last week while sparring with Richart."

Zach's lips twitched. "How did *he* feel about it?"

"He didn't know. He's young enough that he thought I just tired him out. But I wanted to give it a try with someone of your strength to confirm I can use it against Gershom without his realizing what's happening." Leaning forward, he pressed a hand to Zach's chest and infused him with much of the energy he had siphoned away.

Zach sucked in a breath, then sighed. "Much better. Thank you."

Smiling, Seth clapped him on the shoulder.

Zach glanced over his shoulder, then moved to sit with his back against the wall. Stretching out his legs, he crossed his feet at the ankle.

Seth settled himself beside him. He had sat just so with Ami many times since he had rescued her from her torturers. It felt completely natural to do the same with Zach.

"Damn, I'm tired," his friend complained.

Seth chuckled. "Sorry about that. I couldn't return *all* the energy I took because I had to use some of it myself. You're a formidable opponent."

Zach sent him a sardonic smile. "You've only yourself to blame for that. Kicking my ass that time you told me to stay the hell away from Lisette and your Immortal Guardian family really motivated me."

That seemed so long ago, but had only been... what—two or three years? "Yes, well, I'm sorry about that, too."

Zach shrugged. "It didn't stop me from seeing her."

Seth smiled. "I don't think anything could've done that."

"No," he agreed with a smile.

Quiet fell.

Zach's breathing gradually evened out. "So. How are you holding up?"

Seth stared at his boots. "I fear history is destined to repeat itself." A long moment passed. "She's human."

Zach nodded. "You can extend her life."

True, but both knew an extra century would not be enough. Seth wanted forever with Leah, like Zach would have with Lisette.

"I fear Gershom will kill her," Seth admitted.

"You've kept him from killing Ami."

"Barely."

"You can keep him from killing Leah, too. We'll help you keep her safe, Seth. *I'll* help you keep her safe. I owe you"—he shrugged—"everything. You're the reason I have Lisette."

Seth sighed. "You owe me nothing. None of you do. I just want you all to be happy."

"It isn't a matter of obligation. We want you to be happy, too. We want you to have—for however long you can—what we have found. And we'll do everything we can to ensure you will, even if it pisses you off."

Seth rubbed his tired eyes. "Now you sound like Reordon."

"Chris is a good man. One who worries about you." Zach smiled. "He showed me the surveillance video of you and Leah dancing together."

Seth shook his head. Who *hadn't* seen that video? "And?"

"Once I picked my jaw up off the floor, I began to hope every day that you would stop fighting your feelings for her." He shook his head. "I've only seen you like that with one other woman, Seth."

"My wife."

"I didn't understand it then, why you would risk so much to be with her."

Seth snorted. "I know you didn't. You and the Others kept trying to capture me and force me back into the fold."

Zach's lips twitched. "Well, I understand it now. I would risk anything to be with Lisette. And did. I won't let Gershom deprive you of Leah. I will do everything in my power—when you're not draining it, that is—to keep her safe."

Seth forced a laugh. "Thank you."

Quiet fell once more as Seth's mind involuntarily dragged him through possible future scenarios. "You know what will happen if Gershom kills her," he murmured.

Zach remained silent.

"You know what happened the first time." He had been in the city when that atrocity had taken place, far from their home in the country. A man had come to him, begging him to heal his dying child. And Seth had gone, of course.

The child had been moments from death, suffering dreadfully, when Seth arrived. Tears had streaked his pinched little face and stark fear had filled his eyes when Seth knelt beside him. The only gift Seth had revealed to humans at the time was his ability to heal with his hands. Some feared him for it, much as they had Alyssa of Westcott thousands of years later. Some reviled him for not letting them exploit his gift for their own gain. And some regarded him with awe.

Seth assumed this child feared him because of the ugly rumors he'd heard about the source of his gifts. And as he healed the boy, Seth delved into his thoughts to see what rumors had filled his young ears so he could discover who was spreading them. Instead, he made the shocking discovery that the boy's father had poisoned him.

A blade drove into Seth's back and burst from his chest.

"Abomination!" the boy's father shouted.

Roaring in fury and pain, Seth lunged to his feet. Healthy once more, the poor boy scuttled away and cowered in a corner. Using telekinesis, Seth yanked the sword from his back and deposited it in his own hand as he spun to face the father.

Men with swords flooded the domicile. Seth again used telekinesis to thrust the men away from him and strode outside so he could fight them without endangering the child.

Sunshine barely had time to brush his hair before more pain pierced him, stealing his breath. Unbelievable agony swept through him. It felt as though a thousand daggers had all struck him at once. Driven to his knees, he glanced down, found no new injuries, and struggled to understand what was happening.

Then his daughter screamed in his head.

Terror gripped him as he looked up at the boy's father. "What have you done?"

"What we had to," the man snarled, his face a mask of hatred and triumph.

Damning the consequences, Seth teleported to his home. Dozens of men clustered in a circle in front of it. All shouted as they stared at something on the ground. The pain suffusing Seth began to fade as he shoved his way through the throng and stared down in horror. His wife lay in the dirt, one hand clutching a sword, the fingers of the other curled into claws as though she had been trying to pull herself across the grass to their son and daughter.

The heart inside her body did not beat. A dagger had stopped it, the hilt still protruding from her chest. Their son and daughter lay nearby, their dark brown eyes frozen open in death. His daughter's face...

Seth would never forget the pain it portrayed, the tears that streaked her cheeks. Nor would he forget the way her hand had been stretching toward his wife's, her mother's, in a desperate attempt to reach her. His son-in-law lay at her feet, swords still in his hands. He had died trying to protect her but had been overwhelmed by sheer numbers and the incredible swiftness with which these men had struck. His daughter-in-law, whom he had loved as if his wife had born her, lay crumpled on the ground several yards away, his son at her feet. He, too, clutched weapons.

All were dead. The lifeless bodies of several of their attackers littered the ground around them.

Seth bellowed his grief, his fury, and sank to his knees beside his wife and children. He tried to gather them all into his arms, tried futilely to heal them, to bring them back. But his healing gift did not extend to resurrection.

The ground shook violently with an earthquake so strong that the murderers who still stood stumbled into each other and nearly fell. Several men rushed him while he knelt there, his wife and daughter in his arms, his hand clutching his son's shirt, sobs wrenching from his chest.

Swords swung toward him.

Seth threw back his head and roared as power exploded outward from him.

Every blade fell to the ground. Screams of agony erupted as everyone in his sight save his family began to burn from the inside out, their skin first brightening with the color of flames, then blackening and turning to ash. When they threw back their heads and opened their mouths to beg for mercy, flames emerged instead of words.

Rage took control of Seth, burning brightly and searing his insides. He gently laid his loved ones on the ground, then rose.

Swords—nearly six feet in length—appeared in his hands as he strode toward the city.

To this day, he didn't know how many he had slain, how much had burned before David had found him and summoned Zach and the Others to put an end to it. As Seth had confessed to Leah, he hadn't stopped at killing those responsible for the death of his family. He had killed everyone who had harbored hatred in his or her heart. Everyone who had delighted in treating his children like shit because they were different. Everyone who had launched ugly rumors about them, fueling the hatred that had resulted in the day's tragedy. Everyone who had wished him and his family malice, though they had done nothing to deserve it.

"I'm so much stronger than I was then," he told Zach now. "I fear you won't be able to rein me in if…"

"History will *not* repeat itself, Seth."

He shook his head. History *always* seemed to repeat itself. "If Gershom kills Leah, Ami, or Adira, I fear I will become his ultimate weapon. I fear I will succeed where he has failed in launching Armageddon."

"I won't let that happen," Zach vowed earnestly.

Seth hoped with all his heart that Zach was right.

Seth! Aidan suddenly shouted in his head.

Seth straightened. *Yes?*

We've found two more of the missing immortals.

Eyes widening, he leapt to his feet.

"What is it?" Zach asked, alarmed.

"Aidan found two of the missing immortals." He teleported away without another word.

Chapter Twenty

AIDAN EXCHANGED A CONCERNED LOOK with Bastien as the two of them escorted Cliff through the quiet college campus. Most students had long since sought their beds. A few who had either been up late partying or cramming for exams stumbled their weary way back to the dorms.

Cliff walked between Aidan and Bastien, his movements stiff and precise as though he feared if he made a single misstep he would erupt into violence and slay everyone he encountered. A peek into his thoughts revealed a maelstrom of voices urging him on. It was taking every ounce of Cliff's strength to refuse them and fight the sickening desires they incited.

Aidan kept a hand on Cliff's shoulder, infusing him with calm. But it barely made a difference. "How would you like to sit in sunlight for a while, Cliff?" he asked. It had worked well to silence the voices in the past.

A sound reached his ears.

Too late.

"Vampires," Cliff growled in a very un-Cliff-like voice. Shrugging off Aidan's touch, he drew his swords and swung them in arcs and circles as he picked up his pace. A dark smile turned up the corners of his lips. His eyes began to glow bright amber.

A dozen vampires came around the corner of a building up ahead.

Chris, Aidan called telepathically to Reordon and strained to pick up the human's thoughts. Even for a telepath as old as *he* was, such a feat was difficult.

Stay the hell out of my head, telepath.

Cliff is about to launch a bloodbath at UNC Chapel Hill. I see at least two surveillance cameras, and I don't think I'll be able to restrain him long enough to get him and the vampires he intends to slaughter to —

Cliff shot forward.

Ah hell, just get a cleaning crew over here now and have your tech guys get ready to silence whatever shows up on the internet. Without waiting for a response, Aidan raced after Cliff.

Cliff cared nothing about being outnumbered a dozen to one. Such odds didn't even make him hesitate. He just tore into the vampires.

Some of the vamps were well groomed, their clothing neat and clean. Both indicated they had only recently transformed. Good hygiene tended to fall by the wayside once the madness struck. Cliff was a rare exception.

The rest of the vampires were older, judging by their slovenly appearance and the insanity housed in their glowing eyes. Aidan didn't attempt to slay any of them. He merely guarded Cliff's back and fended off any blows directed at himself. Bastien did the same, leaving the killing for Cliff in hopes of silencing the voices.

Aidan's heart sank as he watched. Slaying vampires quickly and cleanly used to bring an end to the violent impulses that plagued Cliff. Simple strikes that would end their lives in less than a minute. Then Cliff had begun to prolong the battles, letting the vampires tire themselves out before he killed them. Now...

Now he ripped them to shreds. And smiled while he did it. There was no denying the madness that glinted in his amber eyes as he slew them.

One by one he took down his opponents, who fought fiercely but could not compete with the strength madness lent Cliff nor the skills Bastien had taught him. Soon only two vampires remained, one tall, one short. Both were pretty damned proficient with the short swords they wielded.

Light reflected off Cliff's blades as he swung them with a flourish and sliced open the shorter vampire's cheek from ear to chin. He nicked the vamp's arm—once, twice—then cut it deeply. The vampire cried out and dropped his sword. Stumbling back a step, he tripped over one of his fallen companions and hit the ground. As Cliff moved in for the kill, the vamp rolled away and lunged to his feet. His baseball cap fell off as he drew a dagger and spun to face Cliff.

Cliff smiled wickedly and raised a sword, preparing to strike a killing blow.

"No!" Bastien shouted. Lunging forward, he halted Cliff's sword with his own.

Aidan stared past him. Long auburn hair tumbled down around the vampire's shoulders as she braced herself to meet the blow. "Shite," he whispered.

When her gaze strayed to Aidan, her face paled.

Cliff glared at Bastien and pushed back against his friend's sword with a snarl.

"Cliff, stop!" Bastien nearly shouted and nodded behind him. "Look."

Cliff did as ordered... and froze.

Blood welled in the deep gash on the woman's face and spilled down her neck. More saturated the torn sleeve of her jacket.

The male vampire lunged forward, intending to strike Cliff while he was distracted.

Aidan threw out a hand and telekinetically plucked the vampire's weapons from his hands, then stole the woman's dagger as well.

Both gaped.

Cliff looked from the woman to Bastien blocking his sword, then back to the woman. Horror dawned on his features. Staggering backward, he dropped his weapons.

"Cliff..." Bastien spoke gently.

Cliff didn't seem to hear him as he looked down at the blood on his hands, then fastened wide eyes on the female.

"Cliff," Bastien repeated, stepping forward.

He shook his head. "Bastien?" His voice was thick with self-loathing. Tears welled in his glowing eyes. "What did I do?"

"Nothing," Bastien replied in the same soothing tone.

But Cliff shook his head. "Did I have another break?"

"No." Bastien slowly walked toward him as Cliff continued to back away. "We were out hunting. We came across some vampires. You did nothing wrong."

The lone male vampire left standing snorted. "Nothing wrong? Look around you! He tore these men apart and damned near killed—"

Aidan darted forward and fisted a hand in the man's shirt. "Shut the fuck up while we handle this," he growled.

The man shoved Aidan away and bent in a blur to grab another weapon.

Aidan telekinetically yanked the weapon from his hands.

The man and woman exchanged an alarmed look, then took a step backward.

Now that he wasn't so focused on Cliff, Aidan recognized them both—the woman *and* the man—as two of Gershom's immortals.

Thrusting a hand out toward them, he once more employed his telekinetic ability and froze them in place.

They gasped.

The woman struggled briefly, her glowing amber gaze fastened on Aidan.

Aidan delved into her thoughts and swore. She thought him the man who had kidnapped her before Gershom had *rescued* her.

Well, he couldn't worry about that right now.

He glanced over his shoulder.

Still shaking his head, Cliff pointed to the woman. "I did that?" His crimson-coated hand shook violently. "I did that, didn't I? I hurt her. I would've killed her if you hadn't stopped me!"

The woman exchanged a confused look with the man.

The man scowled. "What the hell is wrong with him? Is he insane or something?"

Aidan got up in the man's face and glared. "I know Gershom has been fucking with your head and filling it with lies, but show some bloody compassion. Cliff isn't an immortal. He's a vampire."

"Bullshit," the male spat out. "Immortals *kill* vampires." He tried to motion to the dead and decaying corpses around them and cursed when he couldn't move his arm.

"I could've killed her, Bastien," Cliff said in an agonized whisper. "I could've killed her. I could've *killed* her."

"But you didn't," Bastien said.

"Only because you stopped me!"

The woman's brow furrowed. "Why is he so upset over hurting

me?"

Since she thought Aidan the enemy, she couldn't fathom why injuring her would cause his friend such distress.

"Because he's a good man," Aidan explained. "And he's still lucid enough to realize you're one of the kidnapped *gifted ones* we've been trying to locate and rescue."

"Rescue?" she blurted incredulously. "You're the one who kidnapped me!"

"No, I'm not. That was an imposter. You'll understand that in time." He glanced at the man. "You're one of the missing *gifted ones,* too. I recognize you both from your pictures."

"What the hell is a *gifted one?*" the man asked.

"You are. Men and women who were born with special gifts others don't possess. The virus doesn't drive *gifted ones* insane. Our advanced DNA protects us. Humans don't have that protection and suffer progressive brain damage. Cliff was human before he transformed. He joined us years ago. Our doctors have been trying to help him stave off the madness ever since." *Seth!* he called telepathically.

Yes?

We've found two more of the missing immortals.

"I can't do this," Cliff said, his voice full of agony. "I can't do this anymore, Bastien. I don't want to hurt people."

"Cliff—"

"I almost killed her," he continued, more tears spilling over his lashes. "I would've killed her if you hadn't stopped me. I would've cut her throat. I would've killed her. And I would've enjoyed it!"

The sound of a small engine approaching drew Aidan's attention. Glancing to the left, he swore. A golf cart carrying two HPD officers zoomed toward them. They must be working security on campus.

Seth appeared, sword in hand. The devices Aidan and Bastien carried beeped.

The man and woman gasped, eyes flying wide.

"Trouble to your nine," Aidan said.

Seth looked over at the golf cart. A moment later it slowed. The officers' tense faces relaxed. Both men smiled, then chuckled as they turned the cart around. "Damned kids and their stupid pranks," one murmured.

"Yeah," his companion said. "It was a good one though, wasn't it? I thought that shit was real."

As the cart retreated, Seth turned to assess the scene.

Cliff raised red-rimmed eyes to meet Seth's. "I almost killed her, Seth. I didn't mean to. I swear I didn't mean to. I don't want to hurt innocent people. I don't want to be like this anymore."

Nodding, Seth closed the distance between them.

Aidan stiffened.

Bastien did, too. He even tried to step in front of Cliff.

Did Seth intend to slay the vampire and end his torment?

Seth brushed Bastien aside and rested a hand on Cliff's shoulder. He gave it a squeeze. "You did well tonight, Cliff. You kept the vampires busy and killed them all, giving Aidan and Bastien plenty of time to disarm the missing immortals and hold them until I could arrive."

Cliff's tears stopped as he blinked. His features smoothed out, the distress leaving them. "I did?"

"You did. Good job. Why don't you rest now?"

Cliff nodded. "Okay." He closed his eyes. His knees buckled.

Seth caught him before he could fall.

Aidan released the breath he hadn't realized he'd been holding and felt his eyes begin to burn with tears of relief.

His friend would live another day.

Bastien's eyes glistened with moisture, too, as he bent and folded Cliff over his shoulder. Straightening, he swallowed hard and stared up at Seth. "Thank you."

Seth nodded and sheathed his sword. "I know you don't want to abandon hope, Bastien, but there will come a day soon when the kindest thing you can do for Cliff is end his torment."

"I know," Bastien said, his voice hoarse.

"Call me when that day comes and I will do it for you," Seth told him softly. "You shouldn't have to live with that."

Unable to speak, Bastien nodded.

Seth turned to face the male and female immortals.

Aidan released his telekinetic hold on them, giving them the freedom to move. But both still seemed frozen in place.

Because the past few moments had made them question

Gershom's assertion that immortals were cold, power-hungry assholes intent on slaying anyone capable of defeating them while they took over the world?

Utter nonsense. As with Leah, however, Gershom had earned their trust through deception.

Seth approached them slowly, his face somber. "Jordan, Liora, I'm happy to see you both well. Please forgive us for not protecting you better or finding you sooner."

Liora looked at Jordan, then Seth. "What?"

"I shall explain everything once we get you to safety. I trust neither of you has summoned Gershom?"

Jordan scowled at Aidan. "That asshole did something to keep us from moving."

"I fear such was necessary," Seth said, his tone apologetic. "They did not wish to harm you. And had Aidan not disarmed and disabled you, both of you would've attacked while they were distracted, trying to help their friend."

Jordan frowned. "Their friend slaughtered the men you see on the ground around you."

Seth glanced at the decaying vampires. "Were they your friends?"

He hesitated. "No."

"You bear empathic abilities."

Jordan's scowl deepened. "How do you know that?"

"Because I've been watching over you and helping you keep your gift a secret ever since your birth. When you brushed against those men, did your gift convey goodness, happiness, and contentment? Or did you feel malice, anger, and a deep desire to commit violence?"

Jordan opted not to answer.

"As Aidan told you, the virus causes progressive brain damage in humans. Most of these vampires were already beyond our help. The rest were well on their way."

Liora nodded to Cliff. "Isn't your friend there beyond help?"

Seth shook his head. "Cliff is still capable of feeling remorse. He can still discern right from wrong. He's fighting the madness with every ounce of strength he possesses. Most vampires embrace it as soon as the madness begins to erode their impulse control. Cliff didn't."

The low rumble of an engine preceded the appearance of a dark van. Leaving the street, it drove up the wide sidewalk toward them.

Seth caught the eye of the driver and addressed him telepathically. *Thank you for coming. We shall leave shortly. If you need me to return and bury any memories, have Reordon call me.*

The driver nodded and thought, *Yes, sir.*

Seth looked at Aidan. "Take Bastien and Cliff to the network. I'll see to Jordan and Liora."

Nodding, Aidan palmed his cell phone and dialed a number.

"Reordon," the network head answered.

"It's Aidan. Bastien, Cliff, and I are on our way in."

"Okay. I'll turn the alarm off."

Tucking his phone back in his pocket, Aidan clasped Bastien's shoulder and teleported to network headquarters.

⚬◊◊◊⚬

Liora and Jordan gasped. Another look into their thoughts revealed they had believed only Gershom and Seth boasted that particular power.

Before the younger immortals could recover, Seth grasped their shoulders and teleported away. On the off chance that Gershom might be lurking nearby, Seth teleported to multiple locations, one after another, doubling back once or twice, before arriving in Melanie's infirmary on sublevel five of network headquarters.

As soon as he released them, Jordan and Liora staggered away from him.

Liora clenched her teeth and drew in a series of deep breaths.

Jordan bent over and braced his hands on his knees. "Oh, man. I think I'm gonna puke."

Seth grimaced. He'd been teleporting for so many millennia that he sometimes forgot how disconcerting it could be for newcomers. "Sorry about that." Stepping forward, he clasped their shoulders once more. "This should help." A quick infusion of healing energy settled their stomachs.

The large infirmary was empty. Seth's preternatural hearing told him the resident vampires were all in their apartments.

Melanie was in Cliff's apartment, waiting anxiously while Aidan helped Bastien rid Cliff of his clothing and weapons so they could wash the blood off his body and make the sleeping vampire more comfortable.

Seth drew out his cell phone and dialed.

"Reordon."

"We're here. Turn the alarm back on."

"Done. I didn't realize you were coming, too."

"Bastien and Aidan found two more missing immortals. They're with me in the infirmary."

"Excellent. I'll be down in a few to help you get them settled."

"Thank you."

Liora and Jordan shared a look.

"Get us settled?" Jordan repeated. "What does that mean? Where are we?"

Seth pocketed his phone. "You're at the East Coast headquarters of the extensive network of humans who aid Immortal Guardians in our quest to protect humanity from vampires *and* to protect *gifted ones* and immortals like yourselves from discovery and persecution."

Jordan released a derisive laugh. "I'm supposed to believe humans help you? You *kill* humans."

Liora nodded, her brow furrowing. "We've seen your victims."

Seth shook his head as he read their thoughts. "Gershom slew those men and women, then blamed us in order to sway you to his side."

"Bullshit," Jordan blurted. "You hate humans. You think them all beneath you."

Seth heard the elevator at the end of the hallway ding. "I suppose Gershom told you that as well? Just like he told you immortals kill all vampires? You don't find that suspect, considering you met a vampire moments ago whom we are doing our damnedest to save?"

Again they shared a look.

"He's probably just an immortal," Jordan said. "We only have your word that he's a vampire."

Seth motioned to the room in which they stood. "Look around you."

Both surveyed the high-tech infirmary.

"Amongst the thousands of humans who work with us are brilliant doctors and scientists who are learning everything they can about this virus in an attempt to find a cure for it. They're seeking ways to prevent and reverse the madness it causes in humans. They're also hoping they will eventually be able to manufacture a vaccine that will render humans immune to the virus in the future. Give them samples of your blood and they will show you that your DNA is far more complex than that of ordinary humans. Watch them take a sample of Cliff's blood and you will see the difference. Cliff is a vampire, not an immortal. And humans *do* help us."

Boots thudded in the hallway outside.

"I still call bullshit," Jordan muttered stubbornly.

Seth smiled. "Wait for it…"

Chris Reordon strode through the doorway.

Both newcomers glanced over at him.

Chris studied them with shrewd eyes. "Jordan Moore and Liora Duran." He smiled up at Seth. "Excellent. Congratulations on rescuing two more."

He nodded. "Gershom has filled their heads with lies, so they aren't here of their own accord."

Chris snorted. "No big surprise there." He turned to the immortals. "Hi. I'm Chris Reordon. It's good to finally meet you. We've been looking for you ever since we realized you both were missing. I run things here at the East Coast division of the network. I know it sucks that Gershom has lied to you and manipulated you, but we're here to help you get things straightened out."

Liora stared at him. "You're human."

"Yes, I am." Chris sent Seth a questioning look.

He shrugged. "Gershom has convinced them that we kill humans because we think they are inferior, so neither believed me when I told them humans actually work *with* us to help us protect humanity."

Chris's eyebrows flew up. "Didn't they see the cleanup crew?"

Seth shook his head. "We left before the driver parked the van."

Chris turned back to the newcomers. "You think immortals don't like humans?"

Neither responded.

Smiling, he shook his head. "Then staying here is really going to blow your minds. You hear all those voices?" He pointed upward to the four subterranean floors above them and the one floor topside on which hundreds of conversations currently took place. "Those are all humans, with a few *gifted ones* thrown in." He jerked a thumb toward the doorway. "There are more out in the hallway. Immortal Guardians are the good guys, so we humans want to do everything we possibly can to help them. And to help you, too, since you're both immortals." He glanced at Seth. "Do they know they're immortals?"

"They do now."

Chris turned back to them. "If you have any doubts about that, our doctors can clear them up. You can watch them do the blood work yourselves. Until then, I'd like to get you settled. Follow me, please." He turned to leave.

Seth motioned for Jordan and Liora to follow Chris, and they did so, shoulders stiff, faces grim. Both believed Chris would lead them to prison cells or the like.

Out in the hallway, they scowled at the many network guards present. All were clearly human. All issued Seth nods of respect.

"Gentlemen," Seth greeted them.

Jared leaned against the desk down by the elevators and gave them a little wave of greeting.

Chris headed to one of the new studio apartments. Swiping a card, he typed a code into the keypad, unlocked the heavy door, and led them inside. "Are you two a couple?"

Liora frowned. "What?"

"Are you a couple?" He closed the door, which sealed with a *thunk*. "Would you like to stay together or have separate apartments?"

"Together," Jordan immediately responded.

Chris looked at the woman. "Liora?"

She glanced at Jordan. "Together."

Seth read their thoughts. The two weren't a couple, but believed they would have a better chance of escaping if they remained with each other.

Chris met Seth's gaze. Clearly he'd drawn the same conclusion *without* reading their thoughts.

Seth nodded.

"Okay," Chris said. "Then welcome home. I tried to make the place as comfortable as possible for you. I'll have extra food brought in for the kitchen since there will be two of you instead of one. More towels and bath products, too. If you need anything else, just pick up the phone there." He motioned to a white landline phone that only had one button instead of the usual number pad. "It's a direct line to my office. If you change your mind at any time and would like separate living quarters, just give me a ring. If you feel like chatting, there are half a dozen vampires living here. They'll hear you through the walls, and chatting might help alleviate their boredom. I know you guys are listening, so go ahead and say hello."

"Hello."

"Hi."

"Hey, man. How's it goin'?"

"'Sup?"

"Hi. I'm Stewart. Welcome to the network. And for the woman, I'm totally open to dating if you don't mind there being a little insanity in my future. You'll find I'm a lot hotter than the other guys."

"Come on, man."

"Seriously?"

"Stop kidding yourself. I'm way hotter."

Liora stared at Seth.

He shrugged. "If any of them interest you, you are welcome to date them, but" — his voice turned stern as he slid the wall a look — "they will *not* in any way pressure you or sexually harass you or they will answer to me. Understood, boys?"

"Yes, sir," the vampires chorused.

"Good. Liora and Jordan have been through tough times. Both were kidnapped and held by Gershom."

"I hate that asshole," Stewart grumbled. "When he blew up the front of the damned building and sent those vampires in to attack, they killed a lot of good men and women."

"Yeah," another grumbled. "Fuck Gershom."

Surprised, Seth quieted for a moment. He didn't know why he

had never considered that the vampires who resided there might have grown attached to the many men and women they heard converse yet never met in person. But apparently they had.

"Thank goodness the day care is off-site," another vampire murmured, "or they would've killed the children, too."

Liora and Jordan looked more confused than ever.

"It's all right," Seth assured them. "We'll go over that once you've rested. Please, do not try to escape. Doing so would prove futile. Jared, the immortal down the hallway with the human guards, is as ancient as I am and can subdue you with a thought. Should you wish to talk to me, ask him to summon me. Bastien and Melanie are two more immortals who spend much of their time here as well. You met Bastien earlier. Dr. Melanie Lipton is his wife. She will likely want to draw some blood and ensure Gershom has not drugged you. She can also prove to you that you are indeed immortal and not vampire if you wish."

"Monster" began to play.

Seth drew his cell phone from his pocket. He frowned when he saw it was not an immortal calling but a Second. "Yes?"

"Seth," Thomas cried. "Oren is down. Michele is, too. I think Michele might be slipping into stasis. I've never seen so many vampires attack at once!"

Seth looked at Liora and Jordan. "My apologies. I must go. Do *not* harm Chris." Confident that Reordon could take care of himself, he teleported to Toronto.

Chris nodded at Liora and Jordan. "You should listen to him."

Jordan exchanged a look with Liora, then darted forward in a blur and locked Chris in a choke hold. "Open the door."

Chris brought up one hand to clutch the immortal's forearm while he unobtrusively tucked the other in his pocket. Withdrawing an EpiPen-like auto-injector, he flipped the cap up and jabbed the needle into Jordan's thigh.

Jordan jerked. A couple of seconds later, his hold loosened as he began to weave on his feet.

Chris calmly slipped out of his arms and watched the man collapse to the floor.

Liora gaped. "What did you do?" Rushing forward, she knelt beside the unconscious immortal. "Jordan?" She patted his cheek. "Jordan!"

Chris tucked the auto-injector, which she hadn't noticed, back in his pocket. "It's okay. He isn't dead. He's just going to sleep for a bit."

She stared up at him. "How did you do that? You're human."

He shrugged. "While he's out, let me ask you again: Do you want to stay here or would you prefer to have your own apartment? I wanted to ensure Jordan wasn't pressuring you into staying with him."

"I want to stay here. With Jordan."

"Okay. I'd like to ask you to step into the bathroom with me for a moment so I can speak to you privately without the vampires listening in. All bathrooms here at network headquarters are soundproof."

She eyed him warily.

"Please," he said. When she didn't move, he sighed and withdrew the auto-injector. "I sedated him."

"Drugs don't affect us."

"This one does. I'd prove it, but that would be counterproductive. If you come with me, I promise I will keep my hands in your sight at all times so you won't have to worry about my sedating you, too. But be forewarned, if I don't walk out of this room in the next ten minutes, Jared will come check on me and you will be no match for him."

Brow furrowing, she rose and hesitantly followed him into the bathroom.

Chris closed the door and turned to face her, his hands still raised. "Can you tell me in what kind of conditions you've been kept since Gershom kidnapped you?"

"Gershom didn't kidnap me. That immortal Aidan did. Gershom rescued me from him."

"No, he didn't. I hate to be the bearer of bad news, but Gershom can shape-shift. He's been taking Aidan's form and kidnapping women for months. You'll come to realize that eventually. Until then..." He spoke gently. "I don't know what you've been subjected to all this time, if Gershom kept you at his side, if he had you stay with Jordan, or if he locked you in a room full of male vampires. And I apologize if asking this will make you feel uncomfortable, but please know I'm only asking out of concern for you. Were you sexually assaulted while in his care?"

Her eyes widened. "No."

"I don't know you, so I can't tell if that denial was genuine or a knee-jerk reaction because you want me to mind my own business. But if you *were* sexually assaulted, Dr. Lipton can examine you and make sure you're okay. I know you heal quickly and aren't vulnerable to STDs, so physically your body should be fine. But I'd still feel better if she gave you a clean bill of health. We also have therapists on hand with whom you may speak if you've suffered trauma. Anything you need, Liora, we wish to provide. We just want you to be well."

She stared at him. "I wasn't sexually assaulted."

"Okay." Chris was only partially relieved, however. When he left Liora, he intended to ask Jared to delve into her mind and search for any buried memories that would indicate Gershom had been sexually assaulting her without her knowledge. Chris hadn't mentioned that fear to Seth but thought it a possibility they should investigate. They needed to be aware of the full extent of Gershom's vicious mindset. "I'm sorry you're having to deal with all of this. I know Seth holds himself responsible, but watching over *gifted ones* falls under my purview as well. I sincerely apologize for not keeping you safe."

Her frown deepened.

"If you change your mind and wish to speak to Dr. Lipton or one of our therapists, just pick up the phone, call my office, and say *I could really use some chocolate.*"

His words finally succeeded in erasing her frown. "What?"

He smiled. "*I could really use some chocolate.* It'll be our secret code so Jordan won't know what it's about. Melanie loves chocolate. So I'll send her in with some and she'll mention wanting to do a little more blood work. Once you leave the room with her, she'll bring you to my office where we can speak without the vampires or Jordan listening in."

She gave a slow nod. "Okay."

"Just don't use the code in an attempt to escape. That would be a real dickish move because I'm honestly trying to look out for you. Okay?"

"Okay."

"Anything else you want to talk about while the vamps can't hear us?"

"No."

"Okay then. Let me help you get Jordan settled on the sofa." Opening the door, he headed back into the apartment's main living space. Jordan was an inch or so above six feet and muscular like the other Immortal Guardians. Chris grunted as he folded the man over his shoulder and rose. "Sometimes I really wish I had you guys' strength."

"I could've done that," Liora pointed out as she watched him.

"Nah. I'm fine." He dumped Jordan on the sofa. "If you don't want him in bed with you, make him take the sofa. If he gives you any grief, the vampires will tattle on him."

Her head swiveled as she looked at the wall. Her lips twitched.

"Let me guess," Chris said. "They're agreeing?"

"Yes."

"Good. Just don't drive her crazy with your chatter, guys. And give her at least a few days to acclimate before you start hitting on her."

Genuine amusement shone in the eyes she turned back upon him.

"I'm not even going to ask what they're saying now," he said, unable to hear them.

"I wouldn't if I were you."

It was good to see her looking a little less shell-shocked. "Well, I've got work to do, so I'm gonna book." He offered his hand.

She hesitated, then shook it.

"It's good to meet you, Liora, no matter the circumstances. I'll be seeing you again soon." He strode over to the door. Removing the key card from his pocket, he swiped it, then shifted so his back blocked her view and typed in a code. A *thunk* sounded as it opened. "Oh." With one hand on the handle, he turned to face her. "Would you like me to bring Tessa to you once she returns?"

She tilted her head to one side. "Who is Tessa?"

Surprise struck. "You don't know Tessa Hayes?"

"No. Should I?"

Releasing the door, he drew his cell phone out of his pocket. After opening Photos, he scrolled through images until he found one of Tessa. "You've never seen this woman?" He turned the screen to face Liora.

Moving closer, she studied the picture. "I *have* seen her. Just once. But I didn't know her name. Why? Who is she?"

"She's another *gifted one* Gershom kidnapped and transformed. You only saw her once?"

"Yes. She had just been told that Seth killed Veronica and her son Michael. Gershom held her while she wept, then took her away to grieve privately."

His lips tightened. Fucking Gershom. "Was she being held at the same location you were?"

"Yes." Her features hardened. "Until Seth captured and killed her."

"Seth didn't kill her, Liora. She's alive and well and can come visit you if you like."

She stared at him. "Tessa is alive?"

"Yes."

"Veronica is, too?"

He sighed. "No. We weren't able to save Veronica. But Michael is well."

Her face filled with uncertainty.

"Do you know where Gershom was keeping you?"

"No. He always teleported me there because he was afraid Seth would read it in my thoughts if he found me and kill us all."

"He held Jordan there, too?"

"Yes."

"Was it a home or—"

Chris, Jared warned in his head, *don't damage the progress you've made by interrogating her. I will search her memories for the answers you seek.*

Right. He shook his head. "I'm sorry." He sent her a smile. "We don't need to go into that right now. You need rest and time to process all of this. There's nonperishable food in the cabinets. I'll have perishables delivered for the fridge. There are also more satellite television stations than you'll ever need and an iPad loaded with thousands of e-books, movies, and apps if you grow bored. Remember, if you decide you want some *chocolate,* just pick up the phone and call me."

She looked toward the wall. Her lips slowly turned up in a smile as if she didn't want to but couldn't help it. "The vampires said they want some chocolate."

He laughed. "Take it up with Melanie, boys. She'll be back soon." He swung the door open and motioned her closer. "See the big guy down the hallway?"

Cautiously, she approached and poked her head out.

Still leaning against the guards' desk, Jared tossed her a wave.

"That's Jared. He's old as shit and will talk your ear off if you give him half a chance." The multitude of heavily armed guards around Jared all nodded with long-suffering looks that nearly made Chris laugh. "But he's a good guy. If you need anything and for whatever reason can't reach me, just say his name."

"Okay."

Smiling, he stepped out into the hallway. "Try to get some rest, Liora."

She nodded, looking so lost and vulnerable that it broke his heart.

It was hard as hell to close the door, but he forced himself to do it. She needed time.

And he needed to get back to work and help Seth eradicate Gershom once and for all.

Chapter Twenty-One

R ECLINING ON A SOFA, LEAH covered her mouth to stifle a yawn. The hands of the clock that silently kept careful time had long since passed midnight. Then one a.m., two a.m., three a.m., and beyond. Normally, Leah would have to wake, eat breakfast, and open her store in a few hours. Mandy had taken over that task for her temporarily. But Leah still found it hard to stay awake.

She and Seth hadn't slept much last night... or this afternoon. Not that she had any complaints there. She would choose sex with Seth over sleep any day. She had never in her life had so many orgasms so close together. She hadn't even thought it possible. And would love to see if she could again. Just the idea of him running his big hands —

An image of her and Seth sitting beside each other on the edge of a playground sandbox suddenly filled her head, an elaborate sandcastle rising in front of them.

She frowned. That was weird. Why had that —?

A small hand closed over her knee.

Leah glanced down.

Adira stood before the sofa, leaning into Leah's leg and watching her with expectation.

Had she been trying to get her attention while Leah was fantasizing about Seth?

Leah smiled. "I'm sorry, sweetie. What was that?"

Again the image of her and Seth in the sandbox filled her head.

Leah stared at the little girl. Had she done that? "You want to go to the playground again?"

Adira nodded. "Wif Baba."

Leah looked at Ami. "That's amazing."

Sitting on the floor with her husband amid wooden blocks that were stacked in various formations, Ami raised her eyebrows. "Did she show you a picture of it in your mind?"

"Yes."

She nodded. "Adira has strong telepathic abilities. Since she doesn't speak much yet, she tends to communicate with images a lot."

Leah smiled at the toddler. "I'd love to go to the park with you and Baba. Can Aaron come, too?"

Grinning, she nodded.

"Deera," Michael called and held up a block.

Adira returned to building with him and her parents.

Roland and Sarah had claimed spots on the floor as well. Leah suspected neither had wanted to leave while Tessa remained at David's home.

Leah glanced at the woman beside her.

Tessa looked exhausted, both physically and emotionally. Her eyes were still a little bloodshot from crying earlier. And she could barely keep them open. "Adira is a *gifted one*?" she asked wearily.

Ami glanced at Marcus, as though she wasn't sure how to respond.

Leah fought a frown.

"Yes," Marcus said. "She's a *gifted one*."

Tessa stared at the little girl. "I didn't think immortals or vampires could have children."

Again Marcus and Ami shared a look, but Leah didn't think Tessa noticed.

"We adopted her," Marcus said at length.

Tessa seemed to accept that as truth. But Leah knew it to be false. Adira looked too much like Ami to be adopted. And while Seth had spoken freely about *adopting* Ami, he had said nothing about Ami adopting Adira.

As if summoned by the thought, Seth abruptly appeared near the front door.

One look at his grim face lured Leah to her feet.

Some of the tension in his expression eased when he saw her.

Crossing to him, she rose onto her toes and drew him into a hug. Sighing, he wrapped his arms around her and held her tight.

"Tough night?" she asked softly.

He nodded. His lips brushed her neck in an affectionate kiss before he drew back and looked over her shoulder. "How are you feeling, Tessa?"

Leah kept an arm around Seth as she shifted to stand at his side.

Tessa shrugged. "Hanging in there."

He nodded.

Adira raced toward Seth with a big grin. "Baba!"

At last his features brightened as he knelt and scooped the toddler up into his arms. "There's my girl. What are you doing up so late?"

Marcus smiled and shook his head as he began to scoop the blocks into a couple of canvas bags. "We shouldn't have let them nap for so long earlier. They're both still wide awake."

Adira touched Seth's cheek.

He met her earnest gaze. "That was very sweet of you." He bussed her cheek, then set her on her feet. "It wasn't the nap," he told her parents. "She felt Tessa's sadness and hoped to cheer her up."

Tessa looked up. "What?"

Leah stared at the little redhead as she toddled back over to her parents. What a remarkable child.

Roland rose, holding a yawning Michael in his arms. "Now that you're home, I think it's time we get these two to bed."

Sarah, Marcus, and Ami agreed. As soon as the blocks were tucked away, the parents said their good-nights and headed down the hallway.

"Night-night, Baba," Adira called over Marcus's shoulder. "Night-night, Leah."

Leah smiled, her heart turning over. "Good night, sweetie."

Michael was already nodding off, his tousled head rocking on his papa's shoulder.

Once they were out of sight, Leah looked up at Seth. "She's an amazing little girl."

He hugged her close. "Yes, she is." Then he looked over at Tessa.

Tessa rose, eyeing them uncertainly.

"Tessa," Seth began, regret entering his voice, "I'm sorry to ask this of you, but I'd like you to return to the apartment Chris assigned you at network headquarters."

She stiffened. "Of course."

"It isn't for the reasons you think."

Tessa cut a hand through the air. "It's okay. I get it. I'm not one of you. I attacked Leah and —"

"You *are* one of us," he interrupted.

Leah nodded, guessing his reasons for wanting her to stay at network headquarters instead of David's home. "I told you to forget about attacking me. I'm fine, Tessa. I survived. I'm over it. And we both understand why you did it. It's just..." She crossed to the younger woman and took her hands. "Gershom may try to get you back. And — for whatever reason — he hates Seth. It wouldn't be safe for you to sleep under the same roof as Ami and Adira, both of whom Gershom has targeted in the past." She looked over her shoulder at Seth. "Right? It would be too great a lure, don't you think?"

"Such was my concern. We also found two more of the missing immortals tonight."

Leah's eyes widened. "You did?"

He sent her another weary smile. "Yes. They're already settled at network headquarters."

"That's wonderful!" Leah skipped across the room to him and leapt into his arms. "I'm so happy for you, honey."

He squeezed her tight, lifting her feet off the floor.

When she stepped back, he was smiling down at her with an expression she couldn't quite read. "What?"

"That's the first time you've used an endearment when you addressed me."

She grinned. "Actually, I believe I called you buttercup earlier when a certain suspicious throng of immortal warriors threatened to burst into our bedroom."

He laughed. "So you did." Taking her hand, he strolled over to Tessa. "The two immortals we found are Jordan Moore and Liora Duran. Do you know them?"

Tessa shook her head. "I don't think so."

"Liora told Chris Reordon she only saw you once. Apparently

Gershom later told her I killed you."

Leah frowned. "He's such a dick."

Seth laughed. "Yes, he is." But his face gradually sobered. "And he played the same mind games with them as he did with you. Jordan is fighting the truth. Liora seems a little more amenable. If you're up to it, I think your being there willingly would help us sway them to our side."

Tessa rubbed her hands up and down her thighs, her face anxious. "You really think Gershom might come for me?"

Leah's heart went out to her. Poor girl. Her world had been turned upside down tonight, and now she had to worry about Gershom's sorry ass getting his hands on her again, too.

"In truth, I don't know what to expect," Seth answered. "Gershom has proven to be a cunning and unpredictable adversary in the past."

Leah loved that he was honest about it and didn't try to pussyfoot around or offer false promises.

"But if he does," Seth continued, "Jared — an immortal as ancient as I am — will be there at the network to guard you. And he will summon me at the first hint of danger."

Tessa nodded.

Seth turned to Leah. Dipping his head, he brushed her lips with a kiss. "I shall return shortly."

"Okay." Leah stepped away and hugged Tessa. "Good night, Tessa."

Tessa hugged her back. "Good night."

Seth touched her shoulder and teleported away, leaving Leah alone in the huge living room.

Recalling how grim and weary Seth had looked — such a vast difference from how happy and relaxed he had been while they had been ensconced in his bedroom — Leah headed into the kitchen. She had to open a few cabinets to locate a bamboo serving tray. Crossing to one of the two enormous refrigerators the spacious kitchen boasted, she opened the first and gaped at the wealth of food it contained.

"Wow." That much food could feed her for a month.

A hell of a lot of powerful warriors — both male and female — did seem to live here though, so...

Shrugging, she tentatively began to rummage through it.

"Looking for anything in particular?"

Jumping, she spun around.

Sheldon stood in the doorway. He grinned. "Sorry. I didn't mean to startle you."

Resting a hand over her pounding heart, Leah smiled. "That's okay. I was just looking for something to feed Seth when he got back. I doubt he's eaten anything since dinner."

"You haven't either, have you?"

"No."

He headed for the other refrigerator. "Here." He opened one of the double doors. "I always keep a supply of sandwiches on hand for the immortals. Especially for Seth and David. Those two are always go-go-going, and Darnell has a hell of a time trying to get them to slow down long enough to eat a meal."

Leah closed the refrigerator door she held and placed the sandwiches he handed her on the tray.

"Just for future reference, Seth likes lots of veggies and a few spicy peppers on his. All organic." He eyed her carefully. "You aren't going to get your shorts in a bunch about that, are you? Some people do. I don't know why."

"No. I eat organic, too. When my doctor scared the crap out me and told me to start eating healthier, I figured I might as well go all in."

He nodded. "Well, these guys aren't health nuts or anything. They just have supersensitive taste buds and can taste the difference between natural flavoring and the fake stuff." He wrinkled his nose. "And some are simply as hardheaded as everyone else I know. After hundreds or thousands of years of eating nothing but organic food, they tend to dig in their heels if someone suggests they change their diet."

She laughed. "Yeah. I wasn't too thrilled about the idea either."

"Anyway, here's some tea. And a couple of apples. Seth likes the red delicious ones best. That pantry there is stocked from floor to ceiling with chips and other snack foods. Seth tends to gravitate toward either the original flavor ruffled chips or the black-pepper ones. And the deep freeze there is full of ice cream and other frozen treats guaranteed to satisfy any sweet tooth. Speaking of which…"

Crossing to the large freezer, he opened it and drew out two chocolate-covered vanilla ice cream pops. "Tracy sent me to get these," he said with a grin.

Leah smiled.

"Anything else I can do for you?"

"No. This is good. Thank you, Sheldon."

"Anytime." He strolled out of the kitchen.

Leah added some chips to the tray loaded with sandwiches, apples, and tea, then carried it to Seth's bedroom. The door stood open, but Seth wasn't inside. Sheldon must have opened it for her as he passed.

She set the tray on the ottoman.

"Leah?" Seth called softly from the living room.

"In here."

He strode through the bedroom doorway.

She straightened. "Hi, handsome."

His lips curled up in a smile. "Hi, beautiful."

"Is Tessa all settled?"

He nodded. The door behind him swung shut as he shrugged out of his coat.

Telekinesis was so cool. Leah wished *she* could do things like that.

Moving to stand before him, she took his coat and hung it up, then drew him into a hug. "Sorry you had a rough night," she said gently.

He nodded, resting his cheek on her head.

She drew her hands up and down his back in soothing strokes. "Was it Tessa and the other new immortals? Or did something else happen?"

A long sigh escaped him, ruffling her hair. "We came damned close to losing Cliff tonight."

"The vampire you're trying so hard to save?"

"Yes."

He had told her about Cliff after Aidan and Bastien had left earlier to take the vampire hunting.

"I told Bastien I would end Cliff's life for him when it becomes too unbearable for Cliff to continue. I don't want Bastien to have to do it."

She hugged him tighter. "Oh, honey. I'm sorry." He took so much upon himself to try to spare others. When she would've loosened her hold to look up at him, he tightened his arms around her.

"Let me hold you a little longer," he whispered.

Nodding, she relaxed against him.

Several minutes passed while they just held each other.

"You make everything better, Leah," he murmured.

Warmth burrowed through her chest, straight to her heart. "You do, too."

His stomach growled.

Leah grinned. "You really *did* work up an appetite today, didn't you?"

Seth laughed and, at last, loosened his hold enough to step back. "Apparently so."

Some of the shadows, she was pleased to see, had left his deep brown eyes. Perhaps she could eradicate the rest, at least for a time.

Casting him a flirtatious look, she motioned to the tray of food on the ottoman. "What do you say we satisfy *that* hunger" — she touched his chest, drew her fingers down over his muscled abs in a caress that made him catch his breath, then tucked them in the waistband of his cargo pants — "before we satisfy another hunger?"

His eyes brightened with golden light. "What did you have in mind?" His voice, already deepening with desire, sent a sensual shiver through her.

"You, naked in that enormous bathtub, with me riding you until you shout my name."

A growl rumbled forth from him. "Fuck the food," he declared and lunged toward her.

Laughing, Leah planted both hands on his chest to keep him at arms' length. "Nope. You'll have to wait for it. You need to eat." She winked. "Trust me. You're going to need the energy."

Looping an arm around her waist, he pulled her against him and dipped his head. His lips claimed hers in a scorching kiss she felt all the way to her core. His tongue slipped inside to stroke her own. Fire raced through her, stealing her breath. Burying her hands in his hair, she urged him closer, moaning when he slipped a thigh between hers.

Seth drew one hand down to cup her ass and lifted her so she could wrap her legs around him and grind against the hard length behind his fly. "Still want that sandwich?" he asked, nipping the sensitive skin beneath her ear with his teeth.

Leah fisted his hair and drew his head back so she could stare into his luminous eyes. "Fuck the food," she uttered hoarsely.

Laughing, he strode toward the bathroom.

The doorbell rang.

Seth jerked awake, then sighed. Damn it. He really hated for reality to intrude. For a few precious hours, Leah had made him forget everything except the pleasure and happiness she brought him.

"You don't think that's the whole crew out there again, do you?" Leah muttered drowsily as she tugged his arm tighter around her. The two of them lay on their sides with Seth spooned up behind her.

"Maybe." The damned ground still shook and thunderstorms continued to saturate the earth every time they made love.

"Well, I don't know what they have to complain about," she grumbled. "I *told* them to put their rain boots on."

Grinning, he leaned up on one elbow and pressed a kiss to her shoulder. His body responded to the press of hers and already wanted more. "Perhaps it's Sheldon, here to offer us more sandwiches."

Her eyes flew open. Reaching back, she patted his bare hip. "Go get the door, honey."

Laughing, Seth rolled out of bed and tugged on a pair of pants. He waited until Leah drew the covers up over her lovely body, then padded over to the door and opened it.

David stood outside. "It isn't storming outside, so I trust I'm not interrupting anything," he said, a twinkle of amusement lighting his dark eyes.

Seth smiled. "Correct. We were just resting. What's up?"

"Would you and Leah mind meeting me in the study? There's something I'd like to discuss with you."

Seth opened the door wider. "Would you like to talk in here?"

David shook his head. "The study will do." Turning, he strode away.

Curiosity rising, Seth closed the door.

"Just for future reference," Leah said as she sat up, "I know I'm not shy, but I would rather not carry on conversations with your friends and family while I'm naked in bed."

He winced. "Sorry about that. Force of habit. Usually when someone summons me or wishes to speak with me, time is a factor."

Throwing back the covers, she rose. "That sucks. Don't you get any downtime at all?"

As usual, his body instantly reacted to the sight of her naked curves, hardening even more. She was so damned beautiful. "What?"

"Don't you get any downtime at all?"

How quickly did David need to speak with them? It hadn't seemed urgent. He would've spoken to them here in the bedroom if that were the case. So maybe they had time to—

Leah's laughter disrupted his thoughts.

Arching his eyebrows in question, Seth watched her approach. "What?"

Smiling, she rose onto her toes and looped her arms around his neck. "You are too adorable."

Now Seth laughed. "I haven't been described thusly since I was a babe in swaddling clothes."

Still smiling, she rubbed her nose against his and pressed a kiss to his lips. "I love to see you laugh."

He hugged her closer. "And I love to laugh with you." He pressed his hips against hers, letting her feel how much he wanted her. "I love to do other things with you as well."

"But David is waiting."

Nodding, he reluctantly stepped back. "So he is."

"What do you think this is about?"

"I don't know. But I doubt he would've disturbed us if it weren't important."

"That's pretty much what I was thinking." She crossed to the bag of clothes Cynthia had delivered.

Seth tore his gaze away from watching her dress so he could rein in his desire. Now that he had healed her scars, she didn't attempt to shield her nudity at all. And he adored her body. Slender. Lightly muscled. With curves he had spent hours exploring.

He glanced at the clock. Shit. He really *had* spent hours exploring those curves. It was damned near time for the sun to set. Grabbing a black T-shirt from the closet, he drew it down over his head. Once he added socks and shoved his feet into his boots, he drew a brush through his long hair and pulled it back at the nape of his neck with a leather tie. He no longer considered cutting his hair. He enjoyed too much the feel of Leah brushing it in quiet moments.

Behind him, she sighed. "You have the hottest ass."

Grinning, he swung around to face her and discovered she was indeed staring at his ass. "Like it, do you?"

"A *lot*," she said. Instead of her own clothing, she wore black cargo pants similar to his and a black long-sleeved shirt that hugged her breasts and narrow waist.

Shaking his head, he closed the distance between them. "Don't tempt me, minx."

She grinned unrepentantly. "Think it would shock your fellow immortals if I made a habit of grabbing your ass in their presence?"

Again he laughed. "*Everything* you do where I'm concerned shocks my fellow immortals. Did Cynthia not pack any clothing you liked?"

She glanced down. "Actually she did. I just thought I would blend in a little better if I dressed like the rest of you."

"You don't have to do that," he told her softly.

Smiling up at him, she leaned in and claimed another hug. "Maybe I just like to watch that spark of desire light up your eyes the way it's doing now."

He shook his head. "It isn't the clothing I desire, Leah. It's you."

She kissed his chin. "Let's go see what David wants." Stepping back, she took his hand and led him to the door.

Leaving their bedroom — and that's how Seth thought of it now, *their* bedroom — they strode down the hallway to David's study. The house was mostly quiet. Since the sun had not yet sunk below the horizon, all the immortals who lived there likely still slumbered below. Faint tapping sounds carried to Seth's ears as Seconds diligently carried out their duties, handling business for their immortals that must be taken care of during daylight hours.

When he entered David's study, Seth was surprised to find Marcus, Stanislav, and Susan there. He had thought David sought a private conversation.

Susan smiled.

Marcus and Stanislav nodded a greeting, their faces somber.

What was this about?

"Leah," Seth said, still holding her hand, "I know you've met every immortal stationed in the area but thought I would mention this is Stanislav, in case you didn't remember his name."

Her face lit up. "The immortal you thought was dead?"

"Yes."

"Oh my goodness! That's right! Susan found him in her basement." Releasing Seth's hand, she moved forward and hugged Stanislav. "I'm so glad you're safe."

Surprise lighting his features, Stanislav smiled and hugged her back. "Thank you."

When Leah released him, she gave Susan a hug as well. "I'm sorry, Susan. I can't remember—are you a *gifted one* or an immortal?"

"A *gifted one*," Susan said with a glance up at the man beside her. "Stanislav has agreed to transform me and make me immortal, but we're going to wait until after this thing with Gershom is resolved."

"Congratulations."

Susan grinned. "Thank you."

Seth caught Susan's eye and gently reminded her, "Don't read Leah's thoughts."

Susan sent him a worried look. "I promise I won't intentionally read them, but when I sleep—"

"You lose control over your gift and sometimes inadvertently infiltrate the dreams of those who are near you." he finished for her.

"Yes."

"If you wander into Leah's dreams, just exit as soon as you become aware of it. As long as I'm touching her when she sleeps, I don't think that will happen. But if I'm called away..."

"I will. And I won't tell anyone what I see if that happens."

"Thank you." Seth looked at David, who leaned back against his desk, watching them patiently. "What is this about?"

Zach strolled into the room holding Lisette's hand. "Are we ready?"

"Not yet," David said. "Bastien, Melanie, please join us."

Seth was surprised those two weren't at network headquarters. They spent most days there to watch over Cliff and give Melanie more time to work.

The couple strolled in, holding hands like Zach and Lisette.

Straightening, David closed the door with a thought, then addressed Seth. "There is something we wish to show you." He looked at the newcomers. "You, too, Sebastien."

So Bastien didn't know what this was about either? Everyone else seemed to.

"Over here, please." David led them to the large window behind his desk. The curtains were tied back, allowing bright ambient light to enter.

Seth followed the others, bringing up the rear.

Bastien and Melanie peered through the window. Zach stopped beside them, still holding Lisette's hand. David motioned for Stanislav and Susan to stand next to him, leaving a free space for Seth and Leah in the middle.

As Seth joined them, David rested a hand on Stanislav's shoulder.

Stanislav and Susan both smiled as they looked through the window.

Seth peered through the glass, curious to see what was—

His heart stopped. Dread, guilt, and grief suffused him when he spotted Yuri lounging on the wide wooden swing that dangled from a tree in the backyard.

When Seth would've backed away, David clamped his free hand on his shoulder, holding Seth in place. "Let Leah see him," he commanded.

Seth shook his head, a lump rising in his throat.

"See who?" Bastien asked, his brow furrowing as he stared at the swing he thought empty.

Lisette suddenly sucked in a breath. "Yuri," she breathed. Tears rose in her eyes as she stared through the glass at the ghost of her former sports buddy.

Zach rested a hand on Bastien's shoulder, allowing him and Melanie to see Yuri, too.

Both gasped when they spotted their dead friend.

"Seth?" Leah murmured, staring up at him with concern.

But he couldn't find his voice.

"Show her," David repeated.

Seth's arm and hand tingled as he shared his ability to see spirits with her through their touch.

Her eyes widened when Yuri seemed to suddenly appear on the swing. "Who is that?"

"The brother I lost," he finally managed to say, his voice hoarse. "The one who was slain in battle two and a half years ago."

No blood marred Yuri's form. He didn't forever sport the wounds that had killed him as ghosts often did in movies. He looked as though he had just woken up and was getting in some downtime before night fell. His dark hair was short and neatly combed. His body was encased in his usual hunting togs, his skin as healthy as it had been before he'd died. A faint smile even toyed with the edges of his lips as he stared across the lawn.

Seth shot Stanislav a look, but found neither grief nor condemnation on the Russian immortal's face. He also didn't seem at all surprised to see Yuri's spirit. Seth looked at David. "Why are you doing this?" David knew how deeply Seth mourned the fallen immortal.

"Because there is more," David answered simply.

Seth returned his attention to the scene outside the window just as a woman strolled into view. She was pretty, with long brown hair and alabaster skin. But she wore a dress much like those women in England had worn over two centuries ago.

Seth frowned as recognized her.

Bastien's knees suddenly buckled.

"Honey?" Melanie cried in alarm, grabbing him with her free hand and holding him up. "What is it?"

He staggered forward a step. Tears welled in his eyes. "Cat," he breathed.

Melanie's gaze darted to the woman. "Your sister?"

He nodded.

Smiling, Catherine joined Yuri.

Seth stared, astonishment temporarily banishing guilt and self-recrimination as Yuri pulled her down beside him on the swing and ducked his head, capturing her lips in a long, loving kiss. The two murmured words Seth couldn't hear over the pounding of his heart. Catherine said something that made Yuri toss his head back and laugh. Wrapping her in a tender embrace, he set the swing into motion as sunset bathed them in roseate light.

They looked… happy.

They looked as if they were in love.

"Cat," Bastien whispered again. Tears spilled over his lashes and coursed down his cheeks. He glanced at David. "What is this? Why is she here?"

David's expression filled with compassion. "She has rarely left your side since her death, Bastien."

"What?" Bastien's gaze returned to the sister he'd lost so long ago. "No." He shook his head, horror dawning on his features. "No. Please, tell me that isn't true. *Please*. I thought she was gone. I thought she crossed over or whatever the hell you call it after Blaise killed her. The only thing that has gotten me through the past two centuries was the belief—the hope—that wherever she was, she was happy!" His voice rose alongside his agitation.

David motioned to the window. "She *is* happy, Bastien. She loves Yuri." His eyes met Seth's. "And he loves her. It's something they wanted you both to know." He glanced down at Susan. "Tap the glass, please, Susan."

She reached out and rapped her knuckles against the window.

Yuri and Cat looked over at them. Upon seeing their captive audience, the couple straightened, then rose.

Seth looked over and found Stanislav watching him. "You don't seem surprised to see them."

He smiled. "Yuri and Cat had been visiting me in dreams ever since I returned."

Susan nodded. "He's been urging us to find a way to get you to talk to him, so we asked David for help."

Outside, Yuri and Cat linked hands and walked toward them.

David motioned to the other side of his desk. "Let us step back, shall we?" Releasing Seth, he kept a hand on Stanislav's shoulder and guided everyone to the other side of his study.

Moments later, Yuri and Cat passed through the window and joined them.

Cat's eyes glimmered with moisture as she met and held her brother's gaze. "Bastien."

Bastien lunged toward her, his arms outstretched, but stopped short as soon as he broke Zach's hold. "Damn it, where'd she go?"

Zach stepped forward and grabbed his shoulder again so Bastien could see her once more.

Cat hurried to close the distance between them, dragging a smiling Yuri along with her. "Bastien." Stopping a breath away, she raised a hand and rested it on his stubbled cheek.

A sob escaped his lips before he could suppress it. His eyes glowed vibrant amber as more tears slipped over his lashes. "I can't feel you," he whispered hoarsely.

She nodded, swallowing hard. "I know. But now that you've seen me, I can visit you in your dreams tonight and hold you."

Beside her, Yuri nodded. "We feel real to you in dreams."

Bastien barely spared him a glance. "I'm so sorry, Cat."

She shook her head. "Don't be. Blaise fooled us both." Again she swallowed. "I didn't know what he was until that night. I found a dagger that had fallen out of his coat. When I picked it up..." She shook her head. "I saw what he'd been using it for." Cat had been born with psychometric abilities and could glimpse past events that were attached to objects. "I was on my way to tell you when Blaise caught up with me." Releasing Yuri, she raised her other hand to cup Bastien's face. "There was nothing you could've done to save me."

Bastien shook his head. "I protected him," he hissed, self-loathing choking his voice. "After you died, I protected the man who killed you and your babe."

"You didn't know."

When he would've spoken again, she covered his lips with her fingers, careful not to let her hand pass right through him. "No more dwelling on the past." She took a step backward and reclaimed Yuri's hand. "I'm happy now," she said, smiling up at the tall Russian immortal beside her. "And *you're* happy now." Her smile brightened as she turned to Melanie. "Thank you so much for loving Bastien and bringing him the happiness he deserves."

Seth just stood there, his boots cemented to the floor as emotion whorled around inside him.

Yuri caught his gaze. "I'm happy, too, Seth. It's time for you to stop persecuting yourself for shit you could neither predict nor control and acknowledge that. I'm *happy* now, in a way that I couldn't be before. I love Cat. She loves me. And I'm not sorry I died that day because it allowed me to be with her."

Seth shook his head, unable to grasp it.

Stanislav leaned forward. "Seth, Yuri was in love with Cat before the battle took his life."

Bastien frowned. "What?"

Yuri shrugged. "I'm like Marcus. I was born with the ability to see spirits. When Seth transferred me to North Carolina, I stayed here at David's place and" — he smiled down at Bastien's sister — "discovered Cat haunting it."

Catherine wrinkled her nose. "I still don't like that term."

"That's all right." Releasing her hand, Yuri curled an arm around her shoulders. "We haunt it together now." He smiled at Bastien. "Catherine intrigued me from the first moment I saw her. I couldn't help but speak to her. And once I did, I fell in love." Again he stared at Seth. "Dying enabled me to be with her."

Lisette sent Yuri a tearful smile. "I miss watching baseball with you."

He winked. "I still watch it with you sometimes. You just don't know I'm there." When he returned his attention to Seth, all levity fled his features. "So are we good now? Will you stop avoiding me every time you see me?"

"I—"

"Apologize one more time," Yuri warned ominously, "and I will plague you every night with nightmares plucked from Sheldon's weird-ass sexual history."

Zach laughed.

Yuri's expression softened. "I do *not* hold you responsible, Seth. I do not regret dying that day. My *only* regret is not being able to speak with you. And that is something you have the ability to change."

Throat thick, Seth nodded. "Only if you'll come to me in a dream so I can hug you."

Yuri smiled. "That I can do." He turned his attention to Leah. "You'll hold him to that, won't you?"

Leah smiled. "Yes. Thank you, Yuri. Seth may not admit it, but he needed this."

His smile grew. "Seth needed *you* more than anything. Thank you for bringing him the same happiness I've found with Cat." He pressed a kiss to the top of Catherine's head, then straightened and clapped his hands together. "All right, now that the big surprise is over, let's get down to business, shall we? Cat and I have information to share."

Stanislav frowned. "What kind of information?"

Yuri encompassed them all with a look. "We heard Liora and Jordan mention a rendezvous point Gershom designated for them, one where they would meet and he would teleport them to wherever he's keeping them to prevent them from being able to give away its location if captured."

Bastien glanced at Seth, then Yuri. "And?"

"And," Yuri continued, "we took it upon ourselves to haunt that particular location to see if it was true."

Seth frowned. "Is it?"

Yuri nodded. "It is. While we were watching the clearing, two of the missing immortals arrived by foot. One called Gershom on a cell phone. Gershom arrived an instant later, then teleported them away."

Seth met David's gaze. "Then we know where we can catch him."

David nodded. "Precisely."

"Even better," Yuri said. "If we're present when he teleports, we can follow him to his destination much the same way you can, Seth."

Surprise widened Seth's eyes. "You can?" He'd had no idea spirits could do such a thing.

Yuri nodded. "We couldn't at first. But we've been practicing and testing the limits of what this form allows us to do... with the help of Blaise."

Bastien growled as fury darkened his features. "Blaise? That bastard is still around?"

"His spirit is," Cat confirmed.

"Where is he?" he demanded furiously. "Is he here? Is he—?"

Cat held up a hand. "It's all right, Bastien. Blaise can't hurt me anymore. He's…" Her brow furrowed with concentration as she lowered her head and tapped her lips with an index finger. "What's that phrase Sheldon is so fond of using?" Her face lighting up, she snapped her fingers. "Oh yes." She smiled at her brother. "Yuri and I have made Blaise our bitch."

Bastien gaped at her.

Everyone burst into laughter. Even Seth found himself chuckling. Bastien's shock at hearing his timid, proper sister make such a proclamation was hilarious.

Chuckling, Yuri sent Cat an amused look. "That we have, love." Then he spoke to Bastien. "Blaise is terrified of us—mostly of Cat—so we've made him our servant of sorts, forcing him to teach us all his little tricks." He turned back to Seth. "And we finally mastered one of those tricks enough to follow Gershom the last time he visited that clearing."

"And?" Seth prompted.

Yuri's face filled with triumph. "We know where the other missing immortals are."

Chapter Twenty-Two

CONVERSATION ERUPTED AFTER YURI'S ASTONISHING announcement. Leah silently held Seth's hand, smoothing her thumb over his skin, taken aback by the wonder of it all. Just when she thought she knew everything about Seth and his world — or as much as he could share with her — she learned something new. Seth could see ghosts. Seth could allow *her* to see ghosts with a touch. And she was now watching him and his fellow immortals *converse* with ghosts as if it were the most ordinary thing in the world.

Bastien seemed only a little less shocked than she was. Leah's heart went out to the British immortal. He clearly loved his sister and kept darting looks her way as though he feared she would disappear.

Seth spoke. "You saw all of them there? All nine missing immortals?"

Yuri shared a look with Cat. "There are only eight immortals by our count. I thought at first the ninth must be out hunting, but there seems to be no room set aside for a ninth."

Cat nodded. "And we heard no mention of another."

Leah studied them all. "What does that mean?"

Seth shook his head. "I'm not sure."

Melanie bit her lip. "It's possible the ninth *gifted one* didn't survive the transformation."

Bastien shook his head. "Or simply didn't fall into line the way the others did and was slain by Gershom. We know he killed several of the other *gifted ones* he took for that reason... or had them killed."

Leah looked up at Seth.

A muscle in his jaw twitched. "Let's focus on those we can save now. Did Gershom see you, Yuri?"

Yuri shook his head. "He gave no indication that he did. I assumed he could see spirits, since you, Zach, and David all possess that ability, so we did our damnedest to stay out of sight. We also didn't speak. In this realm, when we concentrate, Cat and I can communicate telepathically even though we weren't born with that gift. It's not as clear and direct as it would be if we were actual telepaths, but it's something we've learned to do well enough to get the gist across to each other."

The couple was obviously deeply in love. Leah suspected their knowing each other so well aided them in that silent communication.

"Since we didn't talk and our movements are silent," Yuri continued, "we made no sound Gershom could detect to tip him off that we were there. And we have no natural scent that members of the mortal realm can detect."

Leah smiled. "That is so cool. You're like the perfect spies."

He grinned. "Exactly."

"Such was dangerous," Seth announced grimly.

Leah looked up at him in surprise.

Yuri shook his head. "We're already dead, Seth. What more could he do to us?"

"He could banish you," Seth replied. "Or banish *one* of you so the other would be left behind to grieve and suffer."

If ghosts could blanch, Leah thought both would have done so as they shared a horrified look.

Then Cat straightened her shoulders and stared up at Seth. "Even if I'd known beforehand, I still would've risked it."

"Cat," Bastien protested.

She held up a hand. "I've changed since we last spoke, Sebastien. I've grown. A lot. And you are no longer the only member of our family who is capable of standing up for what's right or who is willing to *fight* for what's right." She again looked at Seth. "You're the reason my brother is happy. You're the sole reason he now has a wife who loves and fulfills him." She shook her head. "And you're the *only* reason civilization has not yet collapsed. Had you not appointed yourself the leader of the Immortal Guardians when you became aware of the virus, gathered the immortals together, trained them, and provided them with the tools they needed to keep the vampire population in check, vampires would have long since slain every human being on this planet."

Leah stared at her. That was sobering as hell. She looked up at Seth, awe trickling through her. "Damn, Seth," she said softly.

He glanced down at her. "What?"

"You saved the world." He really had. He had expressed more than once the importance of maintaining a balance. Had he not pitted immortals against the rising vampire population, there would have been no balance and humans would have all either been slain or transformed. Then those who were transformed — even if they could subsist on animal blood — would've succumbed to madness in just a few years' time.

Humanity would've indeed become extinct.

Seth had *saved* the *world* and was doing his damnedest to save it again.

He frowned as if he were uncomfortable with her thinking such.

"Seth," Cat said, drawing his attention before he could offer a protest, "we know the threat Gershom poses."

Yuri nodded. "We've been present at every meeting you and our brethren have held, both here and at network headquarters." His lips tightened as he sent his leader a disgruntled look. "We just remained out of sight so we wouldn't upset your damned delicate sensibilities."

Zach, Bastien, and Marcus all barked out laughs.

Even Seth laughed, Leah was relieved to see, while David unsuccessfully fought a smile.

"Gershom," Yuri continued, "has proven to be far more dangerous than vampires, more so even than the mercenary groups we've fought in the past. Cat and I wish to do whatever we can to help you stop him. So... yes, had we been aware of the risks, we still would've staked out the clearing and followed Gershom to the place he's holding the missing immortals."

Cat nodded. "And we'll do it again. Whatever you need. We want to help you end this so you can all get on with your lives without anyone else being hurt. Please, let us do this."

A long moment passed.

"Where are they being held?" Seth asked, making no promises.

Poor guy. He even tried to protect *dead* immortals and *gifted ones.*

Yuri and Cat looked over at Marcus.

Marcus crossed to Ami's desk. When he returned, he carried an iPad. "Here." He turned the tablet to face them.

Seth studied the map on the screen. His brows drew down in a scowl. "Seriously?"

Leah studied it. She wasn't very familiar with North Carolina's coast and didn't have Seth's outstanding vision to help her read the tiny print. "Where is it? I can't make out the words."

"Roanoke Island," Seth answered.

Roanoke Island, she silently repeated, then frowned. "The sight of the so-called Lost Colony?"

"Yes," Seth answered with a curl of his lip.

"What an ass," Zach muttered. "Did he think he was being clever, holding them there?"

"I don't know what goes through that bastard's mind," Seth responded. "What kind of building is it, Yuri?"

"The kind that's perfect for his purposes," he answered. "Plain. Nondescript. Set apart from all other homes and structures. Almost no windows."

"Is it military?" David asked.

Yuri shook his head. "I don't think so, but he has convinced the immortals housed there that it is and that the guards present are there to protect them."

"As far as we can tell," Cat said, "the men who guard them are mercenaries."

Seth studied the map. "Chris's contacts should be able to confirm that for us. Are the immortals aware of each other? Liora believes she only saw Tessa and Veronica once. Jordan thinks he saw Veronica once. But I couldn't tell if that was true. If Gershom erased their memories of other encounters, their regenerative abilities would've rid them of whatever scar tissue resulted in their brains."

"Gershom keeps them separated," Yuri answered. "They have almost no contact with each other. I don't know how often

Gershom goes there, but from what we observed, he taps into their minds when he does and erases any doubts or questions that have arisen during his absence." He looked at Stanislav. "Gershom is as adept at manipulating emotions as you are. He constantly fuels their anger and their desire for vengeance and even their patriotism." He again met Seth's gaze. "He's convinced them you're a threat, a power-hungry menace intent on either conquering the world or watching it burn."

Seth shook his head. "When he himself is the one who wants to watch the world burn." He turned to David. "We should act on this now."

Leah stiffened. "What?"

"I agree," David said. "If there's even a slight chance that Gershom saw Yuri and Cat, he may even now be searching for a new place to stash the kidnapped immortals."

Leah's heart began to beat faster with fear. Gershom was supposedly almost as powerful as Seth. "Shouldn't you wait until you have more intel? You know almost nothing about the place."

Yuri shook his head. "We can go with you, Seth, and show you exactly in which rooms the immortals are kept, help you navigate the building, and warn you of approaching guards."

His words didn't dispel her rising panic. "What if Gershom *did* see Yuri and Cat? What if, instead of concentrating on finding a new hiding place, he's laying a trap, knowing you're on your way?"

Zach nodded. "It's possible. Gershom is a wily bastard."

"Which is why," Seth said, "Zach and I will go alone."

"Oh hell no!" Leah blurted. "If you're going to do this, you should take as many men with you as you can."

But Seth shook his head. "If it's a trap, the purpose is less likely to be an attempt to kill or capture me and more likely to be Gershom attempting to lure me away from here so he can nab you, Ami, and Adira. Zach and I will go alone and leave everyone else behind to guard you."

She looked at David, silently beseeching him to back her up.

David sighed. "I don't like it either, but I agree. Gershom has not yet attempted to take Seth's life."

"Not *yet*," she repeated, pouncing on the second word. "He has not *yet* attempted to take Seth's life. That doesn't mean he won't."

David touched her arm. "Thus far, Gershom has merely attempted to set events into motion that even Seth—with all his power and resources—will not be able stop or reverse. Seth would be far less useful to him dead than he would be as a weapon Gershom can trigger by harming those Seth loves."

Leah wasn't even sure what that meant but nevertheless found it unsettling as hell.

"So we're in agreement?" Seth asked.

David looked at Yuri. "Are the missing immortals still there?"

Yuri vanished. A second later, he reappeared. "Yes. They're still there. So is Gershom."

Seth squeezed Leah's hand and turned to Zach. "We go now. Jared."

A man as tall as Seth abruptly appeared in the room with them, not two feet from Leah, startling the hell out of her. "Yes?"

"We've found Gershom. Zach and I are going to confront him and rescue the kidnapped immortals. Do you want to join us?"

Jared's eyes flashed with golden light. "Hell yes!" Two long swords appeared in his hands.

Seth spoke in Leah's head. *Will that put your mind at ease?*

Not really, but she nodded. The last thing Seth needed right now was a distraction. She didn't want him worrying about her while he was confronting his enemy.

"I've awoken the immortals," Seth announced, "and alerted the Seconds. All are arming themselves as we speak. I've also given Reordon a heads-up. He is currently locking down network headquarters in case an attack should ensue while he prepares for the arrival of the new immortals."

Normally Leah would've thought it freaking awesome that Seth could do all that in just a few seconds' time with his mind. But her heart pounded and her thoughts and fears whipped around inside her like a tornado. Seth was really going to do it. He was really going to confront Gershom with just two other immortals.

Marcus took a step forward. "What about Ami and Adira? If this is a trap and Gershom is luring you away…" Fear for his wife and daughter lent his eyes an amber glow.

"If Gershom eludes us and comes here, David and Ami will both call me telepathically the instant he arrives and I will not hesitate to return." He met Zach's gaze. "Give me a minute to arm Leah."

Zach nodded.

Leah gasped when Seth suddenly scooped her up into his arms. The room blurred and wind whipped her face. Seconds later, he set her on her feet. She gaped. The large room to which he had taken her could only be described as an armory. Holy crap, there were a lot of weapons! Men and women garbed all in black darted around the room—some at preternatural speeds, some at mortal speeds—grabbing many of those weapons and strapping them to their bodies.

Seth joined them, swiftly weighing Leah down with shoulder-holstered 9mms and filling her pockets with thirty-round magazines. Daggers appeared in sheaths on her thighs as his hands moved over her. "Gershom has used vampires in the past to attack while I'm distracted. Remember to strike the major arteries if he does so again."

"Okay," she agreed shakily.

Once he finished arming her, he donned a bandoleer loaded with numerous daggers and draped it across his chest. Then he stilled and stared down at her.

Her heart continued to slam against her rib cage. Leaning forward, she wrapped her arms around him and hugged him tight, so afraid for him.

He held her close. "I'll be all right, Leah."

"You'd better be." Rising onto her toes, she captured his lips in a kiss she hoped would convey everything she felt for him. Just in case it didn't, she said, "I love you."

His eyes flared bright gold. Dipping his head, he delivered a scorching kiss of his own. "I love you, Leah." He pressed his forehead to hers. "Please stay safe."

She nodded, a lump rising in her throat. "You, too."

Heavy silence engulfed the room.

Loosening her hold, she looked around.

Every immortal present was staring at their leader.

Aidan stepped forward. "We'll do everything we can to protect her, Seth."

The others nodded.

"Thank you." Seth settled his gaze upon her once more.

Knowing that standing there with tears in her eyes would only make this harder for him, Leah forced a fierce smile and raised a fist in the air. "Go kick his freaking ass!"

Every warrior in the room raised a fist in the air and loosed a battle cry.

Grinning, Seth teleported away.

———◦◦◦◦———

Leaving Leah and returning to David's study was one of the hardest things Seth had ever done. She was so mortal, so fragile despite her bravery. It terrified him, how easily she could be taken from him.

A hand clasped his shoulder.

Seth jumped, startled from his thoughts.

"I know it's hard," Zach said softly, "but erase everything else from your mind and focus on the task at hand. It's the best thing you can do to keep her safe."

He nodded.

Marcus held up his iPad again. "Reordon sent us schematics of the building."

Seth's eyebrows flew up. "He did?"

Yuri moved forward. "I recommend you teleport to just inside this entrance. You'll have a straight shot through to the wing of the building that houses the immortals." He pointed to an area on the east side of the building. "You'll find the first group on this hallway, each in a separate room guarded by armed mercenaries. Then take a right turn up this hallway to find the others." He moved his finger farther along the schematic. "This room here is where we saw Gershom meet with the other guards. If you don't find him with one of the immortals, you'll most likely find him there."

Seth nodded. "Jared, if we don't encounter Gershom where the immortals are housed, I want you to concentrate on freeing them for me while Zach and I continue on to confront him. If Gershom teleports away, we'll follow. We shouldn't have any trouble catching up to him this time because he'll only be a few seconds ahead of us."

He nodded. "If you need my help—"

Seth shook his head. "You'll have your hands full with the immortals since they believe us the enemy. If *you* need help—"

"I can handle it."

"Don't kill them," Seth warned.

"I won't."

Zach shook his head with a wry smile. "He'll just talk their ears off until they *wish* he would kill them, then ask the women out."

Jared laughed.

Seth extended his hands. Two swords appeared in them. "If the guards become a problem, read their minds and kill those who aren't worth saving. Knock out the rest."

All agreed.

Seth met David's gaze.

David dipped his chin in a nod.

Seth looked at the others. "On three. One. Two. Three."

David's study went dark. Then bright fluorescent light showered Seth as he teleported to the hallway just inside the east entrance of the building. Stark white walls surrounded them. White professional-grade epoxy flooring gleamed beneath his feet.

Zach and Jared appeared on his left, Yuri and Cat on his right.

Yelps and curses erupted behind him.

Seth swung around just as half a dozen guards turned their weapons upon him.

Jared darted forward in a blur and knocked every man out with preternaturally fast punches. He stilled. As bodies collapsed to the floor around him, he grinned at Seth. "This is going to be fun."

Yuri pointed down the hallway in the opposite direction. "The immortals are down there."

Vampires, Gershom broadcast telepathically, *arm yourselves. Seth and his Immortal Guardians have found us and have come to kill you all.*

Adrenaline surged through Seth's body.

Gershom was still there. At last, this would end.

"Free the immortals," Seth ordered Jared and raced forward, Zach at his side.

The doors along the hallway abruptly flew open. Men and women bearing glowing amber eyes poured out. Every face filled with hatred as they drew weapons, roared battle cries, and struck.

And all of them targeted Seth.

Seth brought up his swords and managed to deflect most of the daggers that flew toward him. Those he couldn't he gave a telekinetic push at the last moment to keep them from impaling him. Then bullets slammed into him, hitting him in the chest and stealing his breath. Two struck him in the head, scattering his thoughts. He tightened his hold on his swords to keep from dropping them as he stumbled backward, pain radiating through his cranium.

What the hell caliber bullets had those been? It felt like half his brain had just exited the back of his skull.

Zach and Jared leapt past Seth. The clash of weapons erupted as Seth clenched his teeth and bent over, waiting for the fucking damage to his brain to heal. The ground beneath his feet began to tremble as anger rose inside him, barely checked. The floor tiles he stared at reflected the bright golden glow that entered his eyes.

"Seth!" Zach called.

"Don't kill them," he ground out. Metal projectiles fell from his chest and made tinkling sounds as they hit the floor.

More guards ran into view, coming up behind them.

Seth tried to telekinetically yank the weapons from their hands. But the damned head injury he'd suffered was bad enough that it had temporarily robbed him of the ability.

Dropping his swords, he yanked daggers from the bandoleer across his chest and threw them with preternatural speed. All found a home in the guards, whose minds Seth couldn't afford to take time to read first... not that he could probably read them right now anyway.

The pain in his head eased. His thoughts began to clear.

Grabbing his swords, he swung around.

Another bullet struck him in the head. Then another and another. "Fuck!" He stumbled backward. Seth had suffered so few head injuries in his lifetime that he hadn't realized bullets could deprive him — at least for a while — of some of his abilities.

"Get his fucking gun," Zach snarled behind him, "while I handle these two!"

Agony enhanced the rage that suffused Seth. He couldn't think. Couldn't focus. Couldn't restrain the power that rose up inside him and abruptly found release in a roar of fury and burst of energy that radiated outward like the blast wave of a bomb.

Cries erupted in the hallway.

Bodies hit the floor.

"Seth!" Zach dashed up and gripped his shoulder. "Seth, reel that shit in. Now." He cupped the back of Seth's head with his other hand.

Healing warmth slithered into Seth through the touch. The pain in his head swiftly eased. His thoughts realigned themselves. His control returned. "Oh shit." Eyes wide, he spun around.

Every immortal, save Zach and Jared, was down. All lay still, eyes closed, blood trailing from their noses and ears.

Seth's heart began to beat harder with fear and dread. Had he killed them? Had he just slain the immortals he had come here to rescue?

He sent Zach a frantic look.

Zach squeezed his shoulder. "You didn't kill them. Their hearts still beat. Listen."

He did. And some of his fear receded.

"They've all suffered brain injuries," Zach told him, "but they're not life-threatening and can be healed later."

Remorse pounded through him as Seth dragged an arm across his forehead and wiped away the blood that dripped down it. Retrieving his swords, he looked at Jared. "Watch over them."

Jared nodded. "Go."

Seth and Zach raced forward as one.

Three more kidnapped immortals came around the corner.

Their eyes took in their fallen comrades, then flashed amber with hatred as they spotted Seth.

"You killed them!" a female shouted.

All raised their weapons.

Prepared this time, Seth telekinetically yanked their weapons from their hands and sent the swords and firearms flying toward the opposite end of the hallway.

Jared swore and ducked as they sailed past.

Relieved that his telekinetic abilities had been restored, Seth sheathed his own weapons, darted forward, and touched a hand to both male's foreheads. "Sleep."

Their eyes closed as their knees buckled.

Zach grabbed the female and did the same.

Yuri spoke from around the corner. "Guards are headed your way from the next hallway."

Seth and Zach darted around the corner and knocked the guards on their asses before they could even register they were no longer alone.

Yuri and Cat stood at the opposite end of the hallway. Both pointed in the direction Seth should take.

Seth raced down yet another hallway, Zach at his side.

When they reached the closed door at the end, they didn't bother to pause. They just plowed through it... into an empty room.

"Son of a bitch!" Zach shouted.

Seth swung around to face Yuri.

Yuri shook his head. "He was here when we arrived. We'll see if we can pinpoint where he went." He and Catherine huddled together and closed their eyes.

Seth focused on the lingering tendrils of energy he could sense. "Zach."

"I'm working on it."

Yuri and Cat vanished.

David, Seth called telepathically as he worked to determine Gershom's path, *Gershom has fled. We're tracing his path now to determine his destination and follow.*

Silence.

Seth frowned. *David?* he called again.

Still nothing. Had the damned head wound robbed him of his telepathy? "Zach, I can't reach David. I think it's the head wound. Warn him Gershom is on the loose."

Zach nodded. Seconds later, alarm flared in his gaze. "He isn't answering. And I can't reach Lisette."

At the same instant, Seth realized Gershom's energy trail was heading toward David's home. Swearing, he palmed his swords and teleported away.

Chapter Twenty-Three

E THAN AND THE OTHER IMMORTALS in the armory all stared at
Leah after Seth's departure. Though she tried valiantly to keep
her smile in place, she failed. Nor did she succeed in hiding the
anxiety that inundated her. Ethan could practically feel it from
where he stood, and he wasn't an empath.

"Seth, Zach, and Jared just teleported away," Aidan announced.

Ethan wished he could've gone with them. Leaping headlong
into battle alongside his brethren while knowing what to expect
was far preferable to waiting to see if some force would launch an
attack here at David's home while details of the other battle trickled
in. Wherever Seth went, it would be warrior against warrior.
Here... Ethan didn't know *what* might happen. Would an attack
even ensue? If it did, would vampires carry out that attack as they
had in the past? Or would Gershom throw something new at them?

It also wouldn't just be immortal warriors tossed into battle
here. There were two tiny, vulnerable children to protect. And
Leah, who was so very human. And Susan, who was a *gifted one.*
Not to mention Ami and the Seconds.

The other immortals began to file out of the room, the Seconds
following.

Ethan hung back with Heather and sent Leah a smile, hoping to
ease some of her anxiety. "He'll be okay. I know you're worried.
But Seth won't take unnecessary risks. He has you to come back to
now."

Leah nodded. "Thank you."

Ami made her way to them with a sleepy Adira perched on her

hip. Tucking her free hand in Leah's, she led her from the room.

Ethan and Heather brought up the rear, following everyone else upstairs. Every immortal headed into the kitchen to tank up on blood, just in case. Ethan and Heather did the same, then joined the others in the living room.

Leah, Ami, and Adira claimed a sofa and were soon joined by Marcus. Roland, Sarah, and Michael took the sofa across from them. David seated himself in a wingback chair kitty-corner to both while Ethan and Heather found a love seat nearby.

The two toddlers almost immediately slid off the sofas and began to play with their favorite building blocks, scattering them on the coffee table between them.

Heavy silence fell once the rest of the immortals and Seconds found seats. All, like Ethan, covertly watched Leah while they waited, both curious about their powerful leader's woman and concerned for her.

Leah glanced around, her face somber. "I know you told Seth you'd keep me safe, but if it should come down to choosing between protecting me or protecting the children, I want you to protect the children."

Ethan exchanged an uncomfortable look with Heather. Just the possibility of having to make that choice chilled his blood.

"I mean it," Leah said firmly. "If you have to make a choice, choose the children. Seth lost his son and daughter. I don't want him to lose Adira and Michael, too."

Ami swallowed hard, then turned to her husband. "I agree. The children come first, Marcus. If something foul goes down and you have to choose between me and the babies, save the children."

"Ami," Marcus whispered, his expression full of torment, his voice hoarse.

She cupped his face in a small hand. "I know. I love you, Marcus. But we have to keep Adira safe."

Brow furrowed, he closed his eyes and pressed his forehead to hers.

Sarah looked up at Roland. "The children come first. Okay? Promise me."

He swallowed hard, his face grim. "I promise."

Then every female present said the same, ordering the men in their lives to protect the children at all costs. Because they knew the men's first instinct would be to save the women they loved.

"You too, Bastien," Melanie said. The two occupied a sofa across the room. "I need you to promise me. I need to hear you say it."

He studied her, his expression grave. "Why?"

"Because I'm starting to get that feeling again. And this time I don't think it has anything to do with Cliff."

He swore, as did several others present, including Ethan.

Melanie's psychic gift might be muted, but whenever she got one of her *feelings*, serious shit went down.

David rose suddenly. "Seth is speaking to me." He drew two long swords. "Gershom has fled the building. He—"

Gershom abruptly appeared behind David, pressed a gun to his head, and shot him three times.

David's knees buckled as he sank to the floor.

"Oh shit!" Ethan leapt to his feet alongside the others and drew his weapons.

"Sleep!" Gershom bellowed, his face mottling as tendons stood out in his neck.

A tingling sensation struck Ethan's body as a ripple of power passed through him.

Every immortal and mortal in the room closed his or her eyes and collapsed to the floor.

Every immortal save himself. Because Ethan's mind was wired differently, leaving him impervious to mind control.

Shit! Ethan dropped his weapons and caught his wife before she could hit the floor. "Heather?" he called frantically. She was so pale and still that he feared she was dead until he detected her heartbeat.

The cries of a child broke the ensuing silence.

Ethan's head whipped around.

Michael lay still on the floor beside his parents, his eyes closed.

Adira miraculously remained conscious. Crawling over to Ami, she tugged on the front of her mother's shirt, then pressed her face in the crook of Ami's neck as she wept.

"Sleep!" Gershom commanded again with a scowl.

Neither Ethan nor Adira succumbed.

The children come first. Heather's words pounding in his brain,

Ethan fought every instinct that commanded him to get her the hell out of there and lowered her to the love seat.

Protect the children.

Retrieving his weapons, he straightened and faced Gershom. There was no way in hell he could beat the Other in a fight, but he would damned well give his life trying if it would buy Seth enough time to get back here and save everyone.

Ethan tensed, preparing to lunge forward.

David abruptly rose up behind Gershom. Blood coated half of his face and trailed from ghastly exit wounds on the side of his head as he drove a sword through Gershom's back.

Gershom's eyes widened with shock as pain contorted his features. The tip of David's sword emerged from Gershom's chest and twisted sharply.

"Get the children to safety!" David roared, then drove his other sword into Gershom's back. The tip of this one passed through Gershom's heart and exited his chest.

Ethan sheathed his weapons in a blink and raced for the children. Hands shaking, he gathered Michael's limp little body up in one arm and tucked a screaming Adira against his chest with the other. As soon as he was certain he had a secure hold on both, he raced for the door.

Long swords appeared in Gershom's hands as he swung around with a roar, David's blades still embedded in his body.

David drew two more.

Ethan burst through the front door, tears blurring his vision. Every cell in his body urged him to go back for Heather, not to leave her at Gershom's mercy. But she'd made him promise. She'd made him swear to protect Adira and Michael. And he would honor that promise even if it killed him.

Shicks and *tings* reverberated from the house as David and Gershom engaged in a vicious battle.

Ethan sped toward the barn, relieved to see the sun was dipping below the horizon and wouldn't scald his skin. Darkness engulfed him as he ducked inside, but his preternatural vision enabled him to clearly see the many vehicles parked within. He was only a century old and would never be able to outrun Gershom. Bypassing the cars, he stopped beside a tarp. A quick yank on the soft material unveiled David's beloved Tomahawk motorcycle, a monster of a machine with two closely spaced wheels in front and two more in back.

Adira continued to cry disconsolately.

"Shhhh," he whispered. It broke his heart when she instantly clamped her little pink lips together and tried to stifle her sobs. No child so young should have learned to respond to that command.

As swiftly as he could, Ethan cradled both children against him with one arm and awkwardly wound the tarp around himself with the other to bind both close to his chest in a sling of sorts. Climbing onto the back of the bike, he started the engine and tore out of the barn. Down the long driveway he flew. The security gate swung open at his approach and let him pass without slowing. Then he swung onto a narrow two-lane highway. With no cars in sight, Ethan shot forward. His adrenaline levels spiked as he increased his speed as much as he dared, barely managing to stay on the blacktop as he took one curve after another too fast, his knee damned near scraping the pavement, until he reached a major freeway.

Darting through traffic at the signal light, he turned onto the feeder road, entered the wide, straight freeway, and sped forward. A hundred miles per hour. Two hundred miles per hour. Three hundred miles per hour when he reached a long straight strip. Slowing only when he absolutely had to.

Darkness descended, providing him with a little cover as he passed other drivers as if they stood still. Wind whipped him, trying to pluck him from the back of the sleek vehicle. Little Michael remained motionless against his chest. Adira fisted her hands in his shirt and whimpered.

Come on, Seth, he silently chanted, wishing yet again that he were telepathic and could call the powerful leader to his side. But he had to use his phone to do it and didn't dare stop until he placed more distance between the children and Gershom.

He swerved to avoid slamming into the back of a truck as he flew over a rise. Heart racing, scared shitless by the close call, he reduced his speed a bit. When he topped another rise, he swore foully. A sea of brake lights shone in the distance, the flashing lights of an ambulance in their midst.

Slowing even more, he weaved in and out of decelerating traffic and exited the freeway. The feeder road bore only a little less traffic, so he swung right at the first street he came to and tore away again.

Sleep! Gershom's deep voice bellowed in his head.

Shit! How close was he?

Ethan picked up his speed even more. No streetlights illuminated the dark country road, nor did traffic clog it.

Gershom abruptly appeared on the asphalt in front of him and threw out a hand.

Ethan swore as the Tomahawk suddenly braked at the ancient immortal's telekinetic command. The nose froze in place while the rear kept going, tossing Ethan forward like a fucking catapult. Ground and sky repeatedly switched positions as he flew through the air. Dipping his head, Ethan wrapped his arms around the bundle on his chest and brought up his knees to protect the children. Pain crashed through him as he struck the pavement, rolling and skidding several yards. Ribs broke. A kneecap shattered. A bone in one arm snapped. The fabric of his coat tore open, allowing the rough pavement to scrape away skin. His head struck something hard. Sparkling lights clouded his vision like fireworks. Then, at last, he skidded to a halt.

The metallic taste of blood filled his mouth. Groaning, Ethan shifted his hands and slid them over the bundle on his chest. Had he succeeded in protecting the children?

"Adira," he whispered breathlessly.

The bundle shifted. A sniffle sounded. "Unca Eefan?"

Tears of relief filled his eyes. "You okay, honey?"

"Uh-huh," she replied mournfully.

Then Michael shifted beside her, emerging from whatever thrall Gershom had placed him under.

Gritting his teeth against the agony every movement spawned, Ethan drew a dagger from his tattered coat and carefully sliced open the makeshift sling. A moan escaped him as he rolled onto his side and gently dumped the children onto the pavement.

Both little ones sat up. Michael blinked groggily and peered around him. Adira regarded Ethan with big green eyes full of fear and tears. Her little nose was red. Her cheeks glistened.

Ethan tilted his head back and looked up the road.

Gershom strolled toward them as if he had all the time in the world.

At least he tried to. A heavy limp hindered Gershom's ordinarily smooth gait. Blood streaked his bare chest, which bore numerous deep gashes and puncture wounds. One of his dark wings was folded in against his back. The other dragged on the ground behind him, leaving a trail of translucent feathers. His face was a mask of rage and pain. His eyes glowed bright gold.

Ethan rose onto one elbow and looked at the children. "Run," he wheezed. "Hide. Uncle Ethan will find you when it's safe."

Both looked terrified.

"Now," he commanded. "Go."

Adira grabbed Michael's hand and rose, pulling him up. As soon as both were standing, they took off running in that awkward manner of toddlers, toward the dark trees on the side of the road.

Ethan spat blood and drew his good knee up under him. He wasn't sure how he managed it, but somehow he made it to his feet. Or foot. He couldn't put any weight on the leg with the shattered kneecap.

Gershom continued to limp toward him, a warped smile twisting his lips. But his breath emerged in rough gasps. "Still trying to play the hero?" he drawled. Gershom started to stretch his large dark wings out to intimidate him but ended up grunting in pain.

Yeah. His wings were all jacked up. David had really kicked his ass.

Ethan swallowed. Had Gershom killed David?

Reaching into his pocket to retrieve his phone, he instead found only shattered pieces of it. He drew two short swords, grateful that neither had broken or impaled him when he'd crashed.

Every movement birthed greater agony. His head spun. The virus that infected him struggled to make repairs, but the damage was so great it could do little more than stop the bleeding.

Gershom's smile grew when he stood only a few feet away. He motioned to the forest in which the children hid. "There are two donors from whom you can siphon enough blood to heal your wounds. I'd be happy to wait while you partake and bleed them dry."

Protect the children. Whatever the cost, protect the children.

Repeating the mantra in his head, Ethan lunged forward.

Gershom's face twisted in a snarl of malice as he raised his own sword and swung.

⊷◉◉◉⊶

Seth teleported to David's home, followed swiftly by Zach.

Terror struck. Bodies sprawled on the floor of the living room. Too *few* bodies. It took only seconds to realize every man and woman down was either human or a *gifted one*. Not one immortal remained, nor did Leah, Ami, Adira, or Michael.

Zach cast him a look of panic. "Lisette!" he bellowed.

Seth moved forward. Where he should have heard a multitude of heartbeats, he only heard a few. "David!"

No answers came.

Zach blurred as he sped through the hallway and down to the basement. "Lisette!"

The metallic scent of blood hung in the air. Some of the furniture was overturned.

Seth knelt beside Sheldon and Tracy. Sheldon lay partially atop Tracy as though he had tried to shield her from something. Neither displayed any obvious wounds, but blood trickled from their noses and ears.

"Sheldon." Seth gave his shoulder a shake.

Nothing.

When Seth peeled back an eyelid, Sheldon's pupil failed to react. A quick scan of his health drew a curse from Seth's lips. Sheldon had suffered a traumatic brain injury and had sunk into a coma. Seth touched Tracy and discovered the same. What the hell had Gershom done?

Palming his phone, he dialed Chris Reordon.

"Jared just arrived with the immortals you rescued," Chris announced, bypassing a greeting. "I'll get them settled as quickly as I can."

"Gershom attacked David's home while we were gone. The Immortal Guardians who were here are all missing. The children, Ami, and Leah are, too."

~ 374 ~

Chris swore.

"Susan and the Seconds left behind are alive but comatose. All appear to have suffered traumatic brain injuries. Contact the other network heads and have them send you the most powerful immortal healers in their domain."

"All of them?"

"All of them. I need to track Gershom and can't afford the time I would lose healing the Seconds. Nor can I afford to lose the energy such would require. I'll summon some teleporters to bring them to network headquarters."

"All right. I'm on it. Anything else you need, let me know."

Zach returned, his eyes glowing bright gold. "They're all gone. There's no one here. I even checked the escape tunnels."

Seth mentally reached out to David, Ami, Adira, Aidan, Étienne, Lisette. Heather. "None of the telepaths are responding. And I can't sense them." He rose. "I can't sense *any* of them." The ground beneath his feet began to vibrate as he sought to keep his emotions under control.

Zach swallowed hard. "Are they… are they dead? Is Lisette dead, Seth? I can't feel her. I can't touch her mind." And Zach *always* touched her mind when he wasn't distracted by battle. His eyes glimmered with moisture. "There would be no bodies left behind if Gershom slew them. If you can't feel them…"

Seth shook his head. "Look around you. The immortals' clothing would remain, as would their weapons if he'd slain them. And Leah, Ami, Adira, and Michael are mortal. Their bodies wouldn't deteriorate like an immortal's would. Gershom didn't kill them, Zach. He took them." A familiar scent reached him. Striding past Sheldon, Seth dropped to his haunches near a wingback chair. Blood pooled on the floor beside it. "This is David's blood."

Zach joined him, his face grim. "That's not brain, is it?"

Seth hoped like hell it wasn't, but long dreadlocks coiled around the small bits of flesh. He spun, studying the floor. "Gershom's blood intermingles with it." Following the red blotches on the floor, he tracked them through the front door. Whatever wounds David had suffered had not kept him from fighting. The smears left by boots and the damage near the doorway whispered of a very violent battle.

Once outside, Seth scanned every blade of grass in the deepening darkness, searching for more drops of blood or anything else that might guide him.

Wind whipped him, carrying away scents that might have helped as clouds gathered overhead.

Grinding his teeth, he fought the fear and fury that threatened to consume him.

Gershom had Leah and Ami. He had Adira.

A faint thump reached his ears from the direction of the barn—the single, struggling beat of a damaged heart.

His head jerked toward the sound.

Zach's did, too.

Both raced toward it.

David lay on the ground just in front of the barn's entrance.

Seth nearly wept with relief. He'd known David would fight Gershom to the death to protect the others and had feared…

One side of David's head bore three circular wounds where bullets had entered. The other side was a mass of blood and mangled flesh. A fistful of dreadlocks was missing, torn away by the projectiles' exit.

"No wonder he didn't answer me," Seth murmured, rolling David onto his back.

David's hands continued to clutch two swords, never relinquishing their grip.

Seth placed one hand on David's head and the other on his chest. Healing warmth spread from his limbs into David, going first to the head wound.

"He needs blood," he announced as Zach headed into the barn to search it. "I'm going to summon some Immortal Guardians to provide it, so don't kill them when they appear."

Zach grunted an acknowledgment.

Rafe, Seth called telepathically.

Yes?

Come to me at once. I'm at David's home in North Carolina.

Eliana is with me. Should I bring her or leave her?

Bring her.

Zach returned. "No one is in the barn. And David's Tomahawk is missing."

Vicente, Seth called mentally as he continued to heal David as best he could. Brain damage was tricky and should be healed at a much slower pace.

Yes?

Come to me. I'm at David's home in North Carolina.

Mattheus is with me. Immortals worldwide were currently under orders to hunt in pairs.

Bring him, too. Now.

Two heartbeats suddenly joined their own. Then two more. Curses erupted inside the house.

"By the barn," Seth told them.

Grass crunched as the four immortals joined them.

"Oh no," Eliana murmured. Kneeling on David's other side, she curled her hands into fists and rested them on her thighs as she stared down at him.

"He'll survive," Seth told her and withdrew his hands. "Give him your blood." He touched David's jaw. David's lips parted as his fangs descended.

Eliana didn't hesitate to shove her sleeve up and press her wrist to David's lips. She winced when she applied enough pressure for his fangs to sink into her flesh, then relaxed as his fangs carried her blood directly to his veins. She drew the fingers of her free hand over David's dreadlocks. "What happened?"

Seth ground his teeth. "Gershom attacked while Zach, Jared, and I were rescuing the missing immortals." He glanced up. "Zach, bring me Imhotep. He and Chaak are guarding the network."

Zach vanished.

The other three immortals stood sentinel around Seth, David, and Eliana, weapons in hand as they darted David looks of concern. When Eliana paled and began to sway, Seth gently drew her wrist away from David. "Mattheus, you're next."

Mattheus knelt and pressed his wrist to David's lips.

Zach reappeared with Imhotep.

Seth caught Imhotep's eye. "Tell me what happened. It began in the house."

The powerful elder immortal dipped his chin in an abrupt nod and sped away.

Vicente offered his wrist next. The fact that David required so much blood was indicative of the damage done to his brain and body. David was nearly as old as Seth and had incredible regenerative capabilities. A single gunshot to the brain would've only slowed him down. But three gunshots followed by whatever the hell else Gershom had done...

When Rafe would've offered his wrist, too, Seth held up a hand. "He's coming around. Everyone step back."

They barely had time to do so before David's eyes opened and flashed brilliant amber. Roaring in rage, he leapt to his feet, swords at the ready.

The other immortals all hastily gave him room.

"David." Seth spoke calmly.

David spun to face him as Imhotep sped past and disappeared into the barn. "Seth." Blinking, he looked around. "Where are Ami and the children? Where's Leah?"

"Gone," Seth told him. When grief filled David's eyes, Seth hastily held up a hand. "Not dead. Missing. Did you kill Gershom?"

"No. But I came damned close." His brow furrowed as he looked around. "At least I think I did." His thoughts were likely still scattered by the gunshot wounds, the way Seth's had been.

Zach stepped forward. "What happened? Where are the other immortals?"

David looked at Seth with alarm. "They aren't inside?"

Seth shook his head. "We believe Gershom took them. Do you remember what happened?" Seth hadn't had time to heal all of the damage the bullets had wrought. The virus would have to take care of the rest while Seth conserved his energy.

David sheathed his weapons. "Gershom teleported in and shot me in the head three times. I think I lost consciousness for a moment. When I awoke, everyone except Ethan and Adira were down."

Imhotep joined them. "As soon as Gershom shot David, he commanded the others to sleep."

Zach frowned. "Didn't they fight him? How the hell did he manage to touch every one of them and —?"

"He didn't touch them," Imhotep clarified. "He just bellowed the word *sleep* and everyone except Ethan and Adira lapsed into unconsciousness."

Zach stared at Seth in astonishment. "How the hell did he do that?"

Seth shook his head. "I don't know. Even *I* can't command someone to sleep without touching them. He must have been working on building that particular skill for years." He returned his attention to Imhotep. "Ami succumbed to sleep, too?" Ami's regenerative capabilities exceeded even David's. Seth wouldn't have thought it possible for Gershom to mind-control her in such a way.

"Yes," Imhotep confirmed.

And yet Adira hadn't, another indication that the combination of Ami's alien DNA and Marcus's *gifted one* DNA had given the child extraordinary abilities.

"Ethan grabbed the children while David fought Gershom," Imhotep continued, sending David a look of respect. "Even as wounded as he was, David tore that bastard up and came damned close to killing him before Gershom finally managed to land a blow that would knock David out. Ethan bound the children to his chest and took David's Tomahawk. Gershom teleported away with those who are missing, then returned here and followed Ethan."

And he had done it all so swiftly that Seth could not sense a lingering energy trail to follow. "Can you show me where he went when he chased Ethan?"

Imhotep nodded. "This way." Blurring, he shot away.

Seth looked at the younger immortals. "Teleport the injured to network headquarters. I'll summon you if I need you." Without another word, he raced after Imhotep with Zach and David at his side.

It was a long journey. David's Tomahawk had enabled Ethan to cover a lot of ground before Gershom had caught up with him.

Imhotep stopped on a dark country road. "Gershom confronted him here."

Seth looked around. David's motorcycle had crashed in the middle of the road, leaving a long debris trail. Blood streaks on the pavement beyond made his stomach clench. "The children?" he forced himself to ask hoarsely. If they had been bound to Ethan when he'd crashed how much of that blood was theirs?

"They survived the crash intact. Ethan took all the damage and sent them into the trees."

Though the heartbeats he detected all sounded like those of animals, Seth immediately faced the forest. "Adira! Michael!"

"Come to Baba, babies!" David called, taking a step toward the forest. "Come to Abaye!"

Imhotep touched David's arm. "They aren't there. Even as injured as he was, Ethan tried to fight Gershom, but Gershom won."

"Did he kill Ethan?" Seth asked.

"No. Ethan still lives, but he barely escaped losing a limb. Gershom dragged the children from their hiding place in the trees, collected Ethan, and teleported away."

"Do you know where he went?"

"No," Imhotep admitted with regret.

The children must have been terrified. What would Gershom do to them? What would he do to *all* of them? To Leah? To Ami? To Seth's immortal family? How far would Gershom take this hatred of his, this quest to make Seth suffer as the world crumbled around them? "Where was he when he teleported?"

Imhotep guided him to the spot, and though Seth tried, he could find no lingering energy trail to follow.

"Zach?" Perhaps his head wounds had dampened his senses.

Zach walked around the area, his brows drawn down in a deep V. "There's nothing."

Storm clouds gathered overhead. Gershom had Leah, Ami, and Adira. He had Michael. He had so many beloved immortals. Seth had vowed to protect them all. He'd sworn to keep them safe. And they were now at Gershom's mercy.

David shook his head, his face a mask of regret as moisture glimmered in his glowing amber eyes. "I didn't hold him. The head wounds dulled my gifts, so I couldn't—"

Swallowing hard, Seth drew him into a hug. "This is not your fault, David. It is mine. Yet again, I underestimated him." Releasing him, he palmed his phone and dialed Chris.

"Reordon."

"Can you trace cell phones and pinpoint where the missing Immortal Guardians are located?"

"Yes. Whose phone do you want me to trace?"

"All of them. Every immortal stationed locally except for David and Imhotep."

Stunned silence carried over the line. "Shit. Okay. I'm on it. They're all still missing? I was hoping they were off chasing Gershom or something."

"They're still missing."

"Okay. Give me a minute."

Seth paced restively.

Zach did the same, his bright golden eyes reflecting the maelstrom of emotion that buffeted him.

Foul epithets carried across the line. "The phones all appear to be located at David's place," Chris announced.

Seth met Zach's gaze.

Then they had nothing to tell them where to begin their search.

Chapter Twenty-Four

T HUNK. *THUNK. THUNK.*

Leah frowned.

Thunk. Thunk. Thunk. Thunk.

Encapsulated in darkness, she clenched her teeth.

Thunk. Thunk. Thunk.

She didn't know what the hell that sound was, but pain shot through her head every damned time it broke the silence.

Thunk. Thunk. Thunk.

Why were chains rattling between the *thunks?*

She tried to open her eyes, but agony erupted in her head when bright light struck. A moan welled up in her throat and worked its way past the teeth she ground together.

"Easy," a male voice said. It sounded familiar.

"Is it working?" That voice belonged to Lisette, the French immortal.

"I think so," the male replied. Roland. She thought it was Roland.

Fingers touched her forehead. Heat bloomed there.

Thunk. Thunk. Thunk. Thunk.

Grunts and curses accompanied the loud sounds.

The pain in Leah's head receded a little. As it did, she became aware of other things. Her skin was cold, her fingers and toes nearly numb with it. She lay on a hard, chilly surface, her head tilted at an odd angle. She started to straighten it.

"Don't move." Roland's voice sounded strained.

"Honey," Sarah said uncertainly, "are you okay?"

"Yeah," Roland responded.

"You're bleeding," his wife murmured with concern.

"I'm okay," he insisted. "I'm almost done." He didn't sound

okay. He sounded like he was in a great deal of pain.

Leah again tried to open her eyes. This time the bright light didn't feel so much like ice picks piercing her brain.

She blinked, striving to process the sight that met her eyes. She lay in a large room. Plain gray concrete walls. Concrete floor. Concrete ceiling. No windows. One door that was down a short concrete hallway. No window in the door.

Almost all of the Immortal Guardians she had recently met were shackled to the walls around her. Thick manacles encircled every wrist. Heavy chains linked their wrists to thick rings in the concrete above their heads. Some of the immortals were seated. Others stood and were yanking on the chains with all their strength.

She turned her head.

Roland Warbrook was chained next to her, his wife Sarah on his other side. He leaned toward Leah as far as the chains would allow and just managed to brush his fingers across her forehead.

The warmth in her head... He was healing her.

A tapping sound drew her gaze to the floor between them. Blood was drip-drip-dripping from his wrist as he strained to reach her.

"What happened?" she asked, her thoughts sluggish. Where were they? How had they come to be here?

Roland's lips tightened. "Gershom happened. Our best guess is he mind-controlled us, sending us to sleep so he could transport us here without a fight. But you aren't immortal. The mental push caused brain damage and you lapsed into a coma." A muscle in his jaw twitched.

Her gaze again went to the growing crimson stain on the floor. "You're bleeding."

"It's difficult to reach you."

Behind him, Sarah bit her lip.

Leah started to reach and gently push his hand away but couldn't move her arm. Frowning, she looked down. Heavy shackles encased her wrists, the chains attached to them so heavy that—lacking the preternatural strength of the others—she could barely move them. "I'm okay. You can stop healing me."

"One more minute," he insisted. Blood began to trickle from his nose.

"Sweetie," Sarah protested softly, her brow furrowed.

A moment later, Roland withdrew his hand and slumped back against the wall beside her.

Leah stared at him. "Why are you bleeding?"

He motioned to his nose as Sarah gently drew her fingers across the skin above his upper lip, removing the blood. "My nose is bleeding because I'm weakened. If I heal others when I'm not at full strength, the wounds tend to open up on me."

The heavy chain barely impeding her movements, Sarah wiped his blood on her shirt, then cupped his face with that hand and stared into his eyes. "Are you okay?"

He nodded. Turning his head, he pressed a kiss to her palm.

Leah's gaze dropped to Roland's wrist where it rested in his lap. "And your wrist?" she asked as she sat up.

Roland turned his hand palm-up and shifted his arm so his fingers pointed toward her. "These aren't ordinary manacles that just fasten around your wrists like a cuff." He bent his hand back a bit to give her a better look at the place where the manacle touched his wrist. "There's a metal rod that passes through our wrists to the other side. So if we pull too hard, we'll fuck up our hands."

Horror filled her as she stared at his wrist. Blood trailed from the point where the rod pierced his skin. He'd had to stretch to reach her and had torn his own flesh to do it. "I'm sorry."

He shook his head.

She glanced down at the shackles on her own wrists. They chafed and felt heavy as hell but didn't hurt. Were there metal rods piercing her wrists, too? She didn't see any blood, but—

Roland shook his head. "You aren't immortal, so it looks like they gave you the regular shackles. I would've sensed wrist wounds when I healed you otherwise."

"Thank you for healing me."

He dipped his chin in a nod.

Leah glanced around. The men who yanked furiously on their chains in an attempt to pull them out of the wall each gripped the chain they held in a fist to alleviate the pressure on their wrists. Nevertheless, blood speckled the floor beneath them.

She took a quick head count. Roland and Sarah. Bastien and Melanie. Étienne and Krysta. Richart and Jenna. Aidan and Dana.

Ethan and Heather. Lisette and Stanislav. Marcus and Ami.

Thunk. Thunk. Thunk. Thunk.

Leah glanced at Ami, who sat not far away on her other side. "The children?" she asked, fear and dread filling her when she realized they weren't in the room with them.

Moisture glimmered in Ami's eyes. "They're here in the building, but they're being held somewhere else." Her throat moved in a hard swallow. "They're so afraid."

Leah had come to realize that although Ami wasn't immortal, she bore special gifts like the others. She hadn't had time to ask Seth why. Nor was she certain exactly what gifts Ami possessed. Perhaps she shared a mental connection with her daughter that allowed her to see or feel Adira's fear?

Beside Ami, Marcus stood with his booted feet planted as he yanked at one of his chains. His muscles flexed and strained. The cords in his neck stood out.

Thunk. Thunk. Thunk.

Leah hadn't noticed until then that everyone's coats and boots had been removed, leaving most in pants and a T-shirt.

Something about the struggles of Marcus and the other men seemed off. It took her a moment to figure out what. They all only used one hand and only tugged at the chain connected to it. None of them used both hands.

She frowned.

Marcus yanked and pulled and even sat down to prop both feet on the wall, using them to gain more leverage, muscles bulging under the strain. But the chain links held true. Leah looked at his other wrist—the one closest to Ami—and gasped.

Ami followed her gaze, then nodded. Her wrist on that side shared the same manacle as Marcus's, the rod going through his wrist before it passed through Ami's. "Every male here shares a manacle with a woman. Gershom knew the men would risk losing their own hands to escape but wouldn't risk costing us ours."

A glance around confirmed it. Leah was the only female present who wasn't shackled to a male immortal. The married couples present were all manacled to each other. Lisette was manacled to Stanislav. Aidan and Dana worked together to yank on their shared chain with all their might. Leah knew from Seth that both were very powerful. Though tiny cracks formed in the concrete wall above them, the ring to which the chain was attached didn't move.

Leah felt sick.

Marcus's tugs grew more frantic. Desperation and despair painted his handsome features.

"Marcus," Ami said softly, her voice choked with tears. "Please stop. You're hurting yourself, honey. If you lose your hand without Seth here to heal you, you'll lose it permanently."

Thunk. Thunk. Thunk. Thunk.

"Adira is just on the other side of this wall," he ground out.

Thunk. Thunk. Thunk.

A tear rolled down one stubbled cheek. "I can hear her crying, Ami."

Thunk. Thunk. Thunk. Thunk.

"She's calling to us."

Thunk. Thunk. Thunk. Thunk. Thunk.

"I can hear her calling us." He paused a moment, breath coming in gasps, and gripped his wrist. Blood coursed steadily down his arm.

"Marcus, please," Ami whispered. Raising the hand manacled to his, she gripped his T-shirt and pulled him down until he rested wearily on his knees beside her.

"I can hear her crying," he choked out, his eyes glowing bright amber.

"I know." Reaching up with her other hand, she curled her fingers around his neck and drew him close. "I know."

Marcus lowered his forehead to her shoulder, then turned his face into her neck and sagged against her.

Leah felt her own eyes burn with tears. She couldn't hear the toddler, so Marcus's preternaturally sharp senses must be carrying his daughter's voice to his ears. How horrible must it be to hear his baby crying and know he couldn't reach her?

Roland stood on Leah's other side. "Okay. Let's try again."

Sarah rose beside him. Together, they gripped the chain attached to the manacle that bound them and began to yank.

Thunk. Thunk. Thunk. Thunk.

Leah turned back to Ami and met her gaze over Marcus's bent

head. "What about Seth?" Did he know they were gone? That they had been taken? Where they were?

A tear slipped down Ami's cheek. "I can't reach him telepathically. None of us can. Gershom is doing something to block us. We think that while we were unconscious, he injected us all with a drug to keep us weak and tired and mess with our gifts."

Leah looked at Roland. "I don't understand. You healed my head wound."

He sighed. "I was only able to heal *some* of the damage, just enough to enable you to wake from the coma. I'm sorry. Seth will have to heal the rest."

Then Seth was still alive. Relief left her light-headed. Or maybe it was the head wound. She didn't know. But Seth must be frantic, trying to find them.

"He'll come for us," Ami said as she stroked her husband's hair. Leah could detect no doubt in her voice. "Seth will come for us."

Leah nodded. He would. One way or another, Seth would find out where they were and would come for them. But she felt as much anxiety over that as she did over their incarceration. Seth had told her more than once that he would give his life to protect his surrogate family.

Glancing around, she struggled to keep fear at bay.

Leah didn't want him to deliver on that promise.

⋙◈◈◈⋘

The network's infirmary bustled with activity. The wounded mortals Gershom had left behind at David's now occupied every bed. Medical personnel hurried back and forth in a kind of ordered chaos as they made the patients comfortable, ran scans, and rendered aid.

Seth lifted his hand from Darnell's forehead and moved on to the next bed. Lowering his palm to Susan's forehead, he began to painstakingly heal the damage Gershom's powerful command had wrought.

Zach healed Tracy. Jared healed Sheldon. The other immortal healers Chris had summoned at Seth's command healed Cam, Alexei, and the rest of the Seconds.

Seth had insisted David rest. He had been unable to reverse all of the brain damage David had suffered, but David was old enough that the virus coupled with the blood infusions he had received should heal him completely.

Seth glanced at Zach.

His expression tormented, Zach seemed to barely be holding it together.

Seth knew he would see the same anguish in his own countenance if he looked in a mirror.

Yuri and Cat appeared across the room. The couple stood, holding hands as they craned their necks, trying to find —

Dr. Linda Machen walked through them on her way to check on Tanner, one of the fallen Seconds. She and Alleck, a German immortal, had been consulting doctors in Cuba in their attempts to help Cliff and the other vampires but had returned as soon as they heard what had happened.

Cat and Yuri both grimaced as their forms dissipated like smoke then re-formed.

When Cat caught sight of Seth, she pointed. The couple started forward, seeming to walk at a regular pace, but crossing the distance in half the time they should in that odd way spirits could.

Yuri spoke. "Meet us in Chris's boardroom as quickly as you can. Bring David, Zach, and Jared."

Before Seth could question them, they vanished. Hope rose. They wouldn't insist on talking in the soundproof boardroom unless they had discovered something they didn't want Gershom to overhear if the bastard lurked nearby.

As soon as he finished healing Sheldon, Seth looked over at David, where he rested. "David, come with me to Chris's boardroom. Zach, you and Jared come, too." He raced upstairs with the others on his heels. The guards already knew they were on the premises and moving with preternatural speeds as they aided the medical workers, so it didn't alarm them too much.

Chris jumped when Seth, David, Zach, and Jared burst into his office. A foul epithet springing from his lips, he reached for the weapon in his shoulder holster.

Seth raised his hands. "It's us. I apologize for startling you." Since Chris couldn't see the ghosts, he had no idea Yuri and Cat had called a meeting.

Seth caught a whisper of movement behind him.

Chris leaned to one side, his shoulders relaxing. "It's okay, Kate."

Seth turned around and looked past David. His eyebrows flew up.

Kate stood in the doorway, aiming an automatic rifle at them. The tension in her features eased as she nodded and backed out of sight.

Seth's admiration for her went up several notches. Kate really knew how to take care of business.

"What's up?" Chris asked.

"In the boardroom." Seth crossed to the door, opened it, and strode inside.

Yuri and Cat were already there, waiting for them. David entered behind him, then Zach and Jared.

Chris grabbed his laptop and jogged inside. "Is this everyone?"

"For now, yes."

He closed the door. "What's up?" Chris set his laptop on the long, sleek table.

Though no one outside this room could hear what took place within, Chris had a microphone in his office and speakers in here that allowed them to listen to what took place in the rest of the building.

"Can you give us silence?" Seth asked. He wanted no distractions.

Chris crossed to the light switches beside the door and flicked one. Quiet enveloped them. As soon as Chris returned to stand beside him, Seth clasped his shoulder and motioned to Yuri and Cat.

Chris's eyes widened. "Yuri?"

Seth sent the couple an expectant look. "He and Catherine have something to tell us."

Yuri nodded. "We know where they are."

"Who?" Chris asked.

"Everyone Gershom took." Yuri stared at Seth. "When we left you, we ended up in David's home. The humans and *gifted ones* inside were all unconscious. The immortals were missing. Leah, Ami, and the children were, too. David was down outside. And all was quiet. Then Gershom suddenly appeared next to David. He stood there for a moment, as though listening or seeking a scent. Seconds later, he raced down the driveway. We followed him to see where the hell he was going and saw him catch up to Ethan. Even though he was badly injured, Ethan put up a good fight. But Gershom defeated him. When he teleported away with Ethan and the children, we followed him and…" He glanced at Cat.

Both spoke together. "We know where they are."

Emotion inundated Seth. "Do they all still live?" he asked, voice hoarse.

"Yes."

Seth's legs damn near buckled he was so relieved. "Where?"

"Are they all right?" Zach blurted.

Cat nodded. "They've been drugged but are starting to regain consciousness."

David moved to stand beside Seth. "And the children?"

Cat bit her lip. "They're unharmed, but they're terrified."

"And angry," Yuri added. "They're afraid of the bad men, but at the same time want their mommies and daddies and are pissed that they can't see them."

"Where are they?" Seth asked, his stomach burning.

Yuri looked at Chris. "Can you show me a map of Texas?"

Zach frowned. "They're in Texas?"

Chris opened his laptop, typed some keys, and a map appeared on the screen.

Yuri moved toward the table and studied the map. "It took us a while to figure out where we were after we followed him. It's hard to get our bearings when we follow someone who teleports because you don't exactly see scenery rushing past you as you go," he muttered. "And neither one of us was familiar with the area. But it's right about there. Can you zoom in?"

Chris tapped some keys and peered at the image. "I'm not seeing any structures or buildings. Just trees."

"It's there," Yuri said with certainty. "And it's military."

"You're sure?" Seth pressed.

"Yes."

"Shit," Chris spat. "What the hell is it with Texas and secret military bases?"

Jared spoke. "It's a big damned state. You can hide a lot in it."

Seth drew out his phone and dialed a number.

"Yes?"

"General Lane," he said without preamble, "we require your immediate assistance. Are you at home?"

"Yes."

"Are you alone?"

"Yes."

"I'm on my way." Seth glanced at Chris. "Turn off the alarm."

Chris spoke into the walkie at his shoulder.

Seth teleported to the interior of General Lane's house. "I'm downstairs, General," he called.

Rustling sounded on the second floor. Heather's father hurried down the steps, garbed in hastily donned military fatigues. His short hair was a little disheveled. Silver beard stubble coated his cheeks and chin. "What is it?"

"Gershom has taken Heather and a number of other immortals as well as my daughter and granddaughter." He didn't mention Leah, fearing that would lead to questions he didn't have time to answer. "My source tells me they're being held in a military facility in Texas, but it doesn't show up on Reordon's maps."

Alarm and anger entered the general's features. "He took Heather? Ethan, too?"

"Yes. Will you help us?"

"Absolutely." He ducked into his home office, then returned carrying a briefcase. "Let's go."

Seth gripped his shoulder and teleported back to Chris's boardroom.

General Lane glanced around. His eyes widened when they lit upon David. "Are you okay?"

Drying blood coated one side of David's face as well as his head where he was missing dreadlocks. His clothing bore numerous tears and was stained with more blood, both his own and Gershom's.

David nodded.

Though Seth had been shot in the head, too, his exit wounds were on the back of his head and must be fairly well concealed by his hair, because they drew no comment. Seth caught Zach's eye.

"Start bringing in reinforcements." He looked at Jared. "You, too. All elders with gifts that will aid us."

Both men teleported away.

General Lane moved to stand beside Chris and leaned down to examine the map on the laptop's screen.

Chris pointed. "The base where they're being held is somewhere in this area, but nothing shows up on the map."

The general swore. "It's there. Whatever you do, don't have your connections look into it. They'll raise too many red flags."

"You're familiar with it?" Seth asked.

General Lane nodded. "It's military. And it's as classified as the base the vampires attacked the night Heather met Ethan. When we lost that base, this one was repurposed to take its place."

Seth's concern deepened. "They do bioweapons research there?"

"Yes. That's why it's not on the map. If no one knows about it, no one can infiltrate it and walk out with shit we *really* don't want them to get their hands on."

Chris snorted. "And civilians won't complain about a bioweapons lab being too close for comfort?"

"That, too," the general admitted.

Zach and Jared popped in and out, escorting Immortal Guardian elders from around the globe. Every warrior wore hunting garb.

Seth glanced around and spotted Catherine. "Where's Yuri?"

"He went back to the base to keep an eye on Gershom. I stayed behind to answer any question you might have."

"Is the base heavily guarded?"

"Yes."

General Lane—unable to see her—answered, "Yes," believing the question had been directed at him.

Chris straightened. "Are all personnel military?"

The general shook his head. "The guards are mercenary. After what happened at the other base, they decided to contract out security this time."

"Why?" Seth pressed.

More and more immortals began to fill the large room and crowded around the table to listen.

"Should shit hit the fan," General Lane said, "civilians are less likely to care about the loss of mercenary lives than they are about the loss of American soldiers. The former often doesn't even make the news."

Seth studied the trees where the base was hidden. "Have you ever been to this facility?"

"Yes."

"Can you sketch the layout for us?"

"I can try." He seemed doubtful though.

Catherine stepped forward. "I can do it."

Seth regarded her with surprise. "You can?" When the general started to answer, Seth held up a hand and kept his gaze on Catherine.

"Yes," she responded confidently. "I can't hold a pencil, but if you place an iPad on the table, I can run my finger across the screen and produce an image. I've been practicing on Marcus's."

Seth looked at Chris. "Get me an iPad. The largest you have." Seth's knowledge of modern technology was limited, so he wasn't even sure if iPads came in multiple sizes.

Chris left the room. A moment later, he returned with paper, a pencil, and a flat electronic object that was about the same size as his laptop. It was silver on one side and black on the other. He set it on the table, dark-side up, then handed the general paper and pencil.

General Lane bent and began to sketch.

Chris looked up at Seth as he turned on the iPad. "What do you want me to look up?"

Seth clasped his shoulder so Chris could see Catherine as she stepped up beside him.

Catherine motioned to the device. "Open a drawing app for me, please."

Chris did so, then pushed the device closer to her.

Catherine bent over it. Her brow furrowing with concentration, she touched a fingertip to the screen and began to move it. A black mark appeared that soon extended and turned into the outline of a building.

Gasps sounded.

"What the hell?" one immortal murmured.

"A spirit is doing it," another whispered. "A woman."

All crowded closer to watch.

General Lane didn't even look up, concentrating hard on his own drawing, knowing his daughter's life might depend upon his getting it right.

The size of the device and the effort it took Catherine to draw in such a way limited the amount of detail she could provide, but Seth thought she did an admirable job.

"There's only one entrance?" he asked, leaning closer.

"Yes. Here."

General Lane looked over and gaped. He slid his drawing over, placing it beside Catherine's. The two were almost identical, only Catherine had done a better job of marking the interior rooms and hallways. "How did you do that?" he asked Seth.

"I didn't. Two spirits are helping us. Catherine, where are the immortals being held?"

She drew an X on a room in the center of the building. "Here."

"All of them?"

"We believe so."

"The children, too?"

"No. The children are being held here." She drew two small x's on a room right next to the one that contained the immortals.

"There are children being held prisoner, too?" Mattheus asked.

"Yes," Seth answered. "Two toddlers. A girl and a boy. Both are *gifted ones* adopted by immortal couples." Only the immortals stationed in North Carolina knew the truth about Adira, the only child ever to be fathered by an Immortal Guardian. The North Carolina contingent was also the only group to know the truth of Ami's origins—that she had come to them from another planet. "Where are Ami and Leah?"

"They're being held with the immortals," Cat said.

Seth noticed no one asked who Leah was. Word of his relationship with her had traveled fast. He pointed to the two rooms and told those present who couldn't see Catherine, "Ami, Leah, and the immortals are being held here. The children are being held here."

The general studied the map. "The larger room with the immortals was used for prisoner detention before the place was repurposed. Guards will be stationed here, here, here, and here. Here, too. There will be checkpoints here and here. Two more over here. This area will be more heavily guarded. You won't be able to access it without security codes and key cards. But you'll want to avoid that anyway because that's where the bioweapons research takes place."

"All right." Seth straightened.

General Lane did, too, and held up a hand. "There's something else. Because of what happened at the other bases—both the first in which bioweapons research took place and the second that housed prisoners who posed high threats to national security— extra measures have been taken at this one. They wanted to ensure that if the base was attacked, no one could get their hands on the viruses and other bioweapons contained there *or* free the prisoners held there before they could be transferred to their new prison."

Seth frowned. "What kind of measures?"

"The best way I can describe it is fail-safes or booby traps. The place is riddled with them. If it looks like there's been a breach of the base, an alarm will sound and the traps will automatically be activated."

"Do you know what and where these traps are?"

"No."

Chris frowned. "If we kill the alarm, will it deactivate the traps?"

"I believe so, yes."

Nodding, Seth stepped back and addressed the room as a whole. "All right. We don't have time to strategize. I want to strike now before Gershom leaves or has time to kill those he has taken. Chris, can you cut communications to and from the base so personnel can't call for help?"

"Yeah. I'll block landlines, cell phones, sat phones, and fuck up their internet connection. I'll also have my people redirect any satellites aimed at that location." Chris drew out a cell phone and started placing calls.

General Lane's lips tightened, but he voiced no objection.

"Zach, Jared, and I will teleport you all directly into the building here," Seth continued. "While we—along with David—search for Gershom, I want the rest of you to focus on taking out the guards and ensuring *no one* leaves. Telepaths, if you encounter any worth saving, knock them unconscious. We'll sort them out later. Everyone else dies. Understood? Leave no man alive to carry tales."

"Understood," they chorused.

"If I should fall—"

Instant protests erupted.

Seth held up a hand. "If I should fall in battle, help David, Zach, and Jared take out Gershom and rescue those he's taken. You have five minutes to visit the armory on sublevel one to load up on extra weapons."

A wave of black surged toward the door. As soon as they flung it open, noise filtered in.

Amidst the rumble of their retreat, the hubbub created by the network beefing up security, and the medical personnel working hard to aid the injured Seconds, distant roars of rage arose, accompanied by loud crashes.

Cliff.

Seth looked at Zach. "Give me a minute." He teleported to the living room of Emma's home in the country.

Reclining on the sofa in a T-shirt and yoga pants, she shrieked and leapt to her feet at his abrupt appearance.

Seth held up his hands. "Forgive me for startling you. You're needed at the network."

Fear filled her features as she hurried toward him, not even pausing to don shoes.

Clasping her shoulder, he teleported her to Cliff's apartment at network headquarters.

The place looked like a tornado had struck it. Overturned furniture—some splintered into small pieces—cluttered the place and formed drifts and dunes. Shards of glass littered the floor and glittered like diamonds amongst the remains of a coffee table.

Seth spun toward the door and found the source of the thumps and crashes.

Cliff bellowed with rage as he hammered away at the wall with one of the metal coffee table legs. Sweat gleamed on his brown arms, left bare by his T-shirt. White powder clung to the perspiration and speckled his dreadlocks. He had knocked out a large chunk of drywall beside the door and was doing a damned good job of breaking up the heavy concrete it covered. But he would never make it through the titanium reinforcement beneath.

"Let me out!" he roared over and over again. "Let me out!" The other words he shouted were so distorted by rage that Seth couldn't decipher them. A quick examination of the vampire's chaotic thoughts, however, confirmed that Cliff knew Bastien and Melanie had been taken and wanted desperately to help save them.

"Cliff?" Emma said softly. Her heart pounded loudly in the silence that fell.

Cliff spun around so quickly he nearly fell over. His brilliant amber eyes sparked with madness as he regarded them. For one gut-wrenching moment, Seth could discern no recognition in his features. Then Cliff's gaze focused on Emma and his hold on the table leg loosened.

His breath coming in jagged gasps, he stared at them while he fought to subdue the voices in his head that urged him to attack.

Confident that Cliff wouldn't hurt the woman he loved, Seth looked down at Emma. "Calm him. We need his help." An instant later, he grabbed Cliff and teleported all three of them to the boardroom.

The door was closed once more. Chris spoke rapidly into his cell phone. When he saw them, he paused, darted Cliff a concerned look, then addressed Seth. "I have Scott Henderson on the line." Scott headed the Midwest division of the network and presided over the headquarters located in Texas. "He'll have special-ops teams en route in two minutes. My own team is assembling in the hangar."

"Excellent."

General Lane eyed Cliff warily, then added, "My team is on standby if you need them." General Lane's team consisted of half a dozen soldiers who were so loyal they would follow him into hell and back without voicing a single complaint. About a year and a half ago, all six men had extended that loyalty to include Seth after he had healed one soldier's little girl, who had been dying of cancer.

"Thank you." Seth moved to stand nearly nose-to-nose with Cliff, catching and holding his burning gaze. "Bastien, Melanie, and the others are being held in a military facility defended by mercenaries. We're about to descend upon it en force. General Lane believes the alarm will trigger fail-safes or booby traps installed in the base to prevent anyone who succeeds in infiltrating it from leaving alive. I need you to help us pinpoint those fail-safes before we trigger them so we won't lose anyone."

Cliff loved to play the same complex military and action-adventure video games that Darnell and Ami did. And Seth had heard Darnell and Ami both complain about the booby traps they encountered in such. Since he had no idea what to look for himself, Seth figured Cliff might be able to spot something he wouldn't.

Cliff nodded. "I won't let you down."

Emma's face creased with alarm. Drawing Cliff aside, she began to whisper to him urgently.

Seth turned to Zach and David. "Come with me." Clasping David's shoulder, he teleported away.

Chapter Twenty-Five

T HE ROOM THEY APPEARED IN was one Seth had never thought to visit again. It was beautifully crafted from wood and stone. Semicircular in design, it boasted high ceilings, three fireplaces large enough for Seth to stand up in, and a number of sofas, chairs, and coffee tables.

Almost a dozen men — all Seth's height of six foot eight or taller and bearing black hair and dark wings — stood in the center of the room, shouting at each other, their eyes glowing golden.

When Seth, David, and Zach appeared, the group spun to face them. Shock rippled across their faces. Silence fell.

Zach turned to Seth. "Really? You wanted to come *here?*"

Seth released David and strode toward the men Zach sometimes referred to as their cousins. Though they weren't technically kin, all boasted similar origins, so Seth supposed they *were* family of a sort. These men were all as ancient as he. But none boasted his immense power. Seth had spent thousands of years building and increasing his power to keep these very men from killing him or his Immortal Guardians because none of them — none of these *Others*, as he referred to them for lack of a better word — had ever questioned the path they had chosen. That path being to refrain from any and all contact with humanity so they would not influence mankind's destiny in any way. Such influence had wrought cataclysmic results in the past.

Long ago, Seth had shared their beliefs, as had Zach and Jared. Then Seth had fallen in love with a human woman and abandoned that path. He had risked *everything* to be with his wife. Now he would risk everything to be with Leah.

Zach spoke in Seth's head. *Why the hell are we here?*

They have something we need.

More headaches? Zach retorted with a scowl.

Seth shook his head. *More power.*

Realization lit Zach's features, almost bringing a smile to his lips.

Teman strode toward them, his brows drawn down in a deep scowl. "Do you see what you've done?" he snarled furiously. "Do you see what you've wrought?"

Seth darted forward and grabbed the Other by the throat.

Teman had not expected a direct attack and was so taken aback that Seth managed to restrain him with little effort and instantly began to drain his energy. Power surged into him via his hold, so much that it burned Seth's insides like a brand. But difficult tasks lay ahead, and he couldn't afford to let those tasks drain his own energy before his confrontation with Gershom.

He would *not* fuck up again.

Protests erupted from the other men.

When Simon leapt forward, Zach grabbed him and followed Seth's example with a bit more difficulty since he couldn't drain power as quickly as Seth could.

"It's time to choose a side, gentlemen," Seth informed the rest. "Live or die? Support me and you may live. Try to stop me — something that will only empower Gershom — and Jared's vision will come to fruition."

Gideon's frown deepened. "What vision?"

"Before he defected and joined my Immortal Guardians, Jared foresaw Gershom succeeding. He saw Armageddon unfold and everyone — every human, *gifted one*, vampire, immortal, and Other — died."

Teman sagged in Seth's arms.

Gideon's expression darkened as he moved toward them.

David stepped into his path with more speed than any of them anticipated and grabbed Gideon by the throat.

Gideon raised his hands in surrender. "Easy. Teman is depleted. I only wish to offer Seth my own energy if he requires more."

David sent Seth a questioning look.

Seth nodded. "You take it, David."

David's hand began to glow. Then his forearm did, too, as he borrowed Gideon's power.

Jaden cautiously moved forward and retrieved Teman's limp form. After settling the unconscious Other on a nearby sofa, he turned back to Seth. "Do you wish my skills in battle or my power? I've no wish to see Gershom succeed."

"Your power," Seth said. There was too much at stake to toss someone he wasn't certain he could trust into the mix.

When Jaden extended a hand, Seth gripped the man's forearm and swiftly drained his power.

David released Gideon and stumbled back a step. Gideon reached out and steadied him as David leaned forward and braced his hands on his knees, then closed his eyes. His dark-as-midnight skin seemed brighter, as though someone had infused him with light. Seth could actually see the veins in his arms glowing.

David? he asked.

So much power, he responded on their private mental pathway.

Too much?

Almost.

Seth understood. His own skin acquired a golden glow as the power he took from Jaden seared him like flames dancing just beneath his skin.

When Jaden reached out to grip Seth's shoulder in a struggle to remain upright, Seth stopped.

Asher approached and looped Jaden's arm over his shoulder to prop him up.

Zach released Simon, letting him drop to the floor.

Seth eyed the Others. "Be ready. This ends tonight. I *will* defeat Gershom."

Gripping David's shoulder, he teleported back to Chris's boardroom.

Immortals—all geared up for battle—once more crowded the space. But they gave the far corner, in which Emma spoke with Cliff, a wide berth.

Chris and General Lane both jumped at Seth, David, and Zach's abrupt return, then stared at Seth.

The general swallowed. "Are you... glowing?"

Seth glanced down at his hands. "Yes, I am." He turned to Chris. "Are we ready?"

"Yeah."

Seth looked over at Catherine. "Any word from Yuri?"

She shook her head.

Cliff started to move toward him.

Emma caught his arm, then drew him close for a last desperate kiss. Tears glistened in her eyes as she stared up at him. "I love you."

Seth didn't have to read her thoughts to know she thought she would never see Cliff again, that tonight would be his last.

"I love you, too," Cliff said, cupping her face. "Thank you. For everything."

She bit her lip to hold back a sob when he moved to stand with the Immortal Guardians.

"Everyone grab a shoulder," Seth instructed. "We strike fast and we strike hard."

A unanimous battle cry filled the room.

Seth teleported everyone but Zach and Jared to the airplane hangar behind network headquarters. Dozens of human soldiers sporting black fatigues, helmets, automatic weapons, and bulletproof vests faced him. Tanks and Sisu XA-180 military transport vehicles loomed behind them.

Seth raised his hands, silently demanding everyone's attention. "Here we go."

Using the energy that still blazed inside him, Seth teleported everyone in sight, along with the military vehicles, to the classified military base in Texas. It was an incredible exhibition of power, sapping half of what he had siphoned from the Others. Even Zach could not have teleported so many or so much without touching it.

A split second after they appeared outside the base, Seth teleported David, the other immortals, and Cliff inside.

Gunfire erupted outside the building as Chris's special-ops team started taking out the mercenary guards and securing the perimeter.

Seth and the immortals now stood in a wide hallway that ended in a security checkpoint.

Six guards manning the checkpoint gaped at them.

Immortal Guardians surged forward to take out the guards before they could sound an alarm.

Yuri appeared in front of Seth. "Gershom is still here."

"Where?"

"The other side of the building. Follow me."

Seth raced after him, bursting through the first checkpoint. More guards waited at a second.

Immortals surged forward around Seth to take them out and clear his path.

Yuri vanished and reappeared at the end of the hallway, pointing the way. Each time he saw Seth follow, he vanished and reappeared at the next checkpoint or hallway intersection to mark the path.

An alarm blared as they approached the third security checkpoint.

As immortals surged forward, multiple blades suddenly shot out of the walls and impaled them.

Seth threw out his hands to halt the others.

Mattheus clenched his teeth and yanked one of the blades out of his chest. It looked like a dagger without a hilt, the sleek, arrow-shaped metal perhaps five inches long.

Zach cursed. "The fail-safes have been triggered."

"So we bypass them," Jared said and teleported to the other end of the hallway.

If Seth teleported all of them through the base until he reached Gershom, he would expend too much energy. And each time they cleared a hallway, Seth needed two immortals to remain behind and ensure those hallways *remained* clear while the others checked the rooms.

Cliff shouldered his way through the immortals and stood at Seth's side. He studied the floor, then the walls of the hallway. "I don't see anything in the floor that looks pressure sensitive, so there must be motion-activated sensors in the walls that trip them."

He darted forward at preternatural speed, then stopped with a grunt when two blades struck him. Cursing, he yanked them out. "These weren't designed to stop humans. They were designed to stop *us*, or at least to slow us down."

"How do you know?"

"Watch." Turning, Cliff slowly walked up the hallway.

No more blades struck him.

"Shit," Zach murmured beside Seth. "They *are* for us."

"Gershom must have had them modified." Seth spoke to the others telepathically so Gershom wouldn't hear him. *We're going to teleport ahead. Follow as quickly as you can at mortal speeds, but leave every hallway guarded and search every room. We're going after Gershom.*

They nodded.

Seth gripped David's shoulder and teleported to Cliff and Yuri's side. He caught and held Cliff's gaze. *Guide them.*

Cliff nodded. *I'll get them through safely. You won't lose a single immortal tonight.*

Seth didn't want to see the valiant young vampire come to harm, but a quick scan of his thoughts confirmed that Cliff was dangerously close to yielding to the madness that permeated him and wanted this to be the way he went out — the death of a hero, a saver of lives.

Yuri pointed. "Quickly, Seth. He's on the move." He disappeared.

Seth teleported after him, taking David with him. Zach kept pace while Jared remained behind to keep an eye on the immortals as Cliff guided them through the next set of booby traps. When mercenaries appeared and fired their weapons, Seth ignored them and left them to the immortals. Though every impulse urged him to find Leah, Ami, and the children first, he resolutely forged onward, intent on taking Gershom out once and for all.

Thanks to Yuri, they traversed the base in less than a minute. In a moment that felt almost surreal, Seth suddenly found himself standing face-to-face with Gershom... who was shielded by a shitload of human mercenaries.

"Coward," Seth bit out.

Garbed in black leather pants, his wings spread, Gershom crossed his arms over his bare chest and smiled.

The mercenaries opened fire.

Tired of playing by the rules, Seth reached toward the soldiers, curled his hand into a fist, and yanked. Every weapon flew over his head to land with a clatter behind him.

Undeterred, their minds controlled by the powerful being they protected, the humans drew tactical knives and raced forward.

David swept past Seth, knocking them all down in swift succession like a bowling ball toppling pins.

"I see you brought the little one," Gershom commented with apparent unconcern. But fury brightened the eyes he turned on David, who had inflicted so much damage while fighting him that Gershom's arms and torso bore thick ugly scars from it. "Three against one?" he taunted. "Which of us is the true coward here?"

Seth shook his head. "They aren't here to help me kill you." He began to subtly leech Gershom's power as he had when he'd sparred with Zach. "They're here to hold me back."

A flash of uncertainty entered the Other's eyes before he snarled and teleported away. But his energy never left the room.

Swearing, Seth spun.

Gershom appeared behind David just as David dropped the last soldier. Grabbing a fistful of dreadlocks, Gershom yanked David's head back and drew a dagger across his throat, cutting so deeply he nearly severed David's head. "Just evening the odds," he said with a malicious smile.

But David was so full of the energy he had borrowed from Gideon that the wound sealed itself almost as quickly as Gershom inflicted it.

David vanished.

Gershom's eyes widened.

Reappearing right behind him, David grabbed Gershom's wings and twisted, then twisted them again. Bones snapped and feathers flew as Gershom's face contorted with agony.

"Surprise," David snarled. "Not so little now, am I?"

Roaring in pain and rage, Gershom stumbled forward.

Seth drew two swords and swung.

Swords appeared in Gershom's hands just in time to block the blows. Seth steadily siphoned more power from Gershom as he hammered him with strike after strike, keeping him on the defensive.

When Zach started to enter the fray, Seth shook his head. "I've got this."

Boots echoed up the hallway as guards approached. Gunfire

erupted. Bullets buzzed past like bees.

Zach left Seth's peripheral vision. Seconds later, men screamed and the gunshots ceased.

David lingered nearby, never taking his bright amber eyes off Gershom.

Gershom huffed out pained breaths as he fought, his damaged wings dragging on the floor behind him. "You're too late," he growled between bloody lips. "It took you too long to find me. I already fucked your woman."

Seth's heart stopped.

"*And* your daughter," he added with a dark, triumphant smile. "I made those bitches scream."

Despair and fury nearly blinded Seth. Was it true? Had he—?

"He's lying, Seth!" Yuri called over the noise of battle.

David spoke calmly in Seth's head despite the fury Seth read in his features. *Listen to Yuri*, he counseled. *Don't let Gershom get in your head.*

Can you reach them telepathically? Seth asked. He couldn't do it himself while he was focusing so hard on draining Gershom.

No. He must have drugged them.

Or killed them. What if he had done what he'd said? What if he'd—?

"I've never understood your fascination with human women," Gershom sneered, "your attraction to them. But I admit their struggles and cries of agony fired my lust."

The ground beneath Seth's feet began to shake as his control began to slip.

Seth, David cautioned.

The abundance of power fueling him made it more difficult for Seth to keep his fury in check. He clenched his teeth, struggling to block out Gershom's words as he continued to hammer away at him.

An explosion rocked the building. A fail-safe triggered by Cliff? Or were network soldiers forcing their way inside?

Seth's strength and energy surged as Gershom began to weaken, unaware that Seth was steadily draining him.

Gershom attempted to telepathically hurl a dagger at David in an attempt to distract Seth, but it just tumbled to the floor. He frowned, alarm entering his glowing golden eyes. He again tried to use telekinesis—this time to yank Seth's weapons away—but couldn't.

"What's happening?" He tried to teleport away and failed. *"What's happening?"* he bellowed.

Seth swept one of Gershom's swords from his hands. "You're losing," he announced and relieved Gershom of the other sword. Vanishing, Seth reappeared behind him, grabbed a fistful of Gershom's dark hair, and yanked the Other's head back. "Shall I take a page from your book?" When Seth dropped his sword, Zach tossed him a dagger.

Gershom struggled in his grip but had grown so weak he moved like a mortal. "Even if you kill me, you won't win," he snarled.

Seth slowly drew the blade across Gershom's throat, cutting as deeply as Gershom had when he'd done the same to Ami and David, drawing out the pain as long as he could until the blade broke free of his flesh. Stepping back, he released Gershom's hair and gave his head a shove.

Gershom staggered forward, clamping his hands around his neck. Because his energy was so depleted, his wound did not stop bleeding and seal itself the way David's had. Gershom dropped to his knees, his face full of fear and horror. He tried to speak but couldn't.

Pitching forward, he hit the floor hard, squirmed as though trying to get away, then fell still. His eyes closed. But a heart still beat faintly inside that body.

Zach moved to stand over the bastard, then looked at Seth. "Well done."

Only partly relieved, Seth nodded. "Take him to the Others. Make sure they bury him so deep he'll never see the light of day again."

Nodding, Zach reached down and grabbed one of Gershom's mangled wings. Seconds later, he teleported away.

Seth turned to David. "Let's go find the children." Though Gershom's words still echoed in his head, terrifying him and urging him to find Leah and Ami, he knew both women would want him to free the toddlers first.

Seth raced up the hallway. Half a dozen blades shot from the wall and slammed into his side. Swearing, he jerked to a halt.

Beside him, David did the same, sporting as many blades as Seth.

"Damn it," Seth groused, yanking them out. "I forgot the fail-safes are triggered by preternatural speed."

David removed his own. "I did, too."

The two of them continued forward at mortal speeds through hallways that, according to Catherine's drawing, would lead them to the room in which Adira and Michael were confined.

Each time they approached an intersection, Yuri appeared in front of them and pointed. "This way."

Turning a corner, they came upon Mattheus and three other immortals crouched in a semicircle.

They spun to face Seth, weapons raised, then relaxed.

Cliff lay crumpled on the floor before them. Multiple blades protruded from his limbs. One side of his face was scorched and bloody. His clothing bore numerous burned patches.

Mattheus rose, his face somber as he motioned to the fallen vampire. "Cliff insisted on leading us through every hallway, assuming all the risks himself. An explosion ultimately took him down. Should I give him blood?"

Indecision clawed at Seth. Cliff had intended to die tonight. Seth had read it in his thoughts. Cliff was ready to go. He *wanted* to go... before the madness robbed him of the last vestiges of his humanity. And Seth didn't think he should take that right away from him even though the idea of letting the valiant young vampire die ate him up inside.

"No," he forced himself to say. "Let him go."

All nodded grimly. Though none of them knew Cliff personally, word of his courageous struggle had circled the globe.

"We'll stay with him," Mattheus offered, "until the end."

"Thank you."

"I think we've tripped all the fail-safes, so you should be okay from this point on."

Seth shook his head. "David and I just tripped one ourselves. Remain vigilant. General Lane said the traps are connected to the alarm, so as long as the alarm continues to blare, they're still a danger."

"Understood." Mattheus knelt beside Cliff and gently cupped the back of the young vampire's head. Shifting him, he repositioned Cliff so he lay more comfortably on the floor.

Seth forced himself to walk away and leave Cliff behind, regret clawing at him.

"It's what he wanted," David murmured.

"I know." But it didn't make it any easier. Cliff had helped Bastien find his place in the Immortal Guardians' world. He had befriended Ami. He had protected Adira. And he'd saved so many lives when network headquarters had been blitzed. Seth would always lament his inability to save the honorable young man.

As Seth and David followed Yuri through the maze of hallways, they encountered neither military nor mercenary guards. The Immortal Guardians and Cliff must have taken them all out while he was confronting Gershom.

Network soldiers had infiltrated the base and now escorted men and women in white lab coats out, often with immortal escorts. They must be the scientists who were studying the bioweapons.

Ignoring them, Seth strode to the door beside which Yuri stood. He could hear Adira and Michael crying within. Waving a hand, he disengaged the locks and flung the door open.

He and David both started to enter, then stopped short in the doorway. Their eyes widened.

Adira and Michael sat on an exam table that was surrounded by medical equipment one might expect to find in a hospital operating room. Holding hands, the toddlers leaned against each other and wept, their red noses running, their plump cheeks blotchy and tear-streaked.

Above them, three men were plastered to the high ceiling as though someone had Krazy Glued them to it.

As soon as the men saw Seth and David, they began to squirm and reached out to them.

"Help us!" one screamed.

"Make them stop!" the other screeched as his nose began to bleed. "Make them stop!"

"Holy shit," Seth murmured.

David nodded. "Precisely."

"Is Adira doing that or Michael?"

"I think they both are."

As soon as Seth and David moved toward the exam table, the children released whatever hold they had on the adults.

The three men fell like stones, screaming on the way down, and struck the floor hard. Their cries stopped as they went limp. Seth didn't know if the fall had injured them or whatever had made their noses bleed, but all were unconscious and still breathed.

Ignoring them, Seth drew Adira into his arms while David drew Michael into his.

"It's okay," Seth whispered, kissing her hair. "Baba and Abaye are here. It's okay."

Adira clung to him, her little hands fisting in his clothing as she continued to wail.

"It's okay, sweetheart."

Michael clung just as desperately to David.

"It's okay." Seth moved closer to David. "Take them somewhere safe. Somewhere Gershom couldn't have stashed vampires for a secondary attack."

David nodded and shifted Michael to one side.

Seth tried to hand Adira over, but she wouldn't let go of him. "It's okay," he murmured again, giving her another hug and patting her back. "You're safe now, sweetheart. But I need you to go to Abaye so I can find Mommy and Daddy."

Breath hiccupping with residual sobs, she reached out to David.

David gathered her against his chest, holding a child in each arm. "I'll take them to the Others."

Surprise shot through Seth. Then he smiled. "That's brilliant." Gershom should be safely tucked away by now, so the children would be safe from him. And vampires sure as hell wouldn't launch an attack there. "Give them to Gideon and Jaden."

David smiled. "Those were my choices as well. I shall return shortly."

Nodding, Seth turned away and left the room as the three vanished.

Yuri stood in the hallway beside the next door. "Gershom lied, Seth. He didn't hurt Leah and Ami. I'm certain of it. All he did was chain them up, then drug Ami and the immortals to weaken them and prevent them from reaching out to you telepathically."

Seth swallowed hard. "Thank you." As he moved to the bolted door, a tingling sensation crawled up the back of his neck. It wasn't unpleasant, just puzzling. Because if he didn't know any better, he would swear Ami and Adira stood right behind him.

Spinning around with a frown, he half expected David to have returned.

He hadn't.

Immortal Guardians Rafe and Eliana exited a room a few doors down, then passed through the doorway across from it, diligently searching for guards or other personnel who might be hiding. Beyond them—at the far end of the hallway—a male network special-ops soldier helped a pregnant woman in a white lab coat limp past. Or was the woman helping the soldier? Seth couldn't tell. The woman curled one arm protectively around her big belly and kept the other looped around the man's waist. The soldier clutched his chest and urged the woman onward with an arm around her shoulders. He was much taller than she was, his shoulders hunched as he kept his sharp gaze on whatever lay before them. The woman's hair concealed her features, but the man looked pained as they left Seth's view.

Another network soldier jogged past, catching up with them.

"What is it?" Yuri asked.

Seth stared. "Nothing. I just... could've sworn I sensed..."

"What?"

He shook his head as the odd feeling faded. "Nothing."

Turning back to the door behind which his immortals waited, Seth waved a hand to disable the locks.

⸻

Marcus resumed yanking on the chain that bound him. Roland and Sarah did the same on Leah's other side. Aidan and Dana, too. They all paused periodically, their breath coming in gasps.

Was blood loss weakening them? Every single one of them bled from their wrists.

"It's the drug," Ami said.

Leah looked over at her. "I thought drugs didn't affect immortals."

"This one does. Mercenaries have used it on us in the past. I assume that's how Gershom got his hands on it. A strong enough dose will knock immortals out. A lesser dose will weaken them and mess with their gifts. It's why none of us can contact Seth." She frowned. "At least, I think it is. We know Gershom can keep Seth from sensing us. We aren't sure if he can also block the telepaths from speaking to him mentally."

An alarm began to blare.

All movement in the room ceased.

The immortals smiled.

Leah's heartbeat picked up. "Seth is here, isn't he?"

Relief softened Lisette's pretty features. "Yes. Zach and David are, too. And they brought a hell of a lot of reinforcements with them."

The ground beneath them began to tremble.

An explosion shook the walls.

Stanislav's lips stretched into a grin. "Seth is kicking Gershom's ass."

Cheers erupted.

"How do you know?" Leah asked as hope rose. "Can you hear them?"

He shook his head. "There's too much noise. Yuri just popped in and told me."

Yuri the ghost.

Their world was full of wonders.

The quaking of the floor increased.

The immortals still on their feet staggered, then sat down. Spouses leaned into each other.

Leah worried her lower lip. Seth must be furious. And terrified, wondering what atrocities Gershom might have committed in the brief time it had taken Seth to locate him and launch an attack. If Seth couldn't sense them, would he fear the worst? Did he fear them dead? Would that distraction cost him? Because Gershom was not the type to fight fair.

The ground stilled. Eerie silence descended, broken only by the *wonk, wonk, wonk* of the damned alarm.

Stanislav looked up as though someone she couldn't see stood in front of him. He smiled, then swept them all with a glance. "It's over," he announced. "Gershom is down."

Cheers erupted once more.

Leah smiled, their triumph infectious. But she wouldn't relax until she saw Seth and was able to wrap her arms around him. Was he okay? Had he been injured? How badly?

A minute ticked past, feeling more like an hour. Then another.

Marcus suddenly released a harsh sigh. "She's safe." He hugged Ami tightly, burying his face in her hair. "She's safe. Seth and David have Adira and Michael. David is going to take them somewhere vampires can't find them if Gershom has a secondary attack planned. They're safe."

Tears trailed from Ami's eyes as she hugged him back.

On Leah's other side, Roland and Sarah breathed sighs of relief and held each other.

A loud metallic *thunk* sounded.

Leah stared at the opposite wall. One side bore an entrance to a short, narrow hallway no more than five feet long that ended in a metal door.

The door swung open. A large form filled the entrance.

"Seth," she breathed. Relief and elation flooded her as she stared at him.

He was okay. Streaked with blood, but okay.

His gaze skimmed those he could see from the entrance. Some relief touched his face when he found Ami in Marcus's arms. But he didn't truly relax until his eyes met Leah's.

His shoulders loosened. A smile full of love and relief stretched his lips and lit his face as he strode forward.

An odd *twang* sounded, accompanied by a *whhhip*.

Leah thought she saw a brief blur of motion in front of Seth beneath his chin, but it was so fast…

He halted. His smile faltered.

Leah saw movement at his shoulders and glanced at it.

His thick hair fluttered down to the floor as though scissors had cut it.

Uncomprehending, she looked back up at him.

His knees buckled as he sank toward the floor.

Leah lunged up on her own knees. "Seth!"

The men and women around her shouted as he collapsed.

Straining against her heavy chains, Leah felt all breath leave her lungs when he hit the floor. Horror filled her as his head rolled away from his body.

She stared down at him, frozen in disbelief. He'd been decapitated.

Unable to grasp it, she looked above him.

A blade as narrow as a piano wire now extended across the hallway, the center of it dripping with blood.

She looked again at Seth. At his head, separated from his neck, resting in a puddle of hair and blood beside his fallen body. A scream tore from her throat. Then another and another as she began yanking against her heavy chains, trying to reach him.

Chapter Twenty-Six

M ORE CRIES ECHOED LEAH'S, MALE and female, as the immortals began to yank on their chains, too. Blood splashed across the floor as they damaged their hands, desperate to reach their fallen leader.

Leah just screamed. And screamed. And screamed. Her heart breaking. Tears pouring down her cheeks.

Not Seth. Please, not Seth.

David appeared in the doorway. When his gaze fell upon Seth, he staggered back a step. Roaring in agony, his features creasing with grief, he vanished and reappeared beside his fallen friend. Falling to his knees, he pressed his face to Seth's back, wrapped his arms around him in a tight embrace, and began to sob.

Leah's cries grew more frantic. The fact that David didn't even *try* to heal Seth told her there was no hope.

No hope.

Zach appeared in the doorway. His face blanched when he saw David weeping over Seth's body. When his eyes fell upon the sliver of a blade that had taken Seth's head, he yanked it from the walls and dropped it. He then raced across the room and dragged Lisette into a rough embrace. He waved one hand, then hugged her close.

The manacles at Leah's wrists sprang open.

Everyone else's opened as well, freeing them all.

As soon as the heavy chains fell away from her, Leah lunged toward Seth.

In a blur of motion, Zach released Lisette and darted forward to intercept her.

"No!" Leah shouted as he looped an arm around her waist and dragged her over to where Lisette sat, weeping. "No! Seth! *Seth!*"

Zach drew both Leah and Lisette into his arms and held them tightly. Burying his face in Lisette's hair, he whispered over and over again, "I love you. I love you, Lisette. Whatever happens, I love you."

Unable to break his hold, Leah sagged against him. All strength left her limbs as she sobbed so hard she could barely draw in breath. Lisette did the same. As did many others.

A deep rumbling sound filled the air, almost drowning out the anguished cries of Seth's brethren.

The floor began to vibrate.

"Whatever happens, I love you," Zach continued to chant. "I love you, Lisette. I love you. Whatever happens, I love you."

Was Zach like Seth? Did the ground shake when emotion overwhelmed him?

The trembling magnified.

Two network soldiers bearing weapons raced past the open doorway as the alarm stopped blaring.

"Everyone out!" Chris Reordon yelled somewhere beyond her sight. "Now! Go! Go! Go! Into the vehicles! Get as far away as you can!"

More bodies raced past, boots clomping on the quaking floor.

Then Leah could only hear the rumbling, which grew louder and louder.

She didn't know what was happening and didn't care.

Seth was gone.

He was gone.

"Zach!" Lisette cried in alarm when the ground shook so hard they nearly fell over.

"I'm not doing this," he replied, clutching them tighter.

"Who is?" she yelled.

Close your eyes.

Leah sucked in a breath when Seth's deep, calm voice filled her head. "Seth?"

Several others called his name as well.

Hold on tight, he said, *and close your eyes. All of you. Don't open them again until I tell you to.*

"Do it!" Zach bellowed to the room.

Leah closed her eyes.

Zach cupped the back of her head and turned her face into his chest just as light burst into being, bright enough to hurt her eyes despite her closed lids and the protection Zach afforded. Wind blasted her, so strong it would've tossed her across the room if Zach hadn't held her so tightly that he threatened to crack her ribs. The rumbling sound grew deafening. Loud crashes reverberated all around her as if a tornado were striking. Then heat accompanied the wind, steadily increasing until it felt as though flames blasted her.

Thunder roared overhead. Or was the building collapsing around them?

Terrified, Leah squeezed her eyelids together and burrowed as close to Zach as she could get.

Zach just kept repeating, "I love you" over and over to Lisette.

Then everything stopped.

The earthquake.

The thunder.

The crashes.

The wind.

The flames.

The light retreated, leaving darkness behind.

Silence covered them like a blanket.

Leah's heart slammed against her rib cage as she struggled to breathe through her sobs and waited, terrified.

A footstep disturbed the quiet. Then another and another, drawing closer.

Clothing rustled nearby.

"Open your eyes."

Leah whimpered at the sound of Seth's voice.

"Open your eyes, sweetheart."

She did and lifted her head enough to peer past Zach.

Seth knelt beside them, a full moon illuminating him. His black clothes looked as neat as though he had just donned them. His handsome face was free of blood and bore a tender smile. His raven hair fell around his face in silken waves that now only reached halfway to his shoulders.

Leah stared at him, afraid to blink, afraid he would disappear if she did. "Seth?"

"Yes."

Releasing Zach, she reached up and cupped Seth's smooth jaw in a hand that shook. His flesh was warm and firm beneath her touch. His eyes bore a golden glow and held such love for her.

"You're alive?"

He covered her hand with one of his and turned his face to press a kiss to her palm. "I'm alive, Leah."

Another sob burst from her lips as she threw herself into his waiting arms and wept.

Seth wrapped his arms around her. So strong. So real. So alive. He stood, drawing her up with him, and held her tight.

Murmurs rose around them. Then someone large and muscular closed his arms around the two of them in an embrace that constricted her breath.

Prying one eye open, she saw dreadlocks.

David wept as he hugged them.

Then another body crowded against them and another and another until everyone formed a tight knot around the man they had all thought they'd lost.

"You died," she whispered.

Seth pressed a kiss to her hair, then rested his cheek atop her head. "I know."

"I thought I'd lost you." She clutched him tighter, if that was even possible. "I love you."

"I love you, too, sweetheart. I'm sorry I scared you."

David shook his head. "She wasn't the only one you scared," he murmured, voice hoarse.

Seth chuckled as bodies continued to press into them. "All right. All right. Give us some air, would you?"

The close bundle of bodies reluctantly floated away one by one until only Leah still hugged Seth.

Standing nearby, his face tear-streaked, Aidan shook his head. "What the bloody hell, Seth?"

"Where are the children?" Marcus blurted.

"Are the children still safe?" Roland asked at the same time, their words overlapping.

"The children are fine," Seth assured them with a smile. "They're safe."

"Hooooly shit!" Ethan exclaimed, his voice conveying utter astonishment.

"What the hell?" someone else whispered.

Leah finally eased away from Seth but couldn't bring herself to let him go. Keeping one arm around his waist, she leaned into his side. When she finally looked around, she gaped.

The building was gone.

Not damaged, but *gone.* No walls. No doors. No ceilings. No roof. And no rubble. All that remained was the small patch of concrete slab beneath their feet, which had been scoured clean.

By wind? By fire? Both?

No bodies lay about. No vehicles were parked within sight.

They were all alone.

Leah looked up at Seth. "What happened?"

He glanced around with a rueful smile. "My father happened."

Reaching up, she fingered a few strands of his much shorter hair. "You died," she said again, tears blurring her vision.

He grimaced. "A careless error on my part. I didn't expect there to be any fail-safe measures inside your cell."

Zach shook his head, his expression both weary and relieved. "You scared the hell out of me."

"Me, too," David added, the beautiful midnight skin of his cheeks glistening with tears.

Leah released Seth so he could draw David into a bone-crushing hug.

"I'm sorry," Seth whispered.

David shook his head, his fists clenching in the back of Seth's shirt. "Don't ever do that to me again."

Stepping back, Seth cupped the back of David's neck in one hand and stared into his glowing amber eyes. Both were silent for a moment. Then David nodded and smiled.

Ami claimed a hug next. Then Zach. And Lisette.

One by one, the others followed while Leah impatiently waited for her chance to hold him again.

"Your father saved you?" Roland asked as he claimed his own hug.

Seth nodded.

Marcus hugged him next. "Who *is* your father?"

Seth visually consulted David while Leah and everyone else held their breath, awaiting his answer.

"My father," he said at last, "is a Watcher."

Sarah's eyes widened as her jaw dropped. "He's a Watcher?" she asked, her expression incredulous. "Seriously?"

Leah glanced around. Most of those present seemed as clueless as she was. "What's a Watcher?"

Sarah answered, her face still full of awe as she stared up at Seth. "It depends on who you ask. According to religious scholars, ancient scriptures describe Watchers as angels who became enamored of human women and married them. But some historians and scientists believe the Watchers were aliens. Either way, the outcome was not good."

Seth nodded. "Human women bore the Watchers children who were described as giants capable of sorcery."

Leah looked him up and down. "No wonder you're so tall."

He smiled. "Not compared to them. They were giants in the true sense of the word. I'm tiny by comparison. The Watchers and their progeny shared knowledge, sorcery, technology, and more with humanity, corrupting mortals to such an extent that the world had to be wiped clean."

"By the Great Flood," Sarah said.

He nodded. "Those who were more powerful than the Watchers buried them so deeply they would never see the light of day again, then slew the giants they'd fathered."

Leah tilted her head to one side, trying to puzzle it out. "But if your father was one of them..." How had he helped them? And how had Seth escaped death?

Seth shook his head. "I'm not one of the first generation of Watchers' sons. Zach and I and the Others came later. Our fathers didn't wish to meet the same fate as their predecessors, nor did they want us to be slain, so they altered our DNA while we were still in the womb to make us blend in a little better."

Melanie took a step forward, her face full of fascination. "They can do that? They can alter DNA?"

Lisette snorted. "Even so, you and Zach would never blend in.

You're too damned handsome."

Seth grinned. "And we were expressly forbidden from interfering in human affairs."

Zach tightened his hold on Lisette. "Aware of what happened when the first generation of Watcher sons tampered with humanity, we all readily agreed."

Bastien frowned. "No wonder you thought such would result in Armageddon. It already had once."

Seth nodded.

Leah touched his arm. "But you married a human woman."

A smile lifted the corners of his lips as he gave a light shrug. "I suppose I'm too much like my father."

Foliage rustled in the forest fifty yards away.

Everyone spun to face it.

Had any of the immortals borne weapons, Leah knew they would've drawn them. But none save Seth and Zach did, and they kept theirs sheathed.

Leah stared at the dark forest.

Cliff stepped out of the trees, then just stood there, looking dazed.

Bastien and Melanie gasped, then raced toward him.

"What happened?" Cliff murmured as they reached him and drew him into a hug. "Did I have another break?" His clothing bore numerous holes and tears and burn marks. Blood marred his face and arms. "I don't remember what happened. Where are we? How did I get here?"

Melanie shook her head. "You helped Seth save us."

"I did?" Neither his face nor his voice betrayed any emotion. His responses seemed almost robotic.

Bastien nodded.

"Are you okay?" Melanie asked, blinking back tears as she rubbed the vampire's arm.

Cliff glanced down and inspected his torso. "Yeah." He looked around. "My ears feel funny."

Bastien exchanged a concerned look with Melanie.

Melanie gently clasped Cliff's chin and turned his head from one side to the other, then ran her hands along his limbs. Her brow furrowed. "I see blood, but I don't see any wounds."

Seth frowned. "His wounds are all healed?"

Melanie nodded. "There isn't a scratch on him."

The sound of a vehicle approaching distracted Leah.

A Humvee sped into view, kicking up dust on the dirt road. Tires locking, it drifted to a halt inches from the concrete slab upon which she, Seth, and the rest stood.

Leah squinted against the headlights.

Chris Reordon stumbled out, eyes wide, hair mussed. Striding forward a few steps, he stopped, turned in a circle, then met Seth's gaze. "Okay. I don't know how the fuck I'm going to cover this up."

Everyone burst into laughter.

Seth was still laughing when Chris surprised him by closing the distance between them and wrapping him in a bear hug.

"Glad to see you made it," Chris said.

Seth clapped him on the back. "Glad to see you did, too."

Chris had already ordered his men to haul ass and clear the building when Seth had told Leah and the others to close their eyes.

"Did the other Immortal Guardians and network soldiers all make it out safely?" Seth asked when they parted.

"Yeah. They're guarding the prisoners we took a couple miles away. I didn't know what to expect after that big-ass explosion, so I told them to keep their distance and watch the flock while I came to see what had happened."

"There was an explosion?" Leah asked. She had felt wind and heat, but...

Chris stared at them. "Well, yeah. I don't know how you could've missed it. Honestly, I expected all of you to be toast when I came back. It was *that* fucking big. And loud. And bright as hell. It stopped just short of creating a mushroom cloud."

Leah stared up at Seth with wide eyes.

He shrugged, not wanting to go into it. Instead, he addressed Chris. "Don't worry about the cleanup. Have Henderson get his crew back to network headquarters here in Texas and have the teleporters get the rest back to your headquarters in North Carolina. Have Mattheus and the other immortals remain there and guard you all. Gershom is out of the picture, but that doesn't mean he didn't have a plan B waiting in the wings somewhere."

Chris nodded. "I'm on it."

Seth caught his arm as Chris turned away. "Would you take Cliff with you and have Dr. Machen examine him once you're home?"

"Sure." Chris gestured to Cliff as he strode toward his vehicle. "Hop in."

Seth was both surprised and relieved to find the young vampire alive. A quick inspection revealed that Cliff's mind was even wonderfully clear of the voices that had constantly plagued him. Perhaps the brilliant light from the explosion had accomplished what Aidan taking Cliff into sunlight still sometimes did and silenced the voices for a time.

Seth would check on him later just to be sure Cliff hadn't suffered any brain trauma in the blast that might require healing. Right now the vampire just seemed a little dazed, the way he often did after experiencing a psychotic break.

As soon as Cliff ducked into the vehicle, Chris started the engine and sped away.

Bastien and Melanie returned to stand with Seth and the others.

Ami stepped forward. "Seth?"

Gideon, he called telepathically. *Jaden. Bring the children to me.*

The two Others abruptly appeared beside Seth.

Leah jumped and released a yelp of surprise.

Seth slid an arm around her. "Sorry. I should've warned you they were coming." Her nerves were understandably frayed.

Gideon held Adira close to his chest. One large hand cupped her bright orange curls while she leaned against him and played with strands of his long black hair.

Jaden held Michael and shifted awkwardly from one foot to the other.

More reserved by nature, Michael just stared somberly at the man who held him.

Jaden frowned at Seth. "Why does he keep staring at me like that? Am I doing something wrong?"

Before Seth could answer, the children's parents swept forward and plucked the toddlers from their powerful babysitters' arms.

Roland and Sarah fussed over Michael.

Ami and Marcus cuddled Adira.

Happy to be back with her mommy, Adira snuggled against Ami's chest and offered Gideon a smile and a wave.

Gideon's face lit with surprise. Then he smiled back and waggled his fingers.

Seth glanced at David.

David arched a brow. *Will wonders never cease?*

Seth laughed.

"You see?" Jaden complained. "She likes Gideon. Why doesn't the boy like me?"

Gideon snorted. "Because you didn't hide your fear from him."

Seth bit back another laugh. "You were afraid of him?" He knew Jaden had never held a child before, but hadn't thought the powerful warrior would actually be afraid to try it.

Jaden narrowed his eyes, unamused. "No. I was afraid the shit was going to hit the fan when your head left your body."

"We all were," Gideon said. "That scared the hell out of us. Fortunately, it didn't."

Leah's eyes widened. "It didn't?"

Lisette gaped, too, and motioned to the small patch of clean slab, all that remained of the military compound. "This wasn't the shit hitting the fan?"

Seth shook his head. "Believe it or not, no." He and the rest of the Others had always presumed that if one of them—a Watcher's son—was ever slain, his father's response would not be nearly as restrained as Seth's father's had been. It was the only reason Seth had stopped just short of killing Gershom. Those of their ilk, they believed, must be dealt with differently.

Gideon caught Seth's eye and scowled. "Don't do it."

"Don't do what?" Seth asked, feigning ignorance.

Gideon slid their audience a glance. "Don't tell them."

Seth shook his head. "Too late. I've already begun. And they deserve to hear it after everything they've been through."

"The Others won't like it," Jaden warned.

Anger rose. "I don't give a flying fuck what the Others do and don't like. If they had helped me capture Gershom as soon as he defected and I told you he was a problem, none of this would've happened."

When Jaden would've spoken again, Gideon held up a hand to cut him off.

"Understood," Gideon said simply. "We shall take our leave now."

Both men vanished without another word.

"Grab a shoulder," Seth ordered everyone else. Tucking Leah tighter against his side, he waited until everyone present had done as asked. Then he teleported them all to the great hall of his castle in England.

Linking his fingers through Leah's, he led them upstairs through a series of hallways until he came to a closed door. A wave of his hand unsealed and opened it so he could stride inside.

Leah moved forward with him and surveyed the room curiously as she stroked his arm with her free hand.

Seth glanced around and tried to see it through her eyes. Large enough to serve as a ballroom, it boasted no furniture. Nor did it possess any windows. Were it not for the overhead lights that brightened at his telekinetic command, they would be standing in a dark void.

No paintings adorned any of the pale gray marble walls. Nor did tapestries or photographs or flat-screen televisions. The only ornamentation the stark room boasted was an elaborate engraving that whorled across the floor and up three walls.

The one that housed the doorway remained untouched.

Ami entered behind Seth and Leah, Adira cradled in her arms.

Everyone else remained in the hallway, their gazes averted.

Until now, everyone—immortal, *gifted one,* and human—had been forbidden entrance. This had been Seth's room and Seth's alone. Though the large oak door bore no locks, anyone who tried to open it in his absence would've found the task impossible. Even preternatural force and power tools would not have granted them entrance if any had been foolish enough to try.

None had. Seth had expected Bastien to when he had imprisoned the immortal black sheep in the castle for a time. But even Bastien had respected his wishes.

Ami had not known this room was forbidden though and had dared to enter it. She had been so innocent and damaged at the time that he had felt neither anger nor resentment over it. So she was already familiar with the room and many of his secrets, as was David.

"It's all right," Seth told the rest. "You may enter."

Those who could see inside from their positions in the hallway sent the room quick, cautious glances, as though they feared too long a peek would turn them to stone. When Seth didn't do whatever it was they thought he might do, they crept into the room and peered around with interest.

The image on the floor — an enormous tree painstakingly carved by Seth's own hand — drew their fascinated attention.

"Every one of you," Seth began, "has asked me why *gifted ones* are born with such advanced DNA and possess such wondrous gifts." He motioned to the carving. "The answer lies before you." He met Zach's gaze and found only approval and relief in his eyes. Zach had wanted to share this with Lisette ever since the French immortal had stolen his heart.

Seth strolled farther into the cavernous room, drawing Leah with him. "Zach and I and the rest of the Others were the very first *gifted ones*. Less than the giants who came before us, but more than human, we are children born of a union between human women and Watchers, who are far more advanced beings." He glanced at the faces around him. "The rest of you... are my descendants."

Silence engulfed them.

After a moment, Roland spoke. "How is that possible? I thought your children were slain alongside your wife."

"They were," Seth acknowledged with a familiar pang of grief. "But my daughter and son-in-law gave me three grandchildren — two girls and a boy — who managed to escape death that day." He motioned to his second-in-command. "David is my grandson."

Eyes widened and jaws dropped as they all stared at David.

David grinned, amused by their shock.

Ethan looked back and forth between Seth and David, then spoke slowly as though fearing he might offend. "I see the resemblance in your features, but..."

Seth laughed. "You're wondering how I could have a grandson as dark as David?"

"Yyyyyyeah," he admitted.

"My wife, Ayana, was Ethiopian and as dark as David."

Leah squeezed his hand and smiled up at him. "No wonder you were so amused when I asked if I looked like her."

Chuckling, he curled an arm around her shoulders and addressed the others. "Our children were similar in coloring to Darnell. My daughter married an Egyptian man who was as dark as David. And David inherited his father's coloring." He shrugged. "Or my wife's. Or both."

Roland studied him. "Are you infected with the virus, Seth?"

"No. My immortality was bestowed upon me at birth."

Roland nodded slowly. "No wonder I've never seen you infuse yourself with blood." He glanced at the image on the floor. "And this is your lineage?"

Seth nodded. He waved a hand, enabling all of them to read the ancient language he'd used. "You'll find each of your names carved therein amongst the others." As well as dates of birth, dates of death for his descendants who had not become immortal, and notations about each individual's gifts.

Leah moved away but kept a tight hold on his hand.

Seth didn't blame her for not wanting to sever the contact. He deeply regretted frightening her so. He had not expected to die today. He also hadn't expected his father to bring him back if he did.

Drawing him over to the base of the tree, Leah stared down at it. "Your granddaughters weren't immortal?" she asked softly.

He swallowed the lump that always rose in his throat when he thought of the granddaughters he had raised. "No. My children and those who came after them were not granted immortality at birth the way I was. And David was the first *gifted one* infected with the virus. We knew little about it at the time." Until then, none of them had ever sickened or caught so much as a cold. "We saw what the virus did to humans and worried it would drive David insane, too—that it would just take longer." Kneeling, he traced his granddaughters' names. "And immortality lost its appeal when both girls—because of the DNA they inherited from me—outlived the human husbands they loved, then their children and grandchildren and great-grandchildren. Their longer mortal lives brought them great grief, so they didn't wish to extend those lives even more." It had been heartbreaking to lose them.

Leah stroked his hair.

When Seth glanced up, she gave the shorter locks a playful tug. "It's going to take me a while to get used to this."

Trust Leah to always find a way to make him smile. He rose. "It will grow back."

"What's wrong?" Ethan murmured, drawing Seth's gaze.

Standing beside her husband, Heather nibbled her lower lip. She glanced around. "Am I the only one who is quietly freaking out a little over the fact that we're all related?"

"I'm not," Sarah said with a smile. "It's *nice* to discover I have family members I actually like."

Roland laughed. "And who won't try to stab us in the back."

"Exactly," she replied. Both seemed quite pleased by the revelation.

Heather wrinkled her nose. "Yeah. But... we're related to our spouses."

David laughed.

Seth did, too. "Everyone on this planet is related — all descendants of the first man and woman who walked the earth. Some just choose not to acknowledge that fact."

Melanie tilted her head to one side. "I'm guessing the Great Flood narrowed the gene pool pretty dramatically, too."

Seth nodded. "Very few survived. So Melanie and Bastien, for example, are about as related to each other as Bastien is to Chris Reordon."

Bastien grimaced. "Please tell me I'm not related to that bastard."

Everyone laughed.

David smiled at Heather. "Heather, you and Ethan aren't first cousins whose shared ancestor is a grandparent. Or second cousins who have a common great-grandparent. You would have to trace your lineage back thousands of years to find your closest shared ancestor." He motioned to the carving that covered the floor and three walls. "And you may do so if it will ease your concern."

Smiling, Heather leaned into Ethan's side. "You've already eased it."

"None of the men present," Seth added in case any doubts

lingered, "are their wives' ancestors. Only Roland fathered children before his transformation. And Sarah is not his descendant."

Sarah grinned and pretended to wipe sweat off her forehead. "Whew! I didn't marry my great-grandpa!"

More laughter erupted. Then everyone began searching the elaborately carved foliage.

"I found my name!" Krysta called with excitement. "Look, Sean. Yours is here, too. *And* Mom's and Dad's."

Leah leaned into Seth as more exclamations arose.

Smiling, he wrapped his arms around her and held her close.

Gershom was gone. Leah and the others were safe.

It was finally over.

Rising onto her toes, Leah cupped his jaw in one delicate hand and pressed a kiss to his lips. "I like your family," she confided with a smile.

Seth captured her lips in a longer, deeper exploration. "I love you, Leah."

"I love you, too." Tears welled in her eyes. "You scared the hell out of me."

"I know," he acknowledged, riddled with remorse. "Will you forgive me?"

"Yes." She hugged him tight. "Just don't ever do it again."

"I won't."

Chapter Twenty-Seven

THE NEXT EVENING, SETH TELEPORTED into a dark cavern that had never been found or explored by mankind. Heat immediately closed around him, almost robbing him of the ability to breathe as it threatened to sear his skin. Guided by his preternatural vision, he strode forward and followed the tunnel, which had once served as a lava tube.

The channel carried him deeper and deeper into the earth.

The Others had chosen well.

It took some time to reach the end of it. Seth didn't mind. He was in no hurry and could use the extra minutes to tame his emotions. He hadn't wanted to leave Leah and was not looking forward to this. But it had to be done. He had to know.

At last the tunnel ended in a small room as round as a bubble. Seth halted. Only about twenty feet in diameter, it looked no different from the tunnel that preceded it save for the figure chained to one wall.

Gershom's head hung low. His hair covered his face in tangles. The Others had succeeded so well in permanently depleting his power that Gershom could barely raise his head. And his eyes remained a brown so dark they were nearly black instead of flashing with golden sparks at Seth's appearance.

Gershom's lips turned up in a sneer. "I won."

Seth held his arms out away from his sides and made a point of looking around, looking at Gershom in chains, then looking down at himself—clean and strong and free to go wherever he willed. "How do you figure that?"

"I decapitated you. I killed you."

Seth casually seated himself on a nearby rock. Stretching his legs out before him, he crossed them at the ankles. "Actually, you didn't."

"Yes, I did... when you rushed into that cell to save your pathetic little family."

Seth shook his head and sent him a pitying look. "No, you didn't. The United States military decapitated me. That base was used to incarcerate enemy combatants before it was repurposed for the study of bioweapons. It was already booby-trapped to prevent terrorists from breaking in and absconding with the people held there before you took control of it. The fail-safe in that holding room was designed and put there by humans, not you. It responded to human speeds, not immortal speeds. You failed to have them update it because you foolishly believed you would defeat me before I got that far. Your hubris screwed you and robbed you of victory." He gave a careless shrug. "*You* didn't decapitate anyone. The military did, aided by my own carelessness." He glanced down at his healthy body. "And as you can see, I survived."

"Because daddy came to save you," Gershom spat, his face full of fury.

Seth raised his eyebrows and again made a point of glancing around. "Jealous because your daddy hasn't come to save you?"

The verbal barb struck hard, sparking a rant filled with epithets and pointless threats.

Seth shook his head. "Why do you hate me so much, Gershom?" he asked when the Other ran out of breath. He still couldn't puzzle it out. It was the only reason he had come here today. Gershom no longer posed a threat. To *anyone.* He never would again because he would never escape. But Seth needed to know. "Some believe it's because you resent that I was *living* life whilst you merely observed it."

"Because their minds are too small to see the bigger picture," Gershom snarled. "*Living* life," he scoffed. "Soiling yourself with humans. With that offal. It's all your fault," he mumbled. "*Your* fault. It's *all* your fault."

And for a moment, Seth revisited the notion that Gershom had been slowly going insane over the millennia. The Other truly did seem mentally unbalanced.

"What bigger picture?" Seth asked. "What is my fault?"

The veins in Gershom's neck stood out as he roared, "It should have been ours!"

Seth stared at him. "*What* should have been ours?"

The question only seemed to infuriate Gershom more. "Everything!" he bellowed. "Every-fucking-thing! This planet should have been ours! *Ours* to rule over! Not *theirs!* Not *humans,* who are so fucking weak and pathetic and childish in their thoughts and actions!"

"Those weak humans succeeded where you could not," Seth pointed out. "Those weak humans decapitated me, not you." Then he shook his head. "The Earth was never meant to be ours, Gershom. It was meant to belong to humans. We came later."

"And we were better!" Gershom proclaimed, a wild glint entering his eyes. "We *are* better! We are so much more than they will ever be."

"Our mothers were human. Have you forgotten that? Human women bore us. We owe humans our very lives."

"We owe them nothing!" Chains rattled as Gershom gestured weakly. "Humans were given dominion over the Earth. Well, look what the fuck they've done with it! This was a beautiful planet! Perfect in every way! And look how they've soiled it! They're unworthy of it. They're like spoiled fucking children scrapping over toys at the playground, always warring and fighting and stabbing each other in the back in a bid to gain more wealth, more land, more power at the expense of others."

Seth refrained from pointing out that Gershom had tried on at least two occasions to spark wars himself and had repeatedly stabbed Seth in the back.

"It all could've been made right," Gershom ground out, "but you fucked it up."

Once more, Seth found himself shaking his head in bafflement. "I didn't cause—"

"Survival of the fittest," Gershom interrupted.

"What?"

"Survival. Of. The fittest," Gershom repeated as though

speaking to a dimwit. "Nature would've corrected itself, but you wouldn't let it."

"I don't know what you're—"

"The virus. I know its origins."

Seth frowned. "You do?" Even he didn't know that. "Did *you* create it?"

"No. But I saw it claim its first victim. Then another. And another. And I knew." He nodded, his gaze unfocused as if he were peering back into the past. "I knew it for the gift it was. I knew our time had come. I knew the virus would spread. I knew that eventually every human on the planet would either be *killed* by vampires or become one of them. And once only vampires remained, they would slay each other in their insanity." He smiled. "Then only *we* would remain. We, the strongest. We, the fittest. *We* would inherit the Earth."

Seth stared at him.

Gershom refocused his gaze on Seth. His face mottled with rage. "But you fucked all that up. Over a piece of ass! You fucking defected and married a human woman who bore you gifted children. Children with advanced DNA the virus couldn't corrupt. And when David was infected with the virus, he didn't go insane. He didn't die. Nor did the other *gifted ones* who became infected. Even so, nature could've still prevailed. The virus still could've wiped out all the humans. But you pitted your blessed Immortal Guardians against the vampire population to keep it in check and *protect* the humans. The fucking humans who are so fucking far beneath us!" he roared, spittle flying from his lips. "It would've been *ours* if you had just done what you were fucking told and stayed away from humans. It would've *all! Been! Ours!*"

Seth sat there, stunned, for many long moments while Gershom's ragged breathing echoed in the chamber.

Damn, Seth, he heard Leah say again. *You saved the world.*

And all of this—all of the battles and war and pain and death he and his family had endured in recent years—was because Gershom hated him for it.

"It should've been ours," Gershom muttered. "It should've been ours. It should've all been ours. It should've been ours."

He was still repeating it when Seth left and headed back up the tunnel.

———◦◉◦———

Adira's giggles filled the air as Leah trotted up the basement hallway. Bouncing on her back, the toddler wrapped her arms so tightly around Leah's throat that her little fists threatened to choke her. But Leah didn't mind. Making growly monster noises, she stomped up the stairs, adding lots of extra bounce and jounce that inspired more squeals of delight.

She burst into the hallway above.

Richart and Étienne grinned and dodged out of her way as she trotted into the living room.

David's home was packed to the rafters. Every Immortal Guardian stationed in North Carolina occupied the sofas, love seats, and wingback chairs, as did their Seconds. Seth had given them the night off and allowed the network special-ops teams to patrol for vampires instead so the immortals and their Seconds could rest and recuperate.

All grinned when Leah entered with a giggling Adira on her back.

Leah galloped through black-clad bodies and sank to her knees next to Michael, where he and his mother and father were playing with some toy cars.

Ami leaned forward to help Adira dismount.

Leah grinned at her. "Whew! That was quite a workout."

Ami laughed. "I'm sure it was. Adira even runs Marcus ragged, and he's immortal."

The front door swung open.

Leah turned to see who had entered and smiled when she saw Seth step inside. Rising, she closed the distance between them. "Hi, babe. How'd it go?" She knew he'd intended to speak with Gershom.

Ducking his head, he pressed a kiss to her lips, then wrapped his arms around her in a tight hug.

Her smile faltered when that hug went on longer than expected. "That bad, huh?"

A long sigh escaped him. "It went about how I thought it would."

Very bad then. "Did he say anything about the missing *gifted one?*" she asked tentatively. Now that the dust had settled, there was still one unaccounted for.

"No. And asking him would've proven futile."

Leah drew her hands up and down his back in a soothing caress. "Don't worry. We'll find her, honey. Forget Gershom," she declared disparagingly. "He's an ass."

Seth huffed a laugh. "An understatement if ever there was one." Loosening his hold, he leaned back and looked down at her. His somber expression lightened as he brushed a few damp tendrils of hair back from her face. Amusement sparkled in his eyes. "What have you been doing? Your face is flushed."

"I've been giving Adira piggyback rides."

He smiled. "Let me guess. Every time you tried to put her down, she asked for one more?"

She laughed. "Yes."

Looping his arms around her again, he clasped his hands at the base of her spine, pressing her close. "I like it when your cheeks are flushed," he murmured. "You're so beautiful, Leah." *This is how you look when we make love,* he whispered in her head.

Her heart leapt as desire flared to life. Leah rubbed her hips against his, delighting in the hard length she felt rise behind his fly. "Flattery will get you everything."

He arched a brow. "Even a *ride* of my own?"

She grinned. "Hell yes." Breaking his hold, she took his hand and began to lead him through the living room toward the hallway. "Good night, everyone," she said with a wave.

"Good night," several chorused, offering them smiles.

"Wait," Sheldon called. "You two aren't heading to bed already, are you?"

"Yes, we are," Seth confirmed.

Leah could feel his gaze on her ass like a caress as she walked in front of him.

"All right, guys," Sheldon told the room, "you heard them. You know the drill."

Frowning, Leah turned to look over her shoulder, then stopped short and stared.

Every man and woman present reached down beneath his or her

seat. Within seconds, all donned rain slickers and rain boots, then grabbed the arms of their chairs as though bracing for an earthquake.

She burst out laughing.

A look of chagrin swept over Seth's face. And she could've sworn color crept into his tanned cheeks. "Oh, come on," he complained. "It's not that bad."

As if on cue, little Adira and Michael both held up child-sized umbrellas.

Boisterous laughter erupted throughout the room.

Even Seth joined in before Leah tugged him down the hallway and into their bedroom.

She closed the door, ensconcing them in quiet.

Seth shook his head, a smile lingering on his tempting lips. "I'm never going to live this down."

Reaching up, she started to tug off his coat. "Well, it's only going to get worse."

"You think so?" he asked, his eyes glued to the cleavage the V-neck of her shirt exposed.

"Oh yeah," she replied with certainty. Hanging his coat on the hook by the door, she grabbed the hem of his T-shirt and drew it up over his head. "If you think their ribbing is bad now, how much worse do you think it'll be when the thunderstorms and earthquakes stop?"

Seth yanked off his boots and kicked them aside.

Leah drew her fingers over his bare chest, then flattened her hand and felt his heart begin to pound beneath that warm, beautifully sculpted muscle. "You said you think it only happens because it's been so long since you made love." She loved the way he sucked in a breath when she trailed her hand down his washboard abs and unfastened the button on his pants. "And you believe it'll stop once we've been pounding it out every night for however many weeks or months."

Though he chuckled, his eyes flashed with golden light as she slipped her palm down over the hard length still restrained by black fabric. "I don't believe I used that exact phrase." He touched a long, slender finger to her shoulder, then drew it down along the neckline of her shirt in a sweet caress.

Arousal swam through her. "What phrase?"

Sliding his finger back up, he stretched the neckline of her shirt over one shoulder, taking her bra strap with it, and bent to kiss the skin he'd exposed. "Pounding it out."

Her pulse picked up as he pulled the material down even farther, freeing a breast he cupped in one big palm. He tweaked her nipple with his fingers and thumb. Sensation shot through her.

She gasped. "What can I say? I like it when you lose control and take me fast and hard, no holds barred." Tilting her chin up, she sighed as he bent his head and captured her lips in a passionate kiss. Leah rose onto her toes and wrapped her arms around him. "No one makes me feel like you do, Seth," she whispered when she came up for air.

One hand still teasing her breast, he slid the other around to stroke her ass and urged her closer. "Good," he murmured, "because you make me burn." Sweeping her into his arms, he strode across the room to drop her none too gently on the bed. His hands went to his zipper. His form blurred with preternatural speed. When he stilled, he was completely naked and very aroused.

Leah licked her lips. "Awesome. Now do *me*."

Again he blurred. She felt several tugs. And, quick as a blink, she was as naked as he.

She sent him a wicked smile. "Now *do* me." She spread her legs. "Any way you want."

His eyes brightened to brilliant gold. Curling the fingers of one hand around her ankle, he yanked her toward him until her ass hit the edge of the bed.

Excitement skittered through her. Her heart pounded as she spread her arms wide and clutched the bedding in her fists to keep from reaching up and grabbing him. Damn, he turned her on. She could almost come just from looking at him.

As if he had all the time in the world, Seth gripped her hips, then slid his hands up her sides, his thumbs meeting on her stomach. She shifted restlessly, moaning when he moved closer, his cock brushing her clit. He cupped her breasts in his hands, kneading and squeezing the heavy flesh, brushing his thumbs across her sensitive nipples and delivering sharp pinches.

"Seth," she breathed.

Withdrawing his touch, he flipped her over onto her stomach so her torso rested on the soft covers and her toes touched the floor. He pushed a knee between her thighs, nudging her legs farther apart. Her breath quickened as his large hands caressed her ass. He slid one up her back, inspiring shivers. The other positioned his cock at her slick entrance.

"You're already wet for me," he said, his voice deeper with desire.

She moaned when he pressed forward, stretching her, filling her with his long hard length. "Yes," she breathed.

"You're so tight," he gritted, pausing to give her a moment to adjust.

"You're so big," she countered. Unable to remain still—he felt too damn good inside her—she rolled her hips.

Seth groaned and began to move.

"Harder," she pleaded, urging him to lose control, to take her as roughly as he wanted to.

He leaned over her, kissing the back of her neck as he moved in deep, hard thrusts that stole her breath and increased the pleasure. He slipped one hand beneath her and cupped her breast. "You feel so good." He slid the other beneath her stomach and down to stroke her clit in time with his thrusts.

Leah lost the ability to think. Could only feel, moan, clutch the covers, and beg for more as the floor beneath her feet began to tremble. The scent of rain surrounded her, letting her know he'd released his wings. Her breath came in gasps as he thrust harder, deeper, those glorious fingers of his rubbing and stroking and driving the pleasure higher and higher, eliciting cries, until an orgasm crashed through her, so intense she screamed.

Seth stiffened, shouting with his own release.

Leah went limp, breathing hard as little residual twinges of pleasure continued to pulse through her for what seemed like forever.

Seth's hands stilled, then withdrew. He braced his elbows on either side of her and lowered himself over her, letting her feel some of his weight.

She smiled. The first few times they'd made love, he had

worried about being too heavy for her. But he had quickly come to realize that Leah loved feeling all of that hard, heavy muscle pressing down on her. She loved being surrounded by his warmth and scent.

And right now she needed it. Tears filled her eyes. She had come so close to losing him. "I love you," she whispered.

His own breath still choppy, Seth pressed another kiss to the back of her neck. "I love you, too." Then he huffed a laugh. "Damn it."

"What?"

He pressed his forehead to her shoulder. "Now every time I make love with you, I'm going to picture all of them sitting out there in their rain slickers, holding on to their chairs for dear life."

Leah laughed. "Me, too. They do love to tease, don't they?" When Seth withdrew from her body, she rolled over and sat up on the bed. "But I bet I know how to make you forget them."

He arched a brow. "Do you now?"

Grinning, she pointed to the center of the bed. "On your back, handsome."

His smile broadened. "Yes, ma'am."

Leah watched Seth settle himself on his back in the center of the mattress as instructed. Leaning forward, she crawled toward him, drinking in the sight of his big, beautiful, bare body.

Renewed arousal brightening his eyes, he grew hard again as he watched her approach.

She slung a leg across him, kneeling above his waist. Reaching between them, she gripped his cock and played with him until a low rumbling growl spilled from his perfect lips. Then she lined him up with her entrance and slowly sank down on his long, hard length.

He gripped her hips with his hands, face darkening with desire.

"Now," she purred, "let's see what I can do to take your mind off everything but me."

When she rotated her hips, he dropped his head back. "Yes."

⁓✦✦✦⁓

Leah sighed as consciousness beckoned. Sprawled on her back, eyes still closed, she smiled. The muscles in her butt and thighs ached from the vigorous sex she and Seth had enjoyed before she had pretty much passed out from exhaustion. He was such a wonderful lover. Dark and intense during one bout of lovemaking, playful and affectionate the next. And he didn't need time to recuperate after an orgasm, so he could go all night. And day. And always seemed capable of coaxing one more orgasm from her even when she thought it impossible.

She started to stretch but stopped short with a wince.

Yeah. She had definitely overdone it. Even her arms and upper back were a little sore. But damn, it had been worth it. After coming so close to losing him, she had needed his touch, his nearness. She had needed to reassure herself again and again that he was alive and well and in her arms. And he must have sensed it, or maybe felt the same himself, because they had spent most of the thirty-six or forty-eight hours since Seth had defeated Gershom in this bedroom.

A large warm hand slid across her stomach, then around and down, squeezing between her bottom and the mattress. Warmth seeped into her glutes and banished the ache. Next the hand caressed a path down one thigh and up the other, erasing the soreness there as well.

Leah opened her eyes and peered up at Seth.

He lay beside her, his weight propped on one elbow as he stared down at her. "I love you," he said softly.

Smiling, she cupped his face in one hand, his beard stubble rasping in the quiet and abrading her skin as she drew her thumb across his cheek. "I love you, too." She shook her head and again found herself blinking back tears. "I don't know what I would've done if I'd lost you."

Turning his head, he pressed a kiss into her palm, then captured her hand in his and carried it to his heart. "I want to marry you, Leah."

Her heart leapt as joy flooded her. But when she opened her mouth to tell him *Yes*, that she wanted to marry him, too, he released her hand and pressed a finger to her lips.

His look turned somber. "But before I ask you properly... and before you answer, I want you to meet someone."

Some of her joy diminished. "Who?"

"Let's shower and get dressed, shall we? They're expecting us."

Leah did as he asked, anxiety creeping in when he didn't even *try* to fondle her in the shower. Usually Seth couldn't keep his hands off her when she was naked. But he maintained a careful distance this time.

Who was he taking her to see?

Not Gershom, she hoped. She never wanted to see that asshole again.

Seth remained quiet, seeming pensive as she blow-dried her hair. Parting his on the side, he dragged a comb through the thick, not-quite-shoulder-length locks, then left them to dry on their own. He looked good. Leah had loved his hair long, the way it would pool around them like a curtain when he made love to her, the feel of it on her bare skin. But he looked just as heart-poundingly gorgeous with it shorter. And she thought he might be enjoying how easy it was to manage now.

Seth donned his usual black boxers, black cargo pants, and T-shirt. While he tugged on his boots, Leah drew on another set of hunting clothes she'd borrowed from the extensive wardrobe David kept on hand for immortals and their Seconds. She enjoyed seeing little sparks of desire enter Seth's dark brown eyes when he saw her dressed like one of his warriors. He definitely admired strong women.

Grabbing her boots, Leah sank down on the sofa. Seth knelt in front of her and brushed her hands aside. He kept his gaze lowered as he lifted her right foot and slid it into the boot.

Unused to quiet between them, unsettled by it as well, Leah reached out and combed her fingers through his soft, damp locks.

His eyes rose. "Do you miss the longer hair?"

"Yes," she admitted, then smiled. "But I like this, too." She winked. "You make every hairstyle look good."

His lips turned up a bit. "Shall I shave it on one side like Darnell did David's?"

On the side where bullets had apparently blown away a sizable chunk of David's dreadlocks, Darnell had shorn the hair close in a fade, then cut an intricate design into the remaining stubble. The rest of David's dreadlocks remained long. It was a very cool effect.

She winked. "As long as you leave me enough hair to bury my

fingers in."

Seth had a few bare patches of his own in back. She had discovered them while tunneling her fingers through his hair the previous night. And her blood had turned to ice when he'd admitted the missing immortals had shot him in the head multiple times. But the rest of his thick silky hair hid the bald spots.

Catching her hand, he pressed a kiss to it and rose. "Ready?"

"I guess so. Will we be teleporting there?" she asked. Wherever *there* was.

"Yes."

"Okay."

The bedroom around them went black, then sunlight embraced them. Blinking against the brightness, Leah stared at a lovely pale gray cottage with bright white trim. Flowers overflowed hanging baskets on the front porch and proliferated in white window boxes. The neatly mown lawn in front was just beginning to brown with cooler autumn temperatures and bore a dusting of dried leaves.

She looked around but found no other homes or structures in sight, just a plethora of trees. Some of the foliage that adorned them remained a dark, healthy green. Some boasted fiery shades of red, orange, or yellow.

Seth led her up the walk to the front porch and rang the bell.

The door swung open.

A handsome man smiled at them. Clearly he was an Immortal Guardian. His hair was jet-black, his features similar enough to Seth and the others to betray their relation to anyone who looked closely enough. He was perhaps six foot two inches tall with a slender but muscular build and warm brown eyes. And he wore clothing identical to Seth's.

He nodded. "Seth. Good to see you." He turned his gaze upon Leah and offered his hand. "You must be Leah." He spoke with an Italian accent.

Smiling, she clasped his hand. "Yes."

"I'm Tomasso." He carried her hand to his lips for a kiss. "So nice to meet you. I've heard such good things about you."

"Nice to meet you, too." Leah fervently hoped the tales that had reached his ears did not all revolve around the thunderstorms and earthquakes Seth spawned when they made love.

His grin broadened.

Crap. He wasn't telepathic, was he?

"Come in. Come in." Ushering them inside, he closed the door and led them into a quaint living room that definitely bore a feminine touch. "*Dolcezza*," he called to the back of the house, "they're here." He turned back to face them. "May I get you something? A drink perhaps?"

"No, thank you," Leah declined with a smile, wondering why Seth had brought her to meet him.

"No, thank you," Seth seconded, then lowered his voice. "How has she been?"

Though Tomasso's smile remained in place, the light in his eyes dimmed. "She's been well." He shrugged one shoulder. "About the same."

Seth's brow furrowed. "I'm sorry I haven't been by."

Tomasso shook his head. "Don't be. You've had a lot on your plate. And Zach has come by nearly as often as you do to heal her."

Leah studied them both. Was someone ill? Who?

Light footsteps drew her gaze to a hallway that led to the back of the house.

Seconds later, a woman entered the living room. She was slender. Small. About a foot shorter than Tomasso. An oversized cream-colored sweater hung off one delicate shoulder and covered her faded jeans to the thighs. Her long hair was a lovely silvery white with a stray blond strand here and there. A braid began at each temple, drew her hair away from her pretty face, and met at a clasp in back where the rest of the shining waves cascaded down to her waist. Several laugh lines spread out from the corners of her eyes. More lines bracketed her mouth. All deepened as she smiled up at Tomasso.

Susan guessed she was somewhere in the neighborhood of eighty years old. Too old, surely, to serve as his Second.

"Hi, Seth," she said as she joined them.

The smile Seth bestowed upon her was full of affection. "Good to see you." Bending, he pressed a kiss to her cheek.

Tomasso smiled down at the woman and looped an arm around her waist, drawing her up against his side.

Nope. She was definitely not his Second. The two clearly shared an intimacy that went far beyond that.

Leah darted Seth a look.

Try not to stare, he cautioned in her head.

That would've been a lot easier to accomplish if he had given her a little warning. Particularly since she now had a sinking suspicion why Seth had brought her to meet them.

"Leah," Tomasso said, "this is my wife, Cassandra. Cassandra, this is Leah, the human woman who has stolen Seth's heart."

Again Leah darted Seth a look. "So I guess *everyone* knows about us?"

Cassandra's smile broadened. "Word travels fast in the Immortal Guardians world." Unlike her husband, she spoke with an American accent.

Leah winked. "So do the Immortal Guardians."

Cassandra grinned. "And they even *gossip* at preternatural speeds."

Leah laughed, liking her.

Moving forward, Cassandra held out her hand. "Immortals and their Seconds are the biggest busybodies on the planet but will never admit it. It's so nice to meet you."

Leah shook the woman's hand. "Nice to meet you, too." Though Cassandra was clearly in good health, her hand had a little bit of that fragile feel Leah had found in the hands of so many elderly men and women. And now that they were closer, she could see faint age spots peppering Cassandra's pale skin. "I hope you don't mind us dropping by like this."

"Of course not." Cassandra motioned for Leah to have a seat on one of two sofas the living room boasted.

Leah made herself comfortable.

Cassandra sank down on the sofa across from her. "As soon as Tomasso told me Seth had fallen hard for a human woman, I knew he'd bring you to see us." She smiled up at her husband as he sank down beside her and rested his arm along her shoulders. Settling a hand on his thigh, she turned back to Leah. Her smile took on a hint of sadness. "In case you haven't guessed it yet, we're the cautionary tale."

Leah felt her stomach sink and didn't know how to respond to that.

Cassandra sent Seth a narrow-eyed look. "I see he didn't warn you."

Seth shrugged as he sat on Cassandra's other side. "I feared she wouldn't come if I did. How are you feeling?"

"Old and tired. Same as usual."

"Release Tomasso," Seth instructed gently.

She did. Tomasso withdrew his touch and leaned back, stretching his arm along the cushions behind her instead.

Seth placed one hand on Cassandra's upper back, then settled the other on her chest over her collarbones. Both hands began to glow as Leah watched.

Leah glanced at Tomasso, whose gaze remained fixed on his wife. His wife, who could easily be mistaken for his grandmother.

Leah met the woman's pale blue eyes.

We're the cautionary tale. Cassandra was human. And Tomasso was the immortal who loved her.

Cassandra's skin acquired a golden glow. She drew in a deep breath and closed her eyes. Some of the age spots on her skin faded back to her natural pale skin color. But most of the lines in her face remained.

When Seth withdrew his touch, she smiled. "Thank you."

Nodding, he patted her shoulder.

Skillet's "Monster" swam out of Seth's pocket.

Retrieving his phone, Seth glanced at it. "It's Reordon. Forgive me. I have to take this." He answered the call. "How are the new immortals settling in?"

He had spent little time at the network in the two days since he'd defeated Gershom. Leah supposed she should feel guilty about that but instead felt grateful. Seth seemed to understand how shaken up she and his Immortal Guardians still were from watching him die, so he had stuck close to David's instead of diving back into his duties.

"What about Cliff?" Seth asked. "How's he doing?" He frowned as he listened. "Melanie's right. He's usually quiet and withdrawn after a break. And he's convinced he had one back at the base. If it continues, I'll see if anything else is going on. But I don't want to agitate him, so I think I should keep my distance for now."

Leah bit her lip. Seth had told her what had happened, that Cliff had wanted to die back at the compound. Would he hold the fact that he still lived against Seth?

Seth met Leah's gaze. "Will you be all right if I leave you here for a few minutes? Tessa seems to be winning the new immortals over, but I'd like to have a word with them myself."

"Sure," she answered.

"Thank you. I shall return shortly." He rose. "Chris, turn off the alarm. I'm on my way."

In the next instant, he vanished.

Chapter Twenty-Eight

A HUSH FELL IN THE wake of Seth's departure.

Leah wondered if the call from Reordon had been as spontaneous as it had appeared or if Seth had asked Chris to call him so he could leave Leah alone with Tomasso and Cassandra.

"Well, that was subtle," Tomasso drawled with some amusement, breaking the silence.

Smiling, Leah relaxed. "You think he planned the call?"

"Without a doubt."

Cassandra once more rested a hand on Tomasso's thigh. "He clearly loves you," she said gently. "And he must believe you feel the same way or he wouldn't have brought you here."

"I do," she told them. "I love Seth."

Cassandra nodded. "He just wants you to know what you're getting into before..."

Leah raised her brows. "Before I agree to marry him?"

"Yes."

Patting her husband, Cassandra rose and moved to sit beside Leah. "I'm a hundred and fifty-seven years old, Leah."

Leah stared at her. "Wow. You look freaking fantastic!"

The couple laughed.

"Thank you," Cassandra said. "That's Seth's doing. He comes by at least a couple of times a week to heal me and try to stave off as much aging as his gift will allow." She cast her husband a look full of love. "In January, Tomasso and I will have been married for a hundred and thirty-five years."

"That's wonderful," Leah said. Few marriages even seemed to

make it twenty-five years nowadays. "Congratulations."

Cassandra smiled. "I know it sounds cliché, but I love Tomasso more every day I spend with him."

Tomasso's face took on a look of immense tenderness. "I love you more every day, too, *tesoro*."

Leah nodded. "I can believe that." Every minute she spent with Seth amplified the love she felt for him.

Sadness darkened Cassandra's smile a bit as she again met Leah's gaze. "But we both know how this will end."

Tomasso lowered his head.

Cassandra took Leah's hand and gave it a squeeze. "Loving Tomasso is easy. Growing old while he remains young isn't."

Leah swallowed.

"The first sixty or seventy years were fine. I still looked young enough that we didn't draw stares whenever we left the house together. But once Seth could no longer hold back the wrinkles and the white hair... it got harder."

"I don't care what other people think," Leah told her honestly, "as long as Seth and I are together."

Cassandra shook her head. "I thought the same thing when I was your age. When Tomasso and I first married, women were always leering at him and making snide comments about me when they saw us together, because they wanted him for themselves. I couldn't have cared less back then and thought I wouldn't care later. But I do."

Tomasso made a sound of protest but didn't raise his head.

Leah got the impression this was a subject he usually tried to avoid because it troubled him deeply.

"When I was still strong, the gray hair didn't bother me. The nasty looks and comments we drew when we went out together didn't either. But..." She shrugged her slender shoulders. "I'm not strong anymore."

"Yes, you are, *cara*," Tomasso countered.

Cassandra kept her gaze on Leah. "I exercise every day. But even that and Seth can't stop the aging process indefinitely. Despite my husband's claims, I'm physically weaker than I used to be. So when I hear women in their twenties and thirties speculate that I must be rich and Tomasso must be with me for my money because no man in his right mind who is as young and strong and virile as he is would want to have sex with a frail old woman… it strikes a chord." Moisture welled in her eyes. "My body isn't young anymore."

"You have a beautiful body," Tomasso muttered furiously, his eyes beginning to glow.

But Cassandra shook her head. "I'm self-conscious about it when we make love."

"I don't want you to be," her husband said, his voice full of pain as his eyes met hers. "I love everything about you, *cuore mio*. I love your body as much as I ever have. And I keep telling you it would've been no different had I aged alongside you."

"But you didn't," she said, blinking back tears. "And now you have to hold back when we make love."

"I don't."

Cassandra shook her head. "Darling, I've been making love with you for over a century. You think I can't tell when you hold back because you're afraid you'll hurt me if you don't?"

He shook his head, his eyes tormented. "You're my world, Cassandra. You think showing a little restraint takes anything away from what you make me feel when I hold you in my arms? It doesn't." He shifted his gaze to Leah. "It doesn't."

Cassandra returned her attention to Leah, too. "I'm just going to get weaker in the future. I figure I only have another thirty or forty years before I die, if that long."

Muttering what Leah suspected was a curse in Italian, Tomasso rose, stalked out of the house, and slammed the door behind him.

"He doesn't like to think about it," Cassandra said apologetically. When a tear rolled down her cheek, she swiped it away. "But I worry about him."

Leah's throat thickened as sympathetic tears threatened.

"I worry about what it will do to him, watching me wither away until Seth can't stave off death any longer. I know normal human couples have to deal with losing their spouses eventually, too. But Tomasso was alone for three hundred years before we found each other. And he'll be alone for far longer if he can't let go of his grief after he loses me."

"He knew how it would end before he asked you to marry him,"

Leah offered softly.

Cassandra nodded. "I know. I did, too."

Long minutes passed while Leah thought of Seth. "Do you regret it? Do you regret marrying him?"

Cassandra shook her head, finding another smile. "I've had over a century with him. And in that time, Tomasso has brought me more happiness than I could've ever imagined."

Leah squeezed the woman's hand. "You've clearly brought him happiness, too."

Her smile broadened. "Yes. I have." She patted their clasped hands, then withdrew hers. "Now go talk to that stubborn man of mine. Seth wanted you to hear my side of it. I want you to hear Tomasso's as well."

Acting on impulse, Leah leaned forward and hugged the older woman. "Thank you."

Cassandra hugged her back. "Thank you for loving Seth. He needs someone like you in his life."

Leah smiled. "I need him just as much." Rising, she headed outside.

The sun had begun its descent toward the horizon, lending everything a golden glow. All was quiet save the usual birdsong and some scuttling sounds produced by two squirrels that chased each other around and around a tree trunk.

Squinting against the brightness, Leah peered around and finally spotted Tomasso sitting on a wide wooden swing that hung from the limb of a huge evergreen tree. Heavy shade protected him from the waning light of the setting sun.

Grass swished and fallen leaves crunched beneath her shoes as she made her way over to the swing and sat beside him.

Minutes passed while she wondered how to form the questions she wished to ask.

"I do hold back," he admitted, his voice low, before she could speak. "When we make love, I do hold back to ensure I won't hurt her. She bruises more easily now and..." He shook his head. "When you're preternaturally strong, it's easy to inadvertently grip your lover tightly enough to leave marks."

Seth had left a bruise or two on Leah during their tumultuous lovemaking.

"But ensuring I never lose control and take her too roughly doesn't keep me from finding ecstasy in her arms," Tomasso continued. "It doesn't take anything away from what we share."

Leah spoke gently. "She worries it does."

"I know." Rising, he paced away a few steps, careful to remain in the shade. "Cassandra is the strongest woman I've ever known. It breaks my heart to see the insecurities she now harbors. Insecurities that weren't there before." A muscle in his jaw twitched as he lowered his head. "She will only make love with me in the dark now," he confessed, his voice breaking. Shaking his head, he cleared his throat. "She won't do it with the lights on, doesn't want me to see her." He raised a hand and drew it down over his face, loosing a haggard sigh. "Thankfully, she's forgotten how acute my night vision is, or I fear she wouldn't make love with me at all."

Leah didn't know what to say to that and opted to remain silent.

"She can't see herself the way I do," he murmured. "Not anymore. She can't see how very beautiful she is to me. That weighs on my mind as much as how little time we have left together does."

Wispy clouds to the west began to acquire an orange hue.

"And she worries about me," he added. "She worries about what will happen after I lose her, how I will handle the grief."

A third squirrel joined the other two, their little claws making scratching sounds as the chase took them to other trees.

Tomasso returned to the swing and sat beside Leah. Leaning forward, he rested his elbows on his knees and stared at the sunset, his expression pensive.

Leah forced herself to ask him the same question she had asked his wife. "Do you regret it?"

"Marrying a human woman?"

"Yes."

He turned, spearing her with bright amber eyes. "Never. My only regret is that I can't grow old and die with her."

Leah suspected Seth would feel the same.

"I've never loved anyone the way I love my Cassandra. Never experienced the happiness she has brought me all these years." Leaning back, he dragged his fingers through his hair and shook his head. "Being immortal is a double-edged sword. While it will rob me of her in the end, it has also enabled me to have so much more time with her than I would have if I were human."

Leah nodded. Most couples didn't have half the time Tomasso and Cassandra had already shared. "Would you change anything if you could go back and do it all again?"

"No," he responded without hesitation. "Whatever harsh times lay ahead of us are worth the love and happiness we've shared for over a century."

Leah plucked a crisp brown leaf from the wooden slats of the swing and turned it over and over, worrying the edges with her fingers. "I want Seth to be happy."

Tomasso's big hand covered hers, stilling her anxious movements. "You make him happy, Leah. Everyone in the Immortal Guardians world knows that with certainty."

She glanced up at him. "He told me he wants to marry me. But then he brought me here."

"Because he wants you to be happy, too. Seth knows what's in store for you both if you stay with him. It's easy to dismiss a hypothetical future. It's harder to do so when it's staring you right in the face. Cassandra and I are your future if you stay with him. He loves you enough to let you see that and decide for yourself if it will be too much, if it will be too difficult." He patted her hands. "Don't worry. Seth has no doubts about the future he desires with you. He just wants to make sure you don't either. If you ultimately decide that walking away from him will make you happier, he will let you go regardless of how he feels. He loves you that much."

She swallowed. "Which would've been harder for you?"

He smiled. "Watching Cassandra walk away. Being denied the one hundred and thirty-five years I've spent with her."

She nodded. "Thank you."

He brought one of her hands to his lips and pressed a kiss to the back of it. "Thank *you* for the happiness you've brought Seth."

Footsteps crunched in the grass.

Leah looked over and found Seth and Cassandra walking toward them.

Seth sent Tomasso a narrow-eyed look. "I wouldn't have brought Leah here if I'd known you were going to flirt with her."

Leah glanced at Cassandra, concerned the woman might misinterpret the situation.

But Cassandra laughed. "Don't you worry about that handsome rogue. He has a thing for older women."

Grinning, Tomasso rose. "Damned right I do." He swiftly closed the distance between them, captured her lips in a long kiss, then looped his arm around her.

Leah stood and smiled up at Seth as he approached.

Though his own lips turned up at the corners, his dark eyes betrayed uncertainty. Dipping his head, he kissed her lips. "Okay?" he asked softly.

She nodded. "I like your friends."

He curled an arm around her and pressed her close. "Cassandra is a delight," he said with a smile, then feigned a jealous scowl. "Tomasso, on the other hand, is now on my shit list."

The couple laughed, as did Leah.

"You'll stay for supper, won't you?" Cassandra asked.

Seth consulted Leah. *Do you want to?* he asked in her head.

Yes.

He sent the couple a smile. "Thank you. That would be lovely."

And it was. Leah enjoyed the other couple's company immensely. Tomasso and Cassandra shared a warm, affectionate relationship, always teasing each other, always touching. She'd rest a hand on his arm. He's brush a stray lock of hair back from her face. There was no mistaking the love that shone in their eyes whenever they looked at each other.

Clearly, 135 years of marriage had not dimmed the spark between them. They behaved like gloriously happy newlyweds. Cassandra just looked a couple of generations older than Tomasso.

Zach and David must have volunteered to field Seth's calls, because his phone didn't ring once over the next couple of hours. After dinner, the four of them retired to the living room. Tomasso tugged Cassandra down on his lap, then draped his arms around her, looking as though he would rather be nowhere else in the world as they talked and laughed.

Leah was actually sorry to see their time together end when Seth finally rose and suggested the two of them take their leave.

Cassandra hugged Leah goodbye. "Come back and visit me."

"I will."

Tomasso grabbed Seth's arm and tugged him into a man hug. "See you next week?"

"Sooner," Seth promised.

"Thank you."

Leah had already forgotten that Seth had healed Cassandra when they had first arrived and did so on a regular basis.

"And thank you for giving me the night off," Tomasso added. Stepping back, he drew his wife up against his side and sent her a playful leer. "I plan to use it well."

Her cheeks flushing, Cassandra swatted him, then whispered to Leah. "In other words, he plans to use *me* well."

Tomasso grinned. "Hell yes, I do." His eyes twinkled with amusement as he looked at Seth. "And *I* can do it without sparking torrential rainstorms and earthquakes."

Seth groaned.

The rest of them laughed.

"Good night, you two." Seth drew Leah into his arms.

Darkness embraced them, accompanied by that peculiar feeling of weightlessness.

When light flared to life above them, they were back in Seth's bedroom at David's home.

Tilting her head back, she stared up at him. "Thank you for tonight. I really liked them."

Seth drew a hand over her hair, brushing it back from her face. "They liked you, too." His look grew somber. "Did you have a nice talk?"

"Yes." Smiling, she pressed a kiss to his chin. "Now let's get married."

Bright golden light flared in his eyes as he stilled. "You're sure?"

"I'm sure." She studied him closely. "Are you?"

He nodded. "I've been sure for some time now, Leah."

She bit her lip. "You won't mind having to hold back to keep from hurting me when we make love a century from now?"

"No."

"Or making love in the dark when I'm too self-conscious about your still being hot as hell while I'm wrinkled and saggy?"

"No."

"What about when I'm too old and frail to make love at all?"

He shook his head. "It won't bother me, love." Dipping his head, he brushed his lips against hers in a tender caress. "What we have transcends the physical, Leah. Don't you know that? You are so much more to me than an exquisite body upon which I can slake my lust."

"Damn," she murmured. "I don't know why, but your saying that just totally turned me on."

He smiled, his eyes brightening with amusement. "I love you." He claimed her lips in another, longer kiss that carried so much emotion it brought tears to her eyes. "Marry me, Leah."

Reaching up, she cupped his face in her hands and met his alluring golden gaze. "Yes."

His handsome faced creasing with a big grin, he wrapped his arms around her, swept her off her feet, and spun her in a tight circle. *She said yes!* he shouted mentally.

Whoops and shouts immediately bombarded her mind. "What is that?" she yelled over the noise even though she knew it was in her head.

"The telepaths, expressing their happiness for us."

Leah laughed.

As exuberant as a boy who had just gotten the present he really wanted for his birthday, Seth set her on her feet and proceeded to kiss the stuffing out of her.

The floor beneath them began to rumble and vibrate.

Pulling back, she chuckled. "An earthquake? Already? We've barely gotten started."

Seth laughed and shook his head. "I'm not doing it this time."

"Then what—?"

The bedroom door burst open and crashed against the wall, startling Leah so badly she jumped.

Men and women garbed in black rushed inside, vying for position as they surged toward the two of them.

David reached them first and drew Seth into a bear hug.

Ami slammed into Leah, damned near taking her to the floor as she squeezed her tight and offered congratulations.

Then bodies crushed in around them, pressing close.

Leah laughed as she was passed from one immortal to the next.

First the women embraced her, then the men. All overflowed with happiness. All were heartwarmingly thrilled that the man who had watched over them for hundreds and thousands of years had finally found love and happiness.

And all were now *her* family, too.

Seth found Leah again amid the crush of revelers. Bending, he wrapped his arms around her, then straightened, lifting her feet off the floor.

Grinning, happier than she had ever thought she could be, Leah pressed her lips to his. "I love you."

"I love you, too."

Pressing her lips to his ear, she whispered, "You know I'm just marrying you because your boys all make me feel small, right?"

He laughed and tightened his hold. "I don't care why you do it as long as you marry me." Then he kissed her, longer and deeper, firing her blood.

"I get to plan the wedding!" Lisette called behind them.

"I get to help!" Sarah said quickly.

"Me, too!" Ami cried.

Then all the women present were volunteering.

"I want to help," Sheldon tossed in.

"No way," Tracy objected. "You'd line the aisle with creepy blow-up dolls."

Everyone laughed.

Seth smiled at Leah. "Are you okay with that?"

"With Sheldon lining the aisle with creepy blow-up dolls?" she asked with a grin.

Chuckling, he shook his head. "With Lisette and the others planning the wedding."

Shifting, Leah drew her legs up, locked them around his waist, and settled her core against the hard length constrained by his cargo pants. "I'm fine with that." She nipped his earlobe. "We have better things to do."

"Everybody out!" he called, his gaze holding hers as he slid one hand down to cup her ass.

Protests arose.

"You heard him," Leah added with a grin. "Daddy wants to get his kink on."

Several men hooted.

Beside them, David groaned. "Do you know how weird it is to hear someone say that about my grandfather?"

She laughed and reached out to squeeze his shoulder. "Sorry about that, David. I forgot."

Leaning closer with a smile, he kissed her cheek. "Congratulations again. And welcome to the family, Leah."

"Thank you."

"Okay, children!" David called over the din. "Let's go. It's time to begin the night's hunt."

Though some grumbled, all immediately began to file out of the room.

"You'd best hurry," David advised them with a wink at Leah, "and leave before the rain begins."

Now Seth groaned and pressed his forehead to hers.

The door closed, leaving them alone.

She laughed. "You're lucky I'm not the shy type or I'd make you take me someplace remote every time we make love so no one will know."

He raised his head. "Now there's an idea."

"Don't you dare," she ordered with mock severity. "The farmers of North Carolina need you."

Laughing, Seth tossed her onto the bed. "Well, let it never be said that I shirked my duties."

Leah grinned as their clothes fell away.

Chapter Twenty-Nine

S ETH SWAYED ON HIS FEET.
The hand on his shoulder tightened. "Are you all right?"
Felix asked, his deep voice full of concern.

Seth smiled at the Aussie immortal and those clustered around
them. "Yes."

"You should have had someone else teleport us in."

"They're all busy teleporting in the rest," he said with a shake of
his head. "Find a seat."

Felix patted his shoulder, then strode forward. The other
immortals stationed in Australia followed, each offering Seth a pat
or a slap on the back.

As Seth surveyed the scene around him, a peace he hadn't felt
in thousands of years sifted through him. He stood in what
resembled an enormous grassy bowl. Seth had often wondered
over the millennia if the deep indentation in the earth might be the
remnants of a crater blasted into the surface by a meteorite. The
ground curved upward on all sides, no trees marring his view. The
forest didn't begin until you reached the rim. And there it
proliferated, the foliage so dense that even Seth's preternaturally
sharp eyes couldn't penetrate it.

The grass at the base of the *bowl* had been neatly mown. Thanks
to Seth and a handful of immortals whose gifts allowed them to
alter nature, the sloping sides all overflowed with wildflowers.
Hundreds of solar-powered lights and lanterns illuminated the
clearing, twinkling like the stars above them.

Chairs formed row after long row on the lawn, enough to seat every Immortal Guardian on the planet. Even those whom Gershom had transformed with the help of blood stolen from Aidan were present, each assigned to an elder Immortal Guardian.

It was a remarkable experience, seeing his entire family in one place. The males wore sleek black suits. The women wore beautiful gowns. Some of the attire was modern, some vintage formal wear from their mortal days. All looked as happy and excited as Seth felt. *This* — the congregation of powerful men and women before him who spent their nights protecting humanity — *this* was his legacy.

He could not have been more proud.

Seth had never thought to see them all gathered together this way and had Chris Reordon and the other network heads around the globe to thank for making it possible.

"Aren't you tired?"

Turning, he found Zach, Jared, David, Gideon, and Jaden approaching. He had been pleasantly surprised when the last two had asked if they could attend. "What?"

"Aren't you tired after teleporting so many immortals here?" Gideon repeated.

Seth reached out and pressed a hand to Gideon's chest. Energy flooded him.

Gideon staggered.

Grinning, Seth released him. "Not anymore."

The other men laughed.

Zach clapped Seth on the back. "Are you nervous?"

"Hell no. I've been waiting thousands of years for this." He ran a hand down the smooth lapels of his suit. "How do I look?"

"Butt-ugly," Zach retorted. "I don't know what the hell Leah sees in you."

While the other men laughed, David gave Zach a shove and moved forward to straighten Seth's tie. "Ignore them. You look good."

"Thank you." Seth drew a hand over his hair. He was used to pulling his long locks back from his face in a braid or with a tie, but his hair was too short for that now, so he'd opted to leave it loose. "Is her family here?"

David didn't ask whose family. "Yes. They're seated in the front row, everyone except her father, who will walk her down the aisle."

Seth frowned. "I've barely said more than *hello, nice to meet you* to her parents. I should've spent more time getting to know them."

David shook his head. "You've had your hands full with the new immortals. Leah explained everything to her mother and father. They understand."

Not all of the immortals Seth and the others had retrieved from Gershom had fallen into line as quickly as Tessa had. Some had balked, the mind games played on them making the transition to truth difficult. Seth hoped being here tonight would help.

David's eyes twinkled with amusement. "Like Leah, her family is good with different." He glanced at the multitude of immortals taking their seats. Some zipped around at preternatural speeds. "Although their eyes are pretty wide tonight."

Seth smiled. "I bet they are."

Lisette emerged from a white tent located not far away from them but some distance from the last row of chairs. She wore a lovely peach gown that hugged her figure to her hips, then flowed out into a skirt that trailed behind her in the grass.

Zach sent her a besotted smile, his eyes acquiring a golden glow.

She smiled at Seth. "Are we about ready? Leah is driving me crazy."

Unease crept in. "Is she having second thoughts?"

Lisette laughed. "Just the opposite. She cannot wait to make you hers, you handsome devil."

Seth grinned, his heart swelling. "Then let's do this." Turning on his heel, he strode up the center aisle, Zach on his heels.

Every Immortal Guardian still standing blurred and found a seat. Jared, Gideon, and Jaden followed suit.

At the front of the masses, Seth scaled a few stone steps to the large granite dais Zach and David had driven into the side of the hill. Zach positioned himself in the center of the dais while Seth took his place as groom and turned to watch for his bride.

Leah's mother and brother sat in the front row, Ben's wife and Aaron beside them. All looked happy, if a little overwhelmed by the other guests.

Poor bastard, Zach murmured telepathically. *You can't stop smiling, can you?*

No, Seth replied unrepentantly.

A group of Immortal Guardians seated off to one side of the gathering raised string instruments and began to play elegant music.

Seth's heartbeat picked up.

David appeared at the far end of the long center aisle. Ami left the white tent and joined him, so lovely in a peach-colored gown like Lisette's. David smiled down at her as she curled a hand around his arm. Ami's red hair really stood out amid the sea of black around her as David escorted her forward. Her green eyes sparkled with joy.

When they reached the dais, they scaled the steps. Ami stopped before Seth, rose onto her toes, and drew him down so she could kiss his cheek.

"I'm so happy for you," she whispered.

He pressed a kiss to her forehead. "Thank you."

She moved to stand on the bride's side. David moved to stand beside Seth.

Darnell and Lisette appeared at the end of the aisle next, Darnell handsome in his suit, Lisette graceful and alluring in her gown, which matched Ami's.

"Damn, I love that woman," Zach muttered.

Lisette grinned and winked at her husband. She, too, gave Seth a kiss on the cheek upon reaching the dais. "Leah is lucky to have you."

"I'm luckier to have her," he said with a smile.

She moved to stand beside Ami.

Darnell drew Seth into a hug, clapping him on the back, then took his place on David's other side.

The white fabric of the tent on the opposite side of the gathering moved and fluttered. Seth had to struggle not to laugh when he heard Sarah and Roland engage in hasty whispering every immortal present could nevertheless hear. Then little Adira and Michael burst from the tent, giggling as they ran forward.

Sarah and Roland zipped after them, catching them before the toddlers could reach the aisle and charge down it.

The audience chuckled.

Sarah knelt, her gown pooling on the lawn, and whispered to the children, who listened carefully, then nodded.

Turning to face Seth, Adira and Michael began to walk forward with large, slow steps. Adira looked like a little fairy princess, her peach skirt frothing out around her in fluffy layer after fluffy layer. One hand clutched the handle of a pretty white basket decorated with flowers and ribbons that matched the wreath balanced precariously on her fiery curls. Plunging her other hand inside the basket, she drew out a handful of flower petals and scattered them on the ground in front of her.

Michael was equally adorable in a suit identical to his father's. Holding a white satiny pillow in both hands, he marched forward with exaggeratedly somber steps like a little toy soldier.

But there were a lot of immortals present. And the aisle the children had to walk down was a long one. The two soon grew bored and impatient with the slow, stately steps. Adira picked up her pace. Michael cut her a glance and started walking faster, too. Then, as if by some unspoken agreement, it abruptly turned into a contest to see who could reach Seth first.

Both children burst into giggles and took off running up the aisle, Adira flinging flower petals every which way and Michael waving his pillow around like a balloon.

When Roland and Sarah took a step forward to stop them, Seth grinned and held up a hand. "This is a day of celebration," he told them. "Let them have their fun."

Chuckles rippled through the crowd as the little ones ran and giggled and giggled and ran.

Seth descended the steps and caught the two up in his arms. Bussing their cheeks, he carted them safely up to the dais. Adira moved to stand with her mother. Michael moved to stand beside David and leaned into his side.

Seth retook his place and returned his attention to the far side of the clearing.

The tent flaps parted and Leah stepped outside, her hand tucked into the crook of her father's arm.

Seth lost the ability to breathe as he stared, arrested.

She wore no veil as per his request. He had wanted nothing to shield Leah's lovely face and impede his view tonight. Her brown hair was drawn back from her face in a crown of braids from which tiny flowers peeked here and there. The rest cascaded down her back in a sleek, shining curtain. A white gown hugged her figure from breasts to hips, left her soft alabaster shoulders bare, and covered her arms with delicate lace. The skirt flared out from her hips the way Lisette's and Ami's had and trailed behind her as she strode forward with those same strong, sensual steps that had captured his attention from the very beginning.

She was stunningly, ravishingly beautiful.

And she was his.

He heard Leah's mother suck in a breath and guessed his eyes had begun to glow with golden light. But he couldn't help it.

In her free hand, Leah carried a pretty bouquet of wildflowers Ami and the children had picked for her earlier. Even that — choosing something made for her by those he loved over a bouquet that had been carefully crafted by professional florists — made him love her more.

Beside Leah, her father stood tall, perhaps six foot three. The medium brown skin of his head was clean-shaven like Darnell's. His beard, cut in a Van Dyke, bore a mixture of black and gray hairs. His trim, muscular body was clad in a handsome suit. But Seth only saw that from the periphery, unable to drag his gaze away from the woman he loved.

When Leah and her father reached the far end of the aisle, everyone present stood.

Leah's eyes rose and met Seth's.

A lump rose in his throat. Her exquisite face shone with love and happiness and no little excitement. He thought her steps might have even quickened when she saw him waiting for her.

Seth descended the steps but forced himself to wait for her there instead of jogging up the aisle to meet her as he wanted to. When at last she reached him, he managed to drag his gaze away long enough to meet her father's. "Thank you."

Joseph Turner nodded and placed Leah's hand in Seth's. "Make her happy."

"I will."

After kissing his daughter's cheek, Joe turned away and joined his family in the front row.

Seth looked down at Leah.

Her full pink lips stretched in a grin.

Seth's did, too. Ducking his head, he pulled her into his arms and kissed the hell out of her.

Humming her approval, she wrapped her arms around him, parted her lips, and deepened the contact, teasing him with her tongue.

A throat cleared. "I believe you're supposed to wait until *after* the ceremony to do that," Zach drawled.

Leah laughed as Seth raised his head.

The smile he bestowed upon her carried no remorse. "I couldn't wait," he admitted.

"I couldn't either." The moment Leah had seen him standing up on the dais—so damned handsome in his suit, his face full of love for her—she had wanted to follow Adira and Michael's example and take off running up the aisle, impatient to be at his side and make him hers.

His irises glowed as though golden flames flickered behind them. Stepping back, he offered his arm.

Leah curled her hand around it, her heart pounding as he tucked it against his side and strode up the stone steps with her.

Ami moved forward with a sweet smile. Rising onto her toes, she kissed Leah's cheek and took the bouquet. "Thank you for making him happy," she whispered.

Leah gave her a quick hug. "Thank you for helping me find him." If Ami hadn't frequented Leah's store, she never would've met Seth.

Ami grinned as she backed away.

Seth and Leah faced each other in front of Zach, who would officiate the ceremony. Leah could think of no one more qualified to do so than the son of a Watcher who had lived since biblical times.

Little Adira suddenly hurried over to them. Taking Leah's hand in one of hers, she grabbed Seth's with the other and held the two together until Leah twined her fingers through Seth's. Then she wandered back over to her mother's side.

Leah smiled up at Seth. "This is how it all began."

He carried her hand to his lips. "And how it shall be from this day forward."

"I love you so much."

"I love you, too, Leah."

Together they turned to face Zach, eager to begin their future together.

⸺◈◈◈⸺

Leah lost count of the number of men and women who crowded around them to offer their congratulations after the ceremony. All introduced themselves and embraced her with unfeigned affection. After the first three or four dozen, she gave up trying to remember their names. There must be thousands. All Seth's descendants. All powerful, honorable men and women who had dedicated their lives to protecting others.

She stared up at her new husband, knowing her heart was in her eyes.

His was, too, when he smiled down at her as he accepted another hug.

Grinning, she brought her hands together in front of her chin, performed several tiny claps, and mouthed, *I feel so small around these guys.*

He laughed.

When it seemed everyone present had gotten their chance to personally congratulate the newlyweds, Leah looked around. "Where are my mom and dad? I don't want them to feel too overwhelmed, and they've been on their own for quite a while now."

"Sorry about that." Taller than the other Immortal Guardians present, Seth peered around. "There they are, chatting with Darnell over by the drinks."

"There are drinks?"

He nodded. "And food. Chris had one of his restaurants cater it. Zach and Jared teleported everything in after the ceremony concluded. It's over there." He pointed to one side. Then his brow furrowed. "Uh-oh. Sheldon is with them. I didn't know he was here tonight." He had thought Darnell and Tracy would be the only

Seconds in attendance to reduce the crowd size and the number of people who would have to be teleported in. The rest had viewed the wedding through a live internet feed broadcast on one of the network's secure websites.

Leah nodded, unable to see around the tall bodies that surrounded them. "Tracy talked Lisette into letting him play DJ tonight."

"Well, we'd better hurry and join them. I never know what's going to come out of that boy's mouth."

Leah laughed.

Seth wrapped an arm around her and teleported to her parents' side.

Both jumped at their sudden appearance, liquid spilling over the rims of their glasses.

Seth winced. "My apologies. I didn't mean to startle you."

Darnell and Sheldon hastily offered them both napkins.

Leah's mother laughed as she smiled up at her new son-in-law. "Don't worry about it. That whole teleportation thing is very cool, but it's going to take some getting used to."

Leah laughed.

Sheldon smiled and took Tracy's hand, twining his fingers through hers. "Let's go put some music on and give the musicians a break."

"Okay."

"Nice to meet you, Mr. and Mrs. Turner," they said in unison as they backed away.

Darnell shook his head. "I'd better go make sure Sheldon doesn't play anything too outrageous. Nice to meet you, Mr. and Mrs. Turner." He smiled at Leah and Seth. "Congratulations."

Leah and Seth thanked him as he strolled away.

"I like them," her mom proclaimed.

Her dad nodded. "I do, too. I think they were worried we might feel overwhelmed by all this, because they made sure we knew they aren't immortal."

Leah bit her lip. "*Are* you overwhelmed by all this?"

Her dad looked around. "A little bit," he replied honestly, then smiled. "But we couldn't be happier for you both."

Her mom nodded. "No one who sees you two can deny you

belong together. And you couldn't have chosen a better man, sweetie."

Leah sent Seth a loving look. "I know."

He kissed her forehead. "I couldn't have chosen a better woman."

Leah's mother tucked her arm through her father's. She looked so pretty tonight, Leah thought. Though Leah had inherited her mother's straight brown hair and teasing personality, her height had clearly come from her birth father. Because Dorothy Turner was a good foot shorter than Leah's stepdad.

Her mom now stared up at Seth with an expression Leah couldn't decipher. "It's true, isn't it?" She looked up at her husband, then at Seth. "You're him, aren't you?"

Seth sent Leah an uncertain look. "I'm sorry. I don't know what you mean."

Leah studied her parents. She didn't know what her mother meant either.

Her dad spoke. "You're him, aren't you? It took me a while to realize it because — when Leah brought you to meet us — you were wearing jeans and a sweater instead of all black."

When Leah had taken Seth to her parents' house a few days after he had asked her to marry him, he had opted to abandon his hunting garb and dress casually so he would appear more *normal* to them.

"Your hair is a lot shorter now, too," Joe said, "and you don't wear a beard."

Seth stiffened.

Leah looked up at him. "What is it?" When he said nothing, she consulted her parents. "Mom? Dad? What's going on? What are you talking about?"

Her dad alternated between looking at her and looking at Seth. "Do you remember when Ben was born? How he and your mother had to stay in the hospital for a while because he came early?"

"Yeah." She had been ten years old at the time. She couldn't remember what exactly had gone wrong with her mother's pregnancy, but the new brother she had been looking forward to seeing with such excitement had come early enough that he had been placed in the NICU. His lungs had been too underdeveloped for him to breathe on his own. And a host of other problems caused by his premature birth had left doctors and nurses grim-faced. Her mother had cried a lot. Her father had done his damnedest to hide his fear from Leah. But she had seen it nevertheless. And she had heard medical murmurings about Ben's kidneys and bleeding in his brain.

When her father had—at her repeated pleading—taken her to the NICU lobby to see her new brother through the glass window, the number of tubes attached to Ben's tiny body had terrified her.

"There's something we never told you about that," her father said now.

"What do you mean?"

"One night you asked if you could see Ben again. But you were so tired that you fell asleep in my arms before we got to the NICU. And while I stood in the lobby, watching Ben through the window, a man suddenly appeared." He stared at Seth. "He had black hair that fell to his waist, a closely cropped beard, and was dressed all in black. The nurses didn't show any reaction to his abrupt appearance, as if they had no idea he was even there." He shook his head. "I was afraid for Ben. The man looked like a soldier. He even carried sheathed swords on his back. But when I started to call out a warning, he looked right at me and held up a hand."

Leah glanced up at Seth, but he kept his gaze on her father.

"This feeling of rightness filled me," her dad said, "like everything was going to be okay. Then he raised the cover of Ben's unit and rested a hand on Ben's head."

Leah sucked in a breath as she stared at Seth. The only other thing she remembered about that time was Ben improving and growing stronger far faster than the doctors and nurses had expected. "You healed Ben?"

Seth nodded.

"And every other infant in the NICU," her father finished.

"Thank you so much," her mother said, tears welling in her eyes. "Before you came, the doctors warned us that Ben might not survive and that if he did, he would have hearing and developmental problems along with a host of other health concerns for the rest of his life. But he didn't."

Seth sent her a gentle smile. "It was my pleasure."

"Why didn't you tell me?" Leah asked him softly.

He shifted awkwardly. And Leah knew him well enough to realize he wished the conversation hadn't taken such a turn. "I didn't want it to influence your feelings for me," he admitted.

Of course he hadn't. He was clearly uncomfortable with her parents' knowing. So instead of thanking him profusely for saving her brother's life, she shook her head. "No. I mean why didn't you tell me you used to have a beard? That's so hot."

Relief lighting his handsome features, he laughed and pulled her closer.

"Hey, you two," Lisette called as she approached them. "It's time for the bride and groom to share their first dance."

When Leah turned to follow her, one hand linked with Seth's, she was surprised to see that the rows and rows of chairs had been moved to the outskirts and placed around tables, clearing a very large dance area for them.

Her parents trailed behind Leah and her new husband and joined the masses who formed a circle to watch.

Seth led Leah onto the soft, grassy dance floor.

"I'm glad I didn't wear heels," she said with a smile, knowing high heels would've probably sunk into the soil.

"What did you wear?" he asked curiously.

Lifting the hem of her long skirt, she extended a leg and pointed her toes, showing off a pretty ballet slipper.

He smiled. "Perfect for dancing."

Music poured forth from speakers Leah couldn't see, and Etta James began to croon "At Last."

Leah rested her left hand on Seth's shoulder and placed her right hand in his. "*You're* perfect. How's your ballroom dancing?"

"With you in my arms? Exemplary."

She grinned. "That's what I like to hear. Though this dress might hinder me a bit."

Dipping his head, he brushed his lips against hers. "I'll keep it out of your way."

As he swung her into a graceful waltz, Seth kept his promise. Leah didn't know if he used telekinesis or what, but she didn't trip on the long length once while he swept her around the circle. It was like something out of a fairy tale. And Leah soon forgot everything except the joy of being in Seth's arms and knowing he was all hers.

Their dance ended with a romantic dip.

Cheers and clapping erupted.

Straightening, Seth drew her up with him and stared into her eyes. "I love you."

She touched his face. "I love you, too."

———◦❊◦———

Lisette approached them. Like everyone else present, she smiled widely. "You're welcome," she said as she stopped beside them and started to fiddle with the waist of Leah's dress.

Seth smiled. "Thank you. The wedding was beautiful and the song perfect."

"That's not what you're thanking me for."

He eyed her with amusement. "Then for what?"

She winked. "For this." She flicked her hands, almost like someone shaking out a sheet on laundry day before hanging it up to dry.

Leah's long skirt ballooned out, then fell away, revealing a formfitting skirt beneath that only reached halfway down her thighs and left the rest of her long, lovely legs bare.

Leah gaped down at it. "I didn't know it did that!" The skirt bore a layer of the same lace that covered her arms. "Since the wedding was going to be outside, I thought that was just there to keep everyone from seeing my underwear if the wind blew my dress up."

Seth laughed, as did many of the immortals who had overheard.

Then Lisette leaned in and lowered her voice as she caught Seth's eye. "You can thank me later for the lingerie. That and the dress are my wedding gifts to you both."

Seth fastened his gaze on Leah's shortened dress and wished desperately that he could see through it to what lay beneath. "Thank you."

Lisette draped the long skirt over her arm and kissed Leah's cheek. "*This* is Sheldon's gift to you." She dashed away.

Seth looked over Leah's head, past the immortals observing them, and saw Sheldon nod at Lisette. As acting DJ, he had surrounded himself with a plethora of electronic equipment, most of which Seth couldn't identify.

Seconds later, a woman's voice poured through hidden speakers.

"Ooh." Leah smiled. "I love this song."

"What is it?"

"Sean Paul's 'No Lie,' featuring Dua Lipa." She sent him a wicked grin and moved toward him in slow, deliberately provocative steps.

"Leah," he warned sternly, "don't."

"Don't what?" she asked innocently as she rested a hand on his chest, then slipped around behind him, her touch already coaxing his damned body to respond.

"Don't tempt me, minx," he murmured. "Your parents are watching."

"So?" Reaching up, she tucked her fingers in the collar of his suit jacket and tugged it off. "I'm a grown woman. This is my wedding night." Rising onto her toes, she nipped his earlobe with her teeth, sending a shock of pleasure through him. "And I intend to enjoy it to the fullest."

He groaned as she moved back around to face him and held his jacket out to one side.

"Tell Lisette to read my thoughts," she ordered, giving him a siren's smile.

He glanced at Lisette. *Leah wants you to read her thoughts.*

Lisette glanced at Leah. A moment later, her eyes widened and color flooded her cheeks.

What in the world?

Leah's lips stretched in a mischievous grin. "Tell her to do it."

Again, he looked at Lisette. *Whatever she wants you to do, do it.*

Lisette cast her husband an uncertain look, then dashed forward in a blur. The suit jacket Leah held disappeared. Then Seth felt several tugs at his clothing before Lisette zipped back to her husband.

When he glanced down, his eyebrows flew up. His shirt was now untucked and his sleeves rolled back, exposing his forearms.

He looked at Leah.

Winking, she began to move her feet to the music, hips swaying in a way that never failed to stir his blood.

"Leah," he cautioned, trying valiantly to resist her. He really didn't think her father would want to see the two of them dance the way they did in her shop. Yet that seemed to be what the beautiful temptress had in mind.

Ignoring his stern tone, Leah eased forward and reached up. Her tongue darted out to moisten her lush lips as she unfastened the top two buttons on his shirt.

His pulse quickened.

Curling her fingers around the tie just beneath the knot, she loosened it, then tugged him down until their mouths were only a breath apart. "Dance with me, husband," she implored in a sultry voice. It was the first time she had called him that. And it made his heart swell and his body harden.

Closing the last millimeter of space that separated them, Seth locked an arm around her waist and took her lips in a voracious kiss.

Leah was breathless, her cheeks flushed, when he raised his head. And he could see the glow in his own eyes reflected in hers.

Smiling down at her, he shook his head. "All right, wife. You asked for it."

She grinned. "Bring it, handsome."

Seth laughed. Forgetting everyone around them, he began to dance with her the way he enjoyed most, hips moving, bodies brushing, hands teasing. Leah laughed as he spun her around and around, then drew her close again. Her scent intoxicated him — no perfume, just Leah and a hint of the wildflowers she had carried earlier. He slid a hand down her back, his fingers resting on the upper curve of her tantalizing ass as he slipped a thigh between hers. Damn, she felt good.

Winking, she twirled away, then moved behind him. Her full breasts pressed against his back. Her pelvis brushed his ass.

He smiled when she slid an arm around him and splayed her fingers on his chest. He would never get enough of this, enough of her. She was so much fun to be with. So sensual. Her touch sublime. Desire coursed through him anew as she drew her hand down his front. Swearing, he caught it before she could slide it past the waistband of his pants and was glad she'd had the foresight to have Lisette untuck his shirt.

Turning, he sent her a look of mock-admonishment and spoke in her head. *Naughty girl.*

She grinned unrepentantly as he twirled her around and around.

Seth couldn't resist bringing her in close again, once more slipping a thigh between hers as they rocked together to the beat.

"You dropped something," he heard Zach say over the music.

"What?" Lisette responded absently.

"You dropped something."

"I did? What'd I drop?"

"Your jaw," Zach said dryly.

Seth laughed.

"I can't help it," Lisette said, her words full of astonishment. "Seth never danced with *me* like that."

Her husband snorted. "It's a good thing he didn't. I'd have to geld him."

Grinning, Seth once more lost himself in Leah and the dance. Every wink and flirtatious glance filled him with joy. Every brush of her hands, hips, and breasts kindled his desire. He'd played the role of powerful, austere leader for so long that he'd forgotten what it felt like to just be a man in love with a woman who made him laugh and burn and enjoy life.

As the music began to wind down, he spun her in a series of tight, fast turns that left her laughing and breathless, then bent her back over his arm in another dramatic dip.

The song ended.

Seth straightened, keeping her pressed against his chest.

Silence reigned.

Her face flushed with pleasure, Leah looked around. "Um..."

Seth followed her gaze and found a sea of wide eyes and gaping mouths. His Immortal Guardians had rarely seen him relax and had *never* seen their illustrious leader behave in such a wanton fashion with a woman.

He sent her family a quick glance.

Her parents gaped at them, too. A blush darkened her mother's cheeks. Ben was struggling not to laugh as he looked back and forth between Leah and their parents.

"Maybe you were right," Leah murmured. "Maybe they weren't ready to see us like this."

Chuckling, he shook his head. "Too damn bad." Lowering his head, he captured her lips in a long, passionate kiss.

Cheers and applause erupted from the crowd.

All uncertainty left Leah's expression as she grinned up at him.

You're so wrong, he muttered telepathically.

"Why?"

Because I believe I'm supposed to dance with your mother next and now I can't. He didn't have to tell her why. His hips were pressed to hers, allowing her to feel how much she had aroused him.

She bit her lip as though she held back a laugh. "Tell Sheldon to play some big band music."

He looked at Sheldon. *Play some big band music, something we can swing dance to.*

Sheldon gave him a salute. A second later, the thrumming beat of "Sing, Sing, Sing" began to play.

Seth caught Lisette's gaze and waved her forward.

With a little whoop of excitement, she pulled Zach onto the grassy dance floor beside them.

Then Sheldon handed something to Darnell, grabbed Tracy's hand, and jogged forward to join them, too. Ethan and Heather followed.

His heart light, Seth twirled Leah away from him and began to swing dance.

She laughed when he tossed her over his shoulder, swung her around, and landed her on her feet again. "This is so awesome!" she cried over the music, grinning from ear to ear. "Best! Wedding! Ever!"

She looked so happy. Seth always wanted see her thus and felt almost as young and carefree as a boy as they danced and played together.

More immortals raced forward and joined in the swing dancing. Much to his surprise, Leah's mom and dad did, too.

Darnell and Sheldon kept the tunes coming, playing music from many generations.

Seth eventually got to dance with his new mother-in-law while

Leah danced with her father. He also danced with Ben's wife, Abby. And Lisette. And some of the other female immortals present while Leah danced with one immortal male after another.

An hour or so later, he reclaimed Leah and took her to get a drink. "I know the bride and groom are supposed to sneak away fairly early," he said as she drank thirstily, "but…" He took her free hand. "I don't know when we'll all be able to gather together like this again. Would you mind if we stayed a bit longer?"

"Of course not," she replied with a grin. "I'm having a wonderful time. And I don't know if you noticed, but like fifty immortals asked me to save them a dance on our way over here."

He smiled. "I noticed." All were eager to get to know the woman who captivated him. "Are you sure?" He sent her a comical leer. *I don't want you to be too tired to make love with me once we leave.*

She laughed. "*Nothing* could make me too tired for that."

Edward — a young, British immortal who had been stationed in North Carolina briefly — joined them. Bowing, he extended a hand to Leah. "Would you do me the honor of joining me for a dance, Leah?"

Smiling, she took his hand. "I would love to." Handing Seth her drink, she headed back to the dance floor.

The revelry continued until sunrise. Seth thanked everyone for celebrating with them, then asked Zach to begin teleporting them all home. Most would like nothing more than to continue the festivities, but the youngest immortals couldn't withstand more than a few minutes of exposure to daylight.

Seth closed his eyes and drew some cloud cover overhead to give the elder immortals more time to teleport them to safety. Even Roland pitched in and helped now that he could teleport, too.

Leah's parents both looked happy and tired. Ben held his sleeping son against his chest. He and his wife had done their fair share of dancing, too, and appeared worn out.

Leah kissed her mother's and father's cheeks. "Good night. I love you."

"Love you, too, baby," they chorused.

Seth caught David's eye. "Would you take Leah's family home, please?"

"Of course."

Once they vanished, Seth drew Leah close and kissed her forehead. "Ready?"

She nodded.

Darkness embraced them as he teleported away.

Chapter Thirty

SETH APPEARED OUTSIDE TWO LARGE double doors.

Leah glanced around in surprise. "Is this your castle?"

"Yes." Bending, he lifted her up and cradled her in his arms. "The one in England." She had never seen the exterior of it.

"Oh." She stared at the large heavy double doors in front of them. "I thought we were heading back to David's place."

"Not tonight." He wanted neither distractions nor interruptions on their first night together as husband and wife and hadn't even brought his phone with him. Leah had been teasing him with touches and brushes of her body all night. Seth planned to spend the next several hours making love to her with abandon.

The doors swung open at his telekinetic command.

Seth carried Leah inside, flicked on the overhead lights with a thought, then stopped short. His eyes widened.

"Holy crap," she breathed.

The castle boasted very high ceilings. And every single room in sight was packed from the floor to those ceilings with prettily wrapped packages.

Leah looked around. "Are these...?"

"Wedding presents," he replied, overwhelmed by the sheer number of them.

"How many do you think there are?"

Moving forward, he wound his way through the piles and climbed the stairs. "Thousands."

"Wow. It's going to take us a year just to open them all. You're so lucky to have a family that big. Especially one that cares about you so much."

He smiled. "Yes, I am. And they're your family, too, now."

More gifts lined the hallways he traveled and spilled out of the rooms they passed. It would appear every immortal on the planet had sent them at least one gift.

Carrying Leah into his solar, Seth set her on her feet.

"This is your bedroom?" she asked, looking around curiously.

"*Our* bedroom," he said as he tugged at his tie. He hoped she liked it.

Turning to face him, she bit her lip. Her lovely face grew solemn.

Some of his joy faded. She didn't look as though she liked it. "You can redecorate it any way you want," he quickly assured her.

If anything, her brow furrowed more.

Seth paused, still gripping his tie. "Would you rather we go to our bedroom at David's place?"

"It isn't that. It isn't the room."

He lowered his hand, taking the tie with it. "Then what is it? You can tell me anything, Leah."

Her shoulders slumped. "I was wrong."

"About what?"

Releasing a long, weary sigh, she sent him a look full of contrition. "I can't believe I'm actually going to say this, but… I'm too tired to make love. All that dancing has left me exhausted. I'm sorry, Seth. I really am. I don't think I can even dredge up enough strength to shower before going to bed. I just want to dive under the covers and sleep for the next twenty-four hours."

Disappointment flooded him. He had really been looking forward to this, their first night as a married couple. But he made a valiant effort to hide it. He didn't tire nearly as swiftly as a human. And Leah had gamely danced with every immortal who had asked her until they had run out of time. He dropped the tie on the floor and forced a smile as he stroked her arm. "It's all right, sweetheart. I understand. We'll just—"

She burst into laughter. "Ha!" she shouted, eyes sparkling with amusement as she pointed at him. "Got you! I'm just kidding. You should see your face."

Seth laughed. She *had* gotten him. Then he narrowed his eyes. "Oh, you're going to pay for that one," he warned in a sinister voice and lunged toward her.

Leah shrieked and spun away, laughter trailing behind her as she ran.

Of course, Seth was preternaturally fast, so she didn't get very far. Growling in feigned anger, he scooped her up and tossed her over his shoulder. He didn't think he had ever heard Leah giggle before and felt warmth unfurl inside him when she did so now. Damn, he loved her.

"Where are you taking me, caveman?" she cried amid giggles. "And why aren't you naked? I could be grabbing your bare ass right now."

Again he laughed. "Patience, love."

After carrying her into the bathroom, he bent and turned the taps in the large bathtub.

"Still waiting for you to get naked," she mentioned casually, dangling upside down and drumming her fingers on his backside as he adjusted the temperature.

Grinning, he set her on her feet and straightened. "I take it patience is not your strong suit?"

"Nope." She glanced at the steamy water filling the tub, then up at him and arched a brow. "But I'm liking where this is going."

He winked. "You'll like this even more." Seth snapped his fingers.

Their clothing vanished as he teleported it to their bedroom at David's place. All but the delicate white lingerie Lisette had bought her, that is.

Seth's gaze fastened on it — and on the pale, perfect flesh the lace both concealed and revealed. His body hardened as lust struck with a vengeance. His voice deepened an octave when next he spoke. "Remind me to thank Lisette again later."

Leah shifted her weight to one leg. Tilting her head, she sent him a sultry smile and trailed the fingers of one hand over her collarbone, down over the lush mound of one breast. Those fingers paused to tease the pink nipple, then continued onward down her stomach. "You like it?"

He swallowed, his hands curling into fists. "Very much."

She drew her tongue across her lower lip. "You want me?"

"More than anything in this world, wife."

Her face flushed, not with embarrassment but with the passion that had been arcing between them for hours.

She moved forward the same moment he did. They fell into each other's arms, both frantic with need. Seth crushed her lips beneath his own and slid his tongue within to stroke hers.

Leah moaned. Raising one leg, she looped it over his hip and ground her damp core against the erection trapped between them. "Screw the bath," she whispered hoarsely. "I want you. Now." Jumping up, she wrapped her legs around his waist.

Seth groaned and clutched her to him. "This is our first time together as husband and wife." He trailed hot kisses down her neck. "I want to do it right."

Her head dropped back as he lifted her high enough to close his lips around one hard, sensitive nipple. "Who says fast and hard isn't right?" she asked on a moan. "You've been teasing me with touches and brushes and kisses all night. We've had hours of foreplay, so forget the bells and whistles and just take me."

He laughed against her firm, tempting flesh. Shaking his head, he delivered a love bite to her breast.

She jumped against him, then moaned again. "Seth, please. I want you inside me."

More than willing to comply, Seth telekinetically turned off the taps and carried Leah back into the bedroom. Kneeling on the bed, he lowered her to the mattress.

She reached for him before he could pull away, writhing and rolling toward him.

Seth nudged her legs apart and settled himself between them.

"Yes," she moaned when his cock brushed her entrance.

Seth shook his head. "Not so fast, wife." Dipping his head, he closed his mouth around a taut nipple shielded with pretty lace and sucked hard.

Leah swore, squirming beneath him as she buried her fingers in his hair.

He lavished more attention on her other breast, then trailed his lips down her stomach. He teased the warm, soft skin below her belly button with his lips while he slipped a finger beneath the delicate bikini panties she wore and tore them away.

"Oh shit," she whispered. "That's so hot." She groaned when he touched his tongue to her clit, circling it, flicking it, and stroking it while she arched up against him. "You and that mouth of yours. So good." Her fingers fisted in his hair and gave a sharp tug. Lust shot through him, making his cock jump. "Damn, I need your ass." She moaned. "And I mean that literally. I should be grabbing your ass right now."

Seth stopped stroking her long enough to choke out a laugh. "Don't make me laugh, damn it. I'm trying to make this good for you."

"It *is* good," she declared. "It's *better* than good. But I want you buried deep inside me, with all your delicious weight pressing down on me when I come, so I can grab that gorgeous ass of yours and —"

Seth ducked his head, pressed his tongue to her clit and stroked her so swiftly it would feel like he held a vibrator to her.

Leah instantly stiffened, crying out as she arched against him and came hard.

He could hear her heart slamming against her ribs as she slumped back against the covers. Rising above her, he arched a brow. "Better?"

She smiled. "Hell yes. Now take me, handsome."

Shaking his head, he knelt between her thighs instead and sat back on his heels. "Look at you," he murmured, taking in her beautiful body splayed out before him, adorned in delicate lace. Leaning forward, he cupped her perfect breasts in his hands, teased the nipples with his thumbs.

Renewed desire flared to life in her eyes as he drew his hands down her sides to her hips.

His gaze traveled a leisurely path over her body. He was so hard for her. Wanted badly to be inside her. Couldn't believe she was his. That he could be so fortunate.

Shifting his thumbs, he slid them farther down and caressed her clit.

She gasped, arching into his touch. "Seth, please," she whispered.

Nodding, he stretched out above her and settled himself between her thighs.

She smiled. "Finally." Reaching down between them, she curled her fingers around his erection.

Pleasure shot through him as she rubbed the sensitive crown against her entrance.

He met her gaze. "I love you, Leah."

Leaning up, she pressed her lips to his in a kiss that carried as much love and affection as it did passion. "I love you, Seth."

He thrust deep inside her. So tight and hot and ready for him. Then withdrew and drove deep again.

"Yes." Arching up to meet him thrust for thrust, she wrapped her arms around him.

He groaned when her nails scored his back. Then, just as she'd promised, she slid her hands down to grab his ass and urged him on.

"Don't hold back," she pleaded, her breath coming in gasps.

Seth moaned as the ground began to shake. "Leah…"

⸺⊙⊙⊙⸺

Leah jerked awake. Her heart pounded a rapid beat in her breast. What had awoken her?

She lay on her side beneath the covers in Seth's big bed at his castle. After spending all day making love, she had finally collapsed in an exhausted slumber near sunset.

Darkness eclipsed the room now. The covers drooped, allowing cold air to touch her bare shoulders. No warm body curled around hers to keep the chill away. Reaching back, she felt around for Seth but found only covers still warm from where he had recently lain.

Confident that he would return soon, she burrowed beneath the blankets and closed her eyes.

Bright light exploded behind her lids, as blinding as that which had surrounded her and the others right after Seth had been slain. Heat filled her body as though she stood before a roaring fire in a fireplace. At first it felt good, banishing the chill. But within seconds it bordered on pain.

Fear piercing her, Leah opened her eyes… and saw only white. Brilliant white light that banished everything around her. She could make out no walls, no ceiling, no shapes.

"Seth!" she cried, terrified.

I'm here.

"I can't see you!" And just like the night she'd lost him, he spoke in her head.

A sob caught in her throat. Had something happened? Had Gershom escaped? Had she lost Seth again?

"Close your eyes." He spoke aloud this time from somewhere close. His voice was calm, untroubled, as though she had just woken from a nightmare and he were trying to soothe her back to sleep.

The heat intensified. "What —?"

"Close your eyes, Leah. Trust me. Please."

She closed her eyes. Her muscles seized suddenly as though an electrical current touched her. She clenched her teeth. "It hurts."

"I know, sweetheart. But it will be over in a minute." His hand closed around hers, his touch keeping her from totally losing it.

"Don't let go," she pleaded, terrified of losing him again.

His lips touched the back of her hand. "Never."

Then the light vanished. The prickling heat left her body. Her muscles relaxed.

Leah opened her eyes and looked around frantically, her breath coming in gasps. But the light had been so bright that it took her eyes several moments to adjust to the sudden darkness.

Seth sat beside her on the bed, wearing only a pair of sweatpants, his wings a dark shadow behind him.

Leah barely had time to register that before he dragged her onto his lap and cradled her in his arms. Burying his face in her hair, he held her so tightly she suspected he would leave bruises. And his whole body began to tremble.

"Seth?" Concern for him suspended her fear and confusion. Wrapping an arm around him, she cupped the back of his head in one hand. "Are you okay?" She glanced around. The castle bedroom looked the same as it had before they had succumbed to sleep.

He nodded but didn't raise his head.

Alarm returned full force when she felt moisture on her neck and realized he wept. And she could hear his heart pounding in his chest. "Seth, talk to me, honey. You're scaring me. What just happened?"

"My father came," he said, his voice hoarse.

She glanced around the room with wide eyes. "Your father was just here?" His father the Watcher?

He nodded. And she felt him swallow hard as though he fought back a sob.

"Why?" Now that the odd heat had left her, her skin prickled with feeling. And her ears felt weird.

"To give us a wedding gift."

Again she searched the room but found no prettily wrapped package. "What gift?"

At last Seth raised his head. Moisture shone on his cheeks as he cupped her face in both hands and pressed a gentle kiss to her lips. "He granted you immortality, Leah."

She stared at him in shock. "What?"

Moisture welled in eyes that glowed as brilliantly as the sun. "He altered your DNA and made you like me so you would—"

"He can do that?" she blurted.

"Apparently so."

She frowned. "You didn't know he could?"

He shook his head. "I knew he could alter the DNA of babies in the womb, but I didn't know he could alter the DNA of adult humans."

"And yet you don't seem surprised."

"I'm not. My powers are nothing compared to his. His are..." Shaking his head, he shrugged. "Unfathomable even to me."

She cupped his face in one hand. "He didn't do this for your first wife?"

Seth shook his head. "Too little time had passed since the first Watchers' sons had wrought havoc in the world. He believed the same thing Gideon, Jared, and the Others did: that we should keep ourselves separate from mankind and avoid sharing what humans called our *sorcery* with them in order to avoid altering their fate. When I abandoned our self-imposed isolation and not only lived amongst the humans but married one and bred children with her, he feared history would repeat itself. Though he didn't wish to see me suffer, he thought that granting Ayana immortality and gifts she had not been born with would make that a certainty."

Leah struggled to grasp it, all the little implications, the greater ones, too. "I don't understand. The rest of the Others still believe that. Why doesn't your father? What changed his mind?"

He carried one of her hands to his lips and kissed it. "The thousands of years that have passed since then in which I ensured my progeny *maintained* a careful balance in the world instead of tipping it. Gershom may be mad, but there was some truth to his rants."

He had told her what had driven Gershom to hate him so.

Leah nodded. "You and your Immortal Guardians saved the world. You saved humanity." She smiled. "Hell, you're *still* saving it."

"And we stopped Gershom from launching Armageddon. Even some of the Others are beginning to think I chose the right path after all."

As Leah's mind worked to absorb it, her heart began to slam against her ribs. "So... I'm immortal now? I'm not going to grow old?"

Seth blinked back new tears. "You're not going to grow old, sweetheart." He pressed his lips to hers. "You aren't going to leave me."

A sob rising in her throat, she hugged him tight. "I love you so much," she choked out.

"I love you more," he said, voice hoarse.

She emitted a shaky laugh. "I love you most."

Leaning back, Seth smiled down at her. "I'll love you for eternity."

She stared up at him in awe. "We're really going to have eternity together."

"Yes."

"Why does my skin feel so weird? It's prickling or something."

"You're like me now, with my heightened senses, greater strength and speed, and special abilities."

Her mouth dropped open. "*All* of your abilities? Are you kidding me?"

He laughed. "No, I'm not kidding you. But you're going to need me to teach you how to harness and control them, so try not to teleport or shape-shift until I can—"

"I can shape-shift?" she blurted incredulously.

His grin widened. "Yes. But don't try to—"

She glanced down at her arm and thought *cat*. Fur rippled along her skin as her fingernails lengthened into claws. Leah yelped, suddenly afraid.

Laughing, Seth rested a hand on her arm.

Much to her relief, the fur vanished and her nails returned to normal.

His glowing eyes danced with amusement. "As I was saying, don't try to do it until I can give you some direction."

Excitement bubbled up inside her. "This is so cool!"

"Want to see something cooler?" he asked, a twinkle entering his eyes.

"Yes."

Rolling off the bed, he set her on her feet, took her hand, and led her into the bathroom. "Look."

Leah turned toward the mirror and gaped. Her eyes glowed with bright golden light identical to Seth's. "Holy crap! My eyes are glowing!" Peeling her lips back, she studied her teeth.

Seth laughed. "What are you doing?"

"Looking for fangs."

He shook his head. "You don't have any. You aren't infected with the virus, remember? You're like me."

"Oh, right." Spinning toward him, she eyed him speculatively. "So I have superstrength now?"

"Yes."

Deciding to test that out, she placed her hands on Seth's hips and tried to lift him.

Seth's eyes widened as he flew up, crashed through the ceiling, and continued through the ceiling of the room above them.

Leah let out a cry of dismay as she peered up through the ragged holes and tried to glimpse him. "Oh! I'm sorry! I just wanted to see if I could lift you!"

No response came.

"Seth?"

Silence.

She bit her lip. She hadn't actually hurt him had she? "Honey?" she called uncertainly.

He abruptly appeared a foot away from her.

She jumped, emitting a little yelp.

Something powdery covered his hair and shoulders. His eyes narrowed. "Did I or did I not tell you to wait until I've given you some instruction before you — "

Leah couldn't help it. She burst out laughing.

His brows drew down farther, though amusement lurked in his beautiful eyes. "Now you're laughing at me, too?"

"I can't help it. You have plaster and dust and bits of concrete all over you."

He took a menacing step toward her. "Oh, you're going to pay for that."

She winked. "Are you sure? You'll have a harder time catching me this time." Before he could respond, she took off through the castle, running so swiftly the walls around her blurred. It was a heady, exhilarating experience that set her heart to racing.

Seth's laughter followed her, filling her with such happiness that she couldn't stop a broad grin from covering her face... until Seth abruptly appeared right in front of her on the stairwell landing.

Eyes widening, she plowed into him at preternatural speeds. His arms encircled her as the two of them flew out over the great hall. "Oh shit!" she cried. This was going to hurt.

Seth tightened his hold and spread his wings.

Leah relaxed against him as he gently lowered them until their feet touched the floor. "Whew!" She smiled up at him. "That was a close one. Sorry about that."

He smiled. "Don't apologize. This is both new and exciting for you. I had little hope that you'd let me finish my sentence before you began to test your new abilities."

She laughed. "You know me too well."

His look turned mischievous. "I know something else that will interest you."

"Really? What's that?"

Leaning forward, he nipped her earlobe and whispered, "You're going to love immortal sex."

She caught her breath as intense sensation rippled through her body. "Oh wow," she breathed.

"Exactly." He nuzzled her neck and rested his hands on her hips, drawing her closer. "Your senses are all heightened. Your vision…"

"I can see you in the dark now," she murmured, tilting her head to give him better access.

"Your sense of smell…"

When she drew in a deep breath, his scent hit her like an aphrodisiac. Fire licked through her body, luring her into nuzzling *his* neck. "You smell so good."

"Your hearing…"

"I can hear your heartbeat," she whispered. It slammed against his ribs as he trailed his soft lips down to her shoulder and slipped a hand up her side.

"Your sense of touch." He cupped her breast and drew a thumb across the taut peak.

Such pleasure shot through her that Leah's knees nearly buckled.

"You'll feel everything more now," he promised, ducking his head to close his lips over her nipple.

She moaned. The great hall around them fell away, replaced by their bedroom.

Seth raised his head and looked around. His eyes widened. "You teleported us. That was perfect."

Leah drew in his scent again, barely paying attention. "I did that?"

"Yes."

"Good. Tuck your wings away."

His wings vanished.

Desire burning inside her, Leah shoved Seth backward onto the bed.

Though she'd clearly startled him, he offered no protest as he hit the mattress. Instead, his eyes brightened further as Leah climbed on top of him and straddled his big hard body.

"I think I'm going to like this," he said, his voice deepening with desire.

She nodded. "You're going to like this even more."

"What?"

She lowered her lips to his, letting him feel the hunger he inspired as she kissed the stuffing out of him, teasing his tongue with her own. When he would've closed his arms around her, she shook her head and trailed more kisses across his stubbled jaw, along his neck, to his chest.

He moaned when she tongued one of his nipples, then nipped him with her teeth.

"When you listed my heightened senses," she said, "you forgot to mention taste." She heard his heartbeat pick up, thudding rapidly in his chest as she trailed kisses down his rippling abs. "And you taste *very* good."

"I love you so much, Leah," he said fervently, his eyes glowing bright gold.

She grinned. "I love you, too."

Thunder rumbled outside as the castle around them began to shake.

Epilogue

S ETH SMILED. HE AND LEAH had ended their brief honeymoon in England and returned to David's home... though they teleported back to his castle whenever they made love. Now that Leah was like him, the ground shook even more when they made love. So whenever lust struck, he thought it best to place as much distance as possible between them and the immortals who tended to tease.

He would've liked to have had more time alone with her, but Leah—who was as accustomed as he was to being in charge—hadn't felt comfortable leaving her store in the sole care of her employees for very long. Of necessity, she spent less time working now. Her powers and gifts were too new for her to remain long in the company of humans. And too, Seth thought she enjoyed mothering his immortal crew. She was loving the hell out of having such a large family... and delighted in shocking them every chance she could get.

Seth had not felt comfortable shirking his duties either. The fallout from destroying the compound in Texas had been remarkably minimal. Seth didn't know what his father had done, but no one in the military, including Heather's father, retained either a record or a memory of the place. So he was able to concentrate most of his attention on training the new Immortal Guardians and bringing them into the fold.

He and Chris had still not found the last missing *gifted one*. Because twelve *gifted ones* had been missing, Seth had believed all twelve had been taken and transformed by Gershom. But only eleven newly turned immortals had been in Gershom's care. And Tessa and the others had no memory of a twelfth.

Chris believed the woman was dead, executed months earlier by Gershom at the same time Veronica and several other missing *gifted ones* had been.

Since none of his Immortal Guardians had yet encountered a female immortal on their hunts, Seth feared the same. He nevertheless continued to search for her. It was yet another reason he and Leah returned early.

Also, after thousands of years of working almost every minute of every day, Seth just wasn't used to lolling in bed — where he and Leah spent most of their honeymoon — while David, Zach, and Jared fielded his calls. He did work fewer hours though. He was finally getting used to delegating more responsibility. And he liked having the freedom to enjoy more nights like this one.

The Immortal Guardians stationed in North Carolina had all completed their hunts early, thanks to the decrease in vampire population Gershom's defeat had heralded. Now they lounged in David's living room, enjoying each other's company. Conversation flowed freely, interspersed with frequent laughter.

Seth sat beside David on a sofa. The coffee table in front of it had been removed to give Leah room to open more wedding gifts, something he was beginning to believe really *would* take a year. Their castle was still packed with them.

His smile widened. *Their* castle.

Ami and Marcus reclined on the sofa across from him, their sides glued together. Roland sat in a wingback chair kitty-corner to them with Sarah perched on his lap. All laughed as they watched Adira and Michael *help* Leah open the gifts.

Giggling, Adira picked up some curly ribbon and threw it up in the air like confetti.

Michael did the same with several bows.

Then the two applied themselves to tearing pretty paper off a box that was bigger than both of them combined.

Leah laughed and sat back to give them more room to work as it turned into another race to see who could tear off the most paper the fastest. She glanced over and caught Seth watching her. *I love you,* she told him telepathically.

She had been working diligently to hone her new skills. And — as usual — the sound of her voice in his head heated his blood.

She knew it, too. He could tell by the spark of amusement that lit her eyes as he crossed his legs.

Don't tempt me, minx, he warned. *There are children present.*

She grinned. *That's okay. Their rain boots and umbrellas are right by the door.*

He laughed.

Adira suddenly stopped playing with the ribbons and paper. The smile left her adorable face as she looked around as though she had heard something.

Seth watched her, wondering what had caught her attention. One of David's cats, perhaps? Or Susan's dog, Jax? Maybe Marcus and Roland's crazy felines, who persisted in fighting over territory?

Perhaps not. Adira seemed puzzled.

Rising, she tromped across shredded wrapping paper and weaved her way through furniture and black-clad bodies toward the front of the house. One immortal warrior after another reached out and brushed an affectionate hand over her soft curls as she walked past.

Seth leaned a bit to one side so he could watch her.

Adira stopped in front of the bay window. Pressing her little hands to the glass, she peered out into the darkness.

He glanced at her parents.

Marcus shrugged. "Perhaps she heard an animal. We believe her hearing may be more acute than a human's."

Seth hadn't heard anything, but he hadn't really been paying attention and there were plenty of sounds here in the room to distract him from those outside.

"Wow," Leah said. "Look at this, honey." Reaching into the box, she drew out a large, heavy shield that was adorned with ornate engravings.

He smiled. A majority of the gifts they had opened thus far had been weapons and armor of one sort or another. His Immortal Guardians seemed determined to do everything they could to keep Leah safe now that Seth had found her.

The distant sound of a car engine reached his ears. It swung off the highway and began to creep up David's long driveway. Probably one of the Seconds returning from some errand. Or perhaps Chris.

He looked at David. "Think it's Reordon?" Maybe he had some news about the missing *gifted one*. The fact that after all was said and done they had failed to rescue one troubled him deeply.

David shook his head, his brow furrowing. "I can't access the driver's thoughts."

What?

Frowning, Seth reached out telepathically to see who was coming... and found nothing. If Ethan weren't already with them, Seth would've thought it was *him* since Ethan's mind was inaccessible to telepaths. But Ethan stood across the room, laughing at something Heather had said.

"Everyone quiet," Seth ordered, the hairs on the back of his neck prickling.

The room descended into silence. Even Michael fell still, no longer tearing at the wrapping paper or playing with the bows.

Seth looked at Adira, who leaned forward and pressed her nose against the glass. "Adira."

She looked at him over her shoulder.

"Who is it? Who's coming?"

Images flooded his mind... of a man being cut open and dissected on an operating table while still conscious.

Shock tore through him.

"Who is it?" Marcus asked, his hand going to the sword he'd left on a side table.

Seth met his gaze. "It's the man from Adira's nightmares."

Leah frowned up at him. "Adira has nightmares?"

He nodded. "Ever since she was in the womb, she has had nightmarish visions of a man being tortured. We've never been able to discern who it is because the visions are always from his perspective, so we've never seen his face."

Brakes squeaked as the car slowed to a stop outside David's tall security gate.

"I count three heartbeats," David said softly.

Seth did, too.

In the distance, a woman spoke. "Now what?"

A car door opened. Footsteps traversed pavement.

"What are you doing?" the woman asked.

"She's in there," a man said, his voice a deep, guttural rasp. "I know she is."

"You can't climb that," the woman protested.

"The hell I can't." Clanks and clunks sounded, accompanied by pained grunts. Then a heavy weight hit the ground.

David caught Seth's gaze. "Shall we see who it is?"

"May as well," Seth replied as he stood. "He's already made it inside the fence." Waving a hand, he telekinetically opened the gate.

Every immortal in the room rose and reached for weapons.

Beneath the bustle, Seth heard a car door close before the vehicle started forward again.

Marcus gripped his sword. "Whoever it is, Seth, you can't just let him in here."

It sounded as though the man had come for either Ami or Adira. Though Seth was concerned, he remained confident that he and his brethren could keep her safe. *No one* save Gershom could combat them when they had such numbers. And that bastard wouldn't see the light of day again.

Ami gasped suddenly. Face paling, she gripped her chest as though a knife had just pierced her.

Marcus dropped to his knees and reached for her, his brow furrowing with alarm. "Ami? Sweetling?"

For a moment, she looked as though she couldn't breathe. Then air whooshed out through her lips and sucked in again. Tears welled in her eyes.

Frowning, Seth took a step toward her. "Ami?"

Marcus rested a hand on her knee. "Talk to me, sweetling. What is it? What's happening? Are you in pain?" He looked up at Seth. "I think she's in pain."

She did seem to be having trouble breathing. And she kept gripping her chest.

Was this a response to whoever came? Could it be someone who had worked at the facility in which she had been held captive? Ami could feel individuals' energy signatures. If this man and woman had been at that facility, Ami would recognize them. And while she had been at that facility, she had suffered dreadful torture. When Seth and David had found her, Ami's chest had been cut open, her ribs spread, and the bastard scientists had been shocking her heart while she was still awake.

Now she clutched her chest as though she were enduring the same torture again.

Though his concern rose, Seth spoke gently. "Ami. What is it, sweetheart? Do you know them?"

Tears welled in her eyes as she looked at Marcus. "It can't be," she whispered, her face full of torment.

The car's engine grew louder as it pulled up in front of the house.

Adira pressed her nose to the glass again, peering outside. Seth thought it odd that the child seemed unperturbed while her mother experienced such distress. "Baba, look."

Two car doors opened. Footsteps sounded.

"Ami," Marcus said, lips tightening, "did this man—whoever he is—hurt you?"

Anger rising at the thought, at the pain the man's presence now caused her, Seth rounded the sofa and strode toward the front door.

Ami jumped to her feet and rushed past him.

Marcus caught her as she reached for the doorknob. "Ami, wait! We don't know who's out there."

She shook her head. "Let me go. I have to see."

Marcus cast Seth a helpless look.

Frowning, Seth tried to piece it together. Now that the visitors were closer, he discerned that one of the three heartbeats was that of an infant. Surely the man and woman wouldn't have brought a baby if they intended to engage in battle.

"Let her go," he commanded softly.

Marcus shook his head. "Seth..."

"I'll keep her safe," he vowed. "Let her go, Marcus."

A muscle leaping in his jaw, Marcus released his wife and stepped back. But his hand fisted around the hilt of the sword he still carried.

Ami stumbled the final few feet to the door and flung it open.

Seth stared at the two adults who stood outside. A little jolt of surprise shot through him.

He recognized them. The night he had defeated Gershom, he had seen them both at the base in Texas. David had just left to spirit the children away to safety, and an odd feeling had coursed through Seth. He had spun around, half-expecting to see Ami and Adira. Instead, he had seen a network soldier helping a pregnant woman in a lab coat stumble down a hallway. The two had leaned heavily on each other. The woman had been clutching her stomach and the man had gripped his chest much like he was now—much like *Ami* was now—the same pain creasing his face.

But he wore no uniform tonight. Yet another puzzle. Network soldiers tended to *live* in their black fatigues. And his auburn hair was longer than it had been that night. Longer than it could've grown in the brief amount of time that had passed since Seth had last seen him.

Who was he?

Seth glanced at the woman. Who was *she?* The tiny heartbeat he had detected was that of the babe still in her belly.

Were they Gershom's plan B, mind-controlled into carrying out whatever orders he had implanted? Or were they more innocent victims?

A cry escaped Ami.

Seth's head snapped around.

Cupping her hands over her mouth as though to hold back more, she stared up at the man with wide eyes. Tears spilled over her lashes and coursed down her cheeks. Then she lunged forward, threw her arms around the man, and began to sob.

Marcus reached for her.

Seth shot a hand out to hold him back. "Wait."

The man released the pregnant woman and wrapped his arms around Ami. Ducking his head, he buried his face in her hair and began to sob, too.

Seth glanced at the woman.

Pain rippled across her features, mostly hidden by a curtain of hair. Hissing in a ragged breath, she reached out and braced a hand against the doorjamb as she gripped her big belly. But her eyes remained focused on the man.

Seth leaned to one side and caught her gaze. "Are you all right?"

Her heartbeat increased. Fear filled her expression as she glanced at him and the big men behind him. Swallowing hard, she gave him an abrupt nod and released her tummy long enough to draw her hair back from her face and tuck it behind her ear.

More surprise coursed through Seth. She was the missing *gifted one*. At the base, her hair had concealed her features enough for him not to see it, but with the long locks drawn back...

"Ami?" Marcus said quietly, his brow furrowed with concern.

Drawing in a shaky breath, Ami leaned back and looked up at the man who held her. "How is this possible?" she whispered.

He cupped her face in one hand and shook his head, seemingly too overcome by emotion to speak.

"Ami," Marcus repeated, keeping his voice low, "who is this?"

Turning to face him, she kept an arm around the stranger and gave her husband a watery smile. "He's my brother."

Seth stared at the man, stunned speechless. Ami came from another planet. She believed her family didn't know where she was and — since she had no way of contacting them — had never thought to see any of them again.

Her brother tightened his hold on her and studied them with suspicion. He staggered a step to the side, nearly losing his balance. Then his green eyes abruptly rolled back in his head as he sank toward the floor.

Thank you for reading *Death of Darkness*. I hope you enjoyed Seth and Leah's story!

If you liked this book, please consider rating or reviewing it at an online retailer of your choice. I appreciate your support so much and am always thrilled when I see that one of my books made a reader happy. Ratings and reviews are also an excellent way to recommend an author's books, create word of mouth, and help other readers find new favorites.

Thank you again!

Dianne Duvall
www.DianneDuvall.com
Dianne Duvall Books Group

About the Author

Dianne Duvall is the *New York Times* and *USA Today* Bestselling Author of the **Immortal Guardians** series and **The Gifted Ones** series. Audible chose *Awaken the Darkness* as one of the Top 5 Best Paranormal Romances of 2018. Reviewers have called Dianne's books "fast-paced and humorous" (*Publishers Weekly*), "utterly addictive" (*RT Book Reviews*), "extraordinary" (Long and Short Reviews), and "wonderfully imaginative" (The Romance Reviews). Her audiobooks have received three AudioFile Earphones Awards. One was nominated for a prestigious Audie Award. Her books have also twice been nominated for RT Reviewers' Choice Awards and are routinely deemed Top Picks by *RT Book Reviews*, The Romance Reviews, and/or Night Owl Reviews.

Dianne loves all things creative. When she isn't writing, Dianne is active in the independent film industry and has even appeared on-screen, crawling out of a moonlit grave and wielding a machete like some of the vampires she loves to create in her books.

For the latest news on upcoming releases, contests, and more, connect with Dianne online:

Website — www.DianneDuvall.com
Books Group — www.facebook.com/groups/128617511148830/
Blog — dianneduvall.blogspot.com
Facebook — www.facebook.com/DianneDuvallAuthor
Twitter — twitter.com/DianneDuvall
YouTube —
www.youtube.com/channel/UCVcJ9xnm_i2ZKV7jM8dqAgA?feature=mhee
Pinterest — www.pinterest.com/dianneduvall
Goodreads — www.goodreads.com/Dianne_Duvall

Made in the USA
Coppell, TX
22 August 2021

60973527R00298